# Truth

By dhtreichler

Dedication:

This novel is dedicated to Byron Treichler, who believes he knows the truth in any situation. And that truth does not align with that of his parent's perceptions. Through decades of discussions we have come to a common understanding, although non agreement, about how the world may evolve from here. This novel is an attempt to align those disparate perceptions of reality.

This is a work of fiction. Names, characters, businesses, places, events and incidents are either the products of the author's imagination or used in a fictitious manner. Any resemblance to actual persons, living or dead, or actual events is purely coincidental.

# FOREWARD:

<u>Truth</u> is a metaphor for the world we are creating. It is a study of the implications for human relationships in a world with no objective anchors, only those someone else has chosen for us.

As a metaphor, the world depicted lives in the near future. This world has been broken into three spheres of influence known as EuTopia, which comprises the nations of Europe, the Middle East and Africa, UsTopia, consisting of the western hemisphere nations, and UaTopia, which encompasses all Asian nations we know today. While it may seem fanciful that such groups of nations could ever affiliate under single umbrellas, this novel is a bridge between two prior works, <u>Succession</u> and <u>Lucifer</u>. Reading all three works establishes the continuity of the metaphor intended. The common thread is the scenario-based strategic analysis underlying my writings. This story, as is common with the others in my library, depicts a future, where technology has and is changing how we relate to each other. In this novel, most information and knowledge is not transferred in a face-to-face conversation or books. It is read by someone in the background who may or may not find it suitable for posting for others to read and react to. That third party of every conversation is the essence of this novel. It is the world we are inheriting from the sins of our fathers.

The world of today is a foreshadow of the world of tomorrow. The ability to navigate between the shoals of Truth and Reason will be mediated by technologies we can only imagine today. And the fate of mankind lies in the success of us all in how we control the technology mediating our lives. In making decisions that enable each other.

# CHAPTER ONE: BRANDON McINERNY

The embedded images slow down. That only makes it worse. Why does the technology always glitch and leave me staring at the most horrific of scenes? I can't look, but I have to. That's my job. To look. To judge. To make a decision as to what needs to be done. That's what they pay me to do, often seven days a week. Fifty weeks a year. It used to be that we only had to look at this stuff five days a week. Plenty of time to catch up on Monday and Tuesday. But when people started complaining about how many outright lies, how much filth, pornography and hate messaging got through over the weekends, suddenly we were working every day. Someone had to ensure that the worst of what men and women can imagine never is shared or seen by others. If someone got the idea that lies are truth and they could actually go do what these images suggest, chaos would rule the world. Morality as we know it would be dead. Even though there are many who believe that to be the case now.

I don't. Believe morality is dead. There are many things I do believe, but the death of morality is not one of them. If anything, there is all too much morality in the world today. The problem is that someone else's morality isn't yours. Doesn't match up with what you were taught growing up. What you have come to believe since then when your parent's beliefs encountered the world of other parent's beliefs as expressed through their rebelling children. And those expressions were always how 'medieval' parents are. I mean no self-respecting twenty-year-old could ever acknowledge a parent's ideas. Ideas of how the world should work. Ideas different than their own, uninformed by experience.

I'm the same way. Only now there are many a day when I wished I'd listened closer to what they were trying to tell me. Clearly coming to work for the Truth Department in Washington, D.C. wasn't such a great idea. But when I was graduating without a clear notion of who or what I wanted to be when I grew up, the idea of being an arbiter of truth seemed sexy somehow. I could be the wizard behind the screen off to the side of the stage. I could right the wrongs of the world my parents built from the wreckage of the world they inherited. At least listening to them, as I did for way too many years that would be how they wanted me to perceive the task they encountered. And I had different ideas about the world. What it could be, as opposed to what they were passing along to me. At least not while I was a fire brand undergraduate who constantly challenged professors with my ignorance of the world.

The image returns, of a young girl, maybe seven, hidden in the background of a picture of kids playing in a street. The image is seen through a window. I have to magnify to really see it. The picture was served to me to ensure it's what it appears. Arbiter can't make that decision on its own. Not yet. She is blonde, slender and naked, but with her back to me and kneeling on the floor, sitting on her heels. She obscures the view of what appears to be a man she is facing. He is sitting on a bed, but that's about all I can see. The decision, according to the Ten Commandments, should be to delete. It shall not go out over the internet. Following the rule in this case is easy. The picture is not one I want to remember. I have seen way too many like it. I have tried unsuccessfully to forget each and every one of them. And at the end of the day the only thing that helps me deal with this impression, and all the others I have seen and am about to see, is weed. I go home, turn on an old movie. Never the news. Too close to what I see all day. Doubt I could handle another dose of reality. And I take an edible and wait. Wait for the tension to melt away. Wait for the image to move on to an appropriate file cabinet in the back of my mind. A place where, hopefully, it will eventually be erased. From too much weed and increasingly too much alcohol. Someone suggested I drink too much. My response was, what's the problem? That person told me very sternly I was killing brain cells that I'd never be able to regenerate. I started laughing. I couldn't help it. I mean, what the fuck? I'm trying to kill those cells that have all the photos I have to judge for eight to ten hours a day, nearly every day of my life. Get real. If anything, I need to figure out how I can get started drinking earlier in the day.

Another picture. This time the message is hidden well. I have to magnify almost to the max to make it out. Now I can distinguish the embedded image. It's one I've seen a billion times. At least that seems to be how often I see it. A black man hanging from a rope under a big old oak tree somewhere in Mississippi, or Alabama. Maybe Louisiana or Georgia. From the picture I can never tell. But I do know it's not New York or LA. I don't know what I see more now. That situation or one of a man whose head has been severed from his body. Every time a man holds the head by its hair and a blood soaked long sharp knife or short sword in the other hand. I never know which. In any case I never see the head of the beheader. Is that deliberate? Something to make you think at first glance that this is the headless horseman of Ichabod Crane fame? I just want this impression out of my mind. Out of my life. Out of anything I can expect to see in the future. But I've seen both photos so many times that no matter how many edibles or how much alcohol I consume, I can't burn them out. They keep creeping back. Sneaking into my consciousness when I'm trying to concentrate on something important. Something that doesn't set me back on my heels. Something I might have been looking forward to. Something that gives me hope. These pictures only fill me with dread.

Another embedded image. This time the middle-aged naked black guy has his back to me. He is standing over a semi-naked cowering young white woman. She sits on the floor at the end of a bed, arm raised, as if that would be enough to keep this powerful symbol of black manhood from violating what white men seek to protect and keep for themselves. This picture is what I've heard others in my group describe as a 'dog whistle' for every hate group in America. If you don't protect our women, the stud-ly black guys will impregnate them. Fill this country up with bi-racial children, unrecognized by either race. Unloved by anyone other than their parents.

People tell me that's not the way it is anymore. I mean we've gotten so much more sophisticated about all that. A kid's a kid. Right? Black is black and white may be what any other kid is, in their minds. But the sins of our fathers continuously cast that into doubt. What is more likely to be the case is the opposite of this picture. The powerful white guy about to rape a black woman who is totally dependent upon him for food for her family. At least if anyone spends the time to read the sites where these pictures appear, that is what one will never see. The first and never the latter, even though the blood on the hands of our forebears would indicate a much different picture of the interracial relations of the last two millennium.

Why is it all of those who are seeking to influence the national narrative have chosen pictures to be the means of changing opinions? It seems I almost never have to read anything anymore. But I spend most of my days examining in detail the embedded images posted. The media has made this the communications channel of choice. The means of shocking those who have the franchise to select our leaders. Those whose opinions count every other year or every four years when it comes to the knock-out battle to change the composition of the Supreme Court and the national dialog.

I suddenly sit up in bed, sweat soaked, and a headache that just won't quit. Eye lids that know they need to open, but aren't cooperating. I don't want to know where I am, although I know perfectly well. I'm in a seventh-floor apartment five blocks from where I work every day for the Department of Truth in Washington, D.C. From my window I can see the Capitol Building in the distance. The dome more than anything. If I made more money I could have gone up another floor and probably seen more. But there was just no way. I'm barely able to cover my Whole Foods bill as it is. Got to have that high PH water, low fat yoghurt, and exactly three ounces of protein from one of five essential sources. Whole Foods wants me to have seven portions of green something every day. Not going to happen. I hate green. Ever since I read that book. Dress for success. All my friends said I was crazy to read that. Ancient history. But doing what I do all day, I made the assumption that if it was written before Truth became arbitrary it was more likely to be something I needed to pay attention to.

Those same photos parade before me when I close my eyes even for an instant. Why does my dream state mind choose them? Because they're the ones I've seen more than any of the others. Although the others are often even more disturbing. The outright lies and race baiting piss me off. But mutilation always makes me close my eyes and hit the delete button instantly. I can't handle those images anymore.

The sunshine peaks in through the drawn blinds letting me know another day of images are about to overwhelm my senses. It causes me to wonder why I took this job.

## CHAPTER TWO: ELIZABETH WARDEN

My meetings with the President are always orthogonal. I don't say that because I think she's not trying to give me a chance to succeed. But we always seem to be out of synch somehow. Sabr Malik-Goldstein, better known as SMG, defeated me for the presidency in the last election. It wasn't that I didn't give it my all. In fact, probably the only reason she offered me this position in her administration is because I never criticized her. When I lost the nomination I whole heartedly campaigned for her. I never thought identity politics were real until the first ballots were deadlocked. That continued through four rounds. At that point it was clear to everyone in the hall that the most diverse candidate would get the nomination. And who could argue with a black gay Muslim woman whose partner is the son of an Asian woman and Jewish father who is Trans gender? I mean, other than old white guys, who isn't there? When Sabr was nominated I knew my pursuit of the presidency was over. A white woman was never going to be president. So I just needed to get over it and embrace the new reality.

"Elizabeth." There is always something in her voice when she says my name. Something that tells me she would rather not be having this conversation with me. Anyone else, but not me. Is that because she's afraid I'll always want her job? That I'll never really accept her judgment and decisions? I've not given her any reason to think that might be the case. But there's always something in her tone of voice that makes me uncomfortable, believing she's uncomfortable with me.

"Wishing it wasn't so, won't change reality," I respond to the open question she has poised. "The algorithms are not perfect. They never will be. Neither are the human analysts." I point out.

"But I trust people," Sabr looks out the window of the Oval Office towards the Rose Garden. "A black box that just crunches data? I don't like it. Too impersonal. Something could go wrong there and I'd have absolutely no idea how to fix it. If a person screws up I can fire him or her. But a machine? Someone has to come in and figure out what's wrong with the logic. I can't do that. Not what I was trained to do. Do you know what I'm saying? That this whole approach just makes me uncomfortable."

I smile my most reassuring smile, "Madam President, I understand your discomfort completely. I am as much at a loss for understanding how algorithms work as yourself. Maybe even more so. But we've been wrestling for a long time with the burn out rate amongst our analysts, the legal challenges we keep defending."

"To say nothing of the number of times we have to change the Ten Commandments so the analysts will stay in line," Sabr notes ruefully. "Delete what we don't want out there, post our version of the truth, regardless. When we get to just the machine, and we will get there sooner than later, I'll be able to select the truth I want and that will be the truth, no questions asked." Sabr continues looking out the window. I have a difficult time reading her. She just never communicates her thoughts through body or facial expressions. One has to wait for her words to understand her thoughts. That's always made me uncomfortable about her. Maybe that's why she has so much trouble with me. I'm an open book. My every feeling is visible on my face, in my posture, in the tone of my voice. And maybe that's why she made me Secretary of Truth. Because I'd never be able to hide the truth from her.

"Everything's a compromise now. I understand that," Sabr begins. Her voice would make one think she's agreeing with me, but I know better from the sixteen months we've worked together since the election. "But that doesn't make me any more comfortable with the plan. You convinced me at the time it was the best course of action. Made it clear we will eventually reach a tipping point. One where our human analysts simply won't be needed to do the job of finding, judging and disposing of all the postings we don't want out there. But in the meantime they have accelerated since my election."

I have to change the direction of this discussion. It won't lead to anything constructive. I have to keep Sabr focused on the progress we are making. "The theory is if extreme political positions and behaviors disappear from the media that less attention will be paid to them." I wait to see if I have Sabr's attention or if she's still back on control. I've noticed she frequently gets hung up on something. I have to wait for her to move past it if I wish to influence her thoughts.

"Has anyone ever been able to prove that's the case?" Sabr still won't look at me. Not a good sign. Means she's not buying what I'm selling.

"Several scientific papers on the subject have reported encouraging results. That when racist epithets disappear from the media they appear less often in social exchanges that have been studied across America," I inform her.

"Really?" Sabr looks directly at me for the first time today. Guess I finally offered her something she has been looking for. "Make sure Elise has the references on those papers."

Elise is Sabr's speech writer. A good sign.

"What else do you need from me to be comfortable?" I throw out there knowing it's the key elephant on the table at the moment.

Sabr stands and slowly moves toward the window to the Rose Garden. I'm not sure if she's inviting me to follow her out there or she's just restless. But she stops at the window and continues to look out. Shakes her head and finally turns to look back at me but not at me. I can tell the difference. She won't engage my eyes. That makes me incredibly uncomfortable. I don't know what to do about it. No clues have been offered from talking with other cabinet members. The all say they experience the same thing when in a one-on-one with her. In a group she's more than comfortable looking at us directly. But never in a one-on-one. "I know you've given this much more thought than I have,"

Sabr begins. "Looked at the pros and cons. The unintended consequences. The black swans that could occur with just the right alignment of circumstances. I'm completely comfortable that you've done the diligence expected. What I'm not comfortable with is what will really happen the day the machines decide what's true and what's not?"

We're back to square one. We've had this discussion a dozen or more times in just the last couple of months. "Whether people will accept the decision of a faceless algorithm," I complete the thought. "Or blame you for deciding the truth since the machine is your machine."

Sabr nods and turns away from me again since we've had this discussion I can't even count how many times.

"The simple fact is nothing will change. Algorithms identify what should be removed now. The only difference is today that recommendation goes to a person. The person makes the final determination. The goal is to get to the point that the human analysts will rarely over-ride the recommendation of the algorithm. Less than two percent of the time. The current approach is incredibly expensive for us to maintain. If we truly dive deep into the two percent, the overrides will tend to be personal preferences and not mainstream decisions. We can live with two percent getting a day on the internet before another algorithm looks at how it's being accessed and makes a different decision about whether it should stay up. What's the harm of a day or two for two percent?

Sabr continues to look out at the Rose Garden. I don't know what's drawing her attention there. I guess what it is.

"Are you thinking of pulling the plug on the transition because you're afraid of the day after?" I finally ask.

Sabr glances over her shoulder at me, but it's only a glance. "I'm only afraid of one thing..."

# CHAPTER THREE: JURGEN

Meanwhile in Berlin a similar conversation takes place between the slender and owlish looking Javier Santiago, Minister of Truth for the EuTopian nations and the youthful and athletic Jurgen, Chancellor of that federation.

I don't know why Javier feels he must prepare me for what he thinks I need to know. It's not like I don't know what he's doing. Must be he thinks I'll take whatever he's thinking better if he's put it into the proper context. The problem is I never know if the context is real or the one that will lead me to take the action he wants me to take. He knows I hate being manipulated. But that seems to be what everyone thinks they need to do. Just to get what they want from me. Regardless of what I might want to happen. Do they all think I live in a vacuum? That I don't know what's going on?

We're walking the glass walled walkways between the Reichstag buildings. I prefer to talk here as we walk from my office to his. It took a while for security to get the idea that when Javier and I walk they turn off the listening devices. I don't want any record of our conversations and I don't want anyone listening in to know what we're talking about.

"Why are you so slow today?" I finally ask as he seems to be having difficulty getting to the point.

Javier consults a clock on the wall. "You have plenty of time. I checked your calendar." He looks at me now. "You have a half hour before anyone is going to be looking for you. Just because you have a need to make every decision, there are times when you shouldn't."

"What are you trying to say?" He's just annoying me for no good reason.

"We're ready."

Now he has my attention. "No more testing?" I tease him as it seems that every time we got close in the past there was always some issue that would come up. Something he wasn't happy about. Never any details. Just the slipping of a go live date to next year. And then the next year. I'd stopped asking for updates because there was no reason for him to continue telling me the same thing each time.

"No."

"Validations?" I continue the tease.

Javier shakes his head.

"Running parallel?"

Javier gives me that look. The one where he's basically telling me to stop asking questions because the answer won't change.

"Are you going to demonstrate the system's capabilities or are you simply going to throw the switch and toss all those people out of work?"

"The other systems are ready too. But in UsTopia I'm getting conflicting signals," Javier informs me and the tone of voice tells me this is an important point. Like there's something I'm likely going to have to do at some point and he wants me to be prepared.

"Has UaTopia already gone live?" I ask to confirm what he didn't tell me.

"It's hard to tell," Javier has an amused tenor in his voice. "They've had parts of their system operational for years. They keep adding bits and pieces. So you never know quite what they're capable of doing. How much of the analysis has been automated."

"They'll never completely automate," I give him my opinion.

"Because …"

"Xi has a fundamental distrust of everyone and everything. He will never rely on one system or even a system of systems. He will want his lieutenants looking over everything. Answering his questions. Rather than a black box that spits out reports. Particularly when he can't judge their accuracy. No. I don't think we will see a global system operational in Xi's lifetime."

"What about yours?" Javier tests me as he always does, to see if I really believe what I'm saying. That's the problem with someone who's known me as long as he has.

"Tell me how long I'll live and I'll give you an answer," I push right back at him, an answer he hears from me whenever he asks about the future. We've talked more than once about the fact that the future is unknowable. We can create the future or we can let the future create us. I've always taken the first road.

"Then we are likely to be the first," Javier smiles that thin smile I've seen so many times, but only when he thinks he is about to do what no one else has been able to.

"You haven't answered my question," I point out.

"If you wish you may throw the switch, push the button, turn it on. Whatever you wish to call it." Somehow there seems to be a problem with his offer.

"I thought our system was already operational. You told me last time all that would change is turning off the human comparisons. Going without a human look on each and every posting."

"Did I say that?" Javier can be annoying some times.

"You did." I wait for him to respond. He has made his point about being first. That I should have no concerns about turning off the comparative assessments.

"Do you want to establish the truth, or do you want the other federations to tell you what they think it is?" This is the ultimate dare. The question he asked before we started down the path of the single integrated arbiter of truth. An automated system trained on what is the official version of the world my loyal subjects will know and experience. Nothing will post if the system software finds it deviating from my official version of Truth. Any idea or thought not posted on the internet doesn't exist. It's no longer sharable. And if it's not shared it's not an idea, but only a passing thought. And people can have thoughts as long as they are prevented from acting on those thoughts. At least that was the theory. That was the rationale. That was why we started down this road.

We are approaching Javier's office. The wall is a giant integrated screen from which he can look into any database, review any posting, any data stream, any picture and graphic, any representation someone wishes to make of any idea, concept or thought.

"As you can see, our system is working just fine."

I'm not sure how I'm supposed to see that from all he has populated this screen with. He sees it, maybe. I'm never quite sure if when he says that, it's to demonstrate how much the master of the universe he is, or how much I'm dependent upon him for the truth we give to the people. And we do it together. Well... sort of. I give Javier my big ideas. He takes that and runs with it. Populating the criteria for posting removal, whether video, text, picture or graphic.

"How many Truth Analysts are there now?" it suddenly occurs to me to ask.

"Why? Are you afraid to eliminate jobs in a down economy?" Javier isn't happy with this question, particularly now.

"I'm trying to understand how much variation we're going to

eliminate from the system. How many points of entry for terrorist groups that want to change the narrative, tell a different story from the truth."

"Our truth," Javier corrects me.

"Any version of a truth that would cause people to disbelieve the world we have created for them. A world that sustains us. Sustains them in the way we believe they should view their reality."

"Even if it isn't reality," Javier tries to make me see what he sees.

"Well, there's always that," I sort of agree with him, but it doesn't really matter since we are creating their reality.

There's a flashing light in a corner of the screen. "What's that?"

Javier follows my pointed finger. "Oh that. A minor glitch."

"I thought you said it was ready."

"It is. But nothing is infallible. Just like people aren't infallible."

I shake my head, "Don't give me that. What's wrong?"

Javier walks up to the screen and turns off a switch on the side of the monitor. The screen goes blank. "This will take just a minute."

"Reboot?" I ask and watch Javier sheepishly nod, but just once.

# CHAPTER FOUR: ALBERT CARTER

The knock on my door alerts me to the fact that Brandon got my message. Not that I wanted to send that message or any of the others. But what am I going to do? Management gave me no choice.

I look around and there he is; a quizzical smile since I never ask him to come to my office. We always meet either at his cube or at the Starbucks around the corner. But I couldn't have this conversation at Starbucks. That just wouldn't be right. Brandon shuffles on in, his F*CK THIS t-shirt looks like it needs to be laundered or replaced. Either he's worn it way too many times or he's been sleeping in it again. Not that I'm concerned about the shape of his t-shirt. Guess I'm just anticipating his t-shirt expression may summarize his response to the conversation we're about to have.

"What's the occasion?" Brandon drops himself in the one visitor chair in my tiny and barren office. I really hate this space. Maybe that's why I'm usually out on the floor with my team. Any place is better than a tiny place, even if it is all mine and my team has no space that is all theirs. Not that they complain about the space. When they're at their desks they are completely engrossed in the work, in the world the internet has created for them, in the decisions they have to make. I did it for five years, so I know how hard it is. How mentally and morally exhausting. How much it takes from you that you never get back. I've been off the desk for ten years and I still have the nightmares I did when I was out there. Guess I need to answer his question. "Liberation day," I respond cryptically, trying to find a positive spin I can put on the situation. Although I know he and all the others won't see it that way. At least not at first. Maybe in time.

Brandon frowns trying to understand my response. We've been close for all the time we've known each other, probably because we come from the same background. Small rural towns where not much happened. Masters of our universes there. Tight knit families that did everything together. And when we came to the big city we struggled to be seen, to find a place. All because success was our expectation from places where we didn't have to compete for everything we wanted nearly every minute of every day. But because we expected success, we eventually found it. Just not at the level we anticipated. "You giving me the day off?" Brandon's blue eyes sparkle like they do when I've seen him happy about something. A half smile of hope. I learned a long time ago that the one thing everyone on my team wants is time off. To get away from having to decide. From having to read all the fake news. To have to wonder if the world could really be that screwed up. From having to deal with images no one should ever have to see. To have to wonder why people have such extreme reactions to the lives they experience shaped by the forces unleashed by the multitudes around them.

"I'm giving you some time, yes."

Brandon doesn't wait for me to finish, "Good. I really need a break, you know? I don't know what it is, but the determinations of what's fake and what isn't is getting a lot harder. People are getting a lot more sophisticated in the words they use to describe things. Do you know I'm having to go to the dictionary a lot more than I used to just to figure out what people are trying to say? And sometimes I'm finding myself down to the fourth or fifth definition before it's clear what they meant by how they used the word." Brandon laughs at a thought, "You know I decided they must all be lawyers, the people out there who are posting all this shit. I mean who else goes to the fifth definition? I wouldn't have a clue that some of the words they use even had that many meanings. So who are these people? Really? And the photo shopping? I look at some of those images and there's no way I can tell they aren't real. Is that why the algorithms send them to me? Because they can't tell either?"

I'm about to answer, but Brandon doesn't wait.

"You know I was talking with Sheila and she's noticed the same thing. Only she thought the people behind all the fake news had hired former editors. She said with so many of the publishers just shutting down because no one reads anything that's not on line anymore that most of them have been looking for work. What she told me, I didn't know, was she wanted to be one. An editor. She wanted to read the stories people wrote in their raw form. Be able to experience the emotional energy the author wanted to convey before someone else made the story commercial by taking out the parts that don't drive the story forward but show the real state of mind of the author. The parts that reveal the author's soul. You know I'd never thought about that. The author revealing their soul in the parts of the novel the reader never gets to see."

"You ought to spend more time with Sheila. She's a gem." I offer hoping he will take my advice. Sheila, another member of my team, is just a genuinely caring person. I've had to have more than one conversation with her to help her cope with what she reads and sees all day in this job. We even had a conversation that maybe this isn't the right job for her. But she just looked at me with those big brown eyes and told me someone has to do this work. And just because it's hard is no reason. She should dedicate herself to making the world a better place for all of us. Even if that means shielding others from what she has to see. After all, even her name is Sheila. When she said that to me I just stared at her for a long moment. What could I say?

Brandon looks at me as if trying to understand if I know something about Sheila that maybe he should. The fact that he hangs with her more than any of the other girls here tells me he likes her. And I know she likes him because she told me so. But she wouldn't want me revealing that conversation to Brandon. Although with what I have to say to him I doubt he would even remember it later.

"You ought to go easier on her, Albert," Brandon brings me back to his situation, but I'm glad to engage him in a conversation beyond the real reason he is here.

"Did she say something to you?" I decide to ask concerned I've been too focused on my task and not on what is on his mind that I need to know to do the rest of my job.

"Depends on what you mean by say," Brandon responds thinking aloud. "Did she say the words that she needs more time? No. She didn't have to. I see it in her eyes. The ghosts that wait there for her every evening when it's time to go home. I see it in her energy level. You know how she is. Always ready for anything. But she went home after work last Friday. Friday of all nights. If it had been a Tuesday? Well, I could have seen that. But not a Friday. I mean everyone was there. People who only come out on Friday. People who recede into the shadows and only let you see them when something important happens. People who always want to know what's going on for real and are afraid that only those of us who decide what isn't can tell them. You know who I mean. And the people who balance you out by always having some adventure to tell you about. Someplace they've been, or a new restaurant where someone came up with the impossible dish you just have to try. They were all there. For Sheila to not come out on a Friday? That means she's entering into stage three. And that's the beginning of the end."

There are two sets of rules in this business. The Ten Commandments that make up what is true and able to be posted on the internet, and the five stages of burn-out. When all of this truth determination started, most people thought it was another Transportation Safety Administration federal jobs program. Only most of the jobs ended up in the private sector with the media companies. What soon became evident was that what the Truth Analysts were exposed to for endless hours every day affected them in deep psychological ways. No one wanted to admit it, but anyone who entered stage five was at risk of becoming unstable. Some would simply go into catatonic states. Others would run away to rural parts of the country, never to be heard from again. Still others became abusive of family and friends and in a few cases we found them either suicidal or affecting suicide by cop. It was the few who were in that last category that finally brought about access to mental health services for those of us who requested it after ten years of service. However, few have taken advantage of the opportunity. That has led me and several of my peers to acknowledge privately there is an explosion coming. An explosion we need to plan for. And so far none of our superiors have bothered to listen to our recommendations.

"Stage three?" I don't want to admit he could be right. "Was that the first time she chose not to come out?"

Brandon nods. "But I assume that's not why you wanted me to come see you. To give you a heads up about Sheila."

I shake my head, "I'm glad you did, but no. We have to make some changes…"

## CHAPTER FIVE: ELIZABETH WARDEN

I hate vendor meetings. It starts with an excuse and ends with an extension of time, more money or less capability in whatever it is that we're procuring. Why is that? Is it the job of every systems salesman to overpromise and instantly start lowering expectations once I've signed the contract? I'm just glad I don't do this regularly.

"Jocelyn…" I have to interrupt her stream of consciousness because frankly I tuned out a while ago. Now I have absolutely no idea what the latest excuse is, nor do I care. She apparently didn't hear me because she hasn't even slowed down let alone stopped talking. "Jocelyn… I will talk over you if that's what it takes to get your attention."

"…and drives us to a work around that none of us feel…" Kwame pokes her in the side, "…is an acceptable solution." She glances at Kwame, "Why did you do that?"

Kwame, who is her technical sales lead, nods to me without saying a word. "That's no excuse for interrupting me just when I'm coming to the most…"

"Jocelyn!" Now I'm the one who is pushing on her to get her attention. "It's all right. The world won't end if you take a breath. Nor will it end if you actually turn off your transmitter and turn on your receptors."

Jocelyn appears to not understand what I am saying, glances at Kwame and shrugs like 'what did I do wrong?'

"Jocelyn." I push on her again. "I am asking you to go to the ladies room down the hall and stay there until Kwame comes and knocks on the door."

"What?" Jocelyn is either deaf and I'd not realized it earlier, or very hard of hearing. I assume the latter and nod to Kwame to escort her out, which to his credit he does, although Jocelyn is asking him why she needs to leave the meeting since only she has the authority to agree to whatever I agree to.

Once she's gone I sit waiting for Kwame to return. This takes longer than I'd expected. I can be patient about some things even though I'm absolutely not about others.

Kwame returns, closes the door and gives me a half smile that I take as an attempt to apologize for Jocelyn without actually doing so. He sits, "What do you want to know?"

"First of all I don't want Jocelyn returning to this office and I don't want her on my program. Is that clear?"

Kwame closes his eyes. I imagine he is trying to figure out how he is going to make that happen since she is his boss. Not my problem.

"Is that clear?"

Kwame's eyes snap open. "Yes, ma'am."

"And that better be the last time you address me as ma'am. I know it's required in some places, but in this office it is forbidden. Got that?"

"Yes, ma…" Kwame censors himself just in time. He cautiously glances at my expression. "I have it."

"Good. I was beginning to think I needed to terminate your contract since no one there seems to know how to communicate with a customer. And if that were to be the case it would be more than justification."

Kwame's eyes get wide showing more of the whites than usual. And I can see how bloodshot those whites are. He must not be getting much sleep, even though he is not the system architect, nor the lead technical person on the project. He is just supposed to know enough to be able to answer questions. He's not managing the team doing the work and burning the midnight oil to get it done. He is supposed to listen carefully and advise of new scope to be added to the contract which translates into more dollars for the contractor, more hours for the team and more profits in the end. Kwame is very valuable to the company who employs him. He is their best salesman. Although if you asked him, he would tell you he's an engineer and not in sales.

"Kwame," I continue. "We're at a critical juncture here. We've paid you way more than you signed up to deliver. That's not a good deal for the American people. Do you agree?"

Kwame blinks before responding, apparently trying to remember some rote response he's supposed to give when I ask that question. I've been told the contractors often run mock customer discussions to keep the project sold by only telling us what is scripted for them.

"Not what you've rehearsed," I give up waiting. "You're a tax payer. If I collect taxes from you and pay some company twice for something as what you'd pay for the same thing if you went to the store, would you say that's a good deal for you? A good way for me to spend your tax dollars?"

Kwame doesn't blink apparently remembering what he's supposed to say, "We build custom systems. One of a kind. They cost what they cost because no one knows exactly how to build it. We find things as we go we did not anticipate. We assume solutions that sometimes don't work out. We have to try other approaches. Nothing is perfect right out of the box. Nothing that's never been done before is foolproof. That's why…"

"Kwame, I think it's time for you to go take Jocelyn back to work. If you can't have an unrehearsed conversation with me, if you can't tell me the truth, how can I continue to let you build the system that will tell everyone else in the world what the truth is?"

Kwame starts to respond… but stops himself just in time. He looks at me with confusion, apparently afraid to say anything, but also afraid that he is about to be fired for losing the biggest contract his company has ever had.

I wait to see what he does. His facial expressions reveal a set of emotions he probably has no idea he is showing. I wait longer.

Finally Kwame clears his throat, "Ma…" Again he catches himself just in time. "Secretary Warden."

I wait again while he realizes he still has a chance to get out of the box I've put him in.

"This is difficult," he pauses again, then continues. "What was the question?"

"I have another for you. How are you going to finish the project for what I've paid you to date? No more money."

Kwame looks like a fish trying to breathe air. I must wait a good fifteen seconds before he can utter another word, but then it comes, "I am not authorized…"

"I know that. But you do understand the technical requirements, you know where you are against them and you know what it will take to deliver the final system, do you not?"

"Not entirely…"

"I don't care about entirely. I know you're only the messenger. So I expect you to go back to your company, walk into the CEO's office and tell him you have a choice. You can either finish what you're contractually required to deliver as soon as possible for what you've already been paid, or you can continue along as you have on your own dime. Is that clear?"

Kwame apparently can't imagine talking to his CEO about

anything.

"Would you like me to come with you? I'd be happy to do so if that will make it easier. After all, as the Secretary of Truth everyone expects me to tell the truth. So to tell your CEO the truth should be what's expected. You should be able to as well."

Kwame glances at the door like he's wondering about Jocelyn.

"No, she won't be able to help you, because she won't listen to what you have to say, will she?"

Kwame apparently sees the truth in my comment. He looks back at me with a grimace. "Do you have any openings?"

"Why would I want to hire you, Kwame? You don't build anything. You don't have any backbone. You don't or can't tell the truth. How could I possibly hire someone who isn't truthful in the Department of Truth?"

"You have lots of them," Kwame shoots back. "The people on your interface team? They haven't told us the truth since the first day of the project. They promise data we don't get. They promise to complete testing by certain dates that is never done on time. Your people are the reason we are behind and over budget."

"Is that the truth or just the next excuse you've been told to give me?"

# CHAPTER SIX: BRANDON McINERNY

The same image presents itself. The same little blonde girl of maybe seven years of age. Naked with her back to me. Sitting on her heels. She's facing an older man. I don't know how old he is because his face is obscured by the little girl. He's sitting on the edge of a bed. This time I see just a little more than last time. This time I can just make out that the sitting man is barefoot. I know what my mind instantly concludes, but is that what this image is really all about? Some might say it's an art form. But it seems to me that everything I do relates to someone's art. Whether it be images of people doing strange things with all kinds of animals, only some of whom are human, or the words used to express hate, or to inspire fear, or jealousy. Words to incite rage and envy. The words just get me angry because I know what the person who wrote them is trying to do. The images are what keep me awake at night, keep me from the dreamless sleep I've sought through nearly every drug imaginable. And it doesn't get any better. And the dreams don't go away.

I wonder if I've seen that little blonde girl on the street somewhere. If she lives in my neighborhood. I could have walked right past her and not known it was her. Is that the case with all pornography? That the pornographer or his subject is just another person you sit next to at church or pray next to a mosque or who sits at the next table in a restaurant, or who you cheer with at a sporting event? They are clearly amongst us. Friend, neighbor, co-worker. A distant relative maybe.

The more I think about it there is no way I could know if that little girl is someone I've seen anywhere other than in the posting that keeps being made. Keeps presenting itself in hopes that another analyst will let it go out, rather than be swept into the atomized ether of dispersion. Another deleted posting.

The next image is not one I've seen in a while. It's a video clip of a teenager driving a car off a cliff. Thelma and Louise style. One of the Ten Commandments is to delete any posting that shows an actual death, whether at the hand of someone else or self-inflicted. Most of the suicide images we get are of kids or adults jumping off of something, hanging themselves in a room, or using a firearm to end their own life. Usually a clip from a video found at the scene. A clip posted by someone who either comes across it, or planted the camera surreptitiously and ends up with something unexpected. These images come from someone, in my humble opinion, and I could be wrong, who has an ego problem. They are trying to bring down the memory of someone who they were angry with, envious of, or simply didn't like for whatever reason. The color of their hair, maybe. A wart on the nose. A foul body odor. A tendency to laugh inappropriately. Who knows what evil lurks in the hearts of such people? Someone who makes a conscious decision to try to destroy the memory of someone they generally know.

I bring up the zoom. I want to look at his face. See what emotion he is experiencing. Is it relief? Is it fear? Is it resignation? What does someone who is taking their own life feel at that moment when they know the end is about to remove them from this reality? From this life. From all they have known since their birth on this planet. For who really knows whether this is all there is, or this life is just a way station on a much longer journey that takes on many different lives and possibly life forms on this planet or maybe even others somewhere else in the universe. Who can validate that the universe is not connected in some cosmic fashion? That the life forms on one planet in one solar system may not experience their next life on a different planet in a different solar system or maybe even a different galaxy? I'd never really given it much thought. Don't have a belief about what we are in the relativity of the universe. Don't think I've ever even discussed it with Sheila. And she usually wants to discuss things like that. Things that give her hope there is more to life than what we are experiencing.

But then her experience is different than mine. I'm internet. She's broadcast. She spends all day listening to the supposedly live talk shows and newscasts. They are supposedly live, but they are all on a sixty-minute delay. Everything has to be reviewed for content. Nothing can be broadcast if it doesn't meet the Ten Commandments. She tried to explain to me once that things used to be different. There was this requirement of the networks at that time, all before the media companies diversified their platforms. The requirement was known as the Fairness Doctrine. Any network that aired a viewpoint, rather than verifiable facts, had to give an equal amount of time to an opposing viewpoint. That way the audience could make up its own mind about the varying perspectives. The network was neutral. But when the Fairness Doctrine was repealed things quickly deteriorated. People no longer had to consider an opposing viewpoint. They could immerse themselves in a singular drumbeat. Believe the reality as espoused by a single source. The result is the extremes drove out the middle. Polarization became the norm. Both extremes worked hard to exterminate those who held a moderate thought in their head for more than a nanosecond. So Sheila has whiplash of the brain, being pushed from one extreme to the other every sixty seconds. Her job is to search out the opposing viewpoints, compare them and then search for validations that lead to the truth. Under the Fairness Doctrine, extreme positions often were compared to moderate positions which were commonly held by most people. Society moved slowly. It took a lot to get enough people to consider an extreme position and to embrace it. But when the comparison was only widely divergent extremes and no one was left in the middle, the population dug in to their reality. They fought against the change of the other extreme.

This all has made Sheila's job almost impossible. She and the other Truth Analysts frequently have to scrap a planned broadcast entirely because in an hour they can't validate the information presented. And while this has lessened the acrimony of the debates, because they don't get started, it has left most people entrenched where they were when the reinforcing verbal barrage ended.

I remember Sheila and I had a very strange conversation one night shortly after we had joined the department. We were trying to shut down our brains at a local club.

"Where does the truth come from?" she asked me. "Why is there only one truth? And why only the truth as sanctioned by the government? We spend our lives seeing sides of life that only other analysts ever see. It's an ugly hate-filled and fear mongering existence. But is that the only one out there other than the one the government gives us?"

"How does the government give us the truth?" I responded really surprised by her question, especially since it challenged what I thought I knew and made me think in ways I'd practically forgotten I could.

"The Ten Commandments," was her simple reply.

I'd been staring at the truth, or source of the truth, we are given for all the years I'd been an analyst. Yet I had no idea what the Ten Commandments really represents. "But they're just a framework," I pushed back. "There's so much room for interpretation. So many of us that look at them and apply them differently."

"You seem to forget something," she reminded me.

I just shrugged at her because I really had no idea what she was getting at. She looked at me with those big brown eyes. I swear they can look into my soul, if I really have one. She sees me in ways I don't think anyone else can. It seems she knows things about me that even I don't. And in this case she seemed to be looking to see if I really didn't understand or was simply trying to deny what I did know.

"The Arbiter System," she names the server that delivers the proposed postings to us.

"What about it?" I'm still not following why the Ten Commandments are the truth the government gives us.

"The Arbiter System screens everything and applies the Ten

Commandments. It lets things go through and only delivers what we need to review. And what do we review?"

I'm starting to understand her point and I don't like the fact that I'd not seen it before. That answers what she saw when she looked into my eyes. Total and complete blissful ignorance of what I was immersed in. "Only that which Arbiter has already decided should be deleted." I admit. She's got me. The system decides and all I do is confirm a small part of the total postings that will never see the light of day.

And then the recurring image of her appears. The image of her being violently beaten and raped. I can't see who is doing it to her, don't know where I am that I can't stop it. The dream jolts me awake. I'm sweating profusely as I sit up in bed.

## CHAPTER SEVEN: ELIZABETH WARDEN

Lei Lei Wong is probably all of five feet in heels. I have no idea how much she weighs, but it's probably not much more than a sack of birdseed. Lei Lei has a very expressive face, which is usually turned up in a self-satisfied smile. Although as my risk manager I have no idea how she can always be so upbeat. Her job is to figure out what can go wrong. What can keep us from meeting our objectives? And then she comes up with mitigation plans. What can make it better if such and such happens? She has good plans and I'm all about plans. Never met a plan I didn't like if it was well thought out and researched with care. Lei Lei is excellent at both researching and logically working through scenarios to tell me what I should expect and how to make the best of it if it should occur.

Because she is so good, I always listen carefully. I don't always agree with her recommendations. I have been known to send her back to rethink things. But I truly respect her expertise and insights. Maybe because I have so much respect for Lei Lei that I don't quite know what to do when she presents me with a risk I'd not focused on before.

"Burnout leading to violence," hits me like a wet towel in the face.

"What do you mean?" I finally wrap my head around her statement.

"I've been researching our workforce. The analysts in particular stand out," I don't like the way her statement trails off. It's ominous.

"We identified some analysts need counseling in some instances." I remember aloud. "But I thought we'd addressed that."

"Counseling is one thing to help them develop coping skills." Lei Lei acknowledges. "But I'm not talking about drinking too much or drug use. We've become concerned about addiction. However the data gathering about anything medical or illegal is just much harder. No one wants to admit they are."

"Understandable," I indicate I'm following that part, but I'm still wondering where she's going.

"The reports of domestic abuse peaked about two years ago. At the time we thought the new counseling program was having an effect. But what the data shows is it didn't improve. It's being expressed in other ways. Public ways. More disorderly conduct arrests. More public drunkenness, or driving under the influence. More antisocial behavior…"

"Like?"

"Petty theft. Assault. Verbal attacks in public," Lei Lei lays it out there for me.

"Total incidents? Do you have any insight on that?"

"Total incidents are up about ten percent over a year ago," Lei Lei knows the statistics and doesn't have to consult anything to find them.

"Any correlation with average stage?"

"Burnout stage?" Lei Lei seeks confirmation so she doesn't give me the wrong answer.

I nod.

"Burnout average has increased, but less than the violence increase. What I think we're seeing is residual effects among those who have left the Department. Former Analysts that are out there trying to cope. Struggling more than their predecessors. And I think this is just the beginning of what we are ultimately going to see."

"In terms of…"

"Violent acts among those who find they can't cope with what they've been exposed to in any other way."

"What we've exposed them to," I correct her, or at least put my spin on things to gauge her reaction.

Lei Lei thinks about my redirection. I see from her expression she's not sure if she agrees or not. "All we have done is permit them to see what is out there. We have not posted those images, written those words, or expressed those arguments."

"But we have permitted society to degrade to the point that such conditions exist, such thoughts occur to people, such feelings of rage, and anger, and hopelessness pervade corners of every community," I let go of my frustrations.

"When has society ever been this harmonious?" Lei Lei tries to reframe my perspective. "In the history of mankind when has the general public ever been protected from its own basal instincts as it is now? The general public doesn't see what our analysts see and that protects them. It eliminates a questioning of whether this is the best of all possible worlds. It makes the average person more at peace than they ever were when our society was at war with itself. The haves and the have nots. The liberals who wanted to change everything and the conservatives who wanted to go back to the way it was when things were simple. When relative abundance made it possible not to make choices."

"But the problem society encountered has not been a lack of abundance," I counter. "Our industry has produced so much choice that it is impossible to be content. There is always something better available now or coming soon. People who are much better off today are less content than their parents who lived a Spartan life in comparison."

Lei Lei shakes her head, "And that has introduced another of our risks. Namely that people have moved up Maslow's hierarchy of needs. They are searching for the next step above survival. They see others who are self-actualizing and wonder what does it take to get there? To be among those who worry not about health care, or losing a job, or whether aging parents or relatives have what they need to be comfortable. Whether their kids will be able to support themselves when they graduate."

"You've just left out a whole part of us." I note. "Those who don't graduate. Those who aren't on the upward trajectory that is the American dream. All those for whom our society, our community support programs, our jobs creation engine don't work. Those who remain outside the mainstream. What about them? We may protect them from seeing what they would otherwise see every day in the media. But they still see it every day because they are living it. The frustrations, the feelings of inadequacy, the inability to access the door to joining the middle class. What about them?"

"What they live is their reality." Lei Lei nods reflectively. "And you're right. They see a world the rest of us don't. They live a reality different than we show everyone in the media. And to get to a place where most have the means to live a comfortable, if not exciting, life has been our objective. To remove the discomforts, the dissatisfiers, the disappointments and the dislikes from everyday life is a noble objective. And it's why this office and this department of government exist."

Seeing we are in violent agreement I turn back to her original concern, "So you've established the reason why we subject the analysts to the disturbing side of life for eight to ten hours a day for up to seven days a week. But that still doesn't address the trends you have brought to my attention. What's the mitigation recommendation?"

"This is a particularly difficult problem."

I nod, "Although with the Arbiter System going automatic we at least won't be adding to the population who have to cope."

"Maybe." Lei Lei sounds skeptical. "But that doesn't address the millions we have in our midst at the moment. And maybe those who haven't progressed beyond stage three are redeemable. That too is still to be proven, at least to me. It may be stage two where the ability to cope with the public lies, the images and hate speech, the fake news, the perverse fantasies is compromised. But to my way of thinking even those individuals pose a risk to society in the long run. No one knows when these seeds will suddenly manifest themselves in radical behavior. No one knows what the real implications of what we have done to these people will be understood. And this growing and substantial risk is something we need to begin to address more aggressively now. We need a plan, especially for those whose jobs we are eliminating with the Arbiter System go live because it is that transition point when people are most at risk, having an anchor in their lives hoisted. Suddenly they are adrift without purpose, but with very dangerous thoughts in mind."

I understand the perceived risk much better after this discussion, but I'm still not sure what needs to be done about it, other than it needs to be done now.

## CHAPTER EIGHT: SHEILA

I hesitate before knocking on Brandon's door. I've never been to his apartment before. Didn't know where he lives. If Albert hadn't given me his address, I never would have been able to find him. And then he would have simply disappeared without a trace, at least from my life. What am I going to say to him? I'm sorry you lost your job? Why am I here other than I feel sorry for what happened to him? Want to help, but I'm not at all sure how I can… help him.

My knock on the door almost comes involuntarily. I'm so unsure how to handle this that it's almost as if some part of my mind decided I just need to do it even though another part of me isn't ready. The knock is greeted by silence. Is he even home? Did he commit suicide? What am I going to find? I don't know, and that thought scares me.

I hear the lock open. That is followed almost immediately by the door itself. Brandon peeks out. I can instantly tell he's stoned. He won't look at me. Well, at least that's better than some of the alternatives. I guess if Albert let me go I might do the same. No I wouldn't. I'd begin trying to find another job. But that's not Brandon. He needs time to adjust. I don't want to admit it but I probably would too.

"Can I come in?" I ask when Brandon finally looks at me.

He opens the door and steps back to permit me to enter, but continues to look down and not at me. The apartment is small. Barely more than a studio. A big window is the focal point, but he has the shade drawn so I can't tell what he overlooks. And then I realize there is no television monitor, no computer screens. None of the usual media access devices other than a single cell phone on the kitchen countertop. No art decorates the walls. No mementos from places he's visited or posters of a movie, or play. Nothing that would establish his interests. And as I look around, I remember he rarely has talked about anything other than what he's deleted from the internet that day. Only now he won't be deleting anything. So how will he rebalance his life? Regain perspective, mediated from all that he has spent the last several years fighting through?

"I wasn't expecting anyone, so I can't really offer you anything other than maybe an edible," Brandon looks about. "I think I still have a few."

"How many have you had?" I ask trying to understand the depths of his despair.

"Two, three. I don't know. Keeping count wasn't high on my priority list," he seems to grin sheepishly.

"This your usual Friday night meal?" I can't help being a bit pointed with him, hoping he'll bring up his situation rather than me having to.

Brandon nods. "No. I go out with people from work on Fridays. An edible and a glass of red wine. That's Friday. I usually see you out on Friday. But not last week. What's up with that? You sick or something?"

"My sister was in town," I wonder how much to tell him about that visit or whether he will really care. "Haven't seen her in forever."

"I thought you never saw your sister. Something about you really didn't get along," apparently he remembers a least one conversation I had with him when Jules and I were fighting about Mom's health issues. But that was a while ago.

"I never see my sister because she still lives in Oz."

"Australia." Brandon seeks confirmation.

"Where we grew up. I left and she stayed. I got freedom and she got our mother. Sometimes I think she got the better end of that

40

decision."

Brandon looks at me with curiosity. "What makes you think that? I mean you've got your own life here. No one hanging on you. No one telling you what to do. This has got to be better than getting beat up by your old lady because you have a boyfriend she doesn't like or you don't have a boyfriend, and how are you ever going to have kids if you don't get out and mingle."

I'm surprised he remembers my comments, almost verbatim. "That was a long time ago. Even Jules doesn't get that from her anymore."

Brandon nods just once, an exaggerated nod. He then goes and sits on the one couch in the room, ratty flowered cover, which faces the shade drawn window. I'm not sure if he's expecting me to come sit next to him or what.

I see a chair at this breakfast table. I pull that over to face him before I sit on it, backwards, so I can rest my arms across the top of the back.

"What brings you to the slums?" Brandon seems willing to look at me now. Maybe this way of sitting seems authoritarian to him or something. Don't know, but at least he's willing to engage me.

"You," I readily admit but am still trying to dance around the real reason.

"Wanting to know why I didn't come down for lunch with everyone as usual?"

I shake my head. "I know why you weren't there. Albert told me what happened. We're both worried about you."

I see a clarity invade his eyes. I've not seen that until now. It's almost like he'd been looking inward and somehow my comment brought him out of himself, forced him to actually engage me rather than simply ignoring what has happened. "No worries."

"That's my line," I protest. "You can't steal it."

"I wouldn't do that. But I might borrow it until something better occurs to me."

"So I'm supposed to go back and tell Albert that all's good when I don't believe that for a moment."

"I'm not at stage five if that's what you're worried about."

The fact he would go there tells me he's wondering if he is. Not a good sign. But what am I going to do? Challenge him? Make him talk about what he's thinking? What he's feeling? What he's likely to do with all the emotions roiling around in his brain and heart? "Where do you think you are?" I put out there for him to give me his rationale.

Brandon looks away as he answers, "Albert made it possible for me to never have to have another evaluation. So it really doesn't matter. Not his problem, not yours and most importantly, not mine."

"I'm not here to file a report on the state of your mental health. I'm genuinely worried about how you're coping." I decide I have to just lay it out there for him. See what he does with it. If he asks me to leave, then I've done what I could. If he talks, well then, maybe I can help him.

"Coping," Brandon responds still unwilling to look at me, as if he's trying to look past the word, and see what's really behind it. What am I really saying to him? Then something changes. "But you know you're asking the wrong question." His voice has changed as if he's going to tell me something he didn't want to but somehow he's feeling compelled.

"What do you mean?"

"Elizabeth can't see it, but she's got a big problem," He just stops, leaving me wondering.

"What are you talking about?"

Brandon looks at me with the strangest look before answering, "Having time to think. It's not a good thing. But you know what I realized?"

I shake my head.

"I realized if the Department is laying me off, and they lay you off they have a big problem with Arbiter."

"You're just upset about losing your job," I dismiss him without trying to sound that way. More trying to put his situation into perspective.

"Think about it," he watches my reaction, shakes his head then continues, "You don't see it do you?"

"What?" I know that came across harsher than I wanted it to. "I'm sorry…"

"It's right there and no one is using their heads. If they lay us all off, there's no reference group. Arbiter works off learning algorithms. It learns what we, as a group see as acceptable and what's not. If there's no reference group it can't learn. What happens then?"

His observation catches me off guard, "I guess it stops learning."

"Exactly. But we don't stop changing. Don't you see the problem?" He looks at me hopefully.

"Arbiter stops learning so won't post anything it didn't post before because that's the rules it works from."

"Exactly!" Brandon almost jumps off his couch. "It won't post anything it didn't post before, but we keep changing. We keep evolving as people. What's acceptable changes because we change, but Arbiter won't post it. Don't you see? It becomes like a bottle with expanding gases. If there's no release at some point it explodes. That's what will happen if Arbiter can't learn from us. We either invent a new way of communicating not mediated by Arbiter or we storm the barricades to bring it down."

"You want me to go tell Elizabeth?" I'm not sure where this is coming from.

Brandon's enthusiasm seems to be deflated by my question. "If I can't convince you I guess there's just no hope." He sits back down on the couch and seems to withdraw from me.

"You know it just might be better for me to come back when you're not stoned..."

"Stoned? Me?" Brandon acts as if I hurt his pride but I know that's bullshit.

"Yes, you. When you're stoned you're running away from what we've both seen all day long. I understand that. I have my own means of escaping it. But when you're stoned you're not in a frame of mind to have a conversation other than one that acts as a release valve for the reactions you've been sitting on all day long. I get it." I stand up, "When you're not under the influence of one thing or another, give me a call or send me a text. I'll come back. You're important to us. We don't want you to think you're out here all by yourself. We want to help. Help you transition to the next thing, whatever that's going to be. And all I can say for sure is it will be better than what you've done for the last, what is it? Ten years?"

Brandon looks up at me. "Don't go. I didn't want you here when you first appeared at my door. But that was just because I wasn't expecting you. Didn't know what you wanted. This is all very awkward. I wanted to see you so much when Albert gave me the news. But you were also the last person I wanted to see, because I was ashamed about what happened. I'm out but you're still there. Obviously Albert values you more than he does me. I still don't know what to do with that. But the fact that you came to see me. That tells me that maybe

I'm not totally worthless. Someone cares about me. I've not felt that way in a long time. I hate to say that, but it's true. I've been holding down the fort here all by myself for so long I might as well have been on a desert island."

I reach out and tuck a lock of his hair back behind his left ear. Smile at him. "I care." I see the moisture gathering in Brandon's eyes. He tries to blink it away but when his eyes open again I can still see it. See the sadness there. See the pain of rejection; of worthlessness he is apparently feeling having lost his job.

I come sit on his lap, putting my arm around his shoulders, smoothing out his hair. I kiss the top of his head and give him an awkward hug. Not something easy to do from this position. Brandon shakes his head, still looking down. I don't know what else to do to get his attention.

It takes a moment, but Brandon apparently rallies and realizes I'm here. I'm making myself available to him if he's interested. We've never been intimate, although our discussions have touched on intimate things. Likes and dislikes. What turns us on and what turns us off. Things like that. Brandon finally looks up at me and lets me kiss him on the lips. A long and lingering kiss. Our first actual kiss.

After several more long and lingering kisses, Brandon rises with me in his arms. He carries me to the bed on the other side of the room. We slowly undress the other, dropping the clothes onto the floor, looking long and longingly at the other's body as more and more is revealed. Kissing each other's nakedness until all of the clothes are discarded. And then Brandon takes a look at all of me as I look at all of him. I know there is no turning back now. We are able to fire the imagination of the other even when there is nothing between us but air. Brandon steps forward and kisses me as he also moves me slowly down onto the bed.

# CHAPTER NINE: ELIZABETH WARDEN

I hate Sabr's press conferences. She trots me out to take the bullets aimed at her. She does this all too often. But it is what it is. Sabr is answering questions about the state of the economy. Always first on the mind of the Washington press corps. They know people only want to know if the economy is strong. Whether they are likely to keep their job, or the economy is weakening and they may lose their job if things stay bad long enough. Most people on Main Street have no idea why the economy weakens. Why they lose their jobs. Why demand slackens, putting people out of work. None of this makes sense to the average American, Chinese, Indian or European. People make things and people buy things. How hard can it be? If enough people want to buy something that will ensure work for people. Why people stop buying is because they are afraid they may lose their job. Afraid they may not have enough money to feed their family. That's simple economics. That's what people understand. All this stuff about global economy is all theoretical to the average person living just off Main Street in the small towns of America.

The economy doesn't expand exponentially or linearly. It expands and contracts. It is totally unpredictable through all the efforts of millions of people with fantastic tools and massive computers. The economy can't be controlled, although it can be influenced. It can't be predicted, although hundreds of thousands of people are paid a lot of money to do just that. Even though they can't. And through this all, Sabr has to defend an economy that at best she can only influence and not control.

Once the last prognosticator has delivered the advice from on high, the subject seems to turn. Economy is what it's going to be. Okay. "As President you're doing everything you can to extend the economic expansion. Got that. So what's going on with the Department of Truth?"

That's where I come in whether I'm ready or not.

"The Department of Truth is doing everything humanly and machine learning-wise possible to ensure that only the truth is delivered to the American people." What an intro. How am I supposed to build on that? "Secretary Warden is here to answer your questions."

"Secretary Warden, what do you think will be the biggest difference people will see when your new system goes live? When will that happen?"

I look at the reporter who asked this question. Betsy Phillips. She represents a news service. Reuters? I can never remember which one. Probably doesn't make any difference, since if it appears on one news service, anyone can pick it up and repeat it. Viral communications are great except when it works against you. When you'd rather people don't know. But the savior is always the analyst who will deem whatever is being discussed as fake news and delete it. From what I've seen, the analysts have kept more from working against us than stifling what would help us. That's by design.

"Secretary Warden?" Betsy asks again since I've not answered.

"People should not see any difference," I suggest.

"Really?" She challenges me. "How is that possible? People aren't algorithms."

"No, they aren't," I agree. "But algorithms are created by people and reflect the values and sensibilities of people. It's like the old definition of pornography. If I see it, I'll know it. That's the way it is with algorithms. If it sees something that should be removed from the political discourse, or removed from the internet, or removed from the debates about what is appropriate for us politically, that's what it is. An algorithm is as capable of spotting that as a person. Probably more capable, because the same standard is applied in every case. A machine doesn't have a hangover, doesn't have a period, and doesn't have anything that would distract it from the Ten Commandments."

"Do you really believe that?" Betsy Phillips presses her question.

"Don't you?" I push back. "The very nature of your question would indicate you don't. But if that's the case, why do they let you, who apparently represents a viewpoint, ask the questions in the first place?"

"They?" Betsy wonders aloud, looking for me to dig a deeper hole.

"The people who employ you to find the news. Although from what I'm seeing the news would apparently be secondary to what will convince other people to read your blog or listen into your podcast."

"Are you saying I'm biased?" Betsy Phillips continues her challenge.

"I can't tell for sure, but from the nature of the questions you're asking I would have to wonder," I respond neutrally hoping to get some sympathy.

"You have nothing to wonder," Betsy Phillips responds. "We are regulated just as you are. If I ask the wrong question it never gets on the air. If I don't frame the question in such a manner that the news services will want to pick it up, no one will ever know I even asked it. For us, the new reality is even more restrictive than what we had to deal with previously. The world hasn't become friendlier. It hasn't become opaquer. It isn't even translucent anymore. The world has become a dark hole we are all trying to climb out of. The world is the seventh ring of hell, only there is an escape route. Up and over the top. Clear to anyone who understands what is going on just below our feet. And that is the problem for you and me. What is going on just below our feet doesn't look anything like what we are discussing. They are working to make today different from yesterday. Different from the day before yesterday. We are living in an age where you and I are the product of a radically different future. One where we can make a difference. One where the forces of the status quo are having to contest the future where a new organization, a new focus, a new dedication is the result."

"Do you really believe that?" I push back on Betsy Phillips.

"Of course I do or I couldn't do this job. I'd just be another robot. Another drone doing what someone else wants me to do. I have to have autonomy. The ability to ask the questions that matter to me. If not, why would it make any sense for me to continue to do this?"

"Why indeed." I ask her, expecting her to be less than responsive.

"Wait, Madam Secretary." Betsy Phillips isn't happy with my response. "Are you saying that the future is determined by the machine learning algorithms? That the machine will observe us and predict everything of substance about us? Are you saying that freedom will no longer exist because a machine learning algorithm can predict what we will do, regardless of what we may decide, because our tendencies are so well known and so predictable?"

"No, Miss Phillips. That's not what I'm saying." I deflect her question. "The Arbiter system is able today to determine what is socially acceptable. What you and I can see when we go on line? What we can listen to when political figures get on stage and decide to have a debate. The Arbiter System is able to decide what makes sense for you and me to interact with on a daily basis. What will be harmonious with the conventions of the day? What we will find uplifting. Reinforcing of a future of achievement. A future of harmony. A future where everyone is valued equally. Where everyone is compensated equally for the value of what they deliver to the greater good of society. Why are you questioning the value of a system that delivers exactly what we've debated as the most important hallmarks of a democratic society for nearly a century?"

"Why do we need a system to impose on us what we expect to be?" Betsy Phillips asks as if it should be self-evident.

"We have relied on Truth Analysts to deliver this equality for decades." I respond with the safe answer. "The machine algorithms have trillions of data points to learn from. You and I don't have that. Yet society asks us to make those determinations. Why would you think that a human would be better able to make such a decision based on hundreds or thousands of data points in comparison to trillions?"

"No offense, Madam Secretary. But a human can distinguish nuance. Can read between lines. Can see the dimension that algorithms never see. I, for one, would rather stand before a human judge to adjudicate an offense I'm accused of than an algorithm that may have seen a trillion examples of human behavior, but can't look me in the eye to understand my intent."

"Of what are you guilty?" is all I can think of to ask.

# CHAPTER TEN: JURGEN

The makeup artist is having difficulty putting enough powder on my face to keep the sweat from causing shiny spots. Can't have shiny spots on camera. I am the leader of the EuTopian nations. Someone to be feared. Someone who must be reckoned with in any discussion of what the state should or should not do. I am the final decider. Not someone who sweats, or seems anxious. I have to appear supremely confident, not only in my own judgment, but in the correctness of our government's policies.

The makeup artist steps back, smiles at me. She's young. Pretty in an understated way. Apparently she doesn't need a lot of powder to make her look natural. Maybe she should be the one to deliver this address. Answer the questions. The never-ending questions. But the people want to know what the government is doing. Because the government is the only thing we all have in common. So they think it's theirs. And to some extent it is. It governs them. Sets out the rules within which they must constrain their actions in daily life. For the greater good. So that all may live peaceful, harmonious lives amongst a sea of strangers.

"That should do it, Chancellor," she pronounces with a slight accent. She is not from the motherland for sure. I should have realized that. Such jobs as she has, have always been filled by immigrants, who are working their way up. Start out as a technician for a company, learn the trade and then go into business in competition with their former employer. Undercutting the cost, because they have no overhead. No trainees who they must support until they learn the trade. Everyone else supports trainees because they leave as soon as they have a following of customers.

"What's your name?" I ask curious.

"Magritte," she responds proudly. "I have applied your makeup for nearly a year and this is the first time you have noticed me. Did I do something wrong?"

"No, Magritte. As you said, you have applied my makeup for nearly a year and yet I know nothing about you. Your hopes and fears. What's important in your life? What help you need to be happy?"

"Is that your job? To know what I need to be happy?"

I'm surprised at her response. I would have expected her to just tell me something. "It is my job to make sure the government is not making it more difficult for you to be happy."

"Then you are doing your job," she doesn't quite dismiss my concern, but would appear to be dismissing me. "I am happy."

"You like making someone look better than they are in real life," I test her.

"But of course. Isn't that the dream of everyone? To look better than they actually do? Particularly how they look in the morning after a long sleep. Plain. No accents to their features. That's what I do. I add the accents that make them look mysterious. Make them look attractive, and empowered, and desirable."

"And that makes you happy," I conclude.

"Being very good at making people look better makes me happy because I am able to make them happy with how they look. Isn't that enough to be happy?"

I think about her notion of happy for a moment. A thought comes to me, "What would you do to make me look better, if you could do anything. Not just make my face less shiny for the cameras."

Magritte puzzles for a moment, looks closely at my face, steps closer and applies a bit more powder to the left side of my nose.

"Nothing. You have a strong face. If I were to accent your features they would probably make you look older. And that would not be a good thing. You are young and strong and healthy. People like that you are Chancellor and have time to make our lives better."

"Continuity," I suggest. "You would not want someone to be Chancellor who would only be in the job one or two terms?"

Magritte shakes her head. "I see that in other countries. Leaders come and go. The government puts a new program in place. The next government comes in and takes it away. One government reduces taxes, the next increases them. I want things to be predictable. I want to know that things will change, but slowly. I want to know that if I have children I will be able to make a good life for them. Be able to pay for school. Pay for a bicycle, or a video game, or a sports uniform. Whatever he or she would like. Is that so much to ask?"

"What about for other people?" I ask now that I know her political sentiments. "Should the government be doing more for them? Particularly the poor? Or people who have just arrived from somewhere else? People who are struggling or trying to make a new life for themselves and their family?"

"Everything is a balance," She steps forward and applies a little more powder above my right eyebrow. "There, just so," she steps back and continues. "The more you give to someone the more you take from someone else. You increase my taxes I say you take too much. You decrease my taxes I can buy more or save more for my children, but I will still say you take too much. So it is a balance."

"Chancellor," my assistant Dagmar calls me. "It's time."

"Am I ready?" I ask Magritte as I look in the mirror.

"Ready," she confirms.

I realize Magritte is a true believer, and I have need of such people in the plans I am beginning to execute. "Magritte, I may ask you to do something for me."

"Make you look older? I would not want to do that."

I shake my head, "Something that would be different," is all I can say now.

As I join the much shorter Dagmar, I've frequently thought we must look strange that I am constantly leaning over to hear her since she is relatively soft spoken.

She informs me, "You can expect a question from Herr Mustapha about how you are encouraging differing opinions about government policies."

"Immigration policies I assume," hearing that Mustapha is going to ask the question I know it is the same question he comes back to time and time again. When are we going to open up the core to the provinces? I'm not ready to do that having seen it fail everywhere it has been tried, but I can't say that.

"Likely an accurate assumption," Dagmar responds.

I come across the platform and anchor myself behind the podium, looking out on the room with nearly a hundred media personnel manning the cameras, the recorders and the transmitters that will transcribe my responses and submit them for media placement. Their stories will be scanned by my analysts to determine if they have posted the truth as we wish it disseminated. Since the analysts will have not only government policies and the transcription of my remarks for the system to compare, there is little in the way of differences between what the various media outlets will post. That way the people will see the same story regardless of where they get their information.

"Good afternoon. Thank you for coming. Let me begin by saying that the state of our federation has never been stronger. We are at peace. Our economy has continued a strong jobs growth. Our stock market continues to enrich our people. The choices we have in our stores have never been greater. Peace, prosperity, and happiness for everyone. That is our objective and that is what we are delivering today."

A familiar figure rises three rows back. An older gentleman, with longish hair, a full gray beard and rough wool suit. "Chancellor."

So soon? I haven't even reviewed all the progress we made this year on so many fronts. Might as well get it over. Then maybe I can end on a positive note. "Herr Mustapha. Do you have your usual question or another this time?"

Herr Mustapha nods briefly in recognition. "Chancellor. You speak of peace, prosperity and happiness for everyone, but your very statement has excluded a wide swath of the people who reside in the nether reaches of EuTopia. It excludes many in the core. It excludes the very people who work tirelessly at the jobs you are creating, which are not the high paying professional positions people are seeking. These people do not have stock in companies so they are not finding prosperity. And how can anyone be happy with the state of a society that excludes so many who have so much to give and have the energy to truly transform our nation into something more humane, more inclusive and more supportive of individual and group achievement?"

"Herr Mustapha," I begin as I have each and every time, "It is not rational to ask the same question many times and expect a different answer."

## CHAPTER ELEVEN: JAVIER SANTIAGO

I cringe through much of the press conference. Not because I think Jurgen is saying all the wrong things, but because I know he will be coming to see me shortly. That's always the case. Only the Minister of Truth can salvage a poor performance by simply not permitting it to go outside the room where it occurred.

Jurgen comes flying into my office, as expected. He makes a soft landing in the chair he always takes at the round table next to the door. It's his signal for me to come join him. As a Spaniard, I know my place in the hierarchy.

"You are unhappy with your performance?" I start by asking the question I know he will not answer.

"You have removed the Mustapha question from the official version?"

"And his response to your response," I assure him since the revised version is airing as we speak. "But this begs the larger question. How do you address the Mustapha question?" I leave this vague to see where his thoughts are, knowing that as the day progresses, and other issues intervene, his thoughts will change.

"I generally favor cooption. Offer him a low-level position in the Ministry and make him complicit. At that point he is no longer a problem."

This solution has been proposed before, but he generally thinks better of it the later in the day I come back to it. "We have spoken in the past of Internal Security."

Jurgen frowns, so that clearly is not his preferred solution at the moment.

"Why do you not see that now?" I pursue his physical reaction.

"He could become a conduit for information to Radio Free Europe. Ever since the Chinese restarted that old American propaganda machine it has been a growing source of annoyance."

"An alternative truth," I throw out to again fuel his discomfort.

"There is no alternative truth. There is only the truth as I determine it," Jurgen bellows at me. Now I have him where he may listen. Until now it has all been about his instant reaction to Mustapha. Now it will be about ensuring his version of the Truth is all that the people care about.

"Speaking of the truth, Sabr is getting close to fully automating."

That catches Jürgen's attention. "I thought she agreed to slow that."

"She did and she has. Their system has been running in parallel for almost a year."

"I thought after that she was going to have her system make the determinations but have the analysts simply validate machine decisions." Jurgen is testing his memory now. I know he doesn't always listen to the details.

"She moved to that phase six months ago. From what Elizabeth tells me, the correlation has steadily increased. Now she doesn't see a need to keep the man-in-the-loop system in place."

"And Sabr is supporting her recommendation?"

"Apparently it is only a matter of when," I confirm. "I get the impression there will be no announcement as it will essentially be a non-event for most people in her federation."

"Are you having second thoughts?"

I expect this response. "We operate a little differently than they do. We target certain people, like Herr Mustapha, not just his ideas. In a fully automated system that is harder to do without leaving a clear trail of what you are doing. In our system the trail dies with the analyst who has been running that case."

Jurgen nods once, "But why should we care about a trail? No one will ever see it that we don't wish to see it. Why is it an event you are concerned about?"

"History," is my simple response.

"You remind me that history repeats itself, but we live in an age of relativism the world has never seen before." Jurgen is pulling out another of my arguments to use against me. Oh well. "As we more fully control what is truth then that's all there is. If I tell your machine the truth is we never target individuals, the machine will ensure that is the only information discussed, and the only information repeated in the media. So what's the problem?"

"We do not control one-on-one conversations." I point out. "While they lack the pervasiveness of the media, they can still be a very effective means of conveying alternative truths."

"That's how you're planting disinformation elsewhere?"

I nod. "One of many means, and that's part of the issue. We know other nations are planting disinformation here as well. By multiple means. Sometimes even disguised in media postings that the machines and the analysts won't recognize, but the intended audiences will. Like the rumors that music tracks played backwards have hidden messages. Or graphics have multiple images hidden within them. In those cases the media is still the carrier of choice, but we simply don't see or find the seeds of a revolution hiding in plain sight."

"You can't train your algorithms to look for alternative

meanings?"

"We have, but we don't always catch them," I admit to temper his enthusiasm for systems over human analysts.

Jurgen is quiet for a moment, apparently considering either my answers to his questions, or something totally unrelated. I never know with him.

"Are you thinking about our pledge to support the global Truth protocol?"

Jurgen looks up at me, "Should I be?"

"The global protocol requires us to harmonize our system with those of UsTopia and UaTopia. To adopt the statements released in those countries for events occurring there just as they will adopt the statements released here. To harmonize the global understanding of events. To create common enemies and common truths. To praise each of the incumbent governments globally and eliminate criticism."

"Aspirational. Not something we will achieve any time soon," Jurgen dismisses.

I don't mean to surprise him, but... "We could do it today if you chose to."

"I chose to?" Jurgen picks up on the key phrase I wanted him to.

"Sabr and Xi have agreed to go ahead when you decide we will join."

Jurgen rises. He clearly didn't understand where we are. "If we're ready, tell him."

"Even though we aren't fully automated and that is what the protocol calls for."

"How will they know if we are or aren't?"

"The speed with which we respond to their statements," I clarify for him.

"Can't we just accept what they send to us and post them with an initial scan withholding anything that has implications for us?"

"No," I have to make him understand. "That's not the agreement."

"Then why did we sign on?"

"Because we were more concerned about the rest of the world parroting our positions than we were theirs."

"That may have been short-sighted." Jurgen notes, but in an abstract way. "Do we need to have a get together and change the protocol?"

"I wouldn't recommend it," I say in a tone of voice that Jurgen will understand it to not be a good idea.

"Why? What do we have to lose?"

"Support for the whole idea," I explain. "It took a long time to reach this agreement, but it happened when no one was quite sure how it would work. Now everyone has a clearer idea. If we reopen the agreement it is likely to be shelved indefinitely. We have much more to gain by having our citizens hear the same thing when they travel abroad as they do when they are home. That has always been something that introduces instability. When people travel and return with different perceptions of what is happening at home and the impact of our actions as seen in a global context."

"What do we do about Radio Free Europe?" Jurgen puzzles then apparently thinks he sees a different way forward. "What if we meet with Xi and exclude Sabr? Isolate UsTopia?" Jurgen brightens at the thought.

# CHAPTER TWELVE: SABR MALIK-GOLDSTEIN

I nod to Elizabeth as she enters the Oval Office for the call with Jurgen. The only information I received was that Jurgen wants to talk about terrorism, which is why Elizabeth is here. If a terrorist group is operating in UsTopia, Elizabeth should know about them and what their demands are.

"Madam President," Elizabeth greets me as she takes her seat.

A moment later I hear the familiar voice, "Guten Morgan, Madam President."

"Good afternoon, Chancellor," I respond. "This is your call so please proceed."

"I have Javier with me and I assume Elizabeth is brightening your office at this very moment."

"She is," I confirm, surprised at his description, and wait for more explanation.

"You are aware that we are planning a state celebration of the fifth anniversary of my elevation to Chancellor."

"And that is the event you are anticipating the parties of interest are planning to disrupt somehow?" I see where he is going.

"Our counterterrorism teams have identified a dissident group. They appear to be making plans. Although we have not been able to establish targets or dates. The linkage to the state celebration is circumstantial at best. But there have been indications."

"With such tenuous evidence, what do you really know for sure?" I don't want our analysts chasing ghosts. Better that he do more homework before asking for us to apply our intelligence systems to the problem.

"They have attempted to post economic nationalist propaganda," Javier can be heard in the background.

"Nationalist of what ethnic group?" Why are they deliberately making me pull this information from them rather than just giving us the top line to go work?

"Armenian," Jurgen answers this question. Curious.

"So the real grievance isn't against EuTopia so much as it is against the Turks," Elizabeth raises.

"Turkey is a proud member state of EuTopia. A grievance against Turkey is a grievance against the union," Jurgen is adamant.

"Even though it predates the union by a century," I note for them.

"Nevertheless, the state must respond to address their grievances and prevent terrorist activity within the confines of our nations state," Javier recites almost as if he's said it a thousand times or more, which I know he has, having heard it a dozen or more times myself.

"Genocide is a tough grievance to address," I point out, "Especially when you weren't part of or party to it."

"But you are now seen as complicit in that you have brought the guilty nation into the fold along with them." Elizabeth adds to clarify the situation for me. "Both countries are member states of EuTopia so this should be an intra-nations discussion, not the international subject of terrorist activity."

"Tell that to the terrorists," Jurgen suggests sarcastically.

"Their objective would appear to be to bring pressure on your government to force the Turks to the negotiations table," I try to clarify the situation. "Is that what I'm hearing?"

"Evidence we have collected would support that theory," Javier again. He has the specifics that even Jurgen doesn't. I don't know what it is between those two, but Jurgen seems to want Javier to do all the dirty work without getting too close to it.

"Is there an alternative? Elections in Turkey for example?" Elizabeth apparently wants to know more why they think the terrorist group is going after a EuTopian event rather than a Turkish one.

"The Armenians have had lots of opportunity to disturb Turkish elections, but have never chosen to do so. I can't tell you why, other than the Turkish government has dug in its heels on this one. The Turks will simply not admit they were responsible for genocide, even if it was more than a century ago at this point."

"And the Turkish people aren't willing to confront their leaders or admit their complicity to such an act," Elizabeth continues showing her grasp of the situation.

"That is certainly an interpretation that could be drawn from what has transpired." Javier agrees with Elizabeth.

"Do Jurgen and I need to get off this call and let you work this directly?" I suggest.

"I think it important that you and I are part of this discussion." Jurgen throws out there.

"Why?" I push back.

"Are you at all aware of such a terrorist group?" Jurgen asks directly, almost as if he is asking if my government is somehow supporting the group.

"Elizabeth?" I defer to the person on the call who should know.

"Do you have a name for the group?"

"We have given them a code name, but that is internal here. They have not identified themselves with a group or cause name that we have identified." Javier fills in the blanks this time.

Elizabeth starts scrolling on an iPad she carries with her. "That makes it more difficult. I see we have several groups in our global threat database that have advocated for Armenian genocide justice at one time or another. But nothing I am seeing would indicate them as terroristic or suggesting violence in anything they have released or been quoted as saying on the subject."

"Are any of them resident in UsTopia?" Jurgen asks. Why is he drilling in on that particular subject? It almost seems like he is accusing us of protecting terrorists.

Elizabeth scrolls down again. "It would appear that those we are tracking are entirely in Armenia, although we believe they may have individuals here who contribute financially to their cause. Nothing more."

Jurgen has apparently been waiting for that confirmation. "Then I would suggest you need a new Secretary of Truth, Madam President. We have it on very good authority that the group we are tracking is wholly within your borders, that the organizers are American of Armenian descent and that this is not the only cause they are fomenting dissent around."

"A very strong statement on your part, Chancellor. And are you willing to share the evidence you are referring to or are we to simply take your statement as fact and work to validate it completely without the advantage of what you purport to know?"

"You sound skeptical Madam President." Jurgen has thought this out and planned to spring this on us after we confirmed we didn't have whatever information he says he has. But prior experience with Jurgen has bells ringing in my head. He doesn't always come to the table with an airtight case.

"As I should be until my team and I have had a chance to review your evidence."

"Are you not curious as to what else they are advocating?" Jurgen is clearly enjoying informing me about things he thinks I should already know. Demonstrating that his intelligence gathering is at least as good as ours and implying it may be better, at least in this one situation.

"I'm always happy to learn," I respond, not at all eager to have him continue schooling me in intelligence.

"They are advocating the abolition of the position of the Presidency in the US."

"Armenians have taken this position?" I try to clarify something that seems totally orthogonal to the rest of the conversation.

"We found a position paper that had been submitted for publication that asked the question whether the Presidency was necessary in the structure of your government," Javier responds. "The article is on its way to you as we speak."

## CHAPTER THIRTEEN: BRANDON McINERNY

The naked seven-year-old little blonde girl, sitting on her heels, back to me appears again. Why is my mind sending this same image over and over again? Why does it reveal just a smidgeon more each and every time? The large man beyond her is a tiny bit more evident. He has hairy legs from what little of them I can see. Dark hair at that, which would indicate he is dark haired rather than blonde like her. Why does my imagination want to fill in this picture? To know more about the girl. Who she is. Who the man is. What they are doing. And why does my mind instantly run to the worst scenario? Why am I not just assuming the picture is of a man and his daughter? Why do I instantly think the man is too old to be her father? Why do I assume anything? Why can't I just accept the picture for what it is? An incomplete image? Something that is designed to pique my interest. To catch my attention. Isn't that what advertising is intended to do? Don't we pay people who can create curiosity a lot of money to do that? And don't they often have naked or nearly naked women in those images? Why does this image suggest something different? Why do I see it that way without even considering the alternatives? Is something wrong with me? Am I permanently damaged that I can only see the evil side of men? See that which sick minds see? See that which the Ten Commandments tell me are not acceptable for men or women to see, to think about, or to engage in spreading idea viruses.

The image changes to the face of a young woman. Early twenties I would imagine. A black woman whose face is disfigured. Holes in her ears have been widened to accommodate large earrings. Her lips have been stretched out to accommodate what looks like clam shells. A bone pierces her nose, making it appear mis-shapened. She has hooks through her skin at the corners of her eyes. I've seen photos like this before. Pictures of African tribal women for whom these adornments are considered beautiful. To the Western eye they are mutilations. That is exactly what I think, although I know I shouldn't. Who am I to judge the beauty choices of this woman whose life experience is as foreign to me as her appearance? I remember asking about this picture the first time I'd seen one like it. The one thing that stuck with me was that in her culture if she'd not taken these measures to enhance her appearance she would likely never attract a husband. Here she would have difficulty attracting a husband who wished to share his life with a woman who made herself look like this.

I've never understood why women find it necessary to alter their appearance to attract attention. To conform to someone else's standard of beauty. A social convention that may or may not have anything to do with what is important in a relationship. And what she looks like inside. Is she caring? Is she considerate of others? Is she smart and willing to ask questions? Is she willing to challenge the status quo to make things better for others? Suddenly I know I'm thinking of Sheila again. Dangerous thoughts. I can't go there, so I just move on.

A story appears next with a headline of, 'Do we need to bring back the hanging tree?' I already know where this story is going. I don't need to read it. But the person who posted it has already achieved his or her objective. And I'm surprised how often women are now posting unimaginable things in just the few years I've been an analyst. That didn't happen when I started. Didn't happen even a few years ago. And now I have to look at the byline to know. I never did that when I started. And now I don't want to look. But as with so much of what's posted I'm drawn to it. I want to know what kind of sick person posts these things. Why do they do it? To disgust the people who encounter their imagination? To cause us to be repelled and never click on anything that might deliver such a concept to me again? I don't think so. I've come to the conclusion that the people who imagine this sick shit really want to experience it. Or at least watch someone else experience it. And there are a lot of voyeurs out there. People who live through the experiences of others, rather than through their own. Why is that? Is the life that many people make for themselves so boring, so predictable, so void of meaning that they seek something totally different? Something dangerous. Something that might make their lives a whole lot more exciting if they were brought to the attention of authorities? Brought before a Truth Tribunal?

I scan the article. I have to. It's my job. I don't want to, as I don't agree with anything this person is talking about. As I begin to read I find my assumption is wrong. The article is talking about clothes lines. The person who wrote the article is talking about the growing trend of drying clothes outdoors. Says it's a conservation approach. Use less electricity. Makes the clothes smell better. Unless your backyard is next to a processing plant of some kind, or a trash landfill. Always a caveat. Works for some and not for others. The article would appear to make sense. But I'm sure the reason it was flagged and sent to me is because of the headline. It suggests something very different from the body of the article itself. Usually it's the other way around. The headline suggests something that attracts interest. Causes people to want to read it. And the body of the article introduces something very different. Something that is fake news, not the truth or offensive for a million different reasons. So why did this author do the opposite? Why would that person write an article which served as bait for the Arbiter System? Knowing it would be flagged and not posted. The only conclusion I can draw is the author was trying to make a point to the analyst who would read it. And that would be me. Make the point that not everything is what it appears. Make the point that we should not be so quick to refuse a posting. Consider the merits of the message that is being sent apart from the social conventions that push us to take actions to the detriment of the author and her or his audience.

I can accept what this author is trying to do. Fight for the rights of authors. Fight for the right to have their stories considered by whatever audience they might attract.

Another image, this one is a beheaded body. Male. Young. Probably also in his twenties. Standing behind him is a man dressed all in black including a hood so his face is not visible. The man stands before a flag. I've seen that flag in pictures published before the Arbiter

System judged them to carry an undesirable message. A message of inhumanity to men. It represented a sect, loosely affiliated with a radical religious faction. A group of men who so hated western civilization that they took it upon themselves to disrupt that powerful collection of nations. To make its citizens feel unsafe in the world. Just as that radical troupe felt unsafe anywhere they might venture in the world. Unsafe because mighty nations sought to kill the leaders of their nation. Kill in retaliation for an isolated suicidal attack upon the mighty nations.

I look closer at the face of the decapitated figure. I'm instantly repelled as I realize the dead man is me. That's my head. How could someone know who I am? How did someone make this image seem so real that the Arbiter System sent it on for interpretation? This is not an image the system should send on. It never should have gotten to me. Never should have been viewed by anyone after the originator sought to post it. I know I'm over reacting. I shouldn't feel any less secure. This has to be some kind of mistake. That isn't me. Can't be. I need to look at it again. But I'm afraid of what I'll think if I see it really is me. That would mean someone found me.

I look again. Closer this time. The more I look at it I decide it looks a lot like me. Could be me, but it must be someone else. Not me. I'm relieved. So I delete the posting. It doesn't meet the Ten Commandments test in any event. Never post a suicide or dead body. Never show a murder in progress. Don't provide an audience for unspeakable acts. Never give a terrorist a platform.

Deleting this image solves a problem for me. If I don't delete it, but rather hold it in suspense, I'll be tempted to go back and look at it again, and again, and again. Always hoping I can establish beyond a reasonable doubt that it isn't me. Wasn't me. That whoever took the picture modified it and it wasn't the real picture. Someone else's head. Since I'm still here it can't be me. So what am I freaking out about anyway? There. Gone. If only the image it left in my memory was as easy to erase. I know it's not. I know I'm going to be dreaming about that image for a long time to come.

I hear the alarm buzzing. It apparently has been for a while, only somehow my mind blocked it out. My mind wanted me to finish that dream. Was it hoping I'd resolve it? Find that the face wasn't mine? Allow me to move on? There was a time when I had trouble remembering my dreams. I wish I could go back to those days since now I can't forget them. Can't move on beyond the images that keep coming back to me. Only now my mind has started playing with those memories. Started changing what I really saw. Bringing in friends like Sheila's rape. And now it has started attacking me. What's next?

# CHAPTER FOURTEEN: ICHABOD

I watch him approaching. I'm on the street about two blocks from his apartment. I'm standing at the bus stop so he's not looking at me. He's taller than I thought from the pictures. He looks like he had a rough night. Hair uncombed. Hasn't shaved in a few days. Looks like he's been wearing the same clothes for a while. Probably means he's not been out much. And probably wouldn't have gone out today if he'd not run out of edibles. At least that's what he bought. Watched him through the window. Probably running low on cash too since he bought the cheaper grades. Just an impression. I could be wrong. Have been wrong on so many things about this. But the algorithms say he's the one. And who am I to argue with algorithms written by some of the smartest people I've ever met.

He almost seems to be in a daze. Could be he took one of the edibles already. That may help me, but it might also freak him out. Got to be careful. Be totally non-threatening. He's almost here. Time to make my move. "Scuse me?" I attempt to interrupt his high, if that's what it is.

No response, so I've got to be more intrusive, louder. "Scuse me?" I step into his path so he will see me, but hopefully we don't make contact. That would likely make him more defensive.

"You're Brandon," I inform him.

His eyes seem to focus on me, but it appears he is having difficulty deciding how he should respond to me. "Who are you?"

"We have a common friend," is the rehearsed response to his question that we knew would be coming.

"Who?"

"Jackson Bennett," I give him the name of someone I know he will recognize, but is someone he's not spoken to since graduating.

"Jackson?" Brandon struggles to place how such a long-ago name would suddenly be relevant and somehow tied to me.

"He's working with my organization. Said you'd be perfect."

Brandon blinks a few times apparently struggling to make sense of the situation. "Perfect for what?" finally emerges from the cloud that pervades his consciousness.

"That's a longer conversation. I've got the time if you'd have lunch with me, my treat."

"I don't generally eat lunch." Brandon seems to be looking for a way out of this discussion. Got to close him now.

"According to Jackson you have some unique skills we need."

"Unique as in deleting? That's all I do."

"According to Jackson you have a photographic memory." I watch him close his eyes and shake his head.

"That's not a skill, it's a curse," he responds after a long moment.

Curious response. "What if I told you we are working on something that would help you forget either things you don't want or need to remember? And we need someone who can validate our approach works?"

"What are the side effects?" Brandon seems to be focusing better. Either his high is under control or he's deliberately forcing himself to deal with the situation I'm presenting to him.

"Have lunch with me and I can answer all your questions. When we're done you should have enough information to decide whether our opportunity is right for you. If it's not what have you lost other than maybe an hour? You'll need to eat at some point and this would allow you to at least have a good meal."

"I've tried everything." He sounds depressed, like he's given up.

I smile, "I assure you that you have not tried everything." I try to be confident and non-threatening.

"This an experimental drug? I'm not a very good guinea pig. It's my stomach."

"Come have lunch and if you still think it's not for you we're good."

Brandon looks around, apparently thinking about the lunch offer and the opportunity to forget. He won't look at me, then asks, "You know my name. Who are you?"

"People call me Ichabod."

"Ichabod what?"

"Just Ichabod. Never knew my parents. Never wanted to be identified with the people who took care of me as I grew up. So I settled on just Ichabod."

"You're an orphan?"

I nod, even though that isn't the case, but the story evokes sympathy, which is the objective. "Been wandering the world my whole life. As soon as I knew I didn't belong to the people who were trying to make me just like them, well I decided it was time for me to make me into what I wanted to be."

"And that is?"

"Free." I wait a second for that to sink in. "Come have lunch and we can discuss all that. I don't really want to share my story with a bunch of people at a bus stop."

Brandon looks around and apparently realizes we have been standing out on the street having this discussion. "Where do you want to go?"

"There's a sushi place nearby I've found to be good. Called GUI. You know it?"

Brandon nods, "Been there a few times. Not bad."

We walk the few blocks to Guy, mostly in silence as Brandon, I am sure is wondering what he's getting himself into. But then asks, "How do you know Jackson?"

"He's helping us with one of our projects."

"So this super memory eraser thing you're doing, that's not all you're doing?"

"We have a lot of ideas. Some are further along than others. But it's like with anything. When you're trying to do something no one else has done successfully, it's always trial and error until you get it right. But if you keep at something long enough, you eventually find the answer you're looking for."

Brandon regards me suspiciously," I'm not the first person you've asked to do this, am I?"

"We've been at this for a while, so no. You're not the first." I answer truthfully, but I'm not so sure I'll be able to be truthful with the next question I expect he will ask.

"How many have been successful?"

"If we weren't successful, we wouldn't still be doing this, would we?" I respond to his concern. "You can only fail at something just so long before you run out of money and ideas and investors who are willing to keep you going. If you don't establish a track record early on, you never get the chance to change the world."

Brandon stops walking and I have to as well, although now he is behind me. I turn to him.

"Who said anything about changing the world?" Brandon demands of me.

"Any time you introduce something new, you change the world to some extent. People buy your product rather than what they've been using. They start looking for other innovations. Wanting to know what else can make their lives easier, or better somehow. Every new invention can either change the world for some people, or not. We intend to be among those who change the world, at least for some people, and hopefully in a meaningful way. And we make lots of money in the process." I have to add that last part so he won't think my message is too serious.

Brandon looks at me skeptically. If he took an edible, he's not showing the effects of it anymore. Probably a good thing because he will be more likely to understand the pitch and more likely to remember it tomorrow.

"Where is Jackson now?" he keeps coming back to Jackson. Not sure he was such a good candidate to open the discussion with. We'll see.

"San Francisco." I respond although I actually have no idea where Jackson Bennett lives. I can only hope that Brandon has no idea how to reach him either, or won't think about getting in touch with him.

## CHAPTER FIFTEEN: ELIZABETH WARDEN

Maria Xhe is surprisingly tall. She told me she takes after her grandfather who is six foot something. I can never remember exactly how tall he is although Maria has told me on numerous occasions. There are just some things I never forget and others I can never remember. Why is that? Must have something to do with the importance I attach to some fact. Only explanation I've come up with. Maria told me her grandfather played basketball, but another fact that has escaped me is whether it was in college or professionally. She said he was good, but that's all I remember. Maria is also brilliant when it comes to mathematics. She can intuit more than I can calculate with the assistance of a computer. She's also an algorithms expert. She singlehandedly rewrote substantial portions of the Arbiter base code. Made it useful in ways her company had failed to deliver. For that she has my unwavering support and gratitude.

Today I asked her to help me find Jürgen's Armenian Terrorists.

"That's not enough, Elizabeth. I can probably find everyone who lives in this country of Armenian descent, but that won't get us any closer to which of them or people they know might be harboring ill thoughts."

"What do you need to find them?" I ask knowing she's right. She's always right when it comes to what can the system do or not do.

"A signature. Something unique about the group or the members of the group. Something they use when they communicate to confirm to the other members of the group, or the audience they are trying to reach, that the communication is coming from the group."

"I've got nothing like that," I admit and know I have to make a call. I text my assistant and in a few minutes my phone rings.

"Javier, it's Elizabeth and Maria. Sorry to be reaching out so late in the day for you, but we're stuck."

"You know I expected this call several hours ago. It's actually fortuitous you waited as Jurgen had me solving yet another mystery for him until about a half hour ago."

"That mystery have anything to do with disappearing Armenians?" I can't resist asking.

"Only tangentially," Javier responds with that tone of voice I hear when he has told me all I can expect on that topic.

"Maria is looking for a signature. Something this group uses that helped you discover them," I get right to the ask. "What can you tell us?"

Javier doesn't hesitate, "There isn't one we've found."

Maria decides to speed this up by asking directly, "Then how did you discover they exist?"

"All we have is a sample of their work product."

"I don't understand," Maria responds with a quizzical expression.

"Do you have your Arbiter System scan official releases from your Ministries?"

"No," I admit.

"What about analysts? Do you have any of them review your releases before you post them?"

"They're reviewed by the communications teams and a stack of lawyers who fall all over each other trying to ensure even the grammar and punctuation is accurate. Those documents are scrubbed by so many eyes, there's no reason to put them through yet another level of review. But what does that have to do with Armenians?"

"We were the same. Official documents were simply posted after the final legal reviews. But somehow one of our analysts noted something on a posted document. A buried phrase that didn't make sense. When we looked into it, the posted document didn't match the final approved document."

"How is that possible?" I have to ask instantly understanding that if Javier has a vulnerability, we probably do as well.

"It's not." Javier is very explicit in this statement. "And that is what caused us to realize someone has penetrated our systems. Found or is exploiting a trap door."

"Have you found the entry point? Sounds like you haven't," I seek confirmation knowing if he hasn't found it yet, we will likely have as much difficulty, if not more in determining whether someone has penetrated our system.

"No."

"I'm confused." I have to slow this down. Back up for a minute. "If you don't know who has penetrated your system, or how they are doing it, how do you know it's over the Armenian genocide?"

"We don't," Javier confirms. "The embedded message could be explained by someone focused on that event, but we believe that to be a code and not the real message. But if whoever is behind this effort has penetrated your system, that means they may have penetrated your communications as well. They may be listening in on every conversation you have."

"And yours," I push back.

"Possible, although we think we are clean based on the massive work we are doing to sweep the entire network. You can't imagine all the possible points of entry that have to be touched individually to be absolutely sure. We have the usual network sweeps done on unplanned cycles. We have some new technology that attacks breeches from a unique approach. So far we've found nothing. But since you're not doing those same sweeps, our discussion yesterday was intended to set expectations if anyone was listening in."

"Why are we having this discussion if you think we have a leak?" I'm not following him.

"This line is being scanned in real time in hopes of capturing the IP address of anyone who might be listening in. I'm willing to talk about it because our most powerful technologies are telling me this line is clean. And you need to know about the nature of this threat. As Jurgen said, we believe they are resident in the US and are planning to undermine your form of government. We don't know how, but again the coded messages in our official postings can be interpreted that way."

"You've said that several times now. That they are post documents that can be interpreted a certain way. I take it the messages are encoded such that different keys provide differing interpretations."

"These people are very clever," is all Javier is sharing. Apparently he wants us to help find them, but not really understand the threat they pose. I need to test one more thing.

"Javier. What makes you think we would be able to find people you cannot when you have the embedded messages. You have whatever signatures are found in those messages that you say don't exist. But we both know any communication will have certain peculiarities that can be interpreted. So clearly if you're not willing to share the embedded messages then they must not exist."

"The messages are very real. However, I can't share them with you because they reference classified information."

"Javier, we share classified information with you all the time. Does this mean our information sharing protocols are no longer in effect?"

No response. The whole thing about one of the members

publishing a whitepaper advocating that the presidency may no longer be needed. That has to be pure fiction. If all they have is embedded messages they couldn't possibly link any paper submitted for publication unless a message pointed them to such a paper. And that certainly doesn't sound like the case. I also doubt that they have anything linking them to UsTopia. It has to be a pure assumption. A bald-faced lie to get us to use our systems to help them find a threat they can't identify.

"So let me recap," I start to conclude this call. "You have someone or some ones who have somehow penetrated your truth system, planting coded messages in your officially released postings. You don't know how they are doing it or for what purpose. You want our help in finding him or them with just that much information."

"We have given you more than that to work with," Javier knows we understand.

"So you want us to sweep the known universe, uncover anyone who has ill thoughts towards EuTopia. That tells me your system is hosed and you can't admit it."

# CHAPTER SIXTEEN: CHANGING PERSPECTIVES

## JAVIER SANTIAGO

Jurgen apparently entered my office when I was deep in my analysis with my back to the door. I suddenly have my concentration interrupted by him clearing his throat. I swivel around. He is already sitting in his usual chair by the door. "You know I could watch you working for hours, if I had hours to spare."

"You want to know if Elizabeth is working our request," I surmise.

"After I suggested she be replaced. Some people take comments like that personally and then do what they can to ruin your plans."

"She would have to know our plans to ruin them," I clarify for him.

"What will she learn when she looks for our ghosts?"

"She won't look for them as she has concluded they don't exist."

Jurgen rises and glances at the door, "Just wanted to ensure we are on track."

"I would have informed you first thing if there were complications."

"No you wouldn't." Jurgen wants me to know he can read my motivation. "You'd tell me everything was fine and go work the issues behind the scenes. You don't do anything where people can see what you're doing or how you're doing it. That's not a criticism, by the way. That's why I trust you implicitly."

"Not a good recommendation," I try to put the whole thing in perspective for him.


**JURGEN**

Javier is focusing on the tactical aspects of this plan. I need to touch him and make sure he keeps his eye on the bigger picture. "You done bullshitting me?"

"Of course, if you're done looking for me to bullshit you."

Why does Javier always have to get the last word in on any subject? "What's the status on the sleeper cells?"

"They've been deployed for decades." Usual understatement.

"What's their status?" I push him. "Are they ready to start their mission or do we need to initiate them, confirm their readiness, and validate whatever they find?"

"What's so important you would want to expose them now? I can't think of a reason important enough," Javier is very protective of his assets, I understand that, but he has to trust my judgment, which I sometimes wonder if he does.

"If UsTopia goes fully automatic that leaves them exposed as we have determined in our own system. What we need to know is UaTopia exploiting those exposures? They have to see the same things we are. Have you talked with Hwa Kwan recently?"

"I talk to the Dragon Lady frequently, but you are aware of how forthcoming she is. The game never ends. Cooperation is never deeper than the surface to create an impression of a peaceful world. But we are at war. One of the three nations states will eventually be brought into direct conflict with another. Then one of the two nations states will cease to exist. The result will be a bi-polar world. Then we shall face off in the final conflict for global domination. UsTopia may have the military advantage, but they don't have the ideological one."

## ALBERT CARTER

I never want to hear from Elizabeth Warden, but Emily, my assistant, has informed me she is waiting for me to answer my phone. I look at the phone, dreading this conversation for a long moment and then snatch the receiver from the cradle. "Elizabeth."

"Albert, I need a huge favor." Pure Elizabeth. No socializing. No schmoozing.

"Madam Secretary. With what you've left me I'm not sure how I can help you." Got to stake out the situation or she will make the impossible ask, which she always does.

Evidently I caught her by surprise as the silence lasts longer than I expect.

"Maybe not so huge. I need you to give me your top analyst."

She goes right to the jugular. How am I supposed to do my job when I've laid off most of my best people, and those that remain are under water every single day? "My top analysts don't work here anymore. You're the one who gave instructions to lay off all but a small number of them."

"I don't remember that," doesn't sound genuine.

"The world of difference between what you all suppose and what people down at this level perceive to be the truth, given what they see every day." Shit. She'll probably fire my ass. But at this point what do I care? She's just prolonging the inevitable.

"Albert. We're on the same team. Trying to effect the mission. Ensure everyone understands the truth. That's why I need your top analyst."

Can't give her Sheila. Without her I can't do my job even with the Secretary's glorious system. But then again... "Brandon McInerny. He's my top web guy." He's already gone so he won't make what I'm dealing with any worse.

"When can he start?" Elizabeth almost seems to be salivating.


## JAVIER SANTIAGO

Why is it Hwa Kwan is never in her office when I call? What's the likelihood of that? I mean I'm in my office more than I am not. I can't believe she's that much different than I am. Particularly since all the information I need is here.

"Javier?" she finally answers. "What is it you wish to know today?"

"Effectiveness," I respond. "Of your algorithms. How effective have they been in guiding you to the Hong Kong dissidents? Have you been able to find and neutralize all of them, or are the algorithms only sixty percent effective?"

"We are very satisfied with our results."

Bullshit. "I'm satisfied our World Cup team made it further than four years ago. But did they win the cup? Not this year."

"That's only because your team has won it in the past. We have not.

Put that irrelevant complaint aside, "Given what you've done with the Uighur Muslims I would have thought you were the most advanced in the world with your domestic suppression algorithms."

"Thank you." Hwa Kwan apparently didn't understand what I was saying to her.

"You still have riots in Hong Kong." I point out.

"We prefer to consider them as unhappy campers." Where did she come up with that one? It's an American phrase. I'd never use it in conversation with her, so what is she trying to tell me? That they've patched up their differences with the North Americans?

"You saying the UsTopians have come up with something we've not seen?"

"The marketplace constantly innovates," is all Hwa Kwan will tell me. Great.

## CHAPTER SEVENTEEN: SHEILA

The words someone wants me to embrace scroll at the bottom of the screen. The discussion has become a constant torrent of anger and insults. If these people want me to have even the slightest interest in what they are saying they need to dial down the rhetoric. But that's not the conventional wisdom. We live in a society constantly on the brink of conflict. Verbal if not physical. Body language that doesn't mix metaphors. Words that are meant to hold some prejudices tight and exclude those who are the subject of that prejudice. Why is that the rallying cry? Why is the opposition focused on the polyglot of popularism? That everyone should have the keys to the kingdom delivered by the government that everyone, and not them, pays for? The cries that the rich should pay for the poor. And the truth that the middle class gets stuck with the bill while the rich move middle class jobs to the lowest cost country. Welcome to Economics 101. You know the class. The one that everyone running for Congress chose not to take because it was a hard class and could bring down their GPA.

On my desk is a photo. This picture is there for only one reason. To bring me back to the beauty of the world we are so intent on destroying. The photo is of Lake Como in Italy. Taken from a ferry as it approaches Bellagio, the small village where the lake splits into two different areas going south. The photo was shot when the evening lights have come on displaying reflections of the building lights on the water. The restaurants and hotels along the shore are illuminated. The sun has not yet completely set, so the mountains that crest above the lake are still clear and distinct. But the lights of homes up the sides of those mountains identify families that revel in this beauty every day and evening time.

After an hour or so of what the world has become, I glance at that picture for a long moment, take a deep breath, knowing all is not lost.

There is still beauty in the world. There is a place of peace where all the vitriol has not spoiled the existence of mankind. Where someday I will go and see this sight for myself. Where I will experience that peace, that joy, that appreciation for what nature has given us to soak into our soul. To share with others. To make life worth living though all the ugliness, hatred and prejudice.

But then I'm immersed back into the digital representation of humanity. The problem is staying engaged with it so nothing passes by I don't catch. And what 'it' is changes from day-to-day. We have the Ten Commandments. But even they have been clarified periodically since I've been in this job. Although the frequency has increased lately, or so it seems. Slight shifts in what we censor. What we let post or air on the networks. Not that any of it makes a big difference from what I can see. But someone thinks it significant. Otherwise they'd just let it post or air and see what shows up.

DJ Simpson is being interviewed... again. She doesn't have anything new to say so why do they keep bringing her back to trot out the same tired and worn phrases, and ineffective strategies? We tried her stimulus concept. What was that? Two decades ago? Didn't help. Actually increased the deficit that someone's kids will have to repay. So why do they keep putting her on? Must be ratings. Only thing I can think of. But it's a pure mystery why she would generate ratings when even Bernie Sanders is now considered just another voice in the wind, seeking change with no realistic plan for how to achieve the socialist program he espouses.

Oops. DJ is going down that same path. So mark it at the beginning. Let her play it out. How long is this going to go? DJ is longer winded on this topic than usual. Maybe I should back up and mark it earlier. Remove her altogether. But it appears she comes back in later. Would that mean I have to remove the whole discussion? There are comments here that are acceptable according to the Ten Commandments. But it's always an issue of how tight to mark the unacceptable.

I listen to the second response from DJ. No question. The whole thing has to come out. So that means the whole program goes to the nether world of dustbin electrons. Sorry DJ. Nothing personal here, but the Ten Commandments tell me what you have to say is not ready for prime time, or Miller Time or any time for that matter. I touch the delete key. DJ never had the conversation I just listened to. Edited. And finally determined to be beyond the realm of acceptability.

But I wonder. Why did I get the chance to listen to her? Make the decision when the algorithms are supposed to remove everything except the grey areas, the edge cases they call them. Those situations where there may be subliminal messaging the machines don't catch. In this case there was nothing subliminal from DJ. She was forthright and unabashed as she always is. Which is why I was surprised to find I was given a chance to even listen in on her diatribe against the status quo.

A hand touches my shoulder, I assume it is Albert and glance up to confirm my supposition. I'm rewarded with his usual smile. "Let Victoria be lead analyst for now. I need to chat with you."

This sounds ominous. Albert never takes me off line like this when we are in the middle of an election cycle. And the election cycle starts the day after the election. That's the way it's been for as long as I've been on this desk. Never a day when the lead analyst can simply pull out and defer off to another analyst. Something out of the ordinary is happening, but I can't imagine what. Another glance at Lake Como, another emotional dump to put me in the right frame of mind, and I push the toggle that moves my flow over to Victoria, "Sorry, Vik," I say loud enough for Albert to hear, but not enough that he will want to reprimand me for saying it. Albert knows the score. He spent time on the desk. So he knows what we have to deal with every day, for ten hours a day, six or seven days a week.

Apparently Albert doesn't want to talk in my cube. That's an even more ominous sign. We always talk here, where others can see us. Where others will testify that Albert hasn't done anything inappropriate or said anything for which I could bring charges against him. Not that I ever would. Albert could no more harass me than he could his own daughter. Although as I think of it, there has been more than one show about some pervert who was doing his own daughter. Just an inconceivable thought to me. But then again, I guess I'm really traditional in a lot of ways. Maybe that's why Albert gave me the lead analyst job. I represent the middle of American in what I believe, what I value and what I espouse. Albert told me once that I was the original reference for the Arbiter System. What I would delete is what they programmed Arbiter to delete. But that has to be bullshit. If it were the case I never would have seen DJ's proposed broadcast. If that were the case, I wouldn't see anything because the Arbiter system would have disposed of all edge cases before they got to me. So how did they change it? How did they flesh out the criteria for the Ten Commandments? How did Arbiter build a database of unacceptable postings? Unacceptable discussions, unacceptable concepts that allowed things I would reject get to the secondary analyst? None of this makes sense to me. But I'm just an analyst. I'm not supposed to have such deep thoughts. Think about things the government doesn't want me to think. Even though I am the very model of a modern UsTopian. Even though I'm an Australian aborigine raised by a white family. Their values became my values because I was only two when they took me in.

When we arrive at Albert's office he goes behind his desk and motions for me to close the door behind us. This is really serious. He's never closed the door behind us. Too much liability. Too many whispers out on the floor. But I notice how many empty desks there are over on this side. The media side and not live broadcast. I can't wait for him to get to the point because it always take a while. "What's up?"

Albert looks at me like he wished I'd not asked that question, but shakes his head and sits down in the chair behind his messy desk. "The Secretary," is all he says. But that's enough. Whatever he needs is coming from that level. Oh shit. I hope he's not expecting me to go hold her hand and tell her what she really doesn't want to know.

I nod.

"She wants someone. My best analyst. That's you. Always has been. But I'm not about to give you up. If I did I'd never see you again. You'd become one of them. You know. The ones who decide what Sabr wants us to know so she can get re-elected."

Albert is as direct and forthright as ever.

"What if I wanted that?" I push on him. He's making an assumption.

"You don't. Trust me. You don't."

## CHAPTER EIGHTEEN: BRANDON McINERNY

Albert's call is welcome. I'm still trying to decide how to handle what Ichabod discussed with me. Not that I was all that interested in what he had to say. But that's the strange part. I'm still thinking about it. Wondering. He made some linkages that I'd not. Linkages that make sense in the abstract. But life isn't abstract. What he was suggesting made me uncomfortable. And not just because he was informing me of things I probably should have been aware of as an analyst. He was giving me a different world view. A different set of insights into what all the parties to the dance I regulated every day were up to. Good and bad. Right and wrong. Evil and righteous. I'm just so unable to process it all that I've set it aside and let my subconscious worry about it. But that probably wasn't a good choice. My subconscious keeps sending me love letters. Tells me that I've not been paying attention to the important things that are going on out there. I may have been the senior analyst on the media side, but there was so much that escaped my notice. I have a hard time believing it. But Ichabod showed me proof. Like it was no big deal.

I wanted to call Sheila, but Ichabod had warned me not to talk to anyone who was still on the inside. Doing so would only cause a harsh reaction. Those on his side had to ratchet up their defenses, had to ratchet up their subterfuge. Had to ratchet up a means of bringing to a head what would get there on its own if only left alone. That was what they wanted. To be left alone. So they had the time it would take to lay a solid foundation. To have the awareness and commitment of those who believe as they do. While now they are interested. They are not committed. His forces need a little more time to get to the point of inevitability. The point where nothing will prevent ultimate success.

I told him I didn't share his world view. I'm not at all comfortable discussing his conception of the world and what was about to happen.

That was where I got up and left. Ichabod acted as if he expected me to leave. No attempt to call me back. No follow-up calls to ask if I've thought about what he had to say. He has to know that since I have all the time in the world now, that I have nothing better to do than think about his proposal, if you can call it that.

But what am I to do with Albert? Do I discuss it or do I keep it a secret? I really don't know what Ichabod was after, so I don't know how to play it. If I keep quiet is that what he wants? He made it sound that way. But if he really was just planting seeds to get me to talk to the folks inside, he did that just as effectively. I don't know what to do. I've never encountered a situation like this. Whatever I decide will either play into Ichabod's plans or disrupt them, at least at this level. But I've got to be so far down the food chain that at best I'm just a blip on their radar. Doesn't matter what I say or do. Won't change the outcome because all the important things happening are way over my head. I'm just a curiosity. Someone who can divert attention for a while, but not someone who will make any real difference in the long-term outcomes.

At least that's how I see it.

Albert approaches the table where I'm sitting like a man on a mission. In a hurry, but not. Focused on getting to the end of his journey even though it really is just the beginning. He sees me and raises a hand in recognition. I smile to reciprocate and stand to shake hands, which we do as he arrives at the table.

"You okay?" is Albert's first question.

"Every day is a new experience," just comes out unfiltered. I regret it instantly.

Albert nods in understanding but seems at a loss for words as to how to respond to my predicament, which he created by laying me off. There is no question he understands his role in my unhappiness, but he seems strangely comfortable. Not like someone filled with regret that he had to do something completely outside his control. "You have anything you're looking at?" Albert seems curious, put apparently doesn't want to seem intrusive. Thus the round-about question.

"Never thought I'd be here. So, no," I confirm.

"You hoping to catch on with something in the analyst field?" Albert is beating around the bush, feeling me out and trying to get a handle on my state of mind.

"I'm casting a wide net," sounds about right. Not sure it's accurate, but what the hell. It's only Albert.

Albert looks around as if he's uncomfortable as to who might be listening to this discussion. With his job, that's not just paranoia. "I've been asked to give up my best person. I already did that when I had to let you go."

"Give up," I repeat. "That mean to Justice?"

"Higher," Albert confirms. "Working for the Dragon Lady herself."

"Elizabeth Warden?" I have trouble believing she would want anyone like me reporting directly to her. I mean, I've got to be the opposite of all the 'yes men and women' who surround her all day, telling her exactly what she wants to hear.

Albert doesn't deny my guess, which I have to take as an indication that I'm right. I have to think about this. What do I have to gain by working for someone like her? Might be less time on a terminal and more in meetings with boring people who are only there to make sure they know what Elizabeth Warden might be doing. But then again, when one isn't working a paycheck might be a nice addition to my life. Only there was a check there this last week. Probably a final payment, even though I thought I'd been paid out. Exactly my old salary. So probably the case. And now Albert is asking me to take on a totally incomprehensible role for Elizabeth? Well, I don't know quite what to make of that. Do I really have a choice? I mean how does someone say no to an offer from a Secretary level person? The fact that she has absolutely no idea who I am is probably a factor in my favor. If she knew I was just an analyst, even though the lead analyst for media, she'd probably tell Albert to go back and find a real spook. Not some faker who'd just been laid off because he was redundant to the computers now being deployed. That is the case, isn't it?

Albert leans closer to ensure we aren't overheard. "She's looking for an outside validation."

"That she got what she thought she bought?" I guess.

"One way of looking at it." Albert continues checking the crowd in the restaurant.

"How would I know?" I push back on Albert trying to understand what this whole conversation is about, really.

Albert concludes his checking about us, returns his gaze to me. "That's something you need to decide between now and tomorrow at 1:00."

"Where?" I'm caught by surprise and can't think of anything else to ask.

"Her office." Albert looks at me with an intensity I've not seen in a long time, maybe not ever. "You have one opportunity to show her that I am still the best judge of character in her organization... or not, as you see fit."

I shake my head, "Why not Sheila? She was always your favorite. She's still with you, isn't she? You could have let her go when you let me go, but you couldn't do it, could you?"

"Not the issue," Albert deflects my calling him out. "The Secretary asked for my best analyst. That's you. All you have to do is walk across the street and do what you do best."

Nothing to be gained by going down the Sheila trail. I made my point and he's blowing smoke to get me to take this job. Why? What's in it for him? "What if I've already got another job?" I decide to test him.

"Not what I heard, but what is it?" Albert seems to think I'm the one blowing smoke now.

"A chance to change the world. At least that's how it was described."

"You accepted this other job?" Albert seems surprised.

"Told them I wasn't interested, but the offer's on the table."

"The job working directly for the Secretary…" Albert slows as if trying to gather his thoughts. "That's got to be the dream job. You get to know the top people. Work the toughest assignments. Prove you're capable. Someone who can be trusted. You do all those things and your future is assured."

"But what if I don't agree with decisions they make?" I have to know how Albert see this 'opportunity.'

## CHAPTER NINETEEN: ELIZABETH WARDEN

Maria looks uncomfortable. That means she's not confident I'm going to like her review. "So you had a good trip?" I ask of her recent vacation, which was really just a three-day weekend. Getting this close to go live she couldn't be away longer. I simply wouldn't grant her the days off, even though she asked for them.

"Better than nothing, I guess."

I should have been prepared for that response, given I was the one who made it a much lesser event than Maria wanted. But I'm not about to let this project slip even one more day. It was supposed to have gone live almost a year ago. I still have no confidence that we are even one day closer. "What did you do?"

"Went home to visit my parents. They gave me two solid days of nothing. No phone calls, no text messages, no demands that I do anything. I didn't even eat dinner the first day."

"Sounds like it was just what you needed."

Maria's expression tells me she disagrees with my comment but she has apparently decided there is nothing to be gained by telling me so. "Nothing you need to address on the project. We are green across the board – cost, schedule and technical performance."

"Although the schedule baseline has been moved out how many times?" I press.

Maria doesn't blink. She's apparently used to my continued unhappiness about the delays. "We are green to the current schedule," comes with no inflection.

"For how long?" I let her know I suspect she is not giving me the whole story.

"We have mitigation plans for any contingency. We have opportunities to pick up time or cost that we continue to work in parallel. As I said, there's nothing you need to take action on at this point."

"But you're not guaranteeing that there won't be something in the future," I press her wanting her to keep focused, particularly now that she's back from her break.

"With a system this complex there are no guarantees," there is a bit of an edge in her voice now. She's getting tired of my continued pressure to get it done and it better be right the first and every time. "Something could appear tomorrow that we haven't anticipated. But if it does, we will analyze it, decide the best course of action and work it immediately."

I need to let her calm down before I press her on what's really on my mind. At this point with her back already up I likely won't get the insight I need. "How are you doing on staffing the maintenance team?" These are the people who will maintain the system after she turns it over to the Department.

I see the tension fall away and she visibly relaxes. I see it first in her shoulders coming down and then in her face. She's no longer squinting at me. "I've had preliminary conversations with a few of the best people on the development team. Most of them have made no secret of their wish to continue doing development work. Troubleshooting and fixing bugs just isn't the kind of work that gets most of them out of bed eager for the day. But I want to give them an opportunity to be considered in any event."

"So you don't think many will want to join that team." I seek confirmation of what I think she's saying.

"No one has confirmed interest at this point. But as we get closer to the transition, things could change. If you stop and think about it, there likely won't be another project quite like this one in our lifetime."

"I hope not," I confirm my lack of appetite in doing this all again.

"And it's hard for developers to accept this project may be the highlight of their career. It's like an athlete who breaks the world record in their event. Once you hold the world record what do you do next?"

"Interesting you're comparing your developers to athletes," I muse aloud. "In a certain respect they have the same kind of impact on society. They are producing something that will touch everyone's lives. Athletes inspire people everywhere, but not everyone. Your developers are leaving us a legacy that already touches everyone, and hopefully inspires the kind of behavior that will make this a better world for all of us."

I notice Maria doesn't respond to my description. In the past she has also been quiet at such times. Makes me think she's not sold on the value of this system and its impact on the lives of people. She's not the only one on the team who has revealed questions without raising them. Why is it people are afraid to say what they think? I'm certainly not. But then again, I'm the one who decides what gets repeated and what does not. Is that one of the side effects of a more perfect union, a more perfect society and more perfect co-existence for us all? That in order to get along you can't express yourself? Certainly not what we had in mind when we started down this journey. I at least just wanted to end the endless wars. End the race baiting, the insults and denigrating of those who are different, just because they are, different. Why is it people won't take the time to get to know people as people? That was what we all thought would end the divisions. End the two societies, by making everyone tolerant of each other. Willing to accommodate other viewpoints, even though those not acceptable do not gain a wider audience because of the Arbiter system Maria's team is building.

I let the silence sit with us for a moment longer and then ask, "If none are willing to stay on, won't that make it harder for the maintenance team? They won't be familiar with the architecture and logic. The algorithms will be a complete mystery."

"They will figure it out quickly." Maria dismisses. "My current team has a group dedicated to documenting everything so thoroughly that anyone who wants to spend the time will be able to trace out the logic."

I nod once, having heard this particular pitch before, "It's not the logic I'm worried about. It's the algorithms. The learning algorithms. We don't really understand how the machine learns or how it gets to the decisions it makes."

"True, but the algorithms identify the patterns in the billions of decisions our analysts have and continue to make." Maria defends her solution as I knew she would, even if she questions its value. "They simply follow those patterns. And as the patterns change so do the algorithms. That means it never gets out of date. It changes as we change. It learns from our growth as people and stays current with who we are."

"That's a perfect segue into one of the things I've been wondering recently. What is the current fidelity with the human analyst decisions? Last time we talked it was like sixty percent or something."

"It's over eighty now," Maria throws out there, not sure she wants to give me this statistic. I can tell as she won't look at me when she gives me the number.

"What's it going to take to be more consistent than humans?"

Maria glances up at me. She's heard this question since the first day she came into my office and interviewed for the job. "That's nearly a fifty percent improvement in less than a month."

Her defense rings hollow as it tells me we are a long way from being ready to turn on Arbiter without analysts reviewing its recommendations. She apparently knows it as she quickly follows up. "And we should be able to close this gap even faster."

I shake my head, "The last twenty percent is always the hardest."

Maria grimaces and leans forward, clearly unsettled by this part of the conversation. "We have a plan for that."

Where have I heard that before? "I appreciate that you have a plan but how do I get confidence in the plan when all the others have had mixed results? I absolutely can't afford another delay. Can't afford to have Arbiter make one wrong decision. Absolutely need to deliver on the promises I've made to the President and the People of UsTopia."

"You will because I will," Maria responds with determination in her voice and in her eye.

But I also see she is very tired, even after her break. In fact, if anything, she almost seems more tired than before she left. Then she was running on momentum. Having stopped, even if for three days seems to have interrupted that momentum. Now she seems to be struggling to re-engage. I know this is a very difficult assignment, but I can't afford to have the team leader struggling. "How is the team doing?"

"Head down and racing for the finish line."

"Some athletes fade at the end after giving it their all for so long."

# CHAPTER TWENTY: SHEILA

I'm sitting in Elizabeth Warden's office, facing the Secretary of Truth. A very powerful person. Not someone I want to think ill of me. But also not someone I want to hang around with either. She has to have made all kinds of compromises in her life to get to his position. And many of those compromises have to have been difficult personal decisions. Could I live with myself if I'd traveled that same road? Not likely.

"Why didn't Albert recommend you?" she asks out of the blue.

"I thought he did," is all I can say.

"He gave me some other name. A guy I think."

"Brandon McInerny," I suggest.

"I don't remember. I don't want some old white guy who has no appreciation for the complexity of our society, the struggles of people who aren't just like him."

"Brandon is neither old nor completely white. While his father was Irish, his mother is an Indian Hindu. He's also probably the best analyst Albert has."

"I've been told you're better," Elizabeth reveals.

"I don't know who would tell you that, but whoever it is apparently doesn't know Brandon very well." I put out there to make her reflect on her intelligence.

"I've been told that Brandon is absolutely the best media person we have..."

"Had. You laid him off." I see this information catches her by surprise.

"Why would we lay off our best analyst?" Elizabeth pushes back.

"Because you seem to think Arbiter can do what he did better than he did it."

"You don't agree?" Elizabeth isn't asking the question she asked. She's asking something else.

"Do you know what I do all day?" I have to take a different tact to respond to her question.

"You're a broadcast analyst."

I look at her eyes intensely, "Do you have any idea what I do all day? Have you come down on the floor and sat in an analyst's chair? Made the decisions according to the Ten Commandments? Gone home after watching and listening to grotesque discussions that aren't suitable for human consumption?"

"That's not the question," Elizabeth dodges just as she did in the Presidential debates. But this isn't a debate. It's an interview I didn't ask for. It was a summons to take on a different task, but still one focused on finding the truth and eradicating anything that isn't the 'official' truth. Not sure I'm up for this.

"I can't answer your question if you don't answer mine." I don't have anything to lose in this situation so I'm going to play it straight and not pander to her ego.

Elizabeth Warden, Secretary of Truth, sits back in her chair. She just looks at me with a quizzical smile. "Do you have any idea how long it's been since someone said that to me?"

"During the debates I would imagine."

"Not even then. Not since my daughter was three. She asked it out of stubbornness. I wasn't paying enough attention to her. She was right.

I wasn't. She never said that again because I got the message. Tried to be a better mother."

"Does this mean you're going to be a better Secretary of Truth?" I push to see just how far I have to go before she decides I'm the wrong person.

"I'm the best Secretary of Truth our country has ever had," she responds with a baiting tone in her voice.

"Only because you're the only Secretary of Truth our country has had." I point out to show I understood her dodge of another question. "I look at what we're doing and shake my head. Why are we doing this? Has it made our lives any better? Has it changed us as a people into something that was better than what we were before? Are we really sublimating all the base impulses of men and women or are we simply containing them in an artificial way?"

"What do you mean?" Elizabeth pushes back on me.

Now I'm not sure if she really wants to go down this road or is giving me a rope to hang myself with. "I asked if you really know what I do all day for a reason. If you sat in my cube, listened to what Arbiter serves up to me to evaluate, you would know the answer to the question I just asked you. It's clear you don't."

"I think you underestimate what I do and don't know." Elizabeth doesn't like the implication of my challenge to her, but her response is vague enough that it reinforces my opinion of her.

I shake my head. "I know you underestimate what I do and don't know. I listen to and see all the things people want to communicate to other people that you never see or hear. And that's because I follow the Ten Commandments. I make sure they disappear into the ether. Make sure the idea virus is killed before it infects others. But those millions of idea viruses infect me even though I don't want them to. They sit in my head and make me think things no person should ever have to think. They populate my nightmares, but only because nightmares replaced all my dreams a long time ago. They make me question the reality of my reality. Make me question is there a parallel universe out there somewhere that these idea viruses have infected. A parallel universe where a different reality is the norm, where people have these strange ideas and have put them into effect. Demonstrated them. Tested whether they lead to a better life experience than the ones you and Arbiter synthetically establish for all of us who aren't analysts."

Elizabeth Warden pushes her glasses back against her face. That's a nervous habit I noticed during the Presidential debates. A gesture she made when she needed another moment before she launched into a display of anger at how society wasn't her society, or at least the one she would create if she could. And now she is creating that society. "I'm pleased to hear you say that. Do you know why I'm so focused on making Arbiter live as soon as possible?"

Her tone of voice is exactly the opposite of what I expected from my observation of her. Conciliatory. Almost as if she was concerned about what I had to say. Maybe even agreeing with something I said. "It makes no sense to me."

"It's because I think our Truth Analysts like you are getting burned out at an alarming rate." Elizabeth confides. "Doing what you do all day has to take a toll on you personally. It has to be warping your perceptions of society at large. It has to make you wonder who all these people with these strange ideas are. Isn't there someone out there who's normal?"

"I have no idea what's normal," I admit.

"I have an idea I'd like to become the normal for all of us."

"And then what?" I ask to see just how far she's thought this out.

"And then we erase the last ten years for you. From your mind, from your memory. It will be like it never happened. All those images you've observed and judged? Gone. All those expressions of hatred and bigotry? Gone. All that will remain from this time is the loving relationships you've had. The people who are important to you, because in the end all that is important is the people with whom you have relationships."

I've not heard anything about any of this. "Erase my memories?"

"Yes. You won't have to live with it much longer. As soon as Arbiter goes live in fully automatic you can return to a different life. One of normality. One of peace, tranquility and love."

"Normality as you define it," I point out.

"You'll much prefer it, you'll see," Elizabeth tries to reassure, but there's a hollowness, as if she's telling me what she wants to do rather than what she can do.

"So what does any of this have to do with the reason I'm here?"

Elizabeth acts as if she'd forgotten, "Oh yes. I need an analyst who can help me find someone in our media and broadcasts. Someone who is trying to destroy what we are doing here. Someone who is probably the greatest threat to our democracy at this time."

"I'm not a detective," I inform her. "That's not what I do."

"The person or persons we are looking for won't be found by a detective. They are planting seeds in our media. Growing those seeds where they lay, but not harvesting any yet. I need someone to help me filter through all the ideas being expressed prior to Arbiter eliminating so many of them."

This quest doesn't sound right to me.

## CHAPTER TWENTY-ONE: ALBERT CARTER

Brandon is already at Starbucks as I walk up to the corner table he commandeered. He seems to be wearing the same clothes as the last time I saw him. Hair's still rumpled as well. He's clearly not taking care of himself the way he was when he was coming in to work every day.

"Hey," Brandon greets me but doesn't rise or anything. No smile. Just a lethargy I've not seen in him before.

"How you doin'?" I have to ask as I'm more worried about him than I was on the walk over here from the office. I notice he has a coffee for each of us. He knows I like a Frappuccino and that's what's in the paper cup.

"The sun sets. The sun also rises. Not much happens in between anymore."

"You're not sleeping," I interpret from his description.

Brandon shakes his head just once and grimaces.

"Are they getting worse?" I ask about his nightmares. We discussed them many times before I had to let him go, but not since. Guess I need to dive back into how he's handling them since he's clearly struggling,

"They're evolving."

"I don't understand," This is something he'd never mentioned before.

"Same dream only each time there's something about it. Something new I'd not seen the last time. Something that makes that dream stay with me even though I'd rather it just went away."

106

"The blonde girl?" I guess. He'd mentioned her a couple times so I'd assumed the dream was exactly the same. Apparently I wasn't listening.

Brandon shrugs. Seems that dream is not the only one that's evolving on him. "What do you think's changed in the last few days?" I try to clarify what he's saying.

Brandon shrugs again, which tells me he's given up trying to find something that will permit him to sleep a dreamless sleep. I decide it's time to change the subject since I can't help that problem either.

"What was that guy's name?" I ask to get him to refocus.

"What guy?" I should have expected this response.

"The guy who told you about Tortoise."

"Ichabod," rolls off his tongue as if it were a bitter taste. "What about him?"

I take a sip of my Frappuccino to give me a moment to frame my question to him. "He talked about Tortoise. Did he give you any information about what it is they want?"

Brandon half shakes his head and shrugs.

"What did he say about it?"

"Just that there is a group of people out there dealing with the same shit I am."

"And they call themselves the Tortoise?" I'm not quite following this.

"Not the Tortoise. It's more of a code name than anything."

"Code name?" Where is he going with this?

"They're not a group. Not a bunch of people who wear Tortoise tshirts at their Harley Davidson rallies or anything like that."

"You've got to give me more than you're giving me if you expect me to help you understand who these people are, or at least who Ichabod is."

"Did you know someone put a paycheck in my account?"

"Vacation pay or something from the Department?" I suggest.

Brandon shakes his head again. He's been doing that a lot to me today. What's up with the stoic approach? "Who paid you then?"

"Tortoise."

"But what's Tortoise? Who's Tortoise?"

Brandon grins at me, "I was hoping you were going to tell me."

"You're sure the payment came from this Tortoise, whatever it is you want to call them?"

"That was the only identification on the deposit. Tortoise."

"How much did they pay you?"

Brandon smiles again, "Exactly, to the penny, what the Department paid me. Now how would someone know that?"

A very good question. Would mean someone has breached our human resources information system. "I don't know, but I'll be finding out."

Brandon looks away and takes a sip of his coffee, although I'm not sure how he's having it. Looks like a Frappuccino, but you just can't tell. "So you don't know who they are. Even with your great computers and databases on nearly everyone in the fucking world. Every electronic communication that has taken place between two people in the last fifty years. How is that possible?"

"There are people who've been inside and know the system. They could devise ways to avoid detection. If you know what the computers are looking for, you just don't use those in your communications."

"That's right," Brandon looks at me differently for a moment as if he were remembering something. "You were NSA. For what? Like twenty years or something?"

Where did this come from? I haven't said anything about my prior life to him. "My prior experience has been helpful at times given what we do now."

"You sure you're not still working for them? Would make perfect sense to me. You could point your former colleagues where to go look for things."

I can't answer his question since I've spent more than a decade burying that past. "Who told you that about me? Someone's trying to mislead you."

"He said you'd deny it, but he even showed me an identification badge from when you worked there."

"Someone's trying to drive a wedge between us. Don't you see that?"

Brandon shakes his head, "He had no reason to lie to me."

"To win your confidence, maybe?" I suggest. "Since he apparently wants you to do something. What is it Ichabod wants you to do?"

Brandon sits back apparently completely at sea as to what he should believe. "Who's playing me here?"

"I hired you when you were a new grad. I've given you opportunities to prove yourself and you've responded every time. I had to let you go even though I fought against it as long and as hard as I could. Does that sound like someone who is trying to play you? Why am I here? Not to get you to do something, but to help you if I can."

"You wanted me to take a job with the Secretary," Brandon pushes back.

I shake my head this time, "You're out of a job because of me. I'm trying to help you find a new one. How is that playing you?"

"It's who the job is with. Like the Manchurian Candidate. Place me where I can do the most harm."

"Why would I do that?" I can't believe I'm having this conversation. "I work for Elizabeth. If I wanted to do her harm, I'd do it myself, not wait ten years and hope you might be able to do it for me."

Brandon thinks about my response but says nothing.

"Brandon. Listen to me. I didn't have to come today. I was given explicit instructions as to who I had to let go and who stayed if only for a few more months. By the end of the year everyone will be gone, except maybe this one job Elizabeth asked me about. I gave her your name. But since you apparently haven't been contacted that tells me she didn't like you for some reason. Tells me just how much influence I have with the Secretary. Tells me I need to start looking for my next job. None of this is a plot against you. None of this is anything other than a continuation of the automation of more and more tasks that our society has come to depend upon."

Brandon looks at me as if a haze in the room is lifting. "Everyone will be gone by the end of the year?"

I nod.

"That include Sheila and you?"

# CHAPTER TWENTY-TWO: JAVIER SANTIAGO

Elizabeth is a pain in the ass. But sometimes she can be useful. If she takes the bait today, she will prove to be most useful.

"You want more information on the terrorists Jurgen identified on the call. The ones we believe are operating in UsTopia?" I seek to clarify the reason for her call.

"Yes."

This is a secure line so I can talk with her openly. "What do you think you know?"

"That for whatever reasons you don't want to share very much. And that your reluctance is making it real hard for me to find the sonofabitches."

Elizabeth never swears. She must be really agitated with my wild goose chase. "We know they are there," I respond to reaffirm the need for her to persist in this pursuit. "We know they are recruiting assets in your country. Assets capable of disrupting what you're doing, including your Arbiter go live."

Elizabeth considers my additional characterization of the terrorists. "What else can you tell me? There's got to be more to this than a suspicion someone intends to disrupt things here and there. We know those people exist. We know, for the most part, who they are. You and I've been tracking their movements for decades."

"Your government has…" I start to correct Elizabeth.

"Of course. My government has been tracking them. But that's not the point. You make it seem like there's this new group of terrorists, who, for some mysterious reason, is more likely to cause disruption than all of those we've intercepted in the past."

What else do we want to share with her? "Tactics evolve. We've both seen that. The people who watch their fellow terrorists flame out are constantly looking for new vulnerabilities. New ways of attacking us. New ways of embarrassing us in world opinion since, to a man, they all believe world opinion can temper the actions of a sovereign government."

"It has," Elizabeth reminds me.

"You're right. In some rare instances world opinion has shaped the behavior of a nation state. But I can't think of a single incident where it has shaped the actions of a terrorist. Other that is, than to be more daring, more disruptive and more likely to get coverage of their deeds. If only the media would stop covering all these events, they would soon cease, since the events would have no propaganda benefit."

"You control the media in EuTopia. Why do you still cover terrorist actions?" Elizabeth has asked that same question numerous times before.

"You do as well," I let her know the hole in the fabric is also on her end.

"We agreed to coordinate coverage, but you are the ones who have dragged your feet on implementing it," she reminds me.

"The systems aren't ready. There are just too many incidents to be able to coordinate them all without a global system and you know it."

"I'm just saying…"

Why do I even have these conversations with her? "You know who could probably help you more than anyone to find these terrorists in your backyard?"

"Sherlock Holmes?" Elizabeth lets me know she thinks I'm

playing with her which I am but still…

"Hua Kwan," our counterpart in China. "She seems to have a better handle on who is doing what than anyone I know. Just look at the prodemocracy riots in Hong Kong. She was able to shut them down from within without having to resort to the riot police her predecessor used."

"I live in a democracy…" Elizabeth begins her explanation for why Hua Kwan's approach won't work in her situation.

"You don't have to apologize to me about that," I toss back knowing it likely will send her into orbit.

But it doesn't, "…so Hua Kwan's approaches likely won't work here," Elizabeth is emphatic.

"I'd still have the conversation with her. You never know what spark of inspiration you can glean from what someone else is finding successful."

"Apples and oranges." Elizabeth is telling me she's not likely to have that conversation.

"Just tells me you're not interested in solving the problem you're causing us."

"Let me get one thing clear with you. UsTopia is not causing you any problems. If, as you allege, a person or persons living in UsTopia is, or are responsible for terroristic acts anywhere in the world, including EuTopia, we will find them. We will ensure their actions are unsuccessful in terms of disruption."

"Glad I have that on tape for when you run for election next time," I toss at her.

"I'm not running for office any time soon. I am enabling a society that is better, more equitable, more just than any that have come before it. How could I not finish the work I've started? How could I not be the great enabler?"

"Is that what you want on your tombstone? The great enabler?"

"I don't know as that's a noble objective." Elizabeth pushes back. "I'd rather people remember me for solving economic disparity. But that's not going to happen in my lifetime. Despite the proposals I've made. The bills I've introduced. The votes I cast in support of a fairer and more just society."

"As you defined it," she just has so many blind spots I keep exploiting. Hua Kwan does as well.

"No. As I define it. Present tense. We're not talking the past here, yet."

"But we all have just a short window to make the changes we wish to see…" I point out to her.

"Probably shorter for me than for you," she responds soberly. "But that's not the issue. We have to be focused. Do the right things. Build moats around them so they will stand the test of time, and not be reversed by the next inhabitant of the oval office."

"Or Chancellery…" I suggest since she's reminding me that I'm tied to Jurgen. If he is ever pushed aside, surely I will be as well. That's a remote possibility in EuTopia, but a very real one in UsTopia. "So why is Arbiter not operational today?" I decide to push a topic I know to be a sore one for her because she's the reason it isn't.

"It's closer to reality. Operational with a human analyst confirming the recommended actions. But that should no longer be needed soon."

"Soon as in next week, or next decade?" I push her for a status report.

"Sooner than you expect, but not sooner than you hope." Elizabeth responds.

"Welcome to the world of custom-built software," I chide her.

"When is yours going live?" I knew she would ask this at some point.

"It already is live. But we're attempting to make it better," I respond as vaguely as I can and still be truthful. "Just as Hua Kwan's is live and yours is live. Everyone is creeping towards that day when all our systems stand up and talk to each other. Then there will be one global truth, with caveats in each federation. And until that day there is the truth as each of us define it."

"I'm not looking for universal truth." Elizabeth responds. "I'll be just as happy if that day arrives after I've retired to my Boston harbor home. Looking out at the ships bringing in goods for Americans to consume from distant shores. Ships bearing American goods, sailing into the purple-tinted sunset, bound for world markets."

"You are a capitalist at heart," I observe.

"Did you ever doubt it?" Elizabeth responds checking out my perception of her.

"With your famous plans? How could I have assumed that? They were so diametrically opposed to capitalism. Big government for all. Let me solve all your problems even if you were the one who created them in the first place."

"That's not fair."

"Show me how I'm wrong?"

Elizabeth has to reflect on how to answer my question. "I wanted to reform the system not replace it."

"But your reforms would have resulted in something much

115

different. A replacement in fact if not in name. And you had so many examples of alternatives that worked that you would not consider."

"Name one."

"The Mayo Clinic and salaried healthcare rather than medical entrepreneurship."

## CHAPTER TWENTY-THREE: SABR MALIK GOLDSTEIN

Why is Elizabeth so evasive? She's not usually like this. I point to her to get her attention. We're in my cabinet meeting in the conference room just off the Oval Office in the White House.

"The Bergamo Accords are pretty straight forward. I don't understand what the issue is," she responds to my question.

"The issue is someone is questioning whether what was released was the 'official version.' Seems someone thinks there's more than one version of the accords out there. One released by one of the other signatories. Who would have done that? I mean we were very clear about the official version. There may have been side agreements, but they were not part of the official accords and the official press releases that went out. So what's the problem here, folks?"

Elizabeth apparently believes this lies in her domain. "What did the White House release?"

"The official version," I respond without even thinking about it.

"Then that should be the end of it," Elizabeth responds. "One official version. If someone else wants to put something else out there, we simply discredit it."

"Did you talk with Javier Santiago and Hua Kwan?"

"Spoke to Javier a few hours ago. Need to wait on Hua Kwan."

"Why?" I have to know why she's delaying.

"They're in the middle of the night at the moment. Hua is never very forthcoming, especially until her second cup of coffee or glass of fine wine."

"We can't afford to let others determine world opinion on the Accords." I want to make very clear. "It seems to me someone negotiated in bad faith. Did either of them ever intend to abide by the agreements we arrived at in Bergamo? I think it was all for window dressing. Make us think they are going to be cooperative when in fact they intend to enforce the status quo, which favors their interests over ours."

"Would you do any different?" Elizabeth reality tests.

"If the status quo favored us over them? I'd push to make them favor us even more."

"Which China did," Elizabeth points out. "So why are you suddenly surprised? Sounds contrived to me."

"We negotiated a substantial change to the world order," I point out. "And that's the problem. The fact that the Chinese have ignored the world order for decades and we did nothing to call them out for their behavior is our problem and not theirs."

"Exactly. So don't get upset about it." Elizabeth counsels, although I see other opinions around the room based on expressions and body language.

"I'm not upset about the negotiations." I inform her. "I'm upset that someone is undermining the agreement we reached after such protracted exchanges of views. It's getting significantly harder to do that when so much more is at stake every year."

"What's the truth?" Elizabeth asks.

"Truth?" I look at Elizabeth as if she's asking a nonsensical question. "The Truth is whatever I decide it to be. And I expect that is what you will inform the world to be the truth."

"But what happens when the Arbiter system is live?" Elizabeth asks.

I'm not sure I know what she means. "What about the Arbiter System?" This is not a conversation I was planning to have now, but maybe it's time to get this all out on the table.

"It will determine the truth. Based on algorithms."

"No. Arbiter will determine the truth according to what I determine to be the truth. Your algorithms are the red herring. The thing we can point to when someone raises a concern about what we determine we want people to believe. We simply say 'It's the algorithms. They represent decades of machine learning. Decades of studying us and determining what is the truth in any given situation'."

"And at any point you can override the algorithms without anyone knowing." Elizabeth seems to be trying to temper my enthusiasm.

"Elizabeth. Are you a team player or are you going freelance on me?"

Elizabeth sits back in her chair as if I'd slapped her. "Every one of us is expected to deliver certain results," Elizabeth begins. I hate it when she decides it's time for the Harvard Law Professor to give the President of the UsTopian States a lecture. "But each one of us is expected to deliver those results as we deem appropriate. The means, the methods, the investments we make, and the people we hire. Those are all our decisions. You tell me what you want me to deliver and back off so I can do it."

"Back off?" I take umbrage with her words.

"That's what I said."

Elizabeth doesn't appreciate who is in charge here. "I think you and I need a pedicure."

The dreaded pedicure. The time when I either fire someone or give them a redirect that they will either comply with or find another career. I always thought the pedicure was my contribution to the lore of the presidency since none of my male predecessors cared one whit about pedicures. I've only had one with a Cabinet member. My Secretary of Education was a liberal educator who was much better at motivating teachers to pull the right lever in the election booth than at understanding the nuances of educational finance. She never understood that teacher performance in the classroom has nothing to do with educational outcomes of her students. The department of education was established to funnel money to grant writers at the various school districts to put more money in the pockets of teachers who would then reliably vote for a certain party. My secretary thought she needed to establish a legacy of improved educational outcomes. Not something in her job description. But I was willing to see what she could do with the idea until I started getting complaints about her. When the heads of several unions came to me to personally complain, I had to do something. So I told her to back off outcomes-based education. She refused. I had no choice but replace her with the president of the national teacher's union. Someone who understands what our party stands for when it comes to education.

Elizabeth nods just once. "Do you need one that bad?" she asks.

"What are you suggesting?"

"You don't want opposition in the primaries for your re-election." Elizabeth threatens without the courtesy of even masking it in any way.

"Do you really think anyone is going to support an insurgent who got tossed out of the cabinet for disloyalty?" I frame the question for her.

"The truth will win out." Elizabeth responds although I can see she knows the truth of the matter is that I control the truth.

"And the truth is that if the people see a harmonious cabinet, if they see we are creating safety, a stable economy, and opportunity, they could care less about all the other stuff."

"So what's the problem?" Elizabeth asks. "We're doing that. But I am still confused about the Bergamo Accords."

"Foreign affairs," I point out. "Not what the people are concerned about."

"Then what is the truth of the Bergamo Accords?" Elizabeth asks.

"I would assume you read them," I check, just to be sure.

"I did." Elizabeth responds.

"And you read the press releases as Secretary of Truth."

"And approved them before they went out to ensure they were the truth." Elizabeth confirms with a twist of the knife.

"Then what's the issue?"

"I have no idea what the accords accomplish," comes as her complaint. "A statement of principles. Nothing more. I mean we could not adopt them and nothing would change. We adopt them and nothing will change. So why are we holding them out as a great national triumph?"

"It represents the fact that we could get to agreement with nations that have very different interests than our own. Do you have any idea how hard that is? That nations with diametrically opposed interests can find common ground?"

"That's your re-election stump speech? We found common ground?"

## CHAPTER TWENTY-FOUR: BRANDON McINERNY

Another night where I'm suddenly wide-awake. At least I think I'm wide-awake. Maybe in my dream I'm wide-awake. I can't tell anymore. If I am, I look forward to not seeing the images, not seeing the words, not dealing with a world gone mad, or at least as I see the world. But after all this time I can't tell what is mad and what reality is.

But reality is what I live. It's my reality even if it is man-made. Even if it is my reaction to all of the perversion placed before me by the Arbiter system. And then I see her. The young blonde girl. Naked. Her back to me as she sits on her heels. Her hair is different this time. Not stylized. I didn't realize it was so long. Hanging straight back. Further down her back than before. Now I know I'm back in a dream state. I'm not wide-awake. I'm seeing the images that pass rapid fire before me for ten hours a day six days or more a week for a decade at least. I've forgotten just how long it's been.

The man sits on the bed just beyond her. I can see his naked feet. His hairy legs. But the angle of the image doesn't let me see more of him this time. I can't tell much about him since the young girl obscures him almost entirely. Why this image? Why does my mind serve up this image for me to consider? Why does it reveal something different every time, so I study it? I anticipate it. I want to see more. See the young girl. Who is she? See the man beyond. Who is he? What does he want of the young girl? My mind suggests so many things I have to beat them back with a stick. That's not what this image is about. At least that's not what I hope this image is about. And all the time I have the same feelings about the girl as I ascribe to the man on the bed. Feelings I'd never admit to anyone. But there they are. Where did they come from? I'm not like this. I know I'm not. And still…

Another video I've seen before. A man. Back to me. Pants down.

The sheep he has mounted has it's forelegs down on the ground. Its back legs extended to give a straight shot to the man as he has intercourse with the sheep. I don't want to watch, but I do. Until the end. I don't want to watch. And yet I still see the man pull out. See the size of his rod, which probably explains why a sheep is a better partner for him. He is huge. Probably has difficulty finding partners who can accommodate him. I don't see his face. Don't see anything that would identify this individual. But I know I've seen this before. Seen someone having intercourse with a sheep. Why? I don't want to see this. So why is someone posting it on the internet? Why is someone wanting to share this experience with others? It's personal. Shouldn't be something anyone else wants to see, to think about. And now I have to. I have to remember this incident. Not because I want to, but because someone wanted to tell the world that his reality is not ours. That in some instances sheep are the only outlet to someone with a particular … what is it? A particular advantage or a particular handicap? I have no idea how he regards it, as nothing else other than an image is provided for me to consider.

The movie changes again. This time it's someone who is being raped. Tied to a bed. Struggling as a man with his back to the camera approaches the bed, drops his pants and climbs up and over her. Can't I turn this off? I don't want to watch. But I have no choice. No off button. No edit button. No delete button. Nothing that lets me look away. Nothing that lets me escape these images that I don't want in my memory. I see the expression on the young woman's face as the shadowy figure penetrates her. He is not at all concerned for her comfort. He just pushes on in and begins his rhythmic violation of her. Stop! I don't want to watch this. But the image remains. The image shows him violating her ruthlessly. Enjoying the violation more than the sex itself. More than the build and release he achieves at her expense. I close my eyes, but it doesn't make any difference. I still see the horror of the experience on her face. These images are always the worst because someone could stop them. Someone could prevent them. But no one does. No one appears in time to save the young damsel in distress. Is that what my mind is trying to tell me? That no one will magically appear to save me? Is this all metaphorical? Is this image not real? Am I the target of the feelings I have seeing this? Can I save myself from the violations society is perpetrating on me? Am I strong enough to simply say no and it will all stop? But the images don't stop. And that gives me the answer. I can't stop this. I can't change my life so that I will be able to cope with the nightmares that constitute my existence, my reality.

Different clip. A black man with a rope around his neck and his hands tied behind his back. Men whose faces I can't make out are in a circle around him. He sweats and looks down. The men are talking at him, but the black man just looks down. No matter what he says at this point it is all irrelevant. These white men are going to do what they are going to do. No matter what he might want to happen, it won't. No matter how much he hopes a Sheriff or other law enforcement officer might appear, he knows that person won't. Probably because he is one of the men in the circle around him.

One of the men pushes on him. Pushes him so hard he nearly falls. He is able to catch himself and return to his full height. Stand tall. Let them know he's not going to break. He is a powerful young man. He has no regrets about who he is. He has no regrets that he is someone different than them. It's better to be strong and independent than someone completely dependent upon others to validate who he is. Isn't it? That's what he's always believed. But at a moment like this, what can one truly believe that will be a comfort? What can one believe that will make what is about to happen just another incident on a long life towards a fuller universal existence? A being that rises above this earth. A being that incorporates so many diverse experiences that for some role that can't possibly be fathomed at this instant, it will prepare him for a destiny where he will make a transcendent difference in the lives of many. He feels the rope tighten about his neck. Feels the ropes on his hands tighten as if someone has just pulled on them to make sure they are going to restrain him. Make sure he can't work his hands free and prevent the rope around his neck from taking his life.

He closes his eyes, waiting for the momentary jerk that will lead to a release from the mortal body that has so restricted his spirit. So constrained his freedom, self-confidence and mastery of a future he can only imagine. A body that separated him from so many others. A body that limited his potential, not because of his mental capacity, a heart condition, a deadly disease, a physical handicap. But rather a body that limited his potential because of his skin color. The least important of the part of his body. And yet it became a social limitation on an otherwise unlimited future.

Another video clip. A white man in a uniform, down on his knees, hands tied behind his back. The man is looking down at the sand that seems to be infinite. Everywhere one looks. Sand and blue sky. Sand and ancient stone structures. Sand and ancient civilizations that delivered a future state so constrained in comparison to the one that founded the empire of antiquity.

Behind the man stands another. Also in uniform, but with a black mask over his head. Why is it important that we not see the face of the executioner? This coward stands above the humbled soldier who is only here in defense of a concept. Freedom. A concept that organizes the consciousness of a nation and the people who inhabit it. A concept worth fighting for, even though those who he fights have absolutely no idea what the concept means. And that is because they have no concept of what life could be like. They are trapped in a self-reinforcing cycle of deprivation, of limited horizons, of singular conceptions of authority, of religion, or community. How could life be different? The simple answer is it could be a lot worse. Throughout history when things have been bad they have only gotten worse. Good times are rare occasions and only result from piety. From following the instructions of the Imam. From giving complete faith to those who represent God here on earth. How did they get that esteemed designation? I have no idea. Is it important? No, because they have that designation. As an obedient servant of God every Muslim must do as his representative here on earth commands.

The man in the mask holds a very long and sharp sword. Not like a Jedi light sabre. Not like a Gladiator short sword. Not like razor sharp Samurai swords. Not like any of the Hollywood swords that have tried to show us a period in history when civilized men cut limbs from each other. Either very dull blades that hacked each other to death, or razor-sharp blades that cause almost instant release from mortal bonds.

The standing soldier raises his long sword over his head as the bound soldier looks down at that infinite sand, closes his eyes and waits for his release…

# CHAPTER TWENTY-FIVE: ICHABOD

There was something about Brandon that made me think he might not show. He was clearly disillusioned, but not someone who was ready to take up arms against a corrupt regime. He seemed more focused on how to deal with his own dreams than what caused them in the first place. He didn't seem to blame anyone but himself for having taken the job to begin with. That all made me assign a very low probability of conversion. The one thing that made me want to proceed was that he was very loyal. And if we're paying his salary he will feel obligated to do what we ask of him.

I'm sitting with Magritte. Beautiful Magritte, who was abused by her father and has absolutely no self-esteem. She will do whatever I ask, because I've always treated her with respect. Never asked her to sleep with me. Never hit on her, or treated her as someone other than an equal. What is it with abused women? If you give them even token recognition they will think you're a great human being. And that's not how anyone who really knows me would describe me.

Magritte is tall, blonde and almost anorexic thin. She has a cute button of a nose and big lips she constantly covers with bright red lipstick, making her mouth seem enormous. But I'm always drawn to her eyes. They are an impossibly dark blue like the deepest parts of the ocean. There is something behind those eyes she never reveals. A contempt for life maybe? Or maybe a contempt for the father that made her what she is. Rootless, willing and eager to please.

I see Brandon looking into the window. Apparently he's not coming in unless he knows I am here, although he's never met Magritte. Never had the pleasure of being enveloped in her embrace. Trapped in her mesmerizing force of being. All harnessed to our purpose.

"He's here." I tell Magritte. She looks around but apparently doesn't pick him out from my description. She looks back at me and has another sip of her red, red wine.

Brandon approaches but looks unsure. I wave him to join us. "Brandon. This is Magritte, my associate." She looks up at him with those fathomless dark blue eyes, her crooked smile and narrowed eyes as she evaluates him. I'm sure he thinks the evaluation is whether he would be suitable in bed, but I know differently. She's sizing up his willpower. Is he someone who can easily be co-opted or someone who will need to be deconstructed one brick at a time?

Brandon holds out his hand, "Pleasure."

Magritte regards his hand but turns away without satisfying his desire to make contact with her. She's already established that she's in control of their relationship. I see the puzzlement on Brandon's face. Just a flicker and a dismissal. He turns his attention to me. I can see he has decided that for the rest of the evening it's as if she doesn't exist.

"Sit, sit." I command him, but quickly see he's not about to be commanded. He continues to stand.

"Who is Tortoise?"

I look around to see who is listening to this conversation. "Not the place we want to discuss this."

"Fine." Brandon turns and walks away. I'm amazed, this isn't what I expected at all. Do I let him go or how do I get him back to the table? I'm on my feet and quickly overtake him just inside the front door.

"We have friends in many places." I tell Brandon when I spin him around to look at me. "These friends insure we know what we need to know."

"Including my salary, which is one of the most protected databases in the Department."

"Unless you're in the department," is all I'm willing to share. Need to make him understand that we have friends in the right places, but without any indication of who they might be, or why they willingly work with us.

Brandon looks at me and my hand on his shoulder. I remove my hand so he knows he's free to go if that's his choice. I'm not here to stop him. He's only one of many fish I'm trying to reel in at the moment. And by no means the most promising. He's a contingency player. Someone who has information that could be helpful, but not someone we see as core to our mission. So if he walks, I'm not going to worry about it. But he could be helpful enough that it's worth some effort on my part to reel him in.

"Why did you bring her? You think if I sleep with her it will be all over? That I'll give you anything you want?"

I laugh and shake my head. "Magritte hasn't slept with anyone other than of her choosing since she I've know her." He looks at me as if he doesn't believe me. "You want her gone so we can have a conversation, it's done."

Brandon doesn't look back at her, which is what every other man I've introduced to her has done. Instead he looks into my eyes. I have to admit it takes a lot for me to continue to look back at him.

"Why are you paying me when I didn't agree to do anything for you?"

I put my hand on his left shoulder and look into his eyes as earnestly as I can. "Because we believe in you. Believe that once you understand what we want to accomplish you will willingly join us."

"Who is us? You and Magritte?"

I'm the one who looks back at her, hoping he will follow my gaze, but when I turn back to him he's still looking only at me. Waiting. Watching. Evaluating me. I've never run into someone who took this particular approach. Those who simply weren't going to play were already gone. What's the story with this one? Why is he seemingly interested but only on his terms? Is there something he's dealing with that makes him want to find an alternative to what is about to be imposed on society by the Department of Truth? An alternative to whatever it is he's struggling to accept? "You only need concern yourself with me and you. There are others, but they do not affect what you do and will do for us. They believe we can have a different future than Elizabeth Warden sees. A future that addresses your fears, your hopes and your needs."

"You can't help me. No one can." Brandon responds with conviction.

"Come back and sit with me. I'll explain exactly how I can help you. How together we can achieve a different future. We can have dinner. Talk in a more relaxed way than standing here where people coming and going have to step around us."

"Why me? I'm nobody."

"You're someone who has spent his entire career building an expertise. Rising to be recognized as the most proficient of all the analysts the department employs. You're the gold standard. The one everyone else consults if they have questions. You're the one. And that sets you apart. You represent the norm for society. For all of us."

"How do you know that?"

"As I said, we have people on the inside."

Brandon looks away. Thinks about what I've said. "I'm not the one. You're wasting your time on me."

I shake my head, "The question isn't whether you're the one or not. The question is whether you will work with us to change the future."

"I can't help you there. I couldn't even change my own future. My best friend laid me off. The one person in the whole world who believes in me."

"You want to talk about it?" I ask, nod back to the table. "Over dinner?" I have to believe he's hungry living alone and not working.

Brandon glances back at the table, but it's only a glance. Not even sure if he sees Magritte sitting there. "What are you expecting me to do for the money you're paying me? No one gives money away. You have to have something in mind."

"We do. But we understand it takes a while for someone to be comfortable. To embrace the mission. To understand. We're patient. We take the long view."

"That may be your mistake." Brandon warns me.

## CHAPTER TWENTY-SIX: ELIZABETH WARDEN

Even though he wasn't my first choice, Brandon seems to know what he's doing. He's also doing his best to lower my expectations. He is sitting in his new cube and I'm standing looking over the top of the half-height wall.

"Digital footprints is what they're called," Brandon responds to my question. "Something unique about the party you're looking for. And unfortunately we have no idea at the moment what those footprints may consist of."

"So where do you begin?"

"Where every good search begins, with keywords. I'll try to find individuals who are using key words, who they are communicating with and then build influence diagrams of their networks. From there I'll add additional key words and see how the influence diagrams change, who else is brought in, who they communicate with. That way I'll start to see if there is any overlap between the individuals and groups. Overlap in the use of key words that might indicate intent or at least interest in certain subjects."

"How do you winnow it all down?" I'm having trouble seeing how this gets us to a particular group that doesn't want to be found.

"We check the groups and individuals against the current threat databases. See what the history is on each. See what we've monitored in the past. See who is out there that we've not been seeing before, that we're not tracking, and that we were unaware of. Then I'll do more digging. See what can be found on those individuals and groups that haven't surfaced before. The groups that seem to be minimizing their presence, but are using keywords of significant intent."

He at least has a plan, although I was hoping it would be something more unique than the tools and approaches we use all the time. Looking for people and groups we're not tracking. I'll be surprised if he finds much there. We seem to sweep everything and keep it forever, just in case someone expresses something that might crop up later. But that also doesn't explain how kids attempt to post things and end up shooting people in malls a week or more later. We go look at them after the fact. Find we haven't done anything about touching them before something happens. Why is that? Where are the holes in our intent detection vacuums? "What do you think you'll find?"

"Part of the problem is Arbiter," he states matter-of-factly.

I shake my head, "Arbiter is the solution. How can it be part of the problem?"

"Because it never posts things that contain the keywords I'm looking for. So I have to go through the initial registers archives, you know the attempts to post that I used to review or the broadcasts that are made but never aired. But you only keep them for thirty days. After that the registers are deleted. So I only have a thirty-day window to search. If we had the intent to post files going back years this would probably be a much faster process. But with only a thirty-day window I have to keep at it. At least until our party of interest attempts to post something, or uses a keyword in a recorded conversation or broadcast. Until then, the person of interest is invisible in our search."

"What if you don't search the right keywords?" I suddenly realize may be a hole.

"Then we never find him or her."

"You're saying there's a possibility that you'll never find our party of interest?"

"I don't expect to find much to start with," Brandon admits. "It would be an incredibly lucky break that our friend left a footprint I can find with the information I have. I may even look right at the person we seek and not recognize what I'm seeing. It's possible that party works here, knows our systems better than either of us, and will be able to avoid detection indefinitely. It's even possible that the party of interest is you. Since I normally would ignore your use of keywords because of who you are and what you do, I probably would not investigate you further."

"I was going to say…"

"…That you're surprised I would consider you a possible threat?" Brandon looks at me directly, the same way I do when I'm trying to make a point to someone. "Don't be. With the task you've given me, I have to look at everyone and not eliminate a digital footprint for the wrong reason. That's why you brought me back. Because I don't make assumptions. Albert knows that from all the years we've worked together."

He apparently thinks I hired him because of Albert's recommendation. Well, I did in part. But I still think Sheila would have been a better choice for this job. She convinced me to give Brandon a shot. She said she would conduct an independent analysis of the broadcast media in her current role on Albert's remaining team. Thus giving me the best analysts in both spectrums working the search. "What did Albert tell you when he laid you off?"

Brandon hesitates, shows a semi-smile, "That Arbiter no longer needed as many validations so he had to reduce the team. That even though I was his best analyst, he wanted to give me a chance to find another position before all the other analysts flooded the market, which would make it harder."

"What did you think about that?" I wonder what kind of time bomb I might be bringing on.

"That it was bullshit. Albert's been my best friend for a long time. I can tell when he's not giving me the straight scoop. He laid me off because you told him to, which is why I think it's ironic that you brought me back."

"You think I told him to lay you off," I wonder why he ever got that impression. "Why would I do that?"

"I've had a couple weeks to ponder that question." Brandon stops to consider before continuing. "You know, I've not come up with a good explanation. The only thing that makes sense to me is maybe you are in such a hurry to get Arbiter fully on line that you got rid of the analysts who are your benchmarks."

"I'm not following." Why would we do that?

"I was the gold standard. If Arbiter agreed with me then it reached fidelity. The problem was it hasn't. Probably not more than half of the recommendations were consistent with what I did. You know it probably wasn't even fifty percent. Forty maybe."

"I just got a report that it's over eighty," I inform him. "I probably shouldn't tell you that as it's closely held information."

"You can trust me that I won't share it with anyone. But I can tell you, Arbiter is a long way from eighty percent."

"You've been gone for a couple weeks. Isn't it possible the fidelity improved while you were gone?"

"It's possible. Anything is possible. But it didn't improve that much that fast despite the best efforts of all the learning algorithms. The array of cases we see in any given day are just too vastly different. You know the old definition of pornography – I'll know it when I see it? That's the problem we're dealing with. A lot of the stuff we refuse to post are things we've never seen before. And those are the hardest things for Arbiter to deal with. It has no guidance from prior decisions. It has to interpolate and in most instances the interpolations are wrong, at least as far as the analysts are concerned. The Ten Commandments are a framework because they can't give us specific guidance in every situation. Can't see things that are embedded in images in many instances because they are deliberately vague, but suggestive. Arbiter doesn't see those in the same light that a person may. And even among us analysts, some of us see those images and others see what the machine sees. I may delete it, but the analyst sitting in the cube next to me may let it go up."

I'm stunned that Maria isn't telling me the truth about Arbiter, but she can't fake her statistics."

"I know what you're thinking," Brandon interrupts my thoughts. "That the statistics from Arbiter tell you eighty percent. So I would ask, who programmed the machine in how to calculate those statistics? I would bet you're getting only a subset and not the entirety of decisions."

"Why?" is all I can think of to say.

"Profits," Brandon responds immediately. "They need to get to acceptance as quickly as possible to get paid. They need to stop burning programming hours. And it's all because you said you wouldn't give any further contract rebase-linings. Everything beyond the current schedule is on their dollars."

"Didn't know that was common knowledge."

"But there are other reasons your contractor won't tell you the truth."

## CHAPTER TWENTY-SEVEN: SHEILA

I stop by Brandon's cube and find him busy parsing through affinity diagrams. I watch from behind him for a few moments. He's creating the networking diagrams of people who communicate using key words. Not something we do very often as analysts, although from time-to-time we have done such analysis to understand the origins of certain expressions we are seeing on a recurring basis.

"Aaheemmm." I clear my throat loudly since he has his earbuds in, probably listening to music to stay relaxed or hyped up, depending on what he's listening to.

No response, so I tap him on his shoulder.

He jumps and glances over his shoulder with a mixture of surprise and panic in his expression. "Oh. Sheila." He pulls the earbuds out and stands up. "Bet you didn't think you'd see me back."

I give him a hug. "Of course I did. Just knew it would take time."

Brandon looks at the clock on the wall behind me, "You have time for lunch?"

"Thought you'd never ask," I grin at him.

We walk down towards the cafeteria. Quicker than going out. Don't have to ask since the Department subsidizes the cafeteria. While the food's not great, it's at least affordable in comparison with the fast food places around the offices. "You're working directly for the Secretary?"

"Crazy isn't it? I mean who would think I'd get the boot and two weeks later I have this incredible promotion."

"I take it's only a temporary job?"

"No such thing as a permanent job anymore. Even the Secretary serves at the pleasure of the President and the will of the people. We live in a gig economy. So we need to learn how to surf from one job to the next. Start looking for the next job on the day you start this one. You need to think about that because you'll be out of here soon."

We get in line for sandwiches and wraps, "I should be good for a while," I respond but I don't want to say too much.

"Don't bet on it," is his cryptic response.

"Why are you so pessimistic?" I follow as my reaction to his comment.

"Actually I'm optimistic for the first time in weeks. I have a new challenge to focus on. Hopefully that will convince my mind to dream about something else for a while. A better world maybe?"

I let that sit for a bit as we get our wraps and head to a table in the corner, next to the windows that look out on the colorful courtyard garden. I notice the red and blue blossoms set against the green leaves and brown tree trunks. I find myself doing this more and more often. Looking for some normality to help me re-center after a day of extremes. I used to ignore it all. Just do my job. But I can't anymore. I have to take it in smaller bites. Balance things out several times a day. I look at the picture of Lake Como at least once an hour now. I've come to the conclusion I need to add other pictures to my cube. Get more variety of normal. Get more images, totems if you will, that help me put what I'm doing in perspective. Maybe I need to make sure I come down here for lunch every day. Look out at the courtyard, study the trees and flowers, the riot of color. The result of nature's paintbrush.

"You seem lost in thought," Brandon interrupts me.

"What did the Department do for you when they laid you off?" I remember the conversation with Elizabeth Warden that so unsettled me.

"Do for me? Nothing, Why?"

I'm not sure Brandon understands my question. "Did it do anything to help you with your nightmares?"

"Like counseling or something?" he's guessing the intent of my question, but I don't want to come right out and ask.

"Whatever." I finally respond.

"Like I said, nothing." Brandon sounds bitter. "The only one who reached out to me other than you was Albert. We had lunch. He offered to help me get a job. That's probably why I'm here."

"That was it?"

"Look. It doesn't matter. Nothing is as it seems. What the Secretary wants? Well that's just one person's opinion of what needs to be done. There are others out there working for a different future where algorithms don't dictate our decisions. Where we regain the freedoms the systems strip from us. Where we can think what we want and no one is looking over our shoulder herding us into a box of behavior approved by Sabr and her cronies."

I just look at him for a long moment, totally not expecting this from him. "What are you talking about?"

"What the Secretary wants isn't what's important," he continues. "There are others out there working for a just future. One where people like us or algorithms don't tell us what to believe, or what appropriate expression is. And yet that's what our careers have been. Judging others. Deciding what others should know, think or feel. Is that what the world has come to? The Ten Commandments didn't come from you or me. They were handed to us by those who thought they knew what we should think, feel and do. It's like the whole society has been put on weed. Chill everyone. Nothing to get worked up about. Enjoy what you got. Don't worry about what someone else has. That doesn't mean anything to you. You are who you are. You have what you have. That's your lot in life. Enjoy the ride."

I sit back in my chair, trying to understand what's changed. Why is he saying this to me? I hesitate before responding, but once I start… "Are you saying our whole life's work is for nothing? Niente? Really? What we've been doing has contributed to a better world. One where kids, adults and old folks don't have to have their senses assaulted by those who preach freedom as an insult. I can make you feel as bad as I want under freedom of expression. That would be all fine if the internet has a filter that prevents anyone who doesn't elect to see those sites from ending up there. From ending up with the charlatans who just want your money." I stand up and look down at him as he slowly chews his wrap although I haven't eaten. "You better get your head out of your butt and look around. The world isn't ever going to be the place you describe without people like us doing our fair share."

Brandon holds up his hand to keep me from walking away until he can respond, but he is in the middle of a mouthful of food he's been chewing his way through. He finally swallows with much difficulty, takes a sip of vitamin water and looks up at me. "I agree with you. Except that part about getting my head out of my butt. It is up to us and that's why I'm going to make a difference. I'm going to join the revolution. Will you?"

"What revolution? There is no revolution. This is UsTopia. We're a democracy. We work through peaceful transitions of government. We limit our leaders to two terms and then someone else has the chance to change the direction of our country if enough people elect to take a different path. If you're getting involved with the other party, well, that's your choice. I'm not there. At least not yet. I want to see how this all plays out. See if Arbiter can successfully arbitrate expression so we aren't overwhelmed with what you and I have spent our careers preventing from getting into the national consciousness."

Brandon muses over my response. Apparently decides something.

"Sit down." He modifies his directive, "Please sit down with me. I need to talk with someone who understands."

I don't sit, "Understands what?"

"What it's like. The nightmares. The inability to concentrate without unwanted images suddenly interrupting your thoughts. To never get a night's sleep and constantly being in a state of sleep deprivation. To seeing your mind interpret something in a way you never considered."

"Interpret?" He's never said anything about interpreting things.

"Please sit down," he glances around. "People are looking at us, to say nothing of the security cameras."

I glance around and see he is right. People are looking at me standing there. So I sit. "Tell me about interpretations."

"The same image. Recurring. Night after night. But each night there's something new in that same image. Something I'd not seen before. It's like my mind is interpreting something my subconscious wants me to know. Putting it into that image. Making me…"

## CHAPTER TWENTY-EIGHT: 'MARIA' XHE

Elizabeth isn't happy. She called me into her office. I can tell she wants to ask me something, but for some reason she's sitting on it. Deciding not to ask it now. "Something you want know?" I want to get it out on the table. Deal with it so we can move on.

"I'm getting the information I need through other channels."

Cryptic. It's never good when she gets like this. "If you can identify what you want to know I can have the team pull it together."

Elizabeth barely shakes her head, apparently unsure as to whether she wants to respond to my offer. I'll need to ask the team what they're hearing from her other teams. Get ahead of whatever it is she's unhappy about. "Okay. What did you want to talk about?"

"Do you know Brandon McInerny?"

The name is not one I'm familiar with. I shake my head and shrug simultaneously.

"He's working a special project for me and will need full access to Arbiter files and registers. He will need your full cooperation."

"How is this different from the access quality control has? They have full access as you've described."

Elizabeth puzzles for a moment on my clarification. "He needs full access, whatever that means. He needs to review any file, any submission for posting, any broadcast original files as far back as you can provide them."

"That's thirty day currently. Do you want that changed?"

Elizabeth nods with a private thought then looks at me. "For the time being let's not delete any records. What kind of problem does that create?"

"Means I need to add storage, but memory is cheap. Do I have the authority to spend what it takes?"

"Get me a quote and I'll let you know. Do you have a temporary work around? I don't want to lose anything we currently have in memory."

This is odd. "I can probably find excess storage on other systems. Can probably loop it in within a day. Will that work?"

"If it's the best you can do."

"Priority number one," I assure her.

"Go see Brandon. He's on seven. Cube 7B-001."

I nod and excuse myself, take the elevator and walk the short distance to Brandon's cube. I find him engrossed in what looks like the creation of multiple affinity or network diagrams. One appears, he inputs some parameters and another appears. What's he doing?

I approach the cube, knock, but notice he has earbuds in. Probably listening to something. I tug on his right earbud. He glances around, sees me but doesn't respond otherwise.

"Can I talk with you?"

Brandon pulls the earbud out, "Can I help you?"

"Actually the Secretary sent me to help you."

Brandon nods to himself, "Of course. What did she ask you to do?"

The cube has a small table and one chair, he rolls himself over in his chair as I take a seat. "The Secretary said you need full access to all files and registers."

"That would help," Brandon responds apparently not surprised. "Who are you?"

"Maria Xhe. I'm the program manager for Arbiter."

"You apparently know who I am."

"Sort of. The Secretary didn't tell me much. Just that you need unrestricted access."

"To the files but not the programs. I don't need to change anything in the system itself."

"That's consistent with what she said." I note for him. "The Secretary said you're an analyst."

"I was," Brandon responds cautiously. "But I was laid off in the first round. I'm not back on the desk. So I guess that means I'm not anymore."

I think of analyst and instantly ask, "Do you have the dreams?"

"What do you know about my dreams?" Brandon is instantly suspicious.

"I did the interviews with analysts when we were defining the system requirements. I talked with about a thousand analysts then. They all talked about the dreams. How hard it is to do the job because you can't leave it at work. The job takes over your entire existence. Warps your perspectives. Makes you suspicious of everyone and everything."

Brandon nods and looks down. "You didn't interview me. Why?"

I have to think for a moment before answering his question. "As I remember, this was a few years ago now... as I remember it was a

144

random sample. I was just given a list the Department provided. To be sure you'd have to ask Fitch. I don't even remember his first name, but at the time he was the guy responsible for the procurement. He's not on the team anymore. Don't know if he got promoted or left the department, but I've not seen him in a couple years. Sullivan is the current procurement official, but the Secretary is involved in most of the meetings with us now that we're getting close."

"Close?" Brandon asks as if he's confused.

"To the automated go live."

"How close do you think you are?" Brandon asks, but there's something in the tone of his voice. Skepticism maybe? It may be something else but he definitely has an opinion about this topic.

"A matter of weeks now," I give him the same answer I give the Secretary as she may have a conversation with him about this topic at some point and I don't want different dates floating up.

Brandon nods, but doesn't say more about that.

I return to the earlier question about his dreams he didn't respond to. I want to validate that what the others told me is true. "I've heard the stories. I understand the nightmares, the sleepless sweats, and the dry mouth in the morning when all you want to do is get up and vomit to start the day. My algorithms will make it possible that no one will have to suffer like you have or any of the others." I want him to know why I'm dedicated to getting the system operational despite the larger consequences of automating analysis.

Brandon looks down and closes his eyes. I see him shudder and tense up.

In a moment he looks up and glances away, taking a deep breath.

"What is it?"

"Flashback to a particularly gruesome mutilation. This happens to me several times a day, depending on what I'm doing. Stressful days are worse than others. I need to shake it off."

I watch him for a moment and realize he is unsuccessful as the residue remains haunting the periphery of his existence. I see it in his face. In his posture. Mostly it hides in his eyes which seem to be in a perpetual squint.

"What do you need me to do to help you… with your new assignment?"

Brandon tries to work through the remains of the apparently vivid image. He stands up and looks out over the top of his cube. Looks around the room, stretching and cracking his neck as he turns it side-to-side. A deep breath and then he finally refocuses on me. "Help me? You've given me full access?"

"I haven't yet, but will do that as soon as I get back to my office."

Brandon nods. "What else can you do for me?"

"Help you with your dreams."

Brandon looks at me confused. "Nothing helps. I've tried everything."

"Try not taking anything. Don't avoid the dreams. Don't try to shut your mind down with weed and alcohol, the usual courses of action."

"I gave up on that a long time ago."

"You must train your mind to set the images aside, file them away where they won't dominate your thoughts. You have to be strong to do it, but it's the only way."

"How do you know?" Brandon demands of me. "There are so many of us with these dreams."

"Because that was the only approach anyone said actually worked."

# CHAPTER TWENTY-NINE: JAVIER SANTIAGO

I am surprised Jurgen wants to meet with Hua Kwan in his office rather than the formal conference room where we normally meet. This gesture is one of intimacy I didn't think Jurgen felt for the mistress of Chinese intelligence. I have always thought Hua Kwan could be a beautiful woman if she permitted herself the accoutrements of the fashion trade. Instead she downplays her appearance. She seeks to remain in the shadows. Not front and center, which an embellished version of herself would cause whether she wished to be there or not. I am curious as to what has caused her to take this course of action. Possibly forcing men to take her mind seriously? Possibly ensuring that she isn't required to sleep with every bureaucrat between herself and Xi? Now that she's reached the position of power within the Chinese bureaucracy, where she has information that could destroy the career of any individual she chose, no one would dare seek to bend her to their will, with the possible exception of Xi himself.

My speculation regarding Hua Kwan remains with me. I would never share it with Jurgen. It would put him in a position where he would feel compelled to sleep with her out of sheer need to control a powerful person in her own right. Feel it a challenge worthy of his considerable, at least in his own mind, charms. I've watched Jurgen with other powerful women. He is drawn to them like a magnet. Attempts to understand the source of their strength, the location of their weaknesses. And once he understands the delicate balance that makes them powerful, he seeks to exploit any opportunity to change the nature of the relationship to favor his interests. Generally that means sleeping with her, but more recently he has sought more nuanced power.

As I enter Jürgen's office I find him seated behind his immense carved oak desk. The one his grandfather had specially made. To celebrate the initiation of the thousand-year Reich. We are only a little more than a hundred years into that regime, but at the moment it would appear we are well on our way. Hua Kwan sits attentively across from him in the visitor's chair. This is a place of honor that few ever visit. What's the occasion for this treatment? And it seems to be on both sides, as Hua Kwan is dressed in a white silk floor length dress. Her long black hair cascades past her shoulders, framing her pale face with no makeup, no embellishment. A face that could easily disappear in a crowd on any street in China.

"I am a vegetarian by choice, "Hua Kwan is explaining to Jurgen. "Does that make me weak because I am not a predator like you? Someone who must feast from the flesh of animals to maintain your resolve? I think not. I think it makes me more resilient. I can maintain my vigor without the need for a successful hunt. I am not obliged to take the life of an animal that I might live. I am only grateful to a harvest. One of sufficient bounty to enable all to eat. To nourish ourselves before we go back to do battle." I see her glance in my direction with only the most subtle recognition before returning her full attention to Jurgen. "Being vegetarian I can be patient. I am not required to vanquish others to feed my people. I am not subject to discontent among my people when the winter is hard. When there is little reward from the hunt. My people are content for they have full bellies. They are content for they know their adversaries are starving. Their adversaries are discontent. Their adversaries will be weaker when battle inevitably ensues. And rather than wasting energy undertaking ever more arduous hunts, further and further afield, my people sharpen their swords, forge new knives and shields to prepare."

"We no longer live in caves Hua Kwan," I announce my presence. "Those days of preparation for an inevitable fight are passed. Today we are all amongst friends. Our strong military might be a necessary expenditure to keep our people employed, to support new technology development when, if it were for peaceful purposes, it would be criticized as not being in the public interest."

Having caught my entrance earlier, Hua Kwan does not turn to look at me, although Jurgen does. His response is, "Thank you for joining us Minister Santiago. Vice Chairman Kwan was just informing me of why our civilization is doomed from within, all because of our strange proclivity towards eating meat."

"The Vice Chairman of the People's Secretariat has woven her tales of predictive proclivities for me previously. Although I must admit I am beginning to see nuance to her arguments that I did not perceive before." And in this brief response I have just warned Jurgen of the dangers he is playing with by encouraging Hua Kwan to believe she has any particular influence or opportunity to establish such influence with him.

Jurgen sits back, apparently getting the message loud and clear. "I think this is your meeting," Jurgen passes the attention to me to either take control or cede it to her.

"Madam Vice Chairman, thank you for making the arduous journey from Beijing to Berlin. I take it you have had an adequate opportunity to rest before commencing these discussions of mutual interest for both our collectives of nations."

"Minister, thank you for your consideration of my state of being. I am happy to be with you and the Chancellor, grateful for your gracious invitation to have these informal discussions of issues of mutual interest, and ready to begin at your convenience."

"I take it the Chairman is well and enjoying the continuing prosperity and peaceful relationships of your nation states with the rest of the world." These are the required protocol greetings. I have been instructed on more than one occasion to ensure that I follow the protocol lest I upset the delicate balance of our relationships.

"The Chairman is also grateful for the continuing friendship between our nations states and the spirit of cooperation that has enabled a prolonged period of peace and co-prosperity." The latter is a direct rebuke to the UsTopians who abandoned a half century of cooperation in a feeble attempt to cast the UaTopians as free riders on the global economy. After all, the UsTopians had allowed them to be such in order to develop their economy, only to seek to redraw the rules that had enabled that half century of co-prosperity when it threatened their global hegemony.

"Our peoples have long memories," I suggest to show I understand the grievances the Chinese feel towards the UsTopians, who took advantage of a weak China to exploit it and it's peoples fully two centuries ago. And now they wonder why China is unwilling to be subservient to them in the global economy.

"But you have no grievance. After defeating you on the field of battle, they magnanimously helped you rebuild. To become stronger than you had ever been," Hua Kwan notes. "So why do you champion grievances if not to seek advantage for yourselves at our expense?"

I note the raised eyebrow Jurgen hopes to hide from her, but to no avail as she clearly sees it. Hua Kwan is nothing if not extremely observant. She is the ultimate observer, dissecting her adversaries and partners to properly position them for the complete extraction of value. I have warned Jurgen of her ability. Repeatedly warned him and yet he continues to flirt with disaster. That is unless he is simply setting her up so that I might find weaknesses to exploit. I wonder…

"Madam Vice Chairman, we have cooperated with you to establish an exclusion zone around your shores. To weaken the influence of certain other nations amongst your neighbors. To make the nations on your borders more vulnerable to your influence and your economic exploitation. A long time ago, one of your neighbors attempted much the same extension of its influence. They called it an East Asian Co-Prosperity Sphere. I would never use that description because of the historic baggage it carries. But in effect we have assisted you to create your own version of that failed carving up of your neighborhood, so to speak."

Hua Kwan knows exactly what I'm suggesting. I see it in her eyes.

"We acknowledge the role you have played in assisting our expanded global position."

This is the tricky part – our ask. "In exchange for our continued support as you grow your influence we would ask for your cooperation in a sensitive area – algorithms. You are the acknowledged world leader in artificial intelligence and machine learning. Tools to enable unparalleled capabilities in a number of life-altering technologies."

"Algorithms are most useful. They assist us in locating wealth hidden from our taxing authorities." Hua Kwan is understating as usual. "After all, a nation runs on taxes, and automating tax collection expands your resources."

I look at Jurgen, who returns the look with a shake of his head. "Madam Vice Chairman. Your surveillance technology is what interests us most. Your complete suppression of the Uighurs. Your undermining of the Hong Kong protests. You have demonstrated an unparalleled capability that would assist us as we look to the future…"

# CHAPTER THIRTY: SABR MALIK GOLDSTEIN

What is it about Elizabeth? She just never seems to be on the same page with me. It's as if she hasn't accepted that I'm the President and she is the Secretary of Truth in MY cabinet. She is here in my office with me because I chose her, not the people. She didn't win an election that gave her four years of power to do as she pleases within the bounds of a Congress and Supreme Court. If I hadn't chosen her, she would be back in Boston staring out her window on a harbor that seems to only bring in storms that send the local populace scrambling for higher ground. She would be teaching law again to young minds intent on changing the world, without any conception of what it takes to do just that. But Elizabeth would point out that she walked that walk. She followed that idealism to its logical end. And the price you have to pay to gain that power is often not something in your control. Your background, starting with your parents, sets certain expectations. Certain framing opportunities. And the choices your parents made will either set you on the road to greatness, the road to mediocrity, or the road to what every other citizen of our nations experiences. Enough. We experience enough. Nothing more. Nothing less. We are a nation of okay people. We aren't ecstatic. We aren't morbidly depressed. We are healthy enough, but few are great athletes. We can play a mean game of whatever we choose, but we don't win them all. We have a family that can do more than we accomplished in our short lives. But our children may choose to sub-optimize the advantages we give them. Then we spend the rest of our lives apologizing to our friends and family about them. I'm so glad I never had children that would establish what a poor parent I would have been.

Elizabeth waits for me, as she always does, buried deep in her cellphone reading her fan mail, or is it departmental mail? Probably all the same. I can't resist. "Did you read about it?"

"It?" comes as a startled response to my inquiry.

"The shooting in San Antonio," I pronounce to erase all doubt as to what I'm talking about.

"San Antonio," Elizabeth dives back into her phone to bring up the news blogs, sees the gruesome pictures. I watch her pull back, take a deep breath as she wades in to reading the details.

"You simply must keep up with world events, Elizabeth," I scold her.

When she finishes the story she apparently now understands why I called that one to her attention. "I didn't know we have people in San Antonio."

"You don't," I confirm for her since I know all the bloody details. "He lost his job here in your last layoff. He was kicked out of his apartment since he could no longer pay the rent. So he did what you or I would do. He went home to live with his parents – in San Antonio. That's why the shooting took place there. He was living with his parents when the rage overcame his inhibitions. It just burst loose in a rampage that took nearly fifty lives. Fifty votes I need in a state that is teetering between red and blue. Fifty lives, Elizabeth. Fifty votes that could decide whether you and I are back here for another four years."

Elizabeth stares at me that way she does when she is sitting on whatever it is she really wants to say but is afraid of the ramifications of doing so. I never push when I see that expression. I know better having watched her in the debates. She defaults to rage and indignation as a defense. I'm not about to suffer the stings of her loosened rages. So I mitigate. "What are you going to do to ensure this doesn't happen again?"

"You're presuming the media will blame us for what happened, even though my department determines what gets put on the air and what doesn't. What gets pushed to the media and what never is shared between more than two people."

"Yes, I'm making that presumption because your department will tell the world what happened and why. All in the cause of a greater good. All to ensure that others who would suffer because of what our people spew forth into the blackness of the ether, in an effort to save us from those negativities, don't suffer. You will tell the world that one of yours suffered because of them. Suffered to the point he sought out suicide by cop rather than continuing to live with the blackness that resides in the hearts of our people. He did not wish to kill anyone other than himself. We have to continually tell our people who they are. Why the Arbiter project is so essential if we are to change the very nature of us all."

"You're kidding me," is Elizabeth's amazed reaction. "That's not how any of this works. Haven't you been listening? If we tell people who they are we're finished. They will vote for the other guy in a heartbeat. The other guy wants to unleash the beast within. We want to put it into a cage so it can't harm anyone. Which would you rather be? Free to fuck with everyone, or in a cage for the rest of your life?"

Elizabeth puts a challenge out there I have to consider, but I don't have time right now to do that. "Two perspectives on the people who put us here," I throw out there to buy a moment to organize my thoughts. "If you're right then I shouldn't be sitting on this side of the table. I should be sitting over where you are. If I bought into your analysis, then I'd admit I don't understand how I received their votes when you did not. Understand how I was more trusted to deliver a future they sought than the many plans you presented. A clearly defined alternative to the reality they were experiencing. A clear alternative resulting from the path I showed them I would follow. From this brief discussion I would have to say the difference between us, Elizabeth, is that I trust the judgment of the people in a way you do not. I trust that if I show them the alternative, they will embrace what I am offering instead. Whereas you would hide essential truths from them. Truths they understand, and are looking to see if we understand."

"Is this where I leave you and go back to the people to ask the question, do they want my future or your future?" Elizabeth sets her pen down on top of her portfolio. Calmly looks at me waiting for me to blink.

"Are you resigning?" I ask simply since we are now at that point. A ruptured relationship not likely to be repaired. Irreconcilable views of what the people think about the course each of us would chart for their future.

"I'm a team player as long as the team is attempting to reach the same goal," Elizabeth defends herself. "A win. And in this case I'm talking about a win for the people who put us here, regardless of your role in putting me here. I came to Washington because I thought I had a different vision of the future than the man I replaced in the Senate. I came to Washington because I saw how the system didn't work for so many of my fellow citizens. We put our trust in the people we sent to this city. We staked our futures to their reasoned actions on our behalf. And what I came to understand was that many of the people who came here were or became corrupt. They were or became self-centered, rather than servants of the people. Which are you?"

"I'm surprised you would ask that question for you know the answer as well as I do. We're not them. The ones who come here and are lured by the swansongs of the lobbyists. Telling us how if we simply support their causes we will secure economic prosperity for our families and ourselves. Power and economic security for a lifetime, rather than just our few terms in office. That's not us. That's not why we're here. So why are you asking me that?"

"Because you're about to commit suicide by voter, which is the same thing." Elizabeth tries to change my understanding. "If I do what you want, neither you nor I will be here after the next election. Everything we've worked so hard to put in place will be undone four years from now. Will the voters be better off? Impossible. But they have no idea. They can't see what you and I see. If they did they would be here and not us."

I have to step back, consider her perspective. I'm not infallible. I'm not my predecessor, who set policy by twitter in an attempt to keep the people focused on something other than what he was really doing. Elizabeth is expecting me to ask for her resignation so she can be free to unseat me in the upcoming election. I don't think she will succeed. But she could weaken me enough that I might lose the general election. Can't take that chance. "What are you doing for the others?"

"Others?" Elizabeth isn't expecting my question.

"Those you have released who have emotional damage. What are you doing for them? We have to get out in front of the problem you have created."

Elizabeth tries to understand what I've decided. I'm not giving her a hall pass to take future shots at me, whether in private or in public because one follows the other.

## CHAPTER THIRTY-ONE: ELIZABETH WARDEN

Maria. What can I say about Maria? She sits across from me as I sit at my desk. I'm not comfortable talking to her here, but I'm not sure she will feel comfortable if we walk down to the team room where Arbiter is coming alive. Brandon alerted me to the fact that Arbiter is not being reported correctly. My independent assessors have confirmed his assessment. It's not ready for prime time. It's not going to be in the near future. So I'm faced with a Hobson's choice. Continue the current path of rebaselines, pushing a functioning system further and further into the future, or cutting it over now knowing it's not perfect, it's not even good. But it will make determinations that limit the content that is corrupting our community. Many of the worst proposed postings will be prevented from reaching the larger community. Maybe more postings will fall into the trash heap of history than needed, but society will survive. Maybe productive ideas will never see the light of day. But that's clearly better than bad ideas taking us back to the middle ages. And over time, the system will continue to learn, continue to evolve, become higher in fidelity with the human analysts if I leave a reference group. A small reference group in place making human determinations the algorithms can reference. And Sheila is the person I want heading that up. She's the gold standard, not Brandon, no matter what Albert told me. Albert may have been closer to daily traffic, may have watched the two of them day-in and day-out. But I trust Sheila. Brandon seems... what is it? I don't know. But there's something about Brandon that makes me pause when it comes to establishing his sensibilities as being representative of mine.

Maria responds to a text. I give her a minute to finish her message, then, "Let's walk."

Maria seems confused, but she's up following me out the door and down the hallway. The faster we walk the harder it is for the sensors to

TRUTH

follow our conversation. That was confirmed to me by my security experts. If I could run down the halls, that would be the best thing, but a fast walk makes it hard for them to pick up what I'm saying.

"Where are you in fidelity?"

Maria is huffing and puffing already. Out of shape. Not a good thing. "We are making progress."

"Over ninety-eight percent?" I test her.

"On some parameters, not all."

"Which ones?" I push back.

"I would have to consult the test reports." Maria doesn't want to be specific. Got it. But that makes my decision easier in some respects. No uniform performance results.

"What would happen if you threw the switch tomorrow?"

"Tomorrow?" Maria clearly wasn't expecting this question. "Would it decrement our contract?"

"No. You get paid in full. You simply kick up your learning algorithms. We leave a small human analyst team for you to work your machine learning algorithms off and we're done. Fini."

Maria stops, watches me continue on down the hall. I don't look back and I don't wait for her. Either she catches up to me or she doesn't. That's her problem, not mine. In another moment I walk into the Arbiter test lab. It seems the whole room stops breathing. They aren't used to seeing me or any customer representative here. I walk over to the first test station I come to. "What's your name?"

"Brooke," comes the weak response.

"What do you do, Brooke?"

159

She stands up to talk to me at eye level. "I test the algorithm code."

"Is it ready?" I ask simply.

"Ready for what?"

"Deployment. Is it ready to look at internet postings and disposition them as a human analyst would? Is it ready to look at a broadcast and determine what meets the Ten Commandments? Is it ready?"

"I would have to say yes. It can do those things. But will it make the same decisions as any group of analysts? Not going to happen."

"Why?" I push Brooke.

"Because the analysts can't agree. So how's a machine supposed to be this split personality? You know? Able to decide this one is and this other one isn't ready for prime time. It's an impossible task if you ask me. I couldn't do what we're asking the machine to do. But then again, I wonder why we're trying to take all this stuff off the internet, off the broadcasts, off telecommunications in the first place. We're not that country in Huxley's book. What was it? 1984. We're not them. Are we? We're UsTopians. We're better than that. We can be responsible for ourselves. We don't need no big brother telling us what's okay to think or do. Hell, I'll just go do crazy shit sometimes. You know? But it's all in fun. It's all to be free. It's all about being happy, when it gets to the end of the day."

Maria finally arrives huffing and puffing. I look at her and am afraid she's going to have a heart attack. She's flushed. Pasty white under the perspiration and rosy cheeks. I put my hands up for her to stop and breathe. She takes several long and deep breaths. The color seems to be coming back into her face. I wait a bit longer, even though I want to talk to more of her team without her here. I guide her towards the office. "You clearly need to sit down for a bit. Why don't you rest here, and when your breathing is back to normal come out and join

160

me?" I push Maria through the door and close it behind her. I walk over to another nearby desk. I can see the fear in his eyes. He doesn't want to have this conversation, but when I stop at his desk he nods to me and stands up.

"I'm Mo," he tells me.

"Short for?"

"Mohandas Karamchand," he informs me.

"You're here on an HB1 visa?" I ask to confirm he has only a temporary right to work in the US and that will color his responses to my questions.

"Yes, ma'am."

"Okay Mo. Tell me. If you were me, would you say the system is ready to turn on without men in the loop?"

Mo steps back. "Ma'am, you are asking a question I cannot possibly know the answer to. I test. That's what I do. If you ask me is the system doing what I test correctly? The answer is yes. But I only look at a very small part of the software. When we have team meetings my team tells me much the same. But you ask a different question. Will this system make decisions like men without them in the loop? No. It can't possibly do that because men are so different. There is no single standard to test to."

"So the system will never be better than human analysts?" I put the question to him directly.

Mo shakes his head. "You are asking an impossible question."

"So if you were me, would you throw the switch and say the hell with it?"

Mo steps back another step, "Ma'am. You ask another impossible question. I do not have knowledge you have. Nor will I ever. The question you must answer is not one you can ask of another. Only you, ma'am. Only you can and will answer that question."

Mo looks down and won't engage me further. When I move down the aisle I see that he sits back down at his machine.

Maria comes out of the office and eventually catches up to me. "Why are you doing this? They can't answer your questions so why are you keeping them from doing what they know how to do better than anyone else? Make the system fidelity as good as it can get? What is it you want to know?"

"If I throw the switch tomorrow what happens?" I put it out there for her, for all of them.

"Nothing." Maria answers.

I stand there looking at her dumbfounded. "What do you mean nothing?"

"Think about it. Arbiter is operational. It is already making most of the decisions. It tosses the questionable ones to analysts and learns from their decisions. It's already doing the job, just with a little help. Not much, but enough to make it better."

## CHAPTER THIRTY-TWO: BRANDON McINERNY

If I have to create one more affinity diagram I'm going to puke right here. I'm done. This is crazy. I should have known better than to imagine I had any idea how to catch bad guys, let alone even identify them. The more I look the more I realize there are a whole lot of folks who aren't happy. But only a few of them ever post anything that would memorialize that disaffection. Tell the world forever just how they feel about transitory world events and situations.

Closing my eyes I push back from my computer. Chill. It's time to chill. Sheila told me she has this picture she looks at when it gets to be too much. Some place that's just incredibly beautiful. Where was that? I don't remember, but that's not the point. Maybe I need my own quiet oasis. A place I can think about when it all just gets to be overwhelming. Maybe I should ask Sheila… and then I realize she came over when I was let go and I haven't followed up even though she came to find me and we had lunch. I treated her badly. What can I do to make it up to her? That was a great night. Best I've had in I don't know how long. I just pushed it aside because I was sure I couldn't be a reliable partner for her when I didn't even have a job. And now I actually have two, although I still don't completely understand what the other one is paying me to do. I feel guilty taking their money, but I offered to have them cut it off. They haven't. And now I have more money in my bank account than I can ever remember.

Who are these people the Secretary is looking for? It's hard to find a concept in a sea of data, but unfortunately that's about all she's given me. A concept. Bad guys who want to bring the government to its knees. All fine and good. But this isn't getting anywhere. This isn't solving the basic question. And as soon as the Secretary understands there's no possible way I can find the persons of interest I'll be back on the street trying to figure out who am I really?

I sit with my eyes closed, trying to decide how to find a ghost. A ghost is something that doesn't really exist, but it leaves tell-tale evidence that something was there. Evidence that doesn't substantiate the presence of someone so much as the presence of something. And what does that all mean? Something. No digital footprints, but a phrase or word someone uses in just such a manner that it conveys an uncommon meaning only a few people are looking for. How do you program to find that? You can't. Too many variables. Too many key words. Too many players looking for a single word out of context.

And then I have an insight that may help, but isn't a sure thing. A word out of context. How do I find them? I start to create an algorithm for outliers. Words that shouldn't be there. Words that are out of context. Words that common understandings of the phrase would have tossed that word out if the computer was trying to create and validate a sentence.

How do I program this?

I work away furiously trying to capture the concept in an algorithm. Trying to identify outliers. I finish my algorithm and release it. Search all the postings. Search all the broadcasts. Search all the cellular and land line calls in the last thirty day. What are those outliers? What are those words or phrases that have no consistency in the strings they are a part of? Why didn't I think of this before? Why have I been so fixated on the traditional that I've overlooked the obvious? What I'd do if I didn't want anyone to locate what I was doing. And I'm not so special. But maybe the persons of interest are as arrogant as I am. Maybe they think they can hide out in plain sight and no one will see them because we're so focused on looking at something else. Something we've seen before?

The results come back. Just as I feared. Nothing that would identify a group seeking to subvert the government. Just the usual postings of old white guys unhappy UsTopia has become a multicultural community. A land stripped of its former manufacturing glory. A nation that values all and not just people who look like him.

These people make a lot of threats. Say things that are intended to upset. There are a whole series of clues that indicate when they have gone over the line. Nothing shows anyone over that line. Some are getting close. I can see that. But no one I would have referred to investigation in my last position.

So was that all just a wasted effort? Did I just prove to myself that I have no better idea now than I did before as to who I'm looking for? So I dig further at the fringes of conversations. I work off key words that seldom have an immediate threat behind them, but are working towards it. Even here, the nation seems at peace with itself. At least to the extent it has been for the last several years. Five years ago this level would have been alarming. But today, not so much. While I would like to search out Tortoise, I deliberately don't because I don't want any trace that I ever even looked at that in the logs of the machines. And I am careful not to access it in any of my personal searches either. So I have no idea who my two new best friends are or why they have been so interested in the role I have assumed with the Department of Truth. Why they seem so interested that I am interacting directly with the Secretary.

I try to push that all out of my mind. I'm here to do a job and that other paycheck? Well that's just someone who thinks I'm something I'm not. I gave them a reason to stop the payments. Gave them an excuse to cut their losses on me. Told them I have a new job and don't really want their money anymore. I got a job. Got a paycheck. I can pay my bills. So thanks, but I don't need your money. And still it shows up. So what else can I do? I rationalize with myself that I won't spend it. Just let it build up there. When they finally realize they made a mistake I can refund it all to them. That makes the most sense, doesn't it?

I sit back in my chair again. There has to be another approach I can take. But at the moment I have no clue what it might be. And then another key word pops into my mind. If the people we are looking for want to undermine the government, what about the keyword alternative? I've not pursued it because it's just too broad. I mean that word could show up in a conversation about diet pills and I'd be spending the rest of my life trying to parse the difference between the two. But if I pair it with approaches? If I do that it will narrow the alternatives, focus it on approaches and might make the search results manageable, even though a huge file. Or at least I would expect it to be a huge file.

I run it.

The results are daunting so I do a search of this file for safety from this reduced file. Alternative approaches to safety. Not that I think this will cause the intended persons of interest to pop to the surface. This has to be nearly as broad as alternative approaches, but at least it may give me a better indication of who is talking about our safety which seems to be a recurring theme of those who would overthrow our government.

The file comes back. Only a little over a thousand entries, so I start to scan down the list. This isn't the final search. It's only a method of telling me what needs to be eliminated if I want any better idea of where to go from here.

As I scan down I realize alternative approaches to safety can cover the waterfront from emergency response plans to police academy courses and company security systems. Nothing specific to national security. So I back up and input 'alternative approaches to national security'." I'm not prepared for the findings.

Mostly non-governmental agencies debating hypothetical situations.

I'm no closer than I was when I started down the yellow brick road. Why in the world did I think I had the ability to find the needle in the haystack? I don't know anything about this. I need to tell Elizabeth she has the wrong person. I'll never find someone in the maze of data points that constitute the official internet. Whoever is behind this, whatever it is, must be very sophisticated. To be able to hide in plain sight. Not everyone can do that. I certainly can't advise someone where to hide because I can't see them when they are all I'm looking for.

But then I remember advice Albert gave me, not on this subject, but in regards to finding the hidden meanings in pictures people wanted to post. 'Don't look at the picture. Look around it. Look at the context. Does it make sense? Does it fit with everything else you're seeing? If there is any discontinuity, then you're probably looking at the one thing you want to find.' Why was Albert so wise about all that I spent so much time trying to understand?

## CHAPTER THIRTY-THREE: ALBERT CARTER

Sheila and Brandon are the perfect couple. Both brilliant in many ways. Both the absolute best at what they do, although neither can see that. They are also the two people in the whole world who I would put forth as the standards the Arbiter system should be using. But from what I understand that recommendation fell on deaf ears. Sometimes I wonder why I even make suggestions since no one seems to take my insights as being worth anything. I've only been down here in the trenches for fifteen years. Living it. Balancing it. Finding a way to keep it all together and keep my team all together.

We're at Starbucks as that seems to be the only place Brandon can get to and back and still have the semblance of a conversation. Having him back at work has to be good for him. And I know Sheila is keeping an eye on him. So there they are, sitting next to each other like the old friends they are. Friends who grew up together in this crazy job and somehow figured out how to be the absolute best at it. But there's something different about their body language. I don't know what it is, but it's different.

"It's different," Brandon confirms my statement to him that working directly for the Secretary must be a rather dramatic change for him.

Sheila is apparently trying to understand what he means by that response. She looks at him waiting for him to say more. But Brandon is the master of understatement and minimalism. Why use two words when one will suffice. Or no words where a look or gesture gets the point across. Dealing with the written word must have been the catalyst for his response to others. Particularly when those written words are most often laced with homophobic, racist, blatantly misogynistic and disrespectful of human life, communications. I spent five years reading those blogs, tweets and transcripts of communications. And I've spent ten trying to get them out of my head. I was lucky to have only spent five years on the desk, unlike the two sitting across from me who have already been there twice as long as I was.

"Is that in a good way?" Sheila finally gets tired of waiting for more explanation.

Brandon gazes at her as if trying to decide something about her he's not willing to share with me or her, apparently. "Yeah."

"What can you tell us about what you're doing?" I ask, knowing more about the assignment than he probably thinks I do. When Elizabeth asked for my best person she gave me a little background. But not enough to really have a good idea of what he's doing to try to address her needs.

"Nothing. All highly classified. Sorry."

"You don't have a security clearance," I remind him. "So it can't be classified."

Brandon frowns as if he's not sure how to respond to being busted in a lie. And as long as I've known him, I've never detected that he ever lied to me. "Are you saying it's related to national security and shouldn't be talked about in places like this?" I try to help him get off the hook.

"That's about right."

"So who's the bad guy in this instance?" Sheila asks. Apparently she knows more than Brandon thinks she does too. I wonder how that might be possible.

"That's what I'm supposed to discover."

"Who's the bad guy," Sheila reaffirms. "And what is this bad guy doing that we need to find him?"

"That's the part that's so hard about this job. No one seems to know."

"And that's why you can't tell us anything," Sheila apparently is beginning to understand at least a little about why this is so hard to get him to talk about it. "Because you don't know. Must make it really hard to know where to even start looking."

"You have any ideas about that please share them," Brandon says earnestly.

"If there's a bad guy involved, why didn't the Secretary go to her counterintelligence types?" I wonder aloud. "People who find people for a living."

Brandon finishes taking a sip of his Frappuccino before answering. "I asked that question. See I did something right when she finally decided to interview me. And I have no idea why it took her so long getting down to me. But the good news is she finally did. Anyway, she told me those people have been looking for the bad guy and they're having trouble finding the needle in the haystack. The digital footprint of this alleged bad guy. So she wanted someone who was used to looking at the mass of communications out there. Someone who would be more likely to notice something that was unusual. Something that just seems out of place. The counterintelligence types aren't as likely to see something I might see. It's because they've been trained to look for a particular signature. Where I'm not looking for anything like that. I don't care if the person I'm after can write or not. I'm just looking for that one thing that proves they even exist."

"That makes sense, I guess," doesn't sound convincing to me and I'm sure it doesn't to him either. "Anything you can do to help automate your search?"

"I'm doing all the usual filtering and probing for responses, but so far I'm not seeing anything I've not seen before," Brandon sounds tired already.

"Is that part of the problem?" I ask picking up on how he's looking at the data.

"What? That I'm only doing the usual things? Probably the same things the counterintelligence types already did?"

"That's not what I picked up on," I respond hoping to keep his attention as he keeps glancing at Sheila. "If you're only getting back things you've seen before, what are you doing with what you're getting back? Are you using any other tools to take the results you're getting to a different level of analysis?"

Brandon glances back at me. Apparently I did catch his interest with that question. "What are you suggesting?"

"Pattern analysis of your key word search results," Sheila figures out where I was going and answers for me.

Brandon sits back to think about that suggestion. I watch him consider the data in his mind's eye that he reviewed before coming out for lunch. He's looking for patterns in the raw data, but I know he won't see anything because the patterns are either random or intermittent. He blinks at me and then focuses. "I understand what you're suggesting. It's possible, but I'm just not sure."

"Take a look at it when you get back, but in the meantime, what are you doing to decompress?" I try to get him to do what I'm asking about. "You're right back in the middle of all the pressure, the ugliness in this world and the warped perspectives that threaten each of us."

"Decompress? You mean that two-week vacation I just completed wasn't enough?"

"Not a vacation," I point out. "You had to be under more stress than usual and that's pretty damn high to begin with."

"I'm taking a vacation," Sheila moves the conversation along. "Two weeks to St. Lucia."

"You'll regret it," Brandon shakes his head. "After two days there you'll be wanting back at your desk. There's no there, there. What you gonna do? Sit on a beach for two weeks and read novels? That gets old fast."

"You're not me," Sheila reminds him. "I want to slow down. Walk for a while. Not be running to get to work, running to catch the Metro home afterwards. Not be running out to the grocery store or the drug store or the dry cleaners. I think just sitting on a beach is a great thing. And two weeks? For me that's not nearly long enough. I could stay out there for a month if I could get that much time off."

"Take it," I respond to her.

"What?" Sheila looks at me as if expecting me to deny I said what I said, but I just look back in all seriousness. "You'd never let me have that much time off. Not when you're getting ready for a go live event. It's all hands on-deck. You said so yourself."

"If we were about to go live you wouldn't be going anywhere for even a day," I point out to her. "But from what I can tell it may never go completely autonomous. I just don't know how we get there from where we are."

Brandon leans in, "The Secretary told me what Arbiter's fidelity is supposed to be. You know what I told her? From where I sit it's only about half what people are telling her." Brandon looks at Sheila, "A month? A year. Maybe more. I don't think you need to worry about anyone being short-handed. And besides, the day the switch is flipped you're out of a job. So I wouldn't be too eager for them to get it done."

"Maybe you ought to go with her. Make a kid or two. Really destress yourselves."

## CHAPTER THIRTY-FOUR: 'MARIA' XHE

I'm sitting in my office reviewing Arbiter decisions. Elizabeth decided that the system should go live, make the decisions and act. However, we have a team of analysts still reviewing random postings after they have gone up. Since we're most concerned about stopping inappropriate content, we're letting the system be conservative and not post something that actually meets the Ten Commandments, but only marginally.

Of course I didn't agree with this decision, but she's the Secretary… So here I am trying to figure out if her actions have created a nightmare for us. And I'm not comfortable with some of what I'm seeing go up. This system is just so complex, attempting to infer intent in many instances when it is unknown and unknowable. The billions of daily postings simply don't permit us to look at everything, or call up the person responsible and try to understand why they are posting something. This system is awkward enough without adding more layers of complexity.

"Maria?" Sadee, who is the youthful lead of the analyst team we retained today - everyone else is now gone - pokes her head in. "You wanted to see me?"

I motion for her to come on into my tiny barren office and take a seat. She obliges my silent instructions and waits a moment for me to finish reading a short article on dog grooming that got through but was flagged by an analyst. "First of all, thank you for keeping me on…"

A shake of my head indicates I don't want to talk about that. "How big of a hole have we dug?"

Sadee nods once to herself, gathering her thoughts and visualizing something she doesn't share. "The correlation isn't what you thought," she finally decides to be her response, although I can see she's not confident as to how I'm taking it.

"The damn system's live. This is no parallel effort. Arbiter is the arbiter now. So why am I seeing so many analyst rejects on what's already up there?"

Sadee frowns. "You have to understand we're not representative of the analysts who have done the job for decades now. We're all new grads, or practically new grads. Some of us have been out for a couple years, but there's no one on the team who's been doing this work for even six months, let alone ten or twenty years."

"How did that happen?" I'm surprised at her characterization of the team.

"You're on contract to deliver a working system. People with experience are more costly than those of us who are just learning the ropes. So your Human Resources team kept those of us who are at the minimum of the minimum pay grades."

I'm not sure if I should feel good that the analysts aren't representative of the larger pool's interpretations of the Ten Commandments, or angry that HR backed me into a corner where it's harder to verify the system. Either way I'm going to have some explaining to do to the Secretary, and I know she's not going to be understanding.

"How do I salvage this situation?" I ask having no idea what else to do.

"You're asking someone who's barely old enough to be your daughter what you should do?"

I shake my head, "Not a good response. My daughter's only ten. So you don't get off the hook that easy. But I get your point. I'm asking an unfair question. I take it your thought is I need to make the analyst team doing the comparison follow the demographics of the old team.

Then we'd be comparing apples and apples."

"I was positive you'd know what to do. I just don't have the insights you do."

Why am I getting the impression Sadee wants me to know it's not her problem? I get paid the big buck so I need to make the damn decision. I shake my head once more realizing I'm the one who is going to take the fall for the system's performance, so I might as well make sure I at least understand what I'm dealing with. "Riddle me this Batman: I'm sitting here looking at a posting about dog grooming. Arbiter let it pass, but one of your colleagues flagged it and sent a message that it should have been pulled. Why is that?"

"May I?" Sadee asks gesturing to my computer. She comes around the desk and looks at the posting. She scrolls down and looks for a moment at the image of the groomer brushing out the Afghan hound, a tall brown, black and white marked dog with very long fur. I look at it and see what appears to be a perfectly acceptable posting, showing the grooming technique.

Sadee frowns. "Look at the background." I see a series of pictures of dogs hung on the wall. Nothing I wouldn't expect to see in a pet shop where they are grooming dogs.

Sadee expands the image so I can better see the pictures on the wall. The dogs are attacking people of color, bringing them to the ground. Some are standing over prone women and men, all ethnic minorities, Hispanic, African American, Native American and Indian. I'm surprised there are no Muslims among the victims since they seem to be the minority of the moment for the various hate groups and nativists.

"How many people will see that?" I have to ask, trying to understand why the system let this through.

"The people who want to see it will know what to look for. And they're the ones we want to prevent from having access to such images on the internet," Sadee returns to her seat, apparently thinking about something she wants to tell me but is hesitant to say.

"What are you upset about?" I want to know what she won't ask. As someone so young she has to be more objective than I am, who has endured all this most of my life.

"You're Asian," she points out the obvious but bitterly. "Why do you get a freaking free pass? I mean these nativist sonsofbitches go after me and my kind because we're easy to spot. Just look at us. Not many of them have suntans this dark." Sadee is light skinned for an African American. "But you? You stand out in any room. Your eyes give you away. And your long dark hair. But I don't want to sound like I'm one of them. Is that how I'm sounding? They're doing it to us. Making us hate those who aren't like us just because you aren't being treated in the same way…"

"I am," I assure her. "Just not in this posting."

Sadee looks down and shakes her head. "I'm sorry. I know I volunteered for this work. Did everything I could to sell you that I could do it as well or better than anyone on your team. But damn. This is just so hard. I mean my parents did their best to inform me that the world isn't a fair place to be. I can be the absolute best at what I do and still not be chosen for the team anywhere I go. That's just a fact. They tried to tell me things were a lot worse than I imagined, but I thought, girl…you got your shit together. You can do this. Help make the world a better place by making sure all the hate, anger and nativist impulses are stopped dead in their tracks. But that's not what's happening, is it?"

"What's happening is we've made the world a better place." I respond. "There's a lot more darkness in the hearts of people out there, and I'm not just talking about the old white guys who think we should all go back where we came from. I'm talking about our brothers and sisters who think the world would be a better place if the old White guys were all nuked. I'm talking about all the people who think Americans are the devil, who think we are trying to steal their wealth, their heritage, their traditions and values."

"Aren't we, under the guise of economic prosperity?" Sadee shakes her head. "Selling our culture in our movies and media, selling our products to make their lives resemble ours, selling our services so they can wear a fucking Gap t-shirt and look cool like the rich Americans?"

I have to look away knowing I agree with her. "We can sit here and bemoan the state of the world we're trying to navigate or we can deal with what the Secretary is paying us to deliver. A functioning and validated Arbiter system. I'm offering you, Sadee, an opportunity to help me craft a solution to the problem we have created by how we've deployed the system."

Sadee objects, "But we knew…"

"The Secretary knew the system wasn't 98% as the specification calls for. She knew we are a long way from getting there. But she made a decision. Arbiter is making the posting decisions, even though we can see people have found a means to post what they want for their fellow extremists to find. And now they'll think they can get past the human analysts, since they don't now we're no longer in the loop."

Sadee looks at me with a glum expression. "I wish I could help you decide…"

## CHAPTER THIRTY-FIVE: BRANDON McINERNY

How many hours have I been on the desk? When I was an analyst it was contractually limited to ten hours seven days a week, although the standard was six. I've been here at least, what time is it? Ten pm? Damn, I've been here fourteen today alone. How have I let myself put these many hours into finding a solution? Finding the people Elizabeth is looking for, when I don't have any idea who they might be? Nor does she.

I close my eyes and drop my chin to my chest. Time to chill, if even for just a few minutes. I try to relax my shoulders which I've discovered are up almost to my ears. How can that happen and you not even be aware of it? Tension kills, or at least that's what I've read. And I'm way too young to be worried about stress headaches and sleepless nights.

But that's what I'm experiencing. Although the sleepless nights may just be because I'm afraid of the dreams I'll have if I actually go to sleep. I can't have it both ways, so at some point I'm going to need to let go and take the dreams. Take the recurring image of that little girl and the man beyond. The image that suggests so much and yet I have no idea what it really represents.

Bruiser comes by my desk, looks down at me and snorts. Bruiser is a big guy. Body builder I suppose, although I've not had any real conversations with him. As I think about it, I have no idea of Bruiser's real name. Bruiser is his nickname. I have no idea who gave it to him. Although meeting him in the hallway, and the fact he seldom says anything more than a single word in any given conversation, I'd say the name is probably appropriate. And what am I to make of the snort? What's he saying to me? I decide to live dangerously. "Bruiser. What's up?"

He's past my desk and he has a choice to make: ignore the fact I can see he heard me, or he can come back and engage me in a conversation. But that would involve more than a snort. Probably even a word or two. This is a real test. Is Bruiser what he seems, or someone completely differently than I've been led to believe by his behavior. I wait.

Bruiser slowly turns around, regards my cube for a long moment, and then returns to the scene of the crime. "Yeah?"

I hold up my hand to shake his, although I can see if he accepts mine, he is likely to crush it in his mammoth claw. "Brandon."

Bruiser looks at my hand as if he's not sure what he should do. Guess he doesn't have many friends. But that's only an assumption on my part. "Yeah?"

"I'm just curious…"

"Curiosity killed the cat," Bruiser responds. Not a good sign.

"…How I might be your friend," I conclude my statement.

Bruiser looks at me as if I'm a Martian. "I don't have 'friends'."

"Acquaintance?"

"Nice to meet you," Bruiser is about to turn away when I interrupt him.

"Now that we're acquainted, maybe you can help me."

Bruiser looks down at me as if I've got to be the stupidest person on earth. He might actually be right if pursing him is an intelligence test. "How?"

"The legend, which I have no idea if there's anything to it or not, is that you're counterintelligence. That you're probably the best person we've got at putting disparate threads together."

"People shouldn't talk about things they don't know."

He didn't deny it. Wow. Maybe there's something to it after all. "I have this problem the Secretary assigned to me."

"She does that," Bruiser confirms.

"She thinks there's a group out there who wants to overthrow the government."

"More than one," Bruiser confirms.

"Good to know. But how do I find the one group she wants to find?"

Bruiser shakes his head. I'm sure he's about to just walk away, when I see this turn down on the left corner of his mouth. "I can give you five names. One of them will likely be connected to whatever group she's looking for."

I sit there stunned at the implications of what he has just said. "Five people who in some way are connected to all of the terrorist groups in this country?"

"Between them they are connected to the groups of interest. They are only loosely connected to each other."

"But they are connected in some way?"

Bruiser nods. Apparently I don't have a need to know how. "The four who may be your connection are Mai, Sergei, Mustapha and Hilde. I can provide you with sketches on each of them. The problem is we don't know where they are or what they're up to because they are experts at disappearing."

"You said there was a fifth," I point out although I'm still trying to decide how I use this information to solve the puzzle.

"The most likely name you need to know is a man. He calls

himself Ichabod…"

I don't hear what Bruiser says next. Ichabod is the name of the man who has befriended me and is paying me a salary to do something.

But I don't know what that something might be and that's the problem. "Do you have a last name for any of them?"

"The file will give you what we know. The problem is none of these names are their real names. All intended to keep you and me from figuring out who they are."

"Bruiser, if I may…"

Bruiser looks at me without revealing what he may or may not be thinking.

"Why didn't the Secretary hook me up with you in the first place since you clearly know more than I do about this situation?" I'm still swimming with this information. "Would have saved a whole lot of time and effort on my part."

"You'd have to ask the Secretary why she does anything."

I nod in realization that he's absolutely correct. It's unfair of me to ask him a question he would have no way of knowing. "Have you been working this issue as well?"

Bruiser doesn't answer which is a very loud answer in and of itself.

"Do you need an email to know who to send the information to?" I ask.

"You knew who I was. I know who you are for the same reason."

"Of course. I'm sorry to waste your time."

"Apparently the Secretary thinks it's appropriate to waste yours."

Bruiser points out. I have to say I'm surprised to think of it in those terms.

Bruiser looks at me curiously. But then I realize he's not looking at me, but the computer screen behind me. "Ichabod."

I almost swivel my head as I turn to look at the screen. I don't see what he's looking at. The picture is of a restaurant. People I don't know sitting at the bar apparently in conversations. "Where?"

Bruiser steps into my cube and reaches across me to the mouse, clicks on the picture and enlarges it multiple times until the booths behind the bar in the forefront of the picture are all that can be seen. "There."

Bruiser points to three people in a booth in the back of the restaurant. The man to the right is Ichabod. No question about it. To the left is Magritte, his gorgeous lure for the weak of will. What totally amazes me is the third person sitting behind Magritte, who I can barely make out, is Albert Carter. They're having a conversation with Albert, a conversation that has to go almost identically to the one they had with me. We have an alternative future in mind. And while we don't have anything specific for you to do today. At some point we will call on you. And at that point we will expect you to do what we ask with no questions.

Shit.

Why would they go after Albert? But then the answer is so obvious. When Arbiter goes live, the Secretary will have no use for Albert to lead teams of analysts all of whom will be laid off. Why didn't I see this coming? I can't tell the Secretary that he's the one who is making sure the Arbiter system isn't ready for prime time. I just can't do that. Albert is the one person who has believed in me through all the good and bad times. He's the one who's always been there for me. The only one who's always been there.

"Ichabod," Bruiser repeats. "Where is this?"

# TRUTH

I look at the source, it's an Arbiter message. Arbiter sent it to me. Holy shit. Why me? "Last night, Sullivan's in the city, eight o'clock."

## CHAPTER THIRTY-SIX: ELIZABETH WARDEN

Maria is unsettled. I see it in her posture, in her evasive looks, even in her voice, which seems softer than usual, like she's not confident. We are walking back towards my office as I met her unexpectedly in the hallway near the team room, which is now nearly empty. She didn't say why she was there. Probably talking with the maintenance team and the few analysts that she uses to validate as opposed to my team, which has also been greatly downsized. Not a happy task, but one that Sabr has been pushing me to do for over a year. Well, she got what she wants. An autonomous Arbiter system, deciding what meets the test of the Ten Commandments.

I've been waiting for the howls from users, but so far nothing more than the usual protests that something wasn't posted. We get a lot fewer protests that something is up that someone finds offensive, immoral or just plain smut. My husband used to say that people have an insatiable appetite for the lewd, obscene and pornographic, but I don't know about that. It seems that since we've been more effective in keeping that off the internet people talk about it less. And my husband reminds me that just means the strip clubs are doing more business, along with the ladies of the night.

"Is she okay with Arbiter's performance?" Maria finally asks.

"Sabr hasn't said a word. I would assume that no news is good news."

"She knows it's live," Maria wants to confirm.

"She does. I talked to her at length before I authorized the cut over. Wanted her to know that she would be hearing from those whose jobs we eliminated, from those who feel they are being evaluated differently and from those who still can't get their god-awful posts up on the internet."

Maria frowns. I have to ask, "What are you uncomfortable with?"

Maria's eyes dart towards me, but just long enough to gauge my demeanor and then back towards the floor ahead of us. "Fidelity."

"Between the analysts and Arbiter?" I know exactly where she's going and this is the major topic I want to discuss with her.

"The few that are left," she drives a stake into the ground that I don't expect.

"I don't understand the issue," I tell her with an edge that even surprises me. Maybe I'm more concerned about this transition than I thought given how little blow back there's been.

"We didn't reach the 98% fidelity level you specified in the contract."

"I'm aware of that," the edge is still there even though not purposefully, but I can see she's reacting to it as I probably would if I were in her shoes.

"That would imply that either postings or broadcasts are going out that shouldn't or some that should aren't." Maria is trying to play this safe.

"I'm aware of that. And that's why I'm waiting for something to happen. I don't know what it will be, but there will be some kind of ramifications from this. You know the whole action – reaction principle."

"What if there isn't a 'reaction'?" Maria posits for me. "What if... what if nothing happens, but the Arbiter's learning algorithms only learn from itself? Without the analyst reference, it has only itself to learn from. What does that imply? Does that mean it settles in on a standard of the Ten Commandments and it never budges? Our society moves all over the place, changes from day-to-day, in reaction to changing tastes, new technology, the speed of events. We aren't a static people. We change everything about us in reaction to what happens to us. And the rate of change is accelerating."

"You're saying that we need a bigger analyst team for Arbiter to use to continually learn how we as a people change in our values, needs, interests and desires. Change in how we establish relationships and conduct ourselves in those relationships. Change just because we're tired of always wearing black."

Maria's eyebrows rise after that last comment because I'm usually dressed in black, not for any reason in particular other than I think I look good in it. "Not just that."

"What then?" I'm still not seeing what she's thinking.

"How many analysts did you keep?"

"One hundred," I have to search my memory for that statistic.

"We're down to thirty-five and I have to lay off fifteen more next month."

This is news to me, "Why so few?"

"The contract. You eliminated all the analyst positions on my side when we went live. I had to convince management that we needed to keep a few in place to protect ourselves from you,"

"Me? Why would you protect yourselves from me? What am I going to do?"

"Sue us for non-performance."

"Why would I do that? The system has been working in parallel for months…"

"But the contractually mandated fidelity isn't there yet."

"You said you'd reached eighty percent across the board and higher in certain areas." I remember that conversation clearly.

"That means a whole lot of really bad stuff is now making it up on the net that wasn't last week."

"You're saying you think the reason I'm not getting a storm of protest is because people who want to see all of that are happy and those who don't want to see it haven't noticed yet…"

"But they will," Maria shakes her head.

We walk on in silence for a few moments. I understand her concern, but there's got to be more to this story than she's told me so far. "Okay. Suppose nothing happens. Suppose everyone adjusts to the new norm that Arbiter establishes. What's wrong with that?"

"Who did you keep, among the analysts?"

"What do you mean?" I find this a strange question.

"How did you select who stayed and who went?" Her voice is firming. This is something she's really concerned about.

"I'd have to ask Albert Carter. He decided." I really don't know who he kept. I've been so busy on other things I never thought to ask him. Sounds like I probably should have.

"I was afraid of that." Maria is quiet as we walk along for a bit. I keep looking at her trying to understand what's bothering her, but she looks straight ahead without expression.

"Do we need to go see Albert?" I finally ask.

"We?" Maria looks up at me with an expression that tells me she doesn't want to be anywhere near a conversation with Albert and me.

"You're the one who seems to think there might be an issue, and you haven't told me what it is, so you need to be there so I can finally understand the issue." I'm not angry, but I'm certainly unhappy how this conversation is going. She's reinforcing my concerns that something not good is going to result from pulling the trigger.

Maria thinks about my comment for a moment. I see the corner of her mouth curl down in a semi-frown. That's an expression I don't think I've seen before. "Don't get mad."

Oh God, what now? "I promise."

"The thirty-five analysts we kept?"

"What's the issue? They lepers or something?"

"Worse… none are over the age of twenty-three."

I have to think about why she thinks this is something I'll get upset with, but as I reflect on her comments about the system self-reinforcing I think I'm beginning to understand. "A thin slice of what's acceptable content."

Maria nods.

"The reference group should reflect society? Is that what you're thinking?"

"If it doesn't then how can it determine what fits the Ten Commandments?" Maria asks. "We've talked forever about the issues of interrater reliability. Older analysts won't let anything even mildly offensive go up. The twenty-somethings, like my analysts often think those things are hilarious. You need the team to incorporate all those sensibilities if you want what goes up to reflect all those sensibilities in proportion to their numbers in society."

"You'd need a damn rubric's cube to figure that all out."

## CHAPTER THIRTY-SEVEN: SHEILA

I'm always nervous about being summonsed in to see the Secretary. She seems to be understanding and all. But she's just so intense. I don't know how to deal with it. I must be doing okay or she'd never ask me to come back to see her. But after I told her she should hire Brandon because he was more what she needed, I thought I'd just committed suicide. That I'd be on the next layoff list. But somehow I'm still here. Although nearly everyone I worked with is gone now. Just like Brandon. And that's the fluky thing about it all. Brandon is working directly for the Secretary, and now she wants to talk to me again.

"Madam Secretary?" I poke my head through her door as I was instructed by her administrative assistant.

Elizabeth is talking on a cell phone, which is strange given she has a desk phone, but she waves me in. I enter quietly so as not to disturb her call.

"I know. But there's more work to be done. Just because you flip a switch the world doesn't change overnight." She listens to whomever she's talking with before responding. "The contract? Well, yeah. The daily burn rate will drop starting Monday of this week, but it's not over. We have a long tail on this one."

I sit down in the chair as she motions me to do just that. Try to make myself as invisible as possible.

"I know, Sabr. You expect the world to adjust, but sometimes we have to make the adjustments for the world to accept what we've done to it." Elizabeth holds the phone away from her ear and even I can hear the President's response.

"We haven't done anything to the world, other than make it better.

Damn it."

Elizabeth holds the phone against her ear again, "We have. The world is a better place than when we took office. But what I'm saying to you is this is a work in progress. We will be making adjustments for a long time. So don't even begin to think we're done just because you haven't had a tidal wave of people storming the White House when we flipped the switch."

Elizabeth listens for a moment, "Well, if they're out there Arbiter is doing its job because there are no reports of it in the media I review."

A long silence as Elizabeth listens. "I agree. Look, someone just joined me and I need to talk with her about our earlier conversation…" Elizabeth listens to the response. "Right. I'll let you know what I discover and what kind of feedback we get."

Elizabeth clicks off her cellphone and sets it on her desk. "There. Done with my obligatory call for today. Thank you, by the way, for coming back in to see me. I hope you were satisfied that I took your advice not to hire you."

"More than satisfied. Brandon is a much better choice."

I see something in Elizabeth's eye that tells me she may not have the same opinion I do. I wonder what Brandon did or didn't do that has given her that impression. I'll have to ask him the next time I see him.

"I wanted to get some direct feedback. Since we have a relationship I thought you might give me the straight scoop. Not that I think others aren't, but a validation is always a good thing."

I nod, "What can I help you with?"

"How many analysts did we keep?"

I have to think, "Gosh, I don't know. You'd have to ask Albert."

"One hundred?" Elizabeth asks.

I think for a moment, "Hmmm. That might be about right. A few more or maybe a few less. But not the thousands we had."

"How did you decide who stayed and who didn't?"

I look at Elizabeth for a long moment trying to understand why she's asking me this question. "I didn't. That was Albert's decision. He didn't ask for input so I really can't tell you how he decided that."

"Think for a moment if you would." The Secretary asks. "How would you describe the analysts that are still there? Are they all younger than you? Older than you? A cross section of all ages? What's the make-up of our analyst group?"

I let my mind look around the team room. So many empty desks. I've been expecting the Secretary to instruct someone to down size us into a much smaller office space. But that hasn't happened yet. Likely to at any time, but at least not yet. "That's a really hard question. I've not really paid much attention to who's still there since we all expect you to let the rest of us go at any time. I guess I really didn't want to know who made the cut particularly since I don't know what the cut represents."

"That's the problem." Elizabeth responds, almost distracted. "I was hoping you could tell me what I wanted to know without having to ask the question directly. I was hoping that by describing the team that's left in place I wouldn't have to ask this. But since you couldn't… Is the team that we kept representative?"

"Of what?" is all I can think of to say since I really don't know where she's going.

"Of us. Of all the people in our society. Is the reference that the machines are using truly giving them an input that has any fidelity to who we are as a people, as a nation, as human beings?" Elizabeth is clearly passionate about something, but she's not giving me enough to know how to respond to her.

"Us," I try to validate.

Elizabeth nods to me in agreement that she meant us.

I stop to think again about the faces I see. What I know about them. I shake my head. "I can't help you there. Albert's the only one who could answer your question. Sorry."

Elizabeth shakes her head, "No need to be sorry. I respect you acknowledging that you don't know and won't mislead me with a wild estimate. It's okay. I prefer this. So let me change things up. I have another question: What makes you the standard of what should be aired and what shouldn't?"

"The standard." I repeat. "I don't know why anyone would think that."

Elizabeth's eyes are crystal clear. I'd never noticed that before. But then again I've only been sitting across from her once before and she wasn't real happy with me then that I told her that her expectations were wrong. "You and Brandon. That's what Albert has told me since I first moved into this office. He's said you reflect the values of most Americans when it comes to broadcast journalism and Brandon has the bullshit filters that keep all the negative bullshit out of the media."

"But don't you think that's resulted in a Pollyanna America?" I can't help saying.

Elizabeth looks at me, "That's a really obscure simile. I bet most people your age have no idea what you just said."

I grimace at her characterization. "You know what I'm getting at."

Elizabeth smiles at me. "I do, but that's not the point. You think what we do is making our society safer. How many mass shootings have there been in the last year?"

I shake my head, "None?"

"Wrong. There have been one-hundred and thirty-five. We just don't post them. No media coverage. No reinforcement. Keep people from going out in a blaze of glory."

"How many people have died?" I have to ask.

"Too many. One would be too many. But that's not what we're talking about."

"What are we talking about?" I'm out of my depth here.

"The fact that you remove all those mass shootings so people are feeling safe except those who directly experienced the event. They won't forget, but if it doesn't go viral we contain the idea virus."

"That's what this is all about? Idea viruses?"

"How do you decide what goes up and what doesn't? And I'm not talking about the Ten Commandments. What repels you and what are you tolerant of?"

I put my head down for a moment. This is such a hard question. "I don't know how to answer you. I mean I just know."

"Like the definition of pornography. I know it when I see it," she responds.

"The Ten Commandments are the framework. I've internalized it. I apply it against the world as I see it. And that's shaped by my life experiences, my family's values and the times in which I shaped how I embrace life."

Elizabeth looks at me for a long time, at least it seems like a long time to me. "Do you understand how special you are?"

## CHAPTER THIRTY-EIGHT: HUA KWAN

"Why is this meeting taking place in an unsecure room?" I ask Elizabeth. She and Javier turn to look to me as if both are surprised by my question. "As the host, Madam Secretary, I believe it is your responsibility to ensure that we can have a thorough discussion of the trends and players without fear of detection."

Elizabeth nods her understanding of my concern, "This is a secure room. No listening devices, we are aware of, can get through. If you think I'm wrong try your cell."

"As you know we were not permitted to bring our cells in with us so that won't be possible." I'm not sure why she suggested such a test but she is forcing me to be more specific. "You have a monitor on the wall and a land line telephone into the room. Both can be penetrated," I respond.

"The monitor has no connectivity. It's a dumb monitor that can only display from an air-gapped computer resident to this room. It only displays media brought in on a thumb drive…"

"Which can carry malware capable of capturing and broadcasting over Wi-Fi from the computer."

"There is no WIFI in this room, so even if such malware were to be introduced it would not be able to communicate out."

"And the land line?" it seems I have to walk her through technology every time we meet.

"All communications on that phone are monitored and it is not connected to the network until enabled by a human operator. So without a connection, none of your spyware tools will enable monitoring by you or anyone else we are aware of." Elizabeth

194

concludes her defense of her decision to put us in this room.

"And it is the latter parties, the ones you are not aware of, that are my chief concern. Please remove the phone from the room."

Elizabeth raises the phone and in a moment says, "Please have a technician come here and remove this phone," She waits a moment then continues. "Yes, now," She listens further. "We cannot start our discussions until the phone is removed, so yes I need it out immediately." She hangs up and looks back up at me. I can tell she's not happy about my request, but knows when we next meet in Beijing, that she may wish to make the same or a similar request.

"I cannot have anything we say in this room recorded anywhere. If names or tactics or apparent plans should get out, it would interfere with our ability to contain threats." I have to make it clear nearly every time we meet how important complete secrecy is. But then, neither of my colleagues present have a true appreciation for how sophisticated the tools are we are using now to intercept and listen in on their conversations.

"We understand your concerns," Javier responds neutrally. I am sure he thinks I am over reacting, but he has probably the least secure communications having purchased our telephone switching gear for their national networks. We have a trapdoor in every switch that allows us to intercept and monitor all traffic in the various countries that make up his federation. Just as we do in our federation. Only in UsTopia did they refuse to accept our superior technical performance because of security concerns that had been well documented. And yet we were able to convince Jurgen and Javier that those capabilities didn't exist, even though they do. It was the first time we showed technical superiority in a traditional western technology space. And there have been more nearly every year since.

A knock on the door precedes a young woman entering, removing the line at the wall, where she inserts a plug device I recognize. It is designed to ensure no electrons can flow on that line and thus nothing can be conveyed out of the room from that port. She comes to the table and retrieves the handset before exiting. She checks the door is securely closed behind her.

Elizabeth looks to Javier, "Are we ready to begin our discussions?"

Javier looks at me and raises his eyebrow as a question, which I interpret to be am I satisfied?

"Sloth," I begin. "Continues in a recruitment phase. Security cameras have detected meetings between their recruiters and members of our intelligence community. They seem intent on finding and recruiting disaffected workers. Generally approach recently separated analysts. Are you seeing the same?"

"I assume your thoughts are that they approach recently separated analysts who will then use their relationships with those still inside to infiltrate our organizations." Javier is attempting to understand the strategy.

"In part. They are also attempting to understand the vulnerabilities of our systems, how they can hide messages from our analysts and systems."

Javier nods and makes a note on a paper tablet on the table before him. Elizabeth does the same.

"How did you identify the Sloth recruiters?" Elizabeth asks as she finishes her note to herself.

"We set a trap." I respond not wishing to be too specific.

"Loyal employees who you sent home to tell their friends and families they had lost their positions and were unhappy about it." Javier continues to demonstrate his understanding.

"When someone approached them, the employee covertly recorded the encounter, which permitted you to identify that person and that person's network." Elizabeth concludes her understanding of what we did.

"In essence." What I don't tell them is that the employees who have been approached have agreed to work for Sloth and are being paid to do so, but so far none have been given any assignments. It appears we are in a waiting game, but anticipate that when the assignments are made, they will require an immediate response to ensure our plant can't warn us. That's an assumption, but is probably a safe assumption.

Javier glances at Elizabeth and then commences his discussion of Sloth. "We have identified that they are operating in our federation, but we have not identified individuals involved. They have been very careful in their communications. Nothing has come up in any of our filtering. No signatures, nothing that confirms electronic communications between members of the organization."

I nod, "They do not communicate electronically as far as we can tell."

"Then how do they communicate?" Elizabeth wants to know.

It's clear that we know much more about this particular threat than either of them. "Think 1960s."

"John Le Carre tradecraft," Elizabeth responds.

"Slow but sure." Javier finally understands what we understood when we gave them that code name.

Elizabeth makes notes on her pad.

"What of you, Madam Secretary? What do you know of Sloth?" I want to understand what they may be doing in this part of the world.

"We have a team dedicated to finding them."

I wait for her to say more, but she does not. "What progress have they made?"

"We know much more about what they are not doing than what they are," she responds, although it sounds defensive to me. Less to it than she would have us believe.

"Have you confirmed they are operating in your federation?" I push now.

"No. We have not," she admits.

Her response makes me believe the decimation of her intelligence agencies by a prior populist president have blinded her domestically. We have validated their global assets have become almost non-existent. And that actually makes us very nervous. When they have insights into what other international players are doing, they are much more predictable. It's when they are surprised, and subject to reversals as a result of not being aware and or prepared to respond, that they become much more unpredictable. We've even talked about helping them in some instances. Feeding them intelligence that enable them to prepare for events that might otherwise provoke a response that would often be out of proportion to what the situation deserves.

"Do you have any indication as to the goals of Sloth?" Javier asks us both.

"Unfortunately not at this time, but we are working towards that." I confirm.

# CHAPTER THIRTY-NINE: ELIZABETH WARDEN

Hua Kwan always makes me uncomfortable. She shares enough to make it clear we don't know as much as she does, but never the specifics that can enable us to catch up. The whole fit over the room security was unwarranted. She just wanted me to be embarrassed that she knows more about technology than I do. And she does. She grew up in intelligence and technologies. I'm a politician, here because of an election outcome that didn't end up in my favor. This is a consolation job, but I'm trying to make the most of it by putting my stamp on how we arrive at the truth for decades to come.

I decide to follow up on the whole discussion about the potential threat she code named Sloth. Brandon was in his cube when I came in, so I know he's here today. I walk down the hallway to find him, but am intercepted by Danny Martin, a big man who one would expect to find on a football field leading a running back through a defensive line rather than a governmental office.

"Elizabeth…" he's never been one for protocol or deference as a long-time employee of the agency, even before it was renamed Department of Truth. "There's been another event."

Just the way he says that word, 'event', sends chills through me. "What happened?"

"Bricknell. He'd been with us seventeen years on some of the more obscure sites."

I can see the man he's talking about. He was quirky, at least that was what personnel told me about him. They identified him as a stage four risk, who was scheduled for counseling. Stage four meaning he was nearing burn-out. "What happened?"

"Walked into a Mexican restaurant wearing an explosive belt. C4. Enough to level the building and take out everyone including the staff back in the kitchen."

I close my eyes and shake my head. We did this to him. If he had taken any other kind of job he probably never would have ended his own life or those of others this way. "How did he ever get that much C4?"

"We're working that now."

"How many?"

"Dead?" Danny seeks confirmation of what I'm asking.

I nod, just mentally exhausted by the effects of decades of neglect of the people who have been making the internet less hostile to all of us.

"Forty-two including Bricknell," Danny sounds as sad as I am.

"Injured?" I'm afraid to ask.

"Over a hundred."

Oh shit. This was preventable. I shake my head. "Tell Gloria we need to touch all the stage fours and most immediately those who separated in the Arbiter go live. We have no idea how many more time bombs we have walking the streets."

Danny is very solemn in his response, "Too many. This most certainly isn't the end of it."

I'm still trying to deal with the news when I get to Brandon's cube. Not sure I'm ready to learn what he's been able to find. It just seems that nearly everything we do is inadequate. And I need to sit down and figure out how we get on top of the priorities, only there's so many it seems they change relative priority every few minutes. Just now Sloth went from being number one in my mind to something much lower because of one former employee. "Brandon."

He has earbuds in so he doesn't hear me. I touch his shoulder to get his attention. Of course he jumps and spins around. "Morning."

I wait until he pulls the earbuds so he can hear me. I have to motion like I'm pulling imaginary earbuds so he understands.

"Oh, yeah." Brandon remarks and pulls them.

"What's going on?"

Brandon leans back against his workstation desk, reflects on my question, and then responds. "I've worked my way through all the major groups who are leaving footprints. It doesn't appear the parties of interest are embedded in any of them, attempting to mask what they're doing in the midst of the traffic of the larger group."

"What's your confidence level on that statement?" I'm not happy with how vague he is.

"Confidence level? Are you asking am I sure they aren't embedded?"

I nod.

"In this kind of work you can never be absolutely sure. We just don't have enough data to confirm anything."

"Then why did you tell me you didn't think they're embedded?" I'm starting to hear the anger in my voice that I know is more a response to my own inability to better control what's happening. Need to calm down so Brandon doesn't think I'm angry with him.

"I'm telling you I don't think continuing that pursuit is the best use of my time." Brandon is pushing back on my tone of voice by sounding more resolute. "If you want to put someone else on it? Go for it. But since you're looking for quick results, in my judgment I'm more likely to find something to identify them pursuing other approaches."

I relax, pulling my elevated shoulders down consciously,

breathing out. "What do you have in mind?" That comes out better.

"Your persons of interest aren't playing by the rules. So I want to shift to embedded images. See if they may be putting things into the background of images that their followers are looking for, but no one else knows what to look for."

"That doesn't sound like a way to start a movement." I respond unsure why such an approach would be all that effective in growing their membership.

"You think that's their objective? To start a movement?" Brandon seems surprised by my statement. I'm making an assumption from the conversation with Jurgen and Javier who said they thought they were intending to change the government. Maybe I'm assuming that means building popular support for change through violence. I need to reexamine my assumption. Maybe I'm wrong. If I am, I need to have a parallel effort looking into alternatives.

"That's certainly one possibility."

Brandon frowns, "But only one and not necessarily the most likely. The reason I'm saying that is how they're communicating. If they're trying to start a broad-based movement, they need to be on twitter and Instagram and all the other media with their platform. They're not. In fact, they're doing exactly the opposite of a group seeking broad-based support."

He has a point. Unless Hua Kwan's depiction of the group is correct. That they're slow and steady. Building a foundation that will at some point release a torrent of hate across a wide swath of media. Is that why they're recruiting from intelligence agencies? Are they planning to embed people who can shut down the systems from inside and that will make the internet completely open again? Able to post anything anyone wishes.

"Do you need more help?" Occurs to me and just comes out. "You said something about putting someone else on the embedded possibility."

"Depends on how critical you think this effort is. We haven't linked them to any specific events so far…"

His use of the word 'events' brings back the feelings of helplessness about Bricknell. I'm momentarily distracted from what he's saying.

"… So the assumption is that they're in a preliminary state of organizing. If that's the case we have time. And if we have time, then the assets might be better used on threats that are more imminent."

"Of course," I respond, only half listening. But I need to give him my full attention. "What do you need? Anything?"

"There's a tool the Intel guys use on imagery. Automates pattern recognition in the background. If I could have access to it, would greatly accelerate the timeframe for the initial scans."

"The intel guys tend to be protective of those tools as you know." Getting them requires the sign off of the Director of National Intelligence. Not an easy signature to get since he is infamous for not leaving any kind of trail of any kind. He practices the defenses he preaches.

"I'll ask. You know the story."

"I do, which is why I'm asking you." Brandon has apparently already come to the conclusion it's not likely he will get what he's looking for.

"Anything else I need to know?" I'm wondering what I'm not hearing from him.

# CHAPTER FORTY: BRANDON McINERNY

Ichabod and Magritte sit across from me in a tiny Lebanese restaurant in one of the older ethnic neighborhoods. I've never been in the neighborhood, let alone this restaurant. I met Magritte at a bus stop we arranged the last time we met, although I'd expected to meet both of them there. We took the bus and then metro to this area, but still had to walk several blocks. Ichabod was already here when we arrived. He was half way into his ethnic beer, a brand I don't recognize. It makes me wonder, what do I really know about them? They claim not to be a couple, but her body language tells me differently. He is not quite so transparent, but there are occasional glances that reinforce my impression.

"I've ordered for you both." Ichabod starts the conversation. No hand shake, no hello. Right to presumptions about me, about both of us I guess, although he may have told her beforehand that he intended to do so. "Hope you don't mind. Given this is Lebanese, I didn't expect you would be familiar with the dishes."

"Thank you," I respond, "You're probably a much better judge than I would be of what's good here."

"You can tell me if you like it. If not I won't do it in the future."

Since he is business-like in how he's acting, I decide to be the same. "Now that I have a paycheck again, I'm getting a little uncomfortable that you're paying me too. Especially since I'm not doing anything to earn that paycheck."

"Earn." Ichabod muses on my choice of words. "Many people get paychecks that have not earned them. The paycheck may be for work that was done in the past, like a business owner who continues to receive a paycheck after he turns the business over to others to run. Or someone on social security. Same thing. A paycheck for reaching a certain age and having paid into the system over many years..."

"I see where you're going." I don't want to listen to a long rationalization. "But none of those situations apply to me. If you want to keep paying me, I ought to be at least doing something to earn it."

Ichabod acts like he's heard this before. "Consider it a down payment for services you will render to us in the future. You know, like a redshirt freshman, who's on the team, learns the plays, and becomes familiar with the team members, coaches and philosophy of the team. But he doesn't play and doesn't lose a year of eligibility. Think of yourself as a redshirt on our team."

"I can do that..." still not getting a definitive answer. "But you need to redshirt me then. Bring me in on the planning, meet other team members, and give me a high level on the philosophy. Just like you said. I'm a full member of the team who's involved in everything except game day."

Ichabod leans to one side and rests his left elbow on the table and cups his hand over his mouth. A strange reaction to my observation. Ichabod glances around the restaurant and nods to himself. "I admire your work ethic and desire to be worthy of what you earn. But things take time to develop. If we rush into things, things get rushed and what we hope to be the outcome may not be. Do you understand what we're saying? You need to be patient. We are and that's why we're still here, creating the foundation that will be required for success."

"What's success?"

"A favorable change," Magritte responds with an enthusiasm I haven't seen before.

"In what?" I push to understand better what I'm into here.

"All of us," Ichabod appears not to trust Magritte will say what he wants her to say.

She sits back as if she got that message too. "That's about all I can tell you at the moment."

"Why? You're paying me money to do something, but you're not telling me what or when. A hypothetical here. What happens if you ask me to do something and it's not something I feel comfortable doing. Does that mean you're going to want me to payback all the money? Or are you just going to let me keep it and walk away?"

"Walking away never makes sense." Ichabod responds ominously. "But you don't have to worry about that. We know you well enough. You will do what needs to be done when the time arrives."

Magritte places a bag that looks like weed on the table. "For you."

"What is it?"

"Something special that will help you get to a dreamless sleep, something I know you crave."

"They permit a better night's sleep?" I have to admit to being curious.

"Better is a relative term," Magritte looks at me more closely, "But you will have fewer nightmares."

"Will I be more focused at work?" I look closer at the bag, realizing it doesn't look like weed, but a mixture of some sort.

"Sometimes you have to let it work for a while," Magritte is sounding like a doctor. I wonder. "The effects are cumulative. As your body accepts the herbal essences it will accommodate them and enable your peaceful state of being."

"Weed doesn't help. So how is this different than weed?" I react to her description.

"Every herb has a different engagement with your body. Some herbs engage your taste buds, some engage your immune system, and still others act as a cleansing agent, getting the residue of illnesses and organ overuse righted again. These herbs engage your central nervous system. Helps it restore balance in your reactions and perceptions. Shaves the peaks and valleys, if you will, so you can achieve a more harmonious state."

I decide to come right out and ask, "Are you a doctor?"

Magritte does not answer my question directly, "I am an herbalist and a realist. I know what works for different conditions that people have."

"Conditions of the body or conditions of the spirit and soul?" I clarify where I think she's going.

"They are all related. The proper mixture of herbs will improve body functions and improve your spirits and feelings of self-worth."

"Then you'd see yourself more like a shaman or medicine man… woman, than an actual doctor," I seek to clarify.

"Why are you curious about my ability to help you?"

"If you're a medical physician I will have a very different opinion of your concoction than if you are a self-taught experimenter."

"I have studied with many experts," She begins to respond. I'm already judging where I think this conversation will end. "Some are medical experts and they conferred a degree on me. I have studied with herbal experts and they view me as one of them now. I have studied with psychologists who employed me in a mental institution to help patients who were suffering a number of both medical and spiritual disorders."

"So as a doctor, you're telling me your concoction is safe. I should have no side effects from it, and the longer I take it the more likely I am to get to a dreamless sleep."

"As a doctor I can say that none of my herbal blends will have a long-lasting effect upon you. No one who has or is taking them has reported any physical reaction. Is that what you're looking for?"

"One other thing," I don't let her off the hook so easily. "Why is a highly trained physician involved in whatever it is you're planning?"

"I can answer that for her," Ichabod inserts himself back into the discussion. "Because she believes in what we are doing, what we hope to achieve, and how we plan to achieve it."

Magritte's expression tells me she doesn't entirely agree with what Ichabod is saying, but she's also not going to contradict him. I would ask her, but decide to let it go. "If Magritte's a doc, what's your hidden profession?"

"I'm a historian by training," Ichabod offers.

"What is your specialty?"

"Societal transformation."

"Not one country or one era?" I inquire since he keeps the discussion vague.

"History is dead." Ichabod almost sounds bored now. "Studying one country or one era is such a waste of time. But understanding the commonalities of transformational change cross culturally, cross eras, cross stimulating events is fascinating."

"Is that your role here? To use your knowledge to stimulate events that will lead to transformational change?"

"Not to stimulate the change, but to manage the stimulating events that will occur because of the nature of mankind."

"Can you tell me more?"

Ichabod shakes his head. "We've spoken enough of these matters.

You should now know enough to be able to make a decision."

"Decision?" I ask not sure what he's referring to.

"About us," he gestures to indicate the two of them. "Whether we are serious in our intentions, that we have a plan and approach that will succeed, that you can play an integral part in that series of events."

"Why will I want to if I don't know what they are or my role?"

"Because you have been used and thrown away," Ichabod sentences me.

"They brought me back. I wasn't thrown away," I stress 'thrown away'.

"For how long? There were hundreds of thousands of you last week, droning on to make the world ideologically safer for a few who cling to power. This week you're laid off and back on a temporary short-term project. It will last a week, a month? Then what? You're out on the street with the other hundreds of thousands all looking for non-existent work. You've been thrown away and delayed in getting on to your new life, whatever that turns out to be."

# CHAPTER FORTY-ONE: 'MARIA' XHE

My computer desktop alerts me to a falling fidelity ratio. I look and trend the information backwards. The trend has gotten worse hour-by-hour since the go-live event. Assuming the system hasn't changed, as far as I can tell, it would mean that the analysts are viewing things differently, or the learning algorithm has accelerated a learning change for some reason. And if the analysts are in fact acting differently, that would mean Arbiter is moving away from the prior consensus. On top of that, the restricted age range of the remaining analysts skews the determinations even further from the prior consensus.

"Sadee," I call on my cell. "Could you bring the leads to my office?"

Sadee answers on her cell, "Sure. Topic?"

"Fidelity."

It doesn't take long for the five analyst leads to appear and assemble at the table in the small conference room across the hall from my tiny office. Other than Sadee I barely know the other leads as none of them were leads earlier this week. None of them were even here more than a year ago.

I send my desktop to the monitor in the conference room and display the trend chart I'd created. When I walk in Sadee speaks for the group. "You think we have a problem?"

"The data says we have a problem. Doesn't matter what I believe."

Sadee continues as their spokesperson, "What do you think the problem is?"

"I was hoping you could tell me," I toss back at her.

"Something wrong with Arbiter?" Sadee decides to ask first.

"Not according to the run statistics. Appears that everything is operating within the norms." I change the desktop file to the system operating statistics. Everyone looks at the numbers, but I'm not sure if any of them understand what the numbers mean. I do, but that's because I've been here since the beginning.

"Did someone change a setting? Change the software somehow?" Sadee is fishing now and she has apparently come to the same conclusion I have.

"Not that I can find from our diagnostics tools. What are the analysts saying to you?" I go after it indirectly. Don't want to accuse anyone of anything at this point. I may be completely wrong. It's happened many times in my life.

Sadee looks at the others, apparently hoping for a volunteer. None of them exchange the look with her. The most popular thing to look at is my shoes, which aren't all that unusual. So why they pick my shoes, I have no idea. "What they're saying… well, not really saying. More asking. 'When will this job end? If I've only got a week or even a few weeks, all the other analysts have a head start on finding something different."

Deb, another lead who looks to be about twelve, responds, "Mine are telling me there are jobs posted in Europe. They're apparently still hiring over there."

Whitley, the lone male lead shakes his head, "Mine are telling me those are fake ads. There are no jobs. What they're telling me is it seems a lot of the former analysts are trying to get back into school. To retrain for a new career."

"Is anyone doing any work?" I put out there. "Or is everyone into job hunt mode?"

Sadee responds for them again, "Some are working. Wouldn't be a correlation if no one was working."

"But it could explain the falling correlation if few and fewer analysts are working." I put out there to see their reaction.

None of them will look at me. I wait to see if anything changes as the silence grows longer.

Deb finally looks at me. "You going to send the rest of us home?"

"Tell me if I should," I don't expect the answer I get.

"I would," Sadee looks right at me as if she expects me to agree with her.

"Why? Don't you want to keep your jobs?" I react.

"It's like punishment on top of punishment," Deb explains. "You lay off everyone we know, everyone we've worked with since we got here. But it's like you're keeping us after school on the last day of the school year. We know it's over. We know we're next. Why prolong it?"

"How do the rest of you feel?" This never occurred to me.

All nod agreement, even Whitley.

"If I told you your jobs aren't going away any time soon because Arbiter needs a human data set to continue learning, what would you say?"

"Is that true?" Sadee seems skeptical.

"It's true that Arbiter needs a human data set, but I'm still working on the Secretary about job security for you. And the reason for that is your team is not in the contract. Since the go live our company has been eating your salaries from profits because I convinced them it was a risk mitigation strategy. Make sure we can work through the system shortcomings. I've explained that to the Secretary, but she's not committed yet to modifying the contract. That may take a while and I don't know how long the company will continue funding the team, other than you're going down to twenty on Friday."

"That means one of us is going on Friday," Deb informs everyone.

"Not necessarily. So far I've just been given a headcount, nothing about salary grades. I've informed management that I want to keep five teams of four. A lead and three analysts."

"Why would you do that?" Sadee's still not sure she trusts what I'm saying.

"Because I think it will make you a better team, first of all. You'll be able to work closer with each team member, which should lead to better analysis. It also gives me time to develop more of you if I'm successful in getting the contract modified to actually take us back up to fifty or a hundred."

"That's not going to happen," Whitley announces. "Why would they? Arbiter's live. The Secretary has her own small team over there. We're supposed to be for development and testing."

"You're all aware that we went live before the system was finished according to contract standards."

"Even less reason to keep us. They quit development early." Deb seems to side with Whitley.

"What it means is we have to finish up on the maintenance and operations contract. Just moving work to a different contractual phase. Same work's got to be done. Arbiter may be operational, but the fidelity's not. How long can the Secretary let that continue?"

"Why didn't you tell us this before?" Sadee continues her suspicion of me.

"Would it have helped?"

"You're messing with families." Deb responds angrily. "Two of us are pregnant with our first ones. The reduction was a real blow because a bunch of people who are in the same situation are out there about to deliver with no health insurance. What are they supposed to do? Sell their homes so they can pay the hospital to have a kid? They have the kid and have to move to an apartment because that's all they can afford? People are just trying to get by, you know what I'm saying? The secretary makes a decision and then you make a decision and those of us who have to refigure out our lives? Well, we don't have a say in it. So yeah. Telling us the truth would certainly help."

"You have all the information I have. You can tell the rest of the team what I've told you. Tell them I'm working to not only keep them in place, but to bring back at least a few of those who left. Are these jobs going to be careers? That I really can't say because I have no idea how long it's going to take to make Arbiter reach the contracted performance specs. If we're not in full development mode it's going to take a lot longer than it would have had the Secretary just let us finish." I hear my own frustration in the words I chose, but too late now.

"We'll hold a team meeting at the end of the shift," Sadee informs me even though she's not consulted with her peers. "We want you to come and tell them what you just told us. And we'll be listening carefully for any weasel words or changes to the script. 'Cause if you're not telling us the truth there's no reason for any of us to stay on here one more day. You got her team you can use. As much as you make it sound like you think things are all going to work out, I don't trust you, management or the Secretary. We spend our days living with all the people who are posting fake news, and all the other stuff they post, or try to. I guess you could say we don't believe anybody anymore."

"I can do that." I respond calmly and try to make them understand I appreciate their frustrations and perspective. "But first let me ask a question. Have I ever misled anyone in this room?"

"Not intentionally," Deb responds for everyone.

"Have I ever told you something that was a lie?"

Sadee shakes her head and the others just look down.

"I hope you will remember that as together we work our way through this transition in the program. You're not the first team that's been contractually tossed around at the end of a program. I suspect that you're far from the last. What I know for sure is I'm doing everything I can to ensure you all have jobs that as many of your teammates and former teammates have and will have jobs. And one other thing. Deb, if you tell me who else is pregnant, I'll make sure if she's on the list that we take her off."

"What about you?" Sadee asks. "Contract says you go away when the contract is over. It's over and the operations and maintenance manager is supposed to replace you. That's Brooks. Why are you still here?"

# CHAPTER FORTY-TWO: ELIZABETH WARDEN

Trade craft. That's the last thing I ever thought I'd get caught up in. I'm a law professor not a spook. I don't have any idea how to cope with someone who is using such arcane means of communicating. How do you find someone who has taken a step backwards to cope with the modern environment of constant communication and omnipresent surveillance? Brandon may be a great analyst, but this has to be outside his experience. I need to find someone who knows how to maneuver in this space. Find the parties we're looking for.

Who was that staffer to the Senate Judiciary committee when I was on it? He worked for the agency a long time ago. What was his name? Will something… Johnson. I knew it was a common name. I look through the directory in my cell phone. Seems I talked with him a few times on committee business. There he is. William Johnson – Judiciary.

I dial the number and wait.

"Johnson," comes the familiar voice.

"Will…Elizabeth Warden. You have a minute?"

"Madam Secretary. What can I do for you?"

"Tell me all you know about tradecraft."

There's a long silence. Then, "Sounds like you've passed through the looking glass."

"I have, Will. I need someone to help me find persons of interest who we think may be operating using tradecraft."

"No digital footprints?"

"That would be the case."

Again there is a long silence. "Why aren't you going through the Bureau?"

"Suspicions they may be operating globally."

"The Agency then. Not something I'd encourage you to take on. You need more than one expert. The assets you need are available to you if you just ask."

"The problem is one I can't discuss with you over the phone. Can you come by my office? Whenever you get here I'll bring you into a suitable conference room."

"At least you're approaching it in the right way."

"Can you come over?"

An hour later I'm sitting in the secure conference room where I met with Javier and Hua Kwan to address the issue she raised in regards to Sloth.

Will, who is short and stocky with greying hair is shown in. I rise to greet him. "Thank you for coming on short notice."

"For you to rearrange your day is a clear indication of the level of seriousness."

We sit and I slide a file with my notes on Sloth to him. Will scans through the notes and lifts the pieces of paper to look under them. "This all you have?"

"Given that Jurgen got on a call with me and Hwa Kwan says she's penetrated them, I'd say there's enough justification for us to take them seriously."

"A phantom group." Will pronounces. "You know they're out there but you don't know much else."

"You're suggesting bringing in the Agency. As soon as we do that we lose control and that's a concern. This is what I couldn't say on the phone. Jurgen and Javier told me they were aware they may be targeting our government for disruption. Also said they have reason to believe they are headquartered in the U.S. Which makes it all the more curious that we have seen nothing. Yet they are clearly active in other places."

"Not surprising. Such groups often take a lower profile at home to reduce the probability of detection. Think Bin Laden. He was living a mile from the Pakistani Military Academy and yet the Pakistani's said they had no idea he was there."

"I take it you think that highly unlikely," I observe the tone of his voice.

"Impossible is the term I'd choose." Will considers what he's read and learned from me. "You talked about tradecraft. Who brought that up?"

"Hua Kwan. Said they have penetrated the group in China with traps. So they've been able to confirm how they operate, but still have no idea as to their objectives."

"I don't think you have a choice," Will leaves no doubt in his tone of voice. "I know you don't want to lose control, but all that went on before 9/11? It was all the same. No one wanted to give up control to another agency because they thought it was theirs. And yet each of the agencies had different parts of the elephant identified. They just couldn't assemble the bigger picture from the isolated snippets. The whole organization now, with the Director of National Intelligence? That's to break down the barriers to information exchange. You need to bring them in if for no other reason than to let them know the threat exists, supposedly in our backyard, and it's real."

"If I do that I want you to run this for me."

I can't be full time for now. I have some long-standing obligations as important as this could become. That doesn't mean as we get further down the road I can't get more involved. Just not this month."

"I have an analyst working it, but he's just reinforced how useless it is to focus on the traditional means of detecting folks in a situation like this."

"Who is it?"

"Brandon McInerny. His specialty has been on the media side versus the broadcast and signals."

"Maybe alright to establish they exist, but not what they're doing. You really need someone strong on the human Intel side. I know someone I can recommend. Worked with her extensively at the Agency."

"Do we have enough she can actually be productive at this point?"

"Probably not, but getting her on board will give her a chance to get spun up and hit things hard when we do know more."

"What's her name?" I wonder aloud. "Have I heard of her?"

"April Blossom."

"Memorable name." At least I should be able to remember it.

"She's memorable for more than just that. She's absolutely the best I've worked with."

"Contact her and if she's available put her in touch with Gloria in our HR department."

Will takes another long look at my notes, apparently memorizing details since I can't let him take anything with him. "If I think of anything else I'll contact you. In the meantime you'll probably hear from John Spencer. He's Deputy Director for Counterterrorism. I'm actually surprised he's not retired as he goes way back. But he's absolutely the most knowledgeable person they have on tradecraft. Wouldn't be surprised if the Chinese have infiltrated this group that he's aware of them."

"You're going to set up the meeting and give him the unclassified brief?"

"As soon as I can reach him." Will rises, still looking down at the pages. "He travels a lot and I have no idea where in the world he might be."

"I appreciate you helping me out on this one." I shake his hand with regret knowing I've just lost control and have no idea if by doing so this whole thing will blow up in my face. But Will's right. Brandon might be able to establish their existence, but not likely he will find them or gather enough information to understand what kind of threat they actually pose.

I exit the room with Will and leave him at the elevator. It's time for me to check in with Maria on the status of the Arbiter validation.

When I get back to my office there's a note from Maria. She came by at our scheduled time, which was when I was in with Will. She will come back if I call her, which I do. She arrives within a few minutes.

"Maria, what can you tell me about the fidelity numbers I'm seeing?"

"A short-term issue that came up. I believe I have it under control now. We'll give it twenty-four hours to see if the fix holds."

"Software?"

"No, the system is operating as expected. But we have some issues around the analysts."

"What kind of issues?" I pursue.

"They're looking for some kind of assurance that they aren't going out the door next week or the week after that. Everyone is scrambling since so many analysts are suddenly on the street. They're afraid if they don't start looking now all the jobs will be taken."

"That's right," I remember. "You're looking for a contract modification to keep them on."

"We're eating profit on the program by the hour."

"And your folks don't like to do that. I understand. Get with contracts and we'll make it retroactive to the go-live date so you will recover all your lost profits. How does that sound?"

"Send me a note to that effect?" Maria doesn't trust I'll deliver.

"Management doesn't take a verbal on anything... got it. Will that take care of the mutiny you're facing?"

"Not entirely. We have a need to bring back some of the team. Twenty analysts isn't enough for machine learning. I need at least a hundred in addition to your hundred. And if we wanted to accelerate the fidelity match I could use ten times that."

# CHAPTER FORTY-THREE: SABR MALIK GOLDSMITH

Hosting Jurgen and Xi is always problematic. Why they want to meet in Washington escapes me. A neutral city always seems better because then no one is distracted with the safety and security issues I have to worry about here. Getting them into the city from Bulling Air Force Base is not as difficult as from Dulles. Although we still have to run multiple caravans into the city from different directions so no would-be plotters are able to launch a successful ambush. The meetings are all to be held in the Cabinet Room. Once I get them inside the White House their safety is assured. But the issue becomes we cannot host all of their entourages here. That means we have to deal with security folks credentialing and confirming them beforehand. I'm constantly being consulted about one or another member of their staff who happens to be on one or another list we keep of undesirables or persons of interest who we believe have been involved in various terrorist events. And I'm not just talking about Xi. We have the same issues with Jurgen. Surprising, as a Western federation one would think they wouldn't be involved in such activities. On the other hand, while we are not terrorizing anyone, we are trying to influence those events. We're not as heavy handed as we once were. Technology has evolved. The consciousness of the media has grown to the point it is very difficult to play the kinds of roles we used to. Probably better. We are less often found to be in the background, or middle, of events.

As I walk over to the Cabinet Room, my entourage consists of my two translators even though all three of us are fluent in English, Elizabeth and Wilson, my Chief of Staff. Wilson will get the information or background I may need regarding issues that emerge in the discussions.

Today I only have one agenda item I wish to put to bed, although I am sure Jurgen and Xi will have additional items they will add as the talks progress. For some reason Xi always comes with one issue or another we are not prepared to discuss. His issue becomes the focus of the next such meeting.

I enter the Cabinet Room first, followed by Jurgen and finally Xi. The order is determined by the host, the prior host and the next host. That way we rotate through the order and no one is accorded status from the order. It just amazes me the lengths we have to go to sometimes. All to ensure the simplest things we might do will not send signals. Indications for those who spend their lives trying to decipher what is going on between our federations.

When all three of us are present, we come together, first shaking hands and then standing in line for the official photograph. There must be a record of this meeting. The photograph must be posted so that the people of the world know we are meeting to work on issues that will benefit them. Always positive spin to these meetings regardless of what we discuss. Always optimism that while there are tensions between the federations, there is nothing that would lead us to conflicts. Nothing that might lead to war of one type or another. Harmony is the objective along with subjective messaging.

Once the photographs have been taken, the non-participants are excused. The doors are closed. That is all the world will know for sure about this meeting. The topic is one that will not be discussed outside this room for the public to consume. We take our seats and our supporting staff sit in chairs behind us along the walls of this storied room.

I open the meeting, "Chancellor, as host of our last meeting I welcome you to Washington. I look forward to an opportunity to advance our discussions on the topics of importance to our collective federations. Chairman Xi, I welcome you to Washington. This is an opportunity to further understand the issues of concern to all of us, to propose solutions and agree upon actions that will advance the interests of all three federations."

Xi and Jurgen nod their acknowledgement of the formalities. Xi jumps right in. "Frankly Madam President I am having difficulty with the agenda you have set. Why do you believe we should focus on this one issue to the exclusion of those of economics and security?"

I expect this tact on his part since this is our third meeting. "Chairman Xi, what has a greater fundamental impact on our federations than the truth? And when truth varies between our federations that creates dissonance and distrust when our citizens return from visits to your federations. I believe an integration of our vetting systems can and should present a global truth agreed to by us."

"Madam President," Jurgen is not about to sit this one out. "Such an attempt would divert considerable of our personal time from the pressing matters of state to debate and decide on how to present a singular version of the truth amongst our federations. There are so many issues that cut across. We would be held prisoner to the mechanics of achieving your desired end state."

"I agree with the Chancellor." Xi responds. "Better that we continue down our individual paths. Better that we control the truth in our federations as we see fit. It has been a tremendous effort involving thousands of individuals to arrive at this state. And this state is still evolving. We learn new means of arriving at the truth, of the issues we must decide as to what is or should be the truth. This subject is fundamentally transforming our federation, fundamentally establishing the pathways that will lead to a more harmonious society. And that is the goal of all of us, is it not?"

"Gentlemen," I have given them the opportunity to fire their first shots. But this is far from decided. "I understand your reluctance. I have given this subject considerable thought. It is not without a deep understanding of the level of effort such an undertaking would require on the part of each of our nations. However, if you engage our media during your stay here, you will find jarring differences from what you would see and how the same topics are handled in your own federations. And the fact that the world has become so economically integrated, so interdependent on so many fronts, that our citizens spend considerable time in each other's federations. Journalists travel and return home with questions that frankly, I would prefer were not asked. I'm sure you are having the same experience."

"But Madam President." Xi responds. "Are you saying that you have not been able to establish sufficient means of controlling your journalists? Making sure that the differences are not discussed in the media that is posted for the review of your citizens? I for one believe that the issue you wish to solve by harmonizing our systems in not needed. We have the means with the systems we have in place to eliminate the dissonance in the media."

"That is how we are currently handling this particular issue in EuTopia." Jurgen pitches out there for us both to consider.

"We do the same," I admit. "However, there is a considerable discussion of it amongst our corporate travelers. These are the people who influence policy, who are influential with our elected officials. And the hallway discussions of the difference of perceptions and the truth occur every day on Capitol Hill. We have created a state of affairs where those who are most important to our continued prosperity often wonder what the truth of any situation is. That creates a great deal of additional discussion that could be avoided by an integrated world view expressed by the media."

"You are overlooking one thing, Madam President," Chairman Xi cautions me.

"And that would be?" I respond to the implied naiveté he would paint me with.

"It is important for us to focus our populations on an external threat." Chairman Xi continues. "Something that will take away what they have gained so they are not constantly striving to only have more and more. It is essential that we divert the attention of our populations from themselves to the interests of the collective. To mobilize their energies in the advancement of the state and not just their own economic interests."

"Look at recent history," Jurgen interjects. "After the collapse of your antagonist, the Soviet Union, you became the only global superpower. You had no external threat. Nothing to focus your people on external to themselves. So rather than shift priorities to the betterment of your society what did your leaders do? They instantly got into a war with Iraq rather than attempt to return Kuwait to its prior state through diplomacy. As the bully state, you had the arrogance to think you could reverse a military situation through the use of force. You could have done otherwise. Used diplomacy. Isolated Iraq economically. It invaded Kuwait for its oil. If you had only shut down market access for the oil not only from Kuwait but also Iraq, you could have set the world right without expending trillions of your dollars building new military technologies and sacrificing thousands of lives."

This lecture is galling given that Jürgen's grandfather exterminated millions of his nation's Jewish population. But I don't take that bait. Such a discussion at this time and place will not advance a solution to our differences. "We each have to deal with the effects of the polices of those who led our respective federations prior to our administrations. However, at the moment I am only concerned about how we three leaders work together to harmonize the truth to whatever extent we can in the short and longer terms. It may take a multi-stage effort, but I believe it essential to move towards a more uniform understanding of the events of our times, of the forces that are underpinning our economic performance, of the social and moral choices our citizens make each and every day."

"Thank you Madam President for recognizing that a single flipping of a switch will not achieve the global glorification you sought in your opening remarks." Xi is declaring victory already. Even though I've not conceded the point he is assuming I have. "I know the Bergamo

Accords call for a harmonization of our systems to establish the truth in any matter. But that is different than the harmonization of our view of the truth. We absolutely must have the ability to manage public perceptions as we deem necessary in our own domains. Otherwise we are surrendering our national identities to a global cabal. Now that cabal may be the three of us at the moment, but nothing is forever. I cannot leave an unworkable machinery for my successors. And I say that only because while the three of us may see the world in similar, but not the same terms, we have established a history of being able to reach reasonable accommodation. As the Chancellor has pointed out, history shows that not everyone who holds these high offices is willing or able to reach such agreements. I don't want to put into place something that my successor reaches office campaigning against."

"I appreciate your perspective, Chairman Xi…"

Jurgen interrupts, "The Chairman has the right perspective. We cannot, should not put into place something that ties the hands of our successors. A rigid machinery constrains us. We need flexibility to negotiate the needs of our federations in relation to each other. We need freedom to chart independent paths when essential. If we literally implemented the Bergamo Accords we would be creating a world more likely to move toward conflict. There are so many pressure points that would be papered over by a global harmonization that we would not be able to coordinate concerted actions to contain. I for one am unwilling to implement Bergamo all at once. It is not in the interests of my federation."

"Then what is the path forward?" I put out there to see where they believe we are.

"I believe the choice is limited to two options," Still Jurgen. "The first is we do nothing other than complete the deployment of our three different federation systems. We are incrementally moving towards more effective harmonization within our federations. Just the fact that regional and national perspectives will be blended to reduce variation is a good thing. But we will not be trying to achieve singular views across the widest differences in the social and economic diversity we find across the globe. The second option is to create a coordination committee that will study where there are opportunities to harmonize certain views. Issues that are long standing and slow moving. It is the rapidly changing issues where technology enables a difference that will get us into trouble the quickest. We need to permit those changes to develop naturally and determine after a period of study how we wish to address them and whether a global standard is possible."

Xi seeks to put this discussion to bed. "While I came as an advocate of the first position, I am willing to consider the second. In fact, as I consider it further, there may be advantages to show the world we are moving towards Bergamo Accords implementation, cautiously."

## CHAPTER FORTY-FOUR: SHEILA

I consult the Lake Como picture to reset for a moment. Look at the hotels lining the shore. The Italian Alps surrounding the lake. The small ferry boats that crisscross the lakes lined up along the shore, taking on passengers for the short trip across the lake to other small villages. Each village is different from the others. Each unique in many ways. And I need to consider that uniqueness from the positive diversity that is our planet. Why do I need a safe haven? That's the question. What do I need a safe haven from? The cruelty, the insensitivity, the warped perspectives, priorities and desires of so many who haunt the internet and the sites they hope will be visited by those who share their distorted values of humanity. Refuge from those who live next door, down the street, around the corner. And yet when I stare them in the eye, there is no indication of any of the perversion I see them post. No indication they are any different from me. That they have any different values. And yet that is exactly what comes out when they sit alone in a room with a portal to the world. A faceless funnel into the minds of men they also cannot see, but hope will resonate with the message they wish to send.

I look again at the picture on my desk. Bellagio. A small village, totally unlike the resplendent excess of the Las Vegas hotel by the same name. A place of tranquility. A place of solitude, calmness, and beauty. A place where one can nourish one's soul. A place where one can be at peace with him or herself. At peace with those who live next door, with those who say 'Buon giorno' on the street on their way to another day of cappuccino, family, friends great food and happiness.

Why am I doing this job when it would be so much better to live there? To be one with the terroir of the lake. To be someone who gives to neighbors as they give to you. Whether it is a morning greeting, a cup of sugar, babysitting your kids while you have a night on the town or taking care of your animals while you make a trip home to see your family and friends. That obligatory visit you so dread and yet treasure once you've returned home. Being in Washington DC rather than in Sydney, Australia maybe I can understand that better than most. It's a long trip home.

Brandon once asked me why Lake Como? Why not the Sydney Bay Bridge? A famous image with the Sydney Opera House with its flying sail architecture in the background. I have to admit I thought of such a picture. But I decided that Lake Como was something to aspire to. Sydney Bay Bridge would be something to retreat back to. I don't want to go home. That's no longer who I am. That's not what I want to be. I left all that behind for a reason. And that reason was that I wasn't content to be good on a small stage. I needed to prove myself on the larger stage of the federation. A federation where the rules of the world are determined. Not in a remote city where rules are conformed to those of another. I wanted to be at the inception rather than at the conformance. The latter just seemed so unsatisfying.

Now that I've had a break, I return to the broadcast I've been watching. Fox News is hosting a panel of global warming experts. This is not going to be pretty. But they've brought on noted experts. People who know the science, who do the original research, who are attempting to change world opinion such that we as a civilization can survive the effects of the actions we have taken over the last three millennia. And since most change requires twice as long as the causative events, that would indicate that we are screwed as a civilization. Fox News may end up broadcasting from a ship at sea that is anchored over the former studios in New York City. That will be their choice. But the one thing that seems irrefutable is that the changes occurring are not going to be reversed by the deliberate actions of mankind. Not because we are incapable of doing so, not because the task is daunting, but because we will simply choose not to take the necessary actions.

I don't know why it is that warnings go unheeded. The indications of our impact on our environment have been there for decades. But the economy has always been more important than the environment. People have to pay their bills first. If we built in the full cost of the inputs to society, we would still be agrarian. We have blindly ignored the signs. We have chosen to live on the cheap. Raise our own living standards at the expense of all those who are to follow us. It's not a beggar thy neighbor world, it's a beggar thy children world. This is all so hard for me to accept. That my parents kicked the can down to me expecting I will be able to kick it down the road to my children. In some sense that will happen whether I want it to or not. But as I think about the world I've inherited, I have to realistically wonder if I would be better off not bringing a child into this world. It will not be the world of opportunity my parents left me, or thought they were leaving me. It will be a world of increasing constraints. Of increasingly bad alternatives. Of an increasingly more hostile environment. And a government structure that is unable to support itself with the resources it can draw upon from the populace. An increasingly more hostile world, with fewer alternatives, and fewer opportunities for expression, peace or happiness.

If I realize this, why do I stay at my desk? Why am I not on the next airplane to Lake Como? I should be. But then I haven't found the person who would make that trip satisfying to me. I thought it was Brandon, but after our one night together, it's like I don't exist. No calls, no how was your day? When can we get together again? Not even an acknowledgment that it was a special evening. I don't know what to do with that other than to think it wasn't as special for him as it was for me. What else am I to think?

Have I been avoiding him? Not really. But he hasn't made an effort to come find me either. I have to put my expectations back in the jar. Pick myself up and realize he isn't the one special person for me. That's okay. I wish it were different, but I also have to be realistic. What is, is. And if I'm not the one for him? Well, it takes two to tango. I'd have loved to learn how with him. I even imaged us, doing that

232

romantic and daring dance. I've watched movies where the actors sweep each other across the floor. They are so engaged with each other, so attentive. So in synch from their heads to their toes. Maybe that's what I love about the tango. The ability for two souls to fuse into one and sweep across a dance floor in a fluid expression of their passion and love for each other.

Maybe I need to replace Lake Como with a picture of tango dancers. I know just the pose I would choose. Entangled so close, her leg around his, his gaze upon her face, the love and expectation flowing between them. Maybe I'll go find that picture after work, print it out and bring it in tomorrow. Give me something else to focus on. Diversity of diversion. But why do I need that? I've been here ten years, doing the same job. Enduring the same barrage of Ten Commandment decisions, although the barrage has become more focused in the last few years as we stood up Arbiter. Those first five years I didn't need an oasis of calm to reset before wading back into the torrent of tirades. But that was also when the broadcasts were reasonably balanced. There was the good, the stimulating and the repulsive mixed together. It's been a while since I've viewed a thought-provoking piece because Arbiter has already passed those on for broadcast. I will never see those again. And that's where I start needing alternatives to balance out my life. Where I need someone I can go home to. Unburden myself rather than go home, have a glass of wine or smoke a joint or take an edible to return to a centeredness. Seek a balance before I go to bed, sleep it off and start all over again the next day.

I used to wonder about those who have been here longer than me. How can they stand it? When they started the deletions were probably one of twenty-five postings. Maybe less. There was a lot more that was informative and interesting than there was that needed to go to the scrap heap of electrons. But as time has progressed the number of informative and interesting has reduced so that now it's twenty-five probable deletions to every informative or interesting post that I'll approve. It's the nature of learning algorithms. It's the nature of progress. It's the reason why the Department of Truth can do away with us. Arbiter has simply passed on for posting all those suitable for posting. We only get those where there is a question. That means the obvious, the blatant, the crudest postings don't get to us either. Everything we see is subtle. It takes a moment of examination, a moment of thought, a moment of consideration to make the decision. And this where Arbiter struggles. It can't determine nuance. It can't see embedded symbols. It can't see what we see, what we react to that is not up front and blatant.

An image presents itself before me. I'm reviewing a YouTube video channel. A performance artist is posting videos of his or her trend setting forays into the bar and foodie scene in various cities. This one happens to be in the District of Columbia, also known as Washington DC. I'm not sure why Arbiter passed this one along to me as generally there's nothing controversial on these sites. I never go look here for anything when I'm trying to track down the persons of interest the Secretary wants to find. This was passed along to me. So why this one?

I've never heard of this particular performance artist – SoHo Sam. Not a particularly memorable name. Not a particularly noteworthy site. But I learned a long time ago not to make such judgments. You just never know where someone will suddenly blaze to glory for a day, week, month or even years. Some will be with us for a long time, and others not so much.

I watch the video for the issue of concern by Arbiter. So far it's just another small neighborhood ethnic restaurant. From the video I can't tell what kind of food or where it might be other than I know it's in the District. I glance away for a moment to consult the time, because it's kind of boring for a person who is a non-foodie like me. The chef delivers her special plate to the bar. There is an array of celebrity guests, a few of whom I've seen. But if you quizzed me I'd never be able to come up with a name or reason for why they're famous.

One of the celebrities gets up from the bar revealing the table behind them. I have to look twice because it looks like Brandon sitting at that table. It has to be him. Is that why Arbiter sent this one to me?

Brandon having dinner at an ethnic restaurant? Can't be. I look closer. He's sitting in a booth with two other people. One is a gorgeous woman. Probably about my age, although he's not looking at her. He seems engaged in a discussion with an older man. Probably mid to late forties, sitting across from him. Brandon seems to be having an animated discussion about something. I wish I could zero in on that part of the picture, but the sound system only picks up the chef's discussion of her dish.

What is Brandon doing with these people? Why didn't he invite me? Is she the reason? But she doesn't seem to be the focus of his attention. She just seems to be there. What is this?

## CHAPTER FORTY-FIVE: BRANDON McINERNY

The picture of the young blonde girl is suddenly there. I haven't seen it in a while. Why is it posted again? Who's posting it and why? I don't get it. Why is Arbiter unable to determine whether this should be posted? Why is Arbiter continuing to send them to me? Is it picking me out specifically to relook at this one picture? How many times have I seen it now? It seems like a hundred, although that doesn't make sense to me.

This time I see a little more of the man's hair. The girl's blonde hair obscures most of it. In the last picture I could see there was someone, apparently a male beyond her. I could see his feet. See a little of his hairy legs. Maybe that's what convinced me it was a guy she was facing. I instantly thought there had to be some kind of sexual event going on. If you looked at the picture, there was nothing that would confirm that interpretation. Is that why Arbiter sent it on to me? It was unable to determine what the picture was really about. Was this a sexual encounter between an older man and a young girl? Was it a young girl facing her mother? Her father? An older sibling? Who is on the other side of her that has her attention?

Why was I so quick to assume a sexual connotation? Why not assume the innocent scenario? Why not assume this is a picture of a family encounter? I can only assume it's because the young girl is not wearing clothes. She is sitting on her heels looking at someone who is sitting on a bed, facing her. Is that person talking with her? Asking her to do something indecent? Instructing her on something illicit? That is what my mind jumps to, but only because I assume. I can't be sure the person behind her, obscured from my view, is an older man who is also nude. I assume he has ill intentions toward her.

I look closer at the picture. The only thing I can see is the image has been taken from a slightly higher angle. I see a bit of the figure beyond. His head. His hair. But then I realize it could be a woman. That person has brown hair as opposed to the young girl's blonde. Is it a woman's hair? I can't tell. Is it long like a woman or short like a man, although that is not always a good indicator of the sex of the person. In this case the image just doesn't give enough definition to know. I search the rest of the image. Nothing else seems to have changed. I still have no idea what I'm really looking at. Do I post it? Some would say it's art. I don't think so. Someone is testing the limits of our analysis. This is unsuitable for posting because the young girl is nude and suggestive. I have to delete. There. Done with that image. What's next?

The next photo is of a skinhead with tattoos, apparently shouting at someone with longish hair and a smile. I've seen so many pictures like this. Why are they still getting through? I thought they'd all been eliminated by the Arbiter system before now. Again I push delete. Gone in well less than thirty seconds.

Maybe I need to get back to my day job and stop working the analyst desk. But I have this need to immerse myself in it again. The blatant images like that last one are the exception rather than the rule. Arbiter has generally deleted all of them before they get to the analyst. That's what it was intended to do. What it will do as soon as Elizabeth pulls the plug on the remaining analysts. Maybe that's why I'm feeling the need to spend some time on the desk. I'm feeling it's all going to disappear on me. The life I've lived for the last decade. A life of deciding. A life of exposure for a brief period to all kinds of perversion. To all kinds of extreme displays of disgust. And yet when I'm off the desk for more than a few days I miss it. I want the power that comes with saying to whoever it is who is posting this stuff, enough. I will not let it pass. It will not get past me so you will not influence anyone else. Why do I miss that power? I don't know but it's almost like withdrawal. Like I'm not an important or necessary person. When I'm on the desk, I'm all there is between an extreme view of life and one that is conducive of all the values I believe in. All the reasons this can be a better world. When I'm on the desk I'm delivering value to my family, my friends and those who are counting on me to keep from being offended by those who have a distorted perception of the world we inhabit. I'm the gatekeeper, but only when I'm on the desk. Only when I'm pushing that delete key. Only when I look at something, review the Ten Commandments in my head and decide.

A post this time. I read through the usual denials of bias, the usual attempts to slide through the filters by showing inclusive language. But I find repeated hard phrases about the need to earn rights. The need to prove worthiness of being an American. The need for individuals who are recent arrivals to our communities to establish their value before seeking special privilege. All code words for nativist sentiments. Gone. This time in fifteen seconds. I'm not feeling charitable tonight. I'm just doing what I always did on the desk. I blow away anything that anyone could read something into. Blow away anything that could offend. Blow away deviance. And suddenly I realize I'm as bad as those I'm preventing from expressing themselves. I may have the power when I'm on the desk, but I'm no different. I'm taking away the rights of individuals to express themselves. I'm taking away a balanced expression of opinion. I'm the one who is attempting to change the discussion, not them. I'm preventing the larger community from facing the sublimated feelings, thoughts and understandings of their lives. The repression comes from me. The one-sided discussion of a community results from my actions. I am the problem, not the solution. I am not fostering a discussion where people can discuss their insights, their heritage, and their cultures and promote an understanding of each other. I am standing in the door they need to pass through to achieve harmony. The deletion of expression does not promote understanding, it simply suppresses it. And why is that a better state of affairs? Why is that better than the alternative, of the hard work of developing understanding of minority viewpoints? In the push to eliminate hate speech, we have also eliminated the ability to have the discussions as a community where those who post the hate filled speech have to encounter the differences as people and not in the abstract. Sit with someone who looks different, who worships a different god, who observes different traditions, but at the same time just wants a better life

238

for themselves and their children. Who want equal opportunity to achieve that better life. Who want safety and security for their families. Who want to be smiled at when they walk down a street. Where a greeting is 'how is your day?' rather than 'go back where you came from.'

How did I get here? What am I doing this for? What is it I want to achieve? Is it simply I want the same thing as everyone else? That I want to feel safe? That I want to have an opportunity for a better life? That maybe I'll be able to marry and have a family where my kids can have a better life than I'll have?

I disengage from the terminal and sit back trying to understand what I'm feeling. This is not something I've experienced in ten years on the desk. So why is it haunting me now that I've actually had a few days away? I'm finding that I'm experiencing withdrawals and questions as to what I've been doing all this time.

Or is it I was seen as expendable by Elizabeth and the others that represent this government? Used for a decade to deal with the most mind-numbing grotesqueness that was supposed to save everyone else from dealing with it. I was the standard bearer. The one who took one for the team. By doing so I made our federation a better place for all. So if I did the hard work for everyone else, why did I suddenly become expendable rather than rewarded for what I've suffered? The nightmares, the lost weight and appetite. The inability to think at times because my thoughts become crowded out by images no one should have to look at even once. And yet I look at them for ten hours a day every day of the week. Although not so much now. The images are becoming more subtle because Arbiter just eliminates the ones where there is no question. They shall not pass on to the public at large. A machine. I'm cast aside for a machine, but a flawed machine. I can see that. It's a machine with only a limited ability to understand the subtlety of human ingenuity. The ability to disguise, hide or build diffusing patterns around the same content that the Ten Commandments say we should not let others have to deal with. A machine has become more valuable to society than I am. Because I'm suffering from the work I do. Is it any different from those who develop diseases from their occupational exposures? In my case they're not physical as much as emotional disease. I know that now, although for the ten years on the desk I kept denying it. Thought the nightmares and lack of interest in food or exercise was normal. But it's not. I see that now. Elizabeth has done this to me. Made me incapable of many things, whereas I've always thought myself more capable than most. Why have I been living a lie all these years?

I probably should get back to the task Elizabeth has given me. Back to looking in the backgrounds for the indications of an extremist group no one has noticed before. A group with an agenda no one has identified. But a group we all know intends to do something to disrupt the world as we know it. I need to do my job. I go back in and sign out of the analyst workstation.

As I complete my login a YouTube video appears. I don't usually get videos as that's over in the broadcast and signals group. Why? I don't know other than the analytical tools used for static media rather than motion.

I look for a long moment, curious. I'll do just this one. A performance artist is posting videos of his or her trend setting forays into the bar and foodie scene in various cities. This one happens to be local. I'm not sure why Arbiter passed this one along to me as generally there's nothing controversial on these sites. So why this one?

I've never heard of this particular performance artist – SoHo Sam.

I watch the video for the issue of concern by Arbiter, but so far it's just another small neighborhood ethnic restaurant. From the video I can't tell what kind of food or where it might be other than I know it's in the District. The chef delivers her special plate to the bar, where an array of celebrity guests, a few of whom I've seen, but really have no idea who they are. I never watch YouTube or the broadcast media. I'm overloaded when I get home at the end of the day.

# TRUTH

One of the celebrities gets up from the bar revealing the table
behind them. I have to look twice because I'm now sure that I'm sitting
at that table. It has to be me. Is that why Arbiter sent this one to me?
This was my meeting of last night with Ichabod who sits directly across
from me and Magritte who sits between me and the camera person.
Holy shit. Arbiter has found me and is serving me up for a
determination. Does that mean it knows I'm meeting with these people?

## CHAPTER FORTY-SIX: JAVIER SANTIAGO

Jurgen is in rare form. Most of the time he is engaged, but reflects more than he reveals his thoughts. As we sit in his office, alone for a change, he is expansive in his evaluation of the world situation. Maybe, because for the first time in a long time, there is a glimmer of hope that things are moving in our favor. We've been whipsawed by forces we have struggled to shape, but have not been successful.

"Xi played it exactly as we expected. It was almost as if he was reading a script you'd written. He's throwing up roadblocks to Bergamo. Making sure Sabr has to scramble since she'd made a major announcement about how that agreement would reduce tensions between UaTopia and her federation. Now it will be very difficult for her to explain why more progress is not being made."

"But she didn't discuss what Bergamo really means," I clarify. "She has wriggle room by simply playing it that she has met her obligations under the agreement. It is Xi who has chosen not to comply. One he was the principle author of. Makes her look stronger because she is honoring her obligations. She's the strong one because she has nothing to fear from being out front and leading the world to a safer place."

Jurgen half nods showing me that he understands my point but hasn't embraced it quite yet. For whatever reason he still thinks that Xi set up Sabr, and in the process weakened both of them. In that case, I'm the one who's not quite sure. "Xi is pushing a new generation of surveillance systems. Trying to sell them in countries he hopes to exploit. Almost giving the hardware away if the country will but pay a maintenance fee on the software. And that software is full of trapdoors. Xi can have his intelligence service call up any camera they deliver and install anywhere in the world. He can watch traffic on the Strand in

London, lovers stealing kisses as they walk along back streets in Venice or listen in on the President of Argentina as she hatches another plan to steal from her poor shirtless ones."

"And you can shut down the autonomous vehicles on any German autobahn, Los Angeles freeway, or Istanbul arterial road." I remind him. "We all have our systems of influence. Systems we can manipulate in any country we wish since what we have delivered has become the default standard. And once you reach that pinnacle, you're almost unassailable. No one can catch you because you've spread the costs over all the installed systems. Anyone else is going to be playing catch up for years."

"But which systems would you rather have? Those we dominate or someone else's?" Jurgen certainly is open tonight. Unusual. I wonder what's going on.

"It all depends on your perspective," I begin trying to cut this response down as what first comes to mind will take longer than Jürgen's attention span. "For a spook like me, surveillance is the gold standard. Although I think most of Xi's systems are archaic and cumbersome. But if you're trying to dominate the economy it has to be tech. Pushing the state of the art every day of the year. Obsolete devices before the owner has even figured out where he or she put the instruction manual. That's why everything has to be so intuitive. No one reads the instructions. If I can't figure it out by playing with it for five minutes it gets set aside. Just the way it is."

"And we get to sell another one, more expensive, but easier to play with." Jurgen notes. "I love tech. There's a never-ending stream of opportunities, ideas, platforms for new experiences. That's why we have built such a strong economy. Appealing to the sense of cool, of being desirable. Of being mysterious, of being a fashion and social trend setter. We set that up and the people just follow us wherever we decide to take them."

"The UsTopians seem to think they still have a lock on pop

culture. That everything we do is an imitation. They decide what the world will think is cool. But they're not in the forefront anymore. They often skip whole generations of products because they refuse to follow someone else who has set a new standard. We had to do that for decades just to stay in the game. But they think they can innovate away from the new standards we have set."

"In some cases they can still pull it off," Jurgen observes. "But we're winning on that front much more often than we used to. Winning a product generation and establishing the pathway to the next. That's what they used to do so well. Lock us out for multiple generations of a product. Keep us satisfied so we have no interest in even listening to the pitch made by competitors. I'll bet a number of superior new products just sat on shelves because no one would go use them because they weren't Apple. Refused to buy something their friends weren't carrying. None of what we do really makes any sense. The factors that influence decisions are so disparate there's no way to track all of them and build a coherent model that will let you predict the next purchase. All we can do is pile into a short-lived trend. Milk it for all we can get and then go look for the next opportunity to pile in."

I'm not quite sure why he's wrapped up in a social and economic balancing act. Generally he has absolutely no interest in these things. So why tonight? Did someone come give him a class on popular culture and social trends? I wouldn't be surprised as he's constantly trying to understand the things he knows he doesn't. And the longer we've worked together the more he seems to recognize what he doesn't understand. Those first few years he was fearless and would just plunge into any situation and figure it out once he was there. But not anymore. He's become more cautious. Watches much more than he used to. But the one thing that hasn't changed much over time is that he doesn't listen any more carefully. Anything presented has to be quick or he's gone on to the next subject. Another thing that has changed is it doesn't make any difference in regards to the subject. It used to be he would stay engaged all night on some topic he was trying to master, or at least ensure he knew enough to defend himself in any verbal contest. To keep himself out of trouble with the news people. But now that we have our analysts making sure that nothing I don't want out there is out there, he seems a bit less sensitive about that. But all I've really noticed is he harasses me more to make sure I'm on it. Letting me know I don't have a pass on any failures. Something goes wrong and he is exposed in any way will result in a long cold winter some place I'd rather never even visit.

No, Jurgen has no intention of harming me, even if I really screw something up. But he has no compunction about making someone's life miserable if he's been embarrassed or exposed in any way. Maybe seeing what happened to his brother as a result of his own ambition, he simply is not going to give anyone the space to get between himself and the role he plays as leader of what most regard as the least important of the three major federations. We are supposed to be inferior in so many ways to UsTopia. And our economic muscle just can't begin to take on the Asian tidal wave of products, services and protected markets. Take on the protections, which enable nearly anyone in UaTopia to start a business. Grow it. Larger than our largest ones in just a few years. It has nothing to do with product quality. It's all about cost, delivered cheaper because whatever it is never gets packed up on an ocean voyage like products going the other way.

"You're certainly doing a role reversal tonight," Jurgen accuses me. Guess I'd stopped to reflect longer than he was comfortable with.

"I learn from the Master."

"Do you agree about Xi? That's he's backing himself into a corner he hasn't seen coming?"

"Chairman Xi is very astute," I point out. "He has made few mistakes in his long leadership. He's been very skillful at indirect aggression. He seldom confronts, but rather finds a backdoor through which he can present himself as being ahead of you in very unexpected ways."

"You sound like you admire him," Jurgen observes, curiously for I seldom share my impressions of others trying to ensure that they don't come back to haunt me.

"I admire qualities in people, but I broadly admire only a vista or sunset."

Jurgen smiles at me. "That's why you'll never settle down and raise a family."

Where is this coming from? "Since when have you given any thought to relationships?" I confront him which I hate to do, but he set this up. "You've not been in a relationship the whole time I've known you. It's all about conquest as far as you're concerned. Getting her into bed and then once you've had what you want why would you even try again?"

"At least I'm out there pitching myself. Keeping in shape. Burnishing my reputation even if it is mostly the invention of certain journalists."

"You don't let me burnish your reputation." I point out. "The truth about you is that anyone can write what they want and you don't care. Why is that?"

"Legends are never created by a PR firm." Jurgen smiles a Cheshire smile. "They grow in the telling of a simple thing no one can seem to remember. So every person who talks about it makes it greater than it was in reality. I love the legends about me. Why would I want those who take the time to imagine me as something other than I am to stop doing that? Stop because those legends disappear into the ether as soon as they are posted? That's what you are. Someone who used to make people disappear. Now you make their on-line personalities disappear."

"You always get philosophical after you've been with Sabr," I point out. "She must have affected you more than anyone else I can think of."

"That whole persona she created just to get elected? A gay Black Muslim woman married to a Jewish Asian transvestite? I've seen Walter's equipment. She's very happy he never whacked that off. She may like women, but she likes that more. I know from personal experience."

## CHAPTER FORTY-SEVEN: ELIZABETH WARDEN

Lunch at the White House. Only the second time since I came to work for Sabr. The first time was when she asked me to join the cabinet as Secretary of Defense. I told her she wouldn't like what I would do to the place. Her polite and measured response was she was hoping I would defund all the programs the defense contractors love. Then take the heat when all their employees show up in the voting booth having lost their jobs. Just her way of ensuring I'd never get to the Oval Office other than to visit her. But I'd turned the tables by making an unexpected pitch for the vision I'd developed by listening to people on the campaign trail. But it was a vision I couldn't share out there. People were asking for a life insulated from the battering they'd taken from the last president. A mental and moral beat down. They wanted to know that could never happen again. If I'd told them about my plan for Arbiter I would have been finished because it smacked of Orwell's book 1984. Going from one extreme to the other would never get me elected. And yet it may get Sabr re-elected, because people will have the relief they've been searching for. Have the tranquility restored. Life is too fast. Sound bites nip but they don't chew. So in the end, we look battered and bruised, but we are intact. We just aren't happy about how we look or feel. And it's the feel part that has taken the biggest toll on the people of the Federation.

Sabr pats her mouth with her napkin as she finishes chewing the bite from her trout almandine. "You don't think Javier knows his sleeper cells have all been identified?"

"I don't know for sure we have them all," I respond as I swallow a sip of water. "But we've been monitoring them all for nearly six months now. There are no new communications patterns. No reaching out and touching someone we haven't already noticed. Deep cover. Long term assets. It will be interesting to see why he placed them here. What's his expected outcome? He's not going to try to replace a sitting government. He's not going to steal technology secrets when he can simply buy that technology from us with no restrictions. I just don't know why he felt he needed hidden assets."

"I'm much more worried about Xi's people," Sabr refocuses me. "I don't think you really know who he has here ready to do his bidding. It's been a very different relationship. Most of the people most likely to want to play that role are working in our tech companies. Own some of them. And they are given the opportunity to create whole new industries in some instances. Freedom to be something they will never experience when they go home. And yet every year we lose promising minds who do just that. They go home to a very restricted existence."

"But it's home," I point out. "Just as here is your home and my home. I couldn't conceive of moving to China to do research on artificial intelligence. I know they are supposed to be among the world leaders, blazing new paths and finding new frontiers. But still."

"That's because you know the government will find a way to use your creations to control the lives of the people. Create Orwell's 1984 state for real," Sabr notes.

I do a double take at her reference since I've just been thinking about that book. "Our impression, but do we really know what it's like? From what I've read the government has enabled such rapid relative economic prosperity that people are happy to make the devil's bargain. A chicken in every pot, a small but comfortable apartment and a very expensive car in the garage to lure one of the few women available for marriage. A remnant of the one child policy. But even that is changing. The young people are finding they can travel in herds so no one gets left out even though there's not an equal number of men and women. Everyone gets to have time with someone of the opposite sex. They may go home together on occasion, change partners and go home with someone else next time. Or simply go home and relieve oneself. It's all good because the parental pressure to have a family has eased when so many young men can't find a suitable mate interested in the life of parent and poverty."

"You studying up for Secretary of State next?" Sabr gives me a verbal jab.

"I'm curious about everything. I never like to sit down with someone I don't understand. And that means I read everything relevant. Everything that may give me an insight when I need one to plan a successful interaction."

"And has that helped you to find the Chinese sleeper cells?" Sabr isn't letting me get too far away from directly answering her question.

"Yes," I respond and let that sit for a moment because I know that will drive her crazy. I never give her one-word answers for anything.

"How?" Sabr plays the game.

"We closely look at people who bury themselves deeply."

"Meaning?"

"Those who come from large families, but never go home. Those who study the most difficult scientific subjects and then take much less rigorous jobs. Anyone where there is a contradiction between what they were or are and what they become once they complete their preparation. Whether studies or starting a business, or just communicating. The ones who completely cut themselves off are sending a signal to someone. We just have to be smart enough and diligent enough to follow it to conclusion."

Sabr places her utensils on her plate and it is gone immediately. Something about the White House staff. When they only have one person to worry about the service is phenomenal. Sabr nods, "Sounds more like just good psychology than any specific insights about the Asian mind."

"There are twists and turns in any culture."

"All interesting, but not why I wanted to talk," Sabr begins.

But I grab another moment to throw her off stride, "I know you're extremely busy. Just the fact you finally had to break down and buy me lunch rather than harass me on the phone as you're triple tasking. But there are some things you have to be aware of. Not that I expect you to do anything about them. I'm continuing to evaluate all options, but I've crossed into interagency territory and I'm sure you're getting the blow back that I've been sitting on things too long and not acting as a team player. So I wanted to let you know right off the bat, they are correct. I have been sitting on things that I have finally come to the conclusion are better resolved in a cooperative framework rather than using the resources within my department alone. So before you castigate me, mea culpa."

Sabr actually has an amused look. "Mea culpa? Never thought you'd own up to that."

"You gave me a department with deep resources, at least in comparison to the Senate staffers I've lived with the last two terms. I would hope to learn to use them effectively. Solve my own problems without dropping things in someone else's lap."

"What made you see the light?"

"Expertise."

"Tell me more," Sabr thinks that if I can learn something maybe some of her other cabinet members can too. Although I'm not so sure listening to them in cabinet meetings.

"Hua Kwan informed me that persons of interest Javier and Jurgen alerted us to were using tradecraft to communicate."

"She shared that?" Sabr can't hide her surprise. And given how tight-lipped Hua Kwan generally is I can understand.

"A clear indication that she is taking this group seriously and thinks we need to get our act together," I confirm.

"Who is this group?"

I hesitate trying to decide how much I should share not in a secure facility. "We don't know and that's when I realized that even though we have some of our best analysts searching for them, it's not likely they will discover who they are or what their objectives are."

"We still have analysts?" Sabr seems surprised.

"A few," I decide is enough said.

"What happened to that one I read about?"

"The analyst?" I think I know where she may be going but need to validate.

"The one who blew himself up in a Mexican restaurant and took more than a few people with him. What was the story? Thought I heard something about him being a long-time analyst we had just terminated as part of the transition."

"That's the summary description. A little more to it than that. He'd been on Fox monitoring for nearly half his assignment with us. One of the five-year temporaries who stayed on for twenty years and then his job finally disappeared."

"Do you have a problem?"

"Meaning are there others out there we just released who might have a tendency to do something extreme?" I try not to be too blunt.

Sabr nods.

"We don't really know. But with hundreds of thousands of analysts gainfully employed last week who have now been told they are obsolete because a machine can do their job. Well. They've known that for more than a year. Ever since we started the parallel operations. Some left to find other things. Most stayed. It's lucrative work. Stressful. But people seemed to be coping. An occasional suicide mostly. The analysts seemed to internalize what they were dealing with."

"So what changed? Why now?"

"I can only speculate," I know comes across weak, but I really don't have more I can give her I feel confident saying.

"You just learned the lesson about finding external resources to help you deal with your lack of knowledge of tradecraft..."

I nod knowing where she's going.

"You need to reach out to the National Institutes of Health," Sabr mulls as she talks to me. "This sounds like a mental health issue, not a criminal element of society suddenly coming out from behind a curtain they'd raised over themselves as we discovered in an election a few years ago."

## CHAPTER FORTY-EIGHT: ALBERT CARTER

I notice a different look in Brandon's eyes. Maybe it's there and maybe it's not. Hard to tell, really, since he won't look me in the eye. And that's not like Brandon. He also looks more disheveled than usual. Hair not combed the way he likes it. Clothes more wrinkled. That was to be expected when he wasn't working, but he's putting in more normal hours on this gig with the Secretary. And I'd expect he would be trying to keep it together to impress her and hope she will make him permanent. She needs good people. And Brandon is one of the best I ever worked with.

Sheila on the other hand almost seems like she'd rather be anywhere else. Maybe I should have told them I'd invited the other to lunch, but hadn't thought about it since they both work in the same building.

I know this restaurant is not the usual place, which was always Starbucks. But I wanted to actually have something to eat today rather than just a cup of coffee. Since my wife's off at some book club event tonight, I'm on my own for dinner. So thought I'd eat with someone, rather than sit at the counter and eat warmed over leftovers by myself.

"Do you two do anything together?" I finally ask trying to sort out what I'm seeing and feeling but not hearing.

Sheila looks at Brandon, who doesn't look at her and shrugs.

"You know, you two just piss me off. I'd have thought by now you'd be on your second or third kid. That Brandon here would have gotten you off the desk before you totally lost it. And he'd be leaving early to go coach little league or some damn sport kids like these days. You know you're not getting any younger. Time to change your fates is running out."

Sheila glances at Brandon who still doesn't make eye contact with her. There's something going on here that's making them both uncomfortable.

"Okay, what is it? Brandon sleep with your best friend? You suddenly decide gay is in so now is the time to play ball with the other team? Something's going on here and it's killing me to see you not talking."

Brandon finally looks at me, but now I can see his eyes are having trouble focusing. It's almost like he's on something that's whacking him out. Brandon never took anything when he was working. I knew all about the weed and wine and all the prescription drugs after work. Hell, we all did that to try to cope. But this is something else. I snap my fingers next to his left ear. No reaction. Not even sure he heard it. "What's up with you?" I lean across the table to get closer. Look deeper into his eyes. Now I see they're dilated more than they should be. Bloodshot too. "You taking medicine or something?"

Brandon shakes his head. So I know he understands what I'm saying.

"Did you come from work?" I'm right in his face.

Brandon nods.

"You need to go home and sleep off whatever it is you're on. Don't worry, I'll cover for you with the Secretary."

Brandon finally looks at me directly. "You going to buy my lunch?"

Not a tone of voice I've ever heard from him. This is bad shit, whatever it is he's into.

"Sure. What you want?"

Sheila's looking at him like she's afraid to be sitting next to him.

Wondering if whatever he's dealing with is catching.

The waiter comes by. I order three burgers and fries. Not a healthy diet, but at the moment I'm not sure what he needs. "You dealing with something that you took too much medicine or something else?"

Brandon kind of sorta shakes his head. "Dreams."

"What about them? You overdose on something trying to get through the night?"

"Tea."

"To sleep? You're drinking tea to sleep. Tea has caffeine. That's the worst thing you can drink if you're trying to get some sleep," But tea doesn't explain what I'm seeing.

"Herbal," Brandon continues.

Sheila nods, "He said something about that before. Someone gave him some tea bags. Said it would help him sleep without dreams."

"You're only supposed to drink that before you go to sleep." I explain to him. "How many cups have you had today?"

"Six... Seven maybe," Brandon puts his head down on the table.

I see Sheila wants to smooth his hair, starts to reach, but pulls back and puts her hand in her lap.

"Didn't know you could overdose on tea," I note for her consumption since he's totally out of it. "Wonder what kind of herbs were in that tea? Something to make you sleep without dreams? I didn't know anything could do that."

In a moment Brandon's breathing gets heavy and it's clear he's asleep. Sheila does reach out now, smooths his hair. Brandon doesn't wake.

The burgers and fries arrive. "You might as well eat. Looks like he needs the sleep more than food. What's going on between you two?"

"I don't know," Sheila keeps looking at the sleeping Brandon. "We slept together after all these years, and that seems to have ruined everything."

"I was afraid it was something like that." I take a bite into my burger and chew it while I think how to fix this.

Sheila doesn't touch her burger. Continues to look at Brandon.

"Eat up. You only die once. Time to clog up them arteries. Got to have something for all that healthy stuff you eat to clear out for you."

Sheila displays a vague smile so I know she heard me, but it doesn't look like she's going to engage with me either.

"You're going to need to talk to him," I point out.

Sheila nods, looks towards the door, "I probably should get back…"

"Not yet. You and Brandon have danced around each other for a decade, despite my best efforts to break down the Chinese wall you erected between you. You're perfect for each other. I've never seen two people who complement each other the way you do. And yet it's like you're afraid that being together will reveal some deep dark secret that will drive you apart. Let me assure you there is no deep dark secret."

Sheila looks up at me with sorrowful eyes, not the bright sparkling pools I'm used to seeing. "We all have secrets, but the problem is we know each other's secrets because we do the same job. We see the same things. We're inundated with the same…"

"Do you think he's afraid that he's damaged goods? And you think the same thing about yourself?"

"I have the same nightmares, have the same fearful response to closing my eyes. Yeah, I know you think I must be at stage four, but that's what really scares me. I'm not. I'm only in stage three. That means if we weren't live with Arbiter I would probably keep on doing this for three or four more years before anyone would tell me it's time to leave."

Sheila gathers herself before she continues, "I don't know if I can come back from this. I don't know if he can. I mean what's the use? I can't sleep. I can't concentrate. I can't keep my mind from wandering. And all indications are that Brandon is further along than I am. That's what scared us. At least I'm afraid of caring for him more than I do and finding I can't help him because I can't help myself. Do you see what we're running from? We're running from what we've become. And I've not spoken to anyone who's gotten better after it's over. No one who offers hope that we might have a normal life after being exposed to the worst that humanity could ever inflict on another human being for a decade."

"Sheila," I reach across and put my hand on hers. "It's okay. I've been at this longer than either of you. Luckily I've been off the desk for the decade you've been on it. But I've not been away from it. I still put my time in, just not every day and not all day. So I know what you're feeling, what you're experiencing and what you're thinking. It's like Alice in Wonderland. Right now you're through the looking glass, living a distorted and perverted existence. But you're not the victim in that existence because you get to obliterate those images, those words, and that dialog. You're empowered and that's your redemption. Things will get better. I know it takes a long time, but things get better. It takes a lot of work. I'm ten years past the intense phase and still working things out. But they're stable now. I can deal. I can sleep most nights. You'll get there too. You just can't let it get to you. Can't give up in the face of the distress it puts you into."

Sheila looks down at Brandon, still sleeping. She reaches out and touches his hair again, pushing it back into place, even though a hopeless thought as it needs to be combed badly. "I know you're right, but it all just seems overwhelming right now."

"I don't want this to sound like things will get worse, but they will. The time it gets to be the worst is when you come off the desk. I know it's crazy. But that's when things all seem to fall apart. When you're doing the job? You're doing the job and just coping. But when you have time to really think about things? That's the worst. No kidding. But you know, if you prepare yourself for that you get through it. You just don't want to try going cold turkey. You need to work into it. Take a day off here and there when you're getting close. Get through that day knowing you're back obliterating all that evil that resides in us, being powerful. Being in control. Doing the job. And then in another week or so, you take a couple days off, work your way through it. Stay up all night if that's what it takes. Start reading a comedy or listening to music. Stuff that's just the opposite of what you do all day. And then you're back at it. Being powerful again for a few days. Do you see what I'm saying? You work your way out."

"Until you're no longer powerful. No longer a destroyer of all the things that haunt you. And then where are you? You're lost and can't make it go away."

## CHAPTER FORTY-NINE: BRANDON McINERNY

Another night of dreams, but this time I can't move, I can't get comfortable. Why is that? Something's wrong. I'm upside down, drowning in my own words... tying to swim through a tide of hate filled farmers who wash over me, leaving a residue of lost perspective. How did I get here? How did I become another minnow following a school of nativist thinkers? Thinking that everything would be alright if only it were as it was, rather than as it could be. I see my mother, standing on a raft of reason, reading another set of gospel verse as interpreted by Mary Baker Eddy. Telling me that the world is a place filled with wonder, with opportunity and love. A world where I can be anything I desire to be. It's all up to me to simply choose and I'll become. But that's not the way the world works. So why did she mislead me? Why did she encourage me to explore when I was ultimately going to be trapped by a society seeking to transform itself into what it is not? A society where some can have proper thoughts and those who attempt to express something different are labelled deviants rather than free thinkers? Somewhere along the way the two became intertwined. Became fused together in the minds of those who would exploit the weaknesses in the will of individuals to research rather than simply accept the arguments of others at face. And then there's me. The shining star. Able to tell the difference. Able to make the decision, and be happy or willing to ignore the results.

As I float past my mother's raft, she looks at me disapprovingly. "Why have you chosen to forsake my plans for you? Chosen a path that leads to indolence, to indecision and indecency? You were the one. Chosen by God to lead us from ignorance and indifference to a glorious golden garden of earthly delights. Hieronymus Bosh had a conception we should all pause to consider could be our fate. But you have lived in that state of confusion for so long. You have navigated a path not only for yourself, but for those who follow your explorations on the web. And that is good, but insufficient. You could have done more. Could have avoided so much confusion and distress among so many of us, if only you'd have been better."

I'm relieved to have passed by her judgment even though nearly every word has wounded me, left me bleeding in so many places. Left my soul exposed and vulnerable.

My father comes into view. He's sitting in the chair where he always sits after work. Where he reads the newspaper and listens to the television news. I can pass right on by him and he won't even notice. But for some reason he puts the newspaper down, seems to be watching whatever it is that's on the news. What is it? I turn and glance at the screen he watches, but I can't see it from here. Can't tell what it is that attracts his attention when my presence does not.

But I'm wrong. He turns to look at me. "Brandon. Why are you home? You're supposed to be at work, aren't you? You're always at work. At least that's what you tell your mother is the reason you never come home. Never come and tell us what you've learned of the world. Tell us of your plans for the future you are creating for yourself. The place you have taken amongst all those who are engaged in the workaday world. Your place amongst your peers. The place you have assumed in the hierarchy of importance. And you know? It doesn't matter to us what that place is as long as you are doing your part. Making the world a better place. Being a good person. Leading. That's what makes one person stand out. Contributing to the solution and not the problem that others must solve. Come home to see us once in a while. Visit with your mother. She misses learning from you. Sharing the insights she has gained from her readings. Please come home. This is your home."

The television catches his attention again. His gaze passes from me and in a moment the waves of warped wisdom carry me past him to the elementary school I attended. A tiny building today, although when I attended classes there it seemed like a giant place filled with other kids and teachers from nine in the morning until three in the afternoon. Five days a week. And as I grew I could walk the two blocks myself. Initially by cutting through the field between our house and the school, so I only had to cross the one street. Look both ways for any parents who might drive their child. But I lived within walking distance so I never arrived in a big shiny car. Never made a grand entrance. I just arrived. Was that the problem? That I just arrived? Blended in. Entered the building and took my seat. I see Mrs. Daily, my sixth-grade teacher. She was a warm woman, slightly plump, but always hugging us so we knew we were okay. She accepted us for who we were. Gave us opportunity. Patiently explained anything we needed to know. I loved Mrs. Daily because she made me feel important, even though I didn't arrive in a limousine like the others. I didn't come from a wealthy family. I didn't spell every word correctly each and every time. Mrs. Daily gave me the opportunity to be the editor of a school newspaper. Came out every Friday. I wrote most of the articles because no one else wanted to take the time. But from time-to-time one or another would write up something so they would have something to show their parents. I'm sure they only did so because Mrs. Daily sent the newspaper home every Friday. She even let me draw my own comic strip. Create crude images of people discussing topics of the day in our classroom. Questions about dinosaurs or lunar eclipses, or how honeybees carry pollen. You know, the important issues of the day. At least from a sixth-grade perspective.

Mrs. Daily waves good-bye as I continue my floating voyage, my journey to, I'm not quite sure what. Although I know lurking in my mind is all those images and thoughts I don't want to have. All the concepts I visited every day. But no longer. That's not me. Not now. I'm not an analyst. I'm a researcher. I'm trying to find someone who knows how to disappear in plain sight. Knows more than me about how to do that because I've not been able to discover anything that would confirm they even exist. But Elizabeth is convinced. Someone has seen evidence of them, but won't share it. Won't point us in a direction. I wonder if that person has an agenda. Doesn't want us to find the persons of interest, but spend time and effort searching for something that doesn't really exist. Is that what this is all about? And if it is, should I care? I have a job, which I wouldn't have had if I'd not been chosen. I'd be sitting home every day, searching for a position for an out of work analyst, along with all the others who have left the Department. Left all the media companies that were expected to do the first level reviews. Who were supposed to police themselves, but found that even their best tools could only automate a portion of the role. And that's when the government stepped in. Pressured by voters to do something about the problem of hate speech, of white nationalism, of racism, of pornography of so many unacceptable forms of speech and expression. Thought police. That's what we've become. The police who keep you from expressing yourself. Keep you from disgorging whatever horror it is that resides within. And that's all fine. Why should your fellow man have to engage in your nightmare? Be subject to wading through a day populated by your thoughts rather than their own? Why should one person or small group of people steer a much larger group of people in a direction of their choice? Why shouldn't everyone be free to express themselves in whatever way or means that they decide? But then the counter is that an expression opportunity has always been there, but just in the form of art. Hidden messages wrapped in visual and literary expression. So many pictures, paintings and representations of distorted perspective. Novels that ramble through the dark recesses of a very disturbed mind, and yet it is held up as literary genius. I wish I knew what that meant, because I'm sure I've sent those expressions off into the ether when others may have decided to hold them up for all to contemplate. A marvelous encapsulation of experience.

And then I'm floating again. My mind fills with nothing. Is this state Magritte's herbal tea is supposed to transport me to? A state where I don't suffer the ravages of nightmares I can't stop? But it seems it takes nearly a dozen cups for it to bring me here. Is that a good thing? That I have to flood my body with strange medicinal herbs to have even a moment of peace? Albert was trying to tell me something. Was that part of this dreamlike state I'm in? Or am I dreaming now?

Suddenly I'm being sucked down, down, down… accelerating

faster, faster and faster. I can't stop, I've lost control. Who is making all this happen? It can't be me. If it were, I'd be able to stop it. But I can't. Can't even slow the acceleration. Images move past me at such a rate that my eyes can't focus on them. I have no idea what they represent. Should I? Is that what all this is about? A means of communicating with me about something important that I can't perceive? Can't distinguish from the on-rushing images that wash over me in an instant and are gone.

Now I'm on a beach. At least I think it's a beach. Should be. Sun in the sky, sand under my hands as I lie here afraid to open my eyes. Afraid I'm not really here. Afraid I'm not really the man who came to work in the Department of Truth a decade ago to change the world. To establish the truth. Make sure everyone could know it and act accordingly. That was the plan. To change a very corrupt planet into a place of wisdom, truth and happiness. Have I had any impact on that intention? At the moment I'd have to say I have no evidence to support that. No proof I've made a difference in the life of anyone. And that was all I wanted to do. Make a difference.

I discover my legs and arms are staked into the sand with strong ropes. I can't move except my head. Am I Gulliver? A giant in a world of a different perspective? A world where size is a handicap. Where it no longer is meaningful who you are but what you are.

I raise my head and am confronted with a room where a seemingly naked, although I can't be sure tied down here as I am, man is sitting on a bed. Beyond him I can see the outlines of a woman's shape. No. It's a girl's shape. And she may be seven years old, just like the blonde girl in my continuing image. The girl who's virginity I fear for, especially at such a young age. She shouldn't be subject to such coercion. Such expectations. Such adult world obligations. Is this the same picture, image or whatever it is? The same image from a different perspective? But where did it come from? Is it something someone posted? The same person who has posted all the other images of them? And if it is, why is it from this perspective? Why not higher where I can see his face. Or if from this side, hers? Why do I think I know these people, although I can think of no one who even remotely seems like them? But the fact someone keeps serving this image to me would indicate there is something about the image Arbiter has associated with me. Keeps me seeing it, dealing with it. But that's not possible. Arbiter isn't programmed to do that. Isn't capable of independent thought. So how could it possibly find the picture of me in that ethnic restaurant with Ichabod and Magritte? Serve this picture that has some affiliation with me to me, day-after-day, week-after-week?

## CHAPTER FIFTY: 'MARIA' XHE

I look up from my desk to find Elizabeth standing in front of it. She has an expression on her face I've never seen before. Almost like she's stunned or something. Unable to comprehend something. And yet she knows she must go on. How I can read that, I'm not sure. I've never been there. Can't say as I've ever been stunned. But that's all I can read in her eyes and her posture and the fact she's standing before me, but doesn't seem to even see me.

"Madam Secretary?" I ask, not sure what else to say.

Elizabeth continues looking past me for a long moment, but then seems to re-engage with the world, with the room she finds herself in, with me. Although I seem to be an afterthought. In a moment she focuses on me. Something… some thought… some mission returns to her and I can see her posture change as if she finally figures out what it is that brought her here in the first place. "Maria," she says, although I can't read whether it is a question, a greeting or a realization.

"Yes?"

"What's the fidelity level?"

"Seventy-two." I rattle off knowing the statistic by heart and wishing it were much higher. I take it as a personal failure that we aren't even close to the specification.

"Is that good?"

It seems Elizabeth's brain isn't engaged in this conversation. She would know instantly that the spec is 98%. "Improvement is taking time." I offer to keep her engaged, not sure what she will do if she just walks away from me.

"Too much time." Elizabeth replies. But there is no scolding. No reprimand. No anger at my failure to deliver what I promised when I promised it. None of the hostility that has been the core of every meeting since we missed that first schedule milestone. At first I deflected her anger by explaining some things take more time than expected, especially when you are creating something for the first time as we have been with Arbiter. The first few meetings that excuse bought me cooperation. It bought time, such that we were now deeper into the project. More money had been expended. We were getter closer. No one wanted to snatch defeat from the jaws of victory. No one wanted to walk away from a half solution. An opportunity to close the whole thing out if we just keep at it.

Only that's not how complex software driven systems ever end up. There are always bugs to be fixed. Quirks that are unexpected. Annoying. Exasperating. Especially when you're in a bad place and you're praying that software is going to totally upend the best laid plans of the bad guys who are homing in on you. The super tools. That's what we've always been able to invent. Tools to us that were always magic to our adversaries.

But now we're the ones who are encountering magic when our systems break down because we haven't been putting the operations and maintenance dollars in to keep the technology at the forefront of human knowledge. Tools that are our best aren't up to the task of countering Xi's army. Xi's propaganda machine. Xi's plan to decimate us and achieve pre-eminence.

And Arbiter is a classic large-scale systems integration challenge. Make the hardware dance to the tune of the software. Only not only doesn't the software hear the music, but no one bothered to teach it to dance. And the hardware? It has two left feet and try as it may it has no idea how to take software into its arms and make beautiful music together. That's the job of software. Bring the sheet music with you babe.

Elizabeth nods towards the hallway. I rise and follow her out.

"How are you holding up?" she asks, although this is not an unusual question.

"With the go live a lot of pressure is off." I admit. "I'll recover."

"Good to know." Elizabeth seems to still be running on autopilot. We walk further and further from the team room where the remaining analysts are running validation scripts to see if we can tweak the learning algorithm to speed up the correlation process. So far all the gains have been minor. Although some on the team think they have an idea that might get us there faster.

Elizabeth seems to continue to be preoccupied. I'm not sure why she came down and asked me to join her when it seems clear she doesn't expect to engage me in any meaningful discussion. Maybe I should ask. But there's something about the determination in her walk that tells me this isn't a good time to mess with this woman. So I follow along quietly wondering what she's struggling with.

"You said seventy-two percent fidelity."

"Yes," I confirm immediately.

"Can you characterize that seventy-two percent? Is that seventy-two percent of all postings are eliminated or released according to the Ten Commandments, or…"

"Yes." I confirm so she doesn't need to complete the sentence which she seems to labor about. Why? I don't get it.

"Seventy-two percent of all attempted postings are automatically dispositioned by Arbiter in the same way that an analyst would disposition it."

"The average analyst, yes," I confirm.

"But what does that mean?" Elizabeth asks struggling with my response. "Is that good enough? Is it a correlation that would push us towards a more liberal or more conservative society over time? Is that a correlation that would ensure we never progress as a people because a new idea would never see the light of day? What does it mean?"

I pull on her arm to get her to stop, turn and look at me. "What are you trying to tell me?"

"I have to know," Elizabeth responds. "I have to know if there are no more people in the loop, what do we become? Is it different than what we are today? Because we only see something we would see today seventy-two percent of the time? Does that permit us to grow as human beings? To change? To explore new things and decide whether we want to embrace them? Or do we become only what we are seventy-two percent of the time? And twenty-eight percent something else that Arbiter tells us we should be?"

"You're scaring me Elizabeth." I step back from her, afraid she's had a mental breakdown. I've never seen one before, but I've never seen someone act this way before. "What are you trying to tell me?"

"I have to let you go."

"Let me... what are you saying? That I've been fired?" I'm trying to figure this out logically and the emotional reaction is hanging around my ears somewhere, barking at me, but I'm still not paying attention, "You're saying I've been fired?"

Elizabeth shakes her head. "Your positions have been eliminated."

"Eliminated. Just like all the shit you've had us disposition. Is that what you're saying? That I'm no more important than someone's pornographic picture you, or I or Sheila or someone else dispositions at the touch of a finger on a key?"

Elizabeth still seems stunned or something. She finally sits down on the floor, crosses her legs and straightens out the skirt she's wearing, so her knees are covered. She closes her eyes and shakes her head. I hear a deep sigh as she exhales. Letting go of whatever it was she'd

269

been keeping inside. I notice her shoulders drop as the tension releases, her face loses the tension evident there. I let her relax for a long moment.

"So my job's gone. Just like that."

Elizabeth exhales deeply again and seems to settle down. "Not just like that. But it is gone along with your whole team and my whole team."

"What?" I can't believe she's shut the whole project down.

"Arbiter is flying solo tonight," She informs me of the decision. It wasn't just me. It wasn't just my team. Someone, apparently not Elizabeth, decided time was up for good to get better. It was time to start the new day and see what happens.

"We on call back or is this really the end?" I clarify.

"The end. No improvements, no enhancements. No intent to leave the learning algorithms on. So please disable them before your team leaves."

"When?"

"Tonight," Elizabeth sounds like she can't believe it either, but has no choice. The end of the line. Time for all passengers to get off the train to tomorrow.

"I take it you didn't have any warning?"

Elizabeth shakes her head slowly. Can't look at me. Seems still in a state of shock with the realization she has failed. That her legacy will likely cause more tension in the emerging society. And some bright historian will point the finger directly to her and cite this moment as the cause of all the ills the world is suffering at that time. Some place in a future we can't see, but we can predict. The seeds of that future have been planted. It only awaits the decisions of birds who notice the seeds and come pluck them out of the ground to feed themselves in the shorter term than germination takes. I can hope there are plenty of birds these next few seasons. I'm sure Elizabeth is hoping the same.

"What can I do to help you?" I ask.

Elizabeth seems surprised I would ask such a question when she's just told me she's taken my job and my dignity from me. "Help?"

"Are you walking away? Resigning in protest?"

Elizabeth can't look at me, which tells me the answer is no. "Then you need help to wind the project down. I'll tell you what. I'm assuming you're not paying us after tonight, so I need to scrounge a few volunteers. The people on the team who really take a lot of pride in what they do. And that's most of this team, if you hadn't noticed. We may not have gotten you to 98%, but we advanced the state of the art in so many areas. They have a lot to be proud about. So I expect I'll get more than a few who will be happy to come in and wind things down. You know? "

"Why would you do that?" Elizabeth shakes her head.

## CHAPTER FIFTY-ONE: BRANDON McINERNY

I want to drink a cup of Magritte's tea. Want it to take the edge off things. But I'm at work. Sheila told me about falling asleep at lunch. How loopy I was when I was awake. I didn't realize it was having that kind of effect. I need to be more careful. Don't want the Secretary coming by and thinking I'm stoned or something worse. I haven't seen Elizabeth in a while now. She used to come by every day. Wanted to know what I'd found. But not in several days now. I wonder if she's thinking I'm not going to find them. Or maybe she's waiting for me to send her a report.

No tea. Not now. The CIA tool I'd requested finally arrived. It's sped up things unbelievably. It's doing most of the analysis I was having to do manually in only a few minutes. Not on every image, just those Arbiter has sent through for an analyst concurrence. That presumes that Arbiter is picking up on any blatant images and atomizing them. Anything it deems benign it simply posts.

I wait for the program to complete its scans. Looking at today's questionable images first. The tool has flagged only a few images. I look at them carefully. Look for anything that might be a symbol or attempt to communicate anything other than an artistic design. And that's often the hardest part. Deciding what is artistic and what is trying to communicate not an aesthetic, but a concept.

Nothing here. So I start the scan on everything attempted to be posted in the last week. I'll go back to the earliest files we have. This will take a while, but I've got time. Better to be busy than sitting here scratching my head, trying my best to figure out what someone has gone to great lengths to hide.

This scan will take a few minutes so I go into the Arbiter analysis files and realize they are empty. Nothing is being referred for analysis. Must be some system glitch. I look around and suddenly realize I don't hear the usual sounds on the floor. Sounds of analysts talking and working their queues. I don't even hear the air conditioning turning on and chilling the room to keep the temperature bearable with so many people crowded into a relatively small office space.

I get to my feet and walk down the hall. No one is in their cubes. The computer monitors are turned off. No heads down examining postings. No one leaning over the cube to talk to her or his neighbor about one thing or another. It's like a neutron bomb hit this place. It left everything exactly where it was, primed for the next day, but all living things were instantly vaporized, just as the analysts vaporized all those unacceptable postings. Is this someone's ultimate revenge on all of us analysts? Wipe us out in a single gesture just as we wiped out their attempts to influence the thoughts of their fellow countrymen?

This is freaky. I turn and literally run back to my cube. Make sure my monitor is up and the computer doing it's run. Then I get an idea. Maybe I should go down to Elizabeth's office. See if she's still working here. Not that I doubt that, but this is all too weird. Before I do, I look out over my cube to see if I can spot any human lifeforms. Nothing. No one.

Glancing around just in case I missed someone, I leave my machine to complete the run and walk slowly towards Elizabeth's office. I have to exit this wing and go up a flight of stairs. It's not until I get to the next level that I see someone walking. I push through the doors on this floor and follow a guy about my age into the men's room. "Morning." I greet him as he moves in to relieve himself.

"Too much caffeine," is his response as he lets loose with a torrent into the urinal.

"What's going on?" I try to be casual in my question.

"What do you mean?" he answers suspiciously.

"One floor down. You seen it?"

He looks over at me like I'm a nut case or something. "The Arbiter team?" he finally identifies what I'm talking about.

"Yeah. The Arbiter team. There's no one down there. It blow up or something?"

The guy almost laughs, "If it had blown up they'd be scrambling down there," He zips up and heads for the sink. "No. The Secretary got a directive. Shut down the analyst teams. Make it work as it is. So she did. Yesterday I guess if you say there's no one down there now."

"Holy shit," is all I can think of to say.

The guy takes paper towels to dry his hands and takes a look at me. "You weren't on the program or you would have gotten the message. So what's your problem with it being over?"

"That's the problem," I wash and grab the towels to wipe my hands. "It's not over, it's just beginning and there's no one steering the ship."

"That's what it was designed to do."

"But it's nowhere near ready," I inform him.

"Doesn't matter," He opens the door and gets ready to go back to work. "This government has always been the enemy of perfect, or even good. We can't afford perfect. And if it's good now, it won't be for long. Accept it or leave. That's always been the attitude," he steps out and the door closes behind him.

No need to go see Elizabeth now. I have my answer. Suddenly I realize Sheila must be sitting home today. Did she know what was coming yesterday when we went to lunch with Albert? Is that what they talked about when I passed out? I still don't know what happened. All I know is one minute I'm trying to have a conversation and the next it's dreamland. At least it wasn't nightmare city. As so many nights have been. Even though, I'm feeling edgy. Like I can't think straight. I can react. Do what I need to, but it's not like normal. Albert told me I'd be confused for a while after leaving the desk. I guess I just accepted his warning and have gone along with it. But I hope this passes soon because I keep having all these strange thoughts I never had even when I was on the desk for days and weeks at a time. Immersed in the worst images and accusations anyone could make about another human being. Thoughts that maybe I'm the one who is wrong, trying to change the natural order of the world by not letting people express themselves. That I need to do something about it. Why do I keep thinking I need to do something about Elizabeth and the people like her who are trying to change the right of freedom of speech to be the freedom to post your speech knowing that someone else will decide whether anyone else should ever see it? But if Arbiter went live yesterday, then there's only a machine between you and what you want the rest of the world to know. A machine! And that machine doesn't evaluate or make decisions about you the same way another person would. The decision is the result of an algorithm. Machine learning from a sample of human decisions. And even after that they couldn't get the fidelity of decisions to be anything close to a human's interpretation. I'm unfortunately starting to think like all those people whose outraged blog posts accuse the government of spying on us; of plotting to take guns from those of us who have them; to ship our good paying jobs overseas so someone who will take half the pay we've earned can do our jobs and leave us working as Walmart greeters.

I finally leave the men's room. Begin to walk back to my desk. Back down the stairs and into the ghost town that is now the floor where I work. Or at least where I think I still work. Will have to wait and see if I was among those terminated and just didn't get the message. I wonder what precipitated the termination of the development phase. Must have been something rather dramatic as I don't think anyone saw that coming. I sure didn't. But why didn't I? Albert terminated me weeks ago as part of the first phase of reductions. But it seemed that they were going to keep the small validation teams in place for the foreseeable future. Guess that future arrived a lot quicker than anyone anticipated.

Walking past the empty cubes makes me uneasy. I wonder about the people who were sitting in them yesterday. Where are they today? I know intellectually they must be home, in complete shock, or denial or whatever stage they may have reached in their psychological adjustment to the new reality that is their lives. They're probably doing exactly what I did that first day after. I didn't shower or shave. No need to. I didn't eat breakfast. Just wasn't hungry. I watched the news to see if there was any discussion about the reduction that had taken place. There wasn't. I should have known there wouldn't be because Arbiter wouldn't let any coverage of such an event pass. I scrolled through the news feeds I subscribe to, also to see if there was any reports about Arbiter. And of course nothing appeared. And of course I spent much more time reviewing what Arbiter and the remaining analysts let through than I normally would have. Busman's holiday I guess. Looking at the end product I rarely see anymore, rather than the inputs that may, or most likely, wouldn't make it out.

I sit back down at my desk. The routine is complete. I review the rest of the month of background pattern analysis. A few things, but I doubt any of them have anything to do with my persons of interest. The symbols that appear are subtly racist. If I were on the desk I wouldn't let them pass. But since I'm reviewing input postings rather than those that actually went up I can't tell what Arbiter did with these. As standard race baiting there are probably thousands of individuals out there who would have delighted in seeing these images. What they would have done other than have a moment of self-satisfaction that such images are shared sentiments, I have no idea.

I scroll through the department internal blog to see what it says about the reductions in force from yesterday. Probably shouldn't be surprised to find there is no mention of it. Just the usual notices about retirement counseling, debt reduction workshops and the upcoming all department family picnic. Don't think I'll be attending this year. But then I remember I did attend it last year with Sheila. We had a good time. It was nice to relax in a green field, sun on our faces, the sounds of kids running about, laughing and calling out to each other as they played their games. The Secretary was there with her husband. I had an opportunity to talk with him for a bit. Actually a nice person for a Harvard Law Professor. Notorious for being a hard grader. I wonder whether he will be there this year. Probably. Wonder what Sheila will do instead, since she won't get the invitation, even though she dedicated herself to this work for more than a decade. Used up and disposed of. That's just not right.

## CHAPTER FIFTY-TWO: SHEILA

I must look a fright. But I don't know what I can do about it now. I've been walking the streets since I left the department with my few possessions. Basically my picture of Lake Como, tissues, hand lotion and eye drops. Why is it I never took anything else to work since that's where I spent most of my waking hours? Unable to see the sun from my cube. Nothing green to look at until I went to the toilet. A fake plant greeted us coming and going. Never figured out if it was supposed to be symbolic or just some department mandate. Probably was some kind of air freshener given where it was located.

The light rain in my face makes me realize the picture of Lake Como will probably get ruined if I don't get in somewhere out of the mist. I don't want to go back to my apartment. Just can't face that yet, knowing it will be my only day time destination for as long as it takes to find another job, another career, another identity. I know where I want to go, but after the condition he was in at lunch with Albert, I'm afraid what I'll find. Probably a dead body where there was once a brilliant analytical mind.

I step into a shop entranceway, so I can get out of the rain for a moment to think. I glance at the shop windows. Formal wear. I have no occasion to wear such clothes. Frankly I'm surprised there are enough occasions for people to buy such clothes that a shop like this could stay in business. But formal wear isn't something you would buy over the net and have delivered. You want to try it on. See how it looks on you. Make sure they do any tailoring needed. The last thing you want when you're trying to look your best is for it to be too tight in the wrong places and just hang on you in others. So that all makes sense. A shop for formal wear is more to tailor the dress than sell it.

I briefly try to remember the last time I dressed up. And the longer

I think about that question the more it becomes clear that I have had no occasion to dress up in the entire time I've been in this country. Not since I graduated university in Sydney. They had that graduates ball they called it. I went with Alistair even though he really wanted to be there with Traci and everyone knew it except me. He spent the whole evening watching her and Roger. I wonder what ever happened to all of them. My classmates. People I spent years with, learning about myself and what I was good at doing. Learning how to work with others on team projects. Finding the strengths in each of us so the team project could be as good as possible. Standing here in the dark entranceway of a closed clothing shop I'm filled with memories of a time that was full of expectation, anticipation and hope. A time of laughter, learning and self-doubts that we all masked but carried with us every day. Why did we do that? I don't know, but I always felt it when we had late night conversations about what we thought the future held for us. Brave ambitions, but lesser expectations fueled by that lingering self-doubt. I've not had to prove anything yet, other than my ability to master academic concepts.

The rain is getting heavier. I can't stand here all night. Either I go and face Brandon or go back to my apartment, lying awake all night in my bed, unable to sleep. That's just not something I want to do right now. I spend most of my life alone. At this moment I just want to be with someone. And the only person I want to be with is the Brandon I knew from before the layoff. I just hope he's still somewhere to be found.

I dash between the rain drops to the street corner, look up at the sign to figure out where I am. Probably better to Uber since I'm not really sure where his apartment is in comparison to where I am. So I go back to the formal wear store entryway and call for a car.

Fifteen minutes later I'm standing outside Brandon's apartment door. I'm still soaked, with long stringy wet hair falling back, although water still gets through and runs down my neck. I feel the cold wetness down my back. While it isn't cold, it is cool enough that I'm shivering. I'm trying to decide if I should knock or not when the door opens. Brandon is looking at me first with a puzzled look, then one of concern, and finally relief. "I found you," he says and wraps his arms around me, folding me into him and warming me with his body heat. "You're shivering. Come in here so I can get you into something dry and warm."

I follow his lead as he still has an arm around me. This is the Brandon I was hoping to find.

He helps me out of my wet clothes, joins me in the hot shower, hugging me at first to warm me with his body heat, soaps me up and lets me rinse off. Then, he towels me off and lets me dress myself. His blue jeans pulled in with a belt so they will stay up, and a flannel shirt I've seen him wear a hundred times or more. I think it must be his favorite shirt, but only in the cold weather, which in Washington is most of the time. With the exception of those hot muggy summer days between July and August. Don't think I've ever seen him wear this shirt either of those months. He usually comes in with just a golf shirt, similar to the ones I wear, only in basic colors like white or gray. Don't think he even has one in a pastel like I wear those months.

Once I'm dry and dressed, with heavy wool socks on my feet that he wears with work boots on the snowy days, I feel the tension begin to drain from me. Warm and comfortable with my best friend. Maybe I can put all that's happened today out of my mind and just not think. That is what I want more than anything. To just be for a while.

I sit on the floor in front of his ratty old couch with a flower bedspread thrown over it. Brandon brings out two big steaming mugs. I smell the Chicken Noodle soup. He knows it's my favorite as it's what I always have for lunch on those cold wintery days at work. He passes one to me and joins me on the floor. I instantly begin to warm my hands against the mug. Absorbing the heat, pulling it into my soul. Wanting to melt the lump in my stomach. To just let it all go.

"Better?" he asks me with that smile I know so well, having studied it for a decade from across the room.

I nod and take a sip of the hot broth, only to find it still very hot, so I need to let it cool a bit before I try that again. "Are you?" I ask.

"I don't know what happened yesterday. But I was just out."

He apparently isn't going to share what he really thinks happened. There's a new cautiousness about him. He would tell me anything before. Whether he believed it or not. Often just to see what I'd say. Then he'd pick apart my arguments just for fun. Never seriously. And the more absurd the explanation, the more fun it would be. Then it would be my turn to cut up his explanations and see who could get to the most ridiculous explanation first. It would usually take us a while to declare a winner. We are both very competitive. And maybe that's why he has never wanted to take our relationship further. At least that's my guess. That he's too competitive and feels our relationship would dissolve into a competition to see who's right. I don't buy that. When we are together we banter and joke, but never seriously go head-to-head.

"Albert was trying to figure out how to get you home. Whether he was going to have to carry you out to an Uber."

Brandon laughs at that thought since Albert is shorter and probably forty pounds lighter than Brandon. But he almost instantly shakes that image off and comes back to look at me. "I'm sorry about yesterday. Not only because of my behavior, but because I wasn't there for you at the end of the day."

"Tough day," is how I sum it all up.

"Did you go home last night?" Brandon reaches behind him and brings out the soaked picture of Lake Como. "I like how you incorporated the rain so it looks a little more realistic."

He hands the picture to me. I look at it knowing it will never be the same. "Might as well throw it away. It's served its purpose."

I hand it back to him expecting him to toss it in the waste basket next to him, but he doesn't. Instead he takes a long look at it and then sets it on top of an end table. "We'll save that just in case you need it again. On another rainy day like this one."

"I don't ever want to be in this position again," I share with him, but not wanting to give him any more explanation. Having just been through this himself, I'm sure none is needed.

I reflect on the long night and day since Elizabeth came into our area and asked to speak to all of us at once. I found her approach unusual and her manner hesitant. As if uncomfortable about what she had to tell us. I was right as she even told us this action was not one she wanted to take at this time. However she had no choice. She wanted us to know she would ensure alternatives would be made available to us in time. "We were given five minutes to gather our possessions. That was it. Stop in the middle of whatever we were doing. No need to leave notes. No need to do anything other than shut off our machines."

Brandon nods in understanding of my feelings. He moves closer to make contact with me as we both sip our soup in silence. After a moment I jostle him with my elbow. "Mind if I ask you a personal question?"

Brandon hesitates. Another change from before. He glances at me to gauge my intent and shrugs.

"Who is she?"

"She?" Brandon didn't see this one coming.

"Arbiter sent me a clip. You were sitting next to this attractive woman…"

"Arbiter sent it to you?" It sounds like he can't understand how a clip of him ended up in Arbiter's decision files. "Who tried to post it?"

"Is she the reason you've withdrawn from me?"

Brandon has to think about my question. I don't like where this conversation is going. "She makes the tea that helps me not dream."

That's not an answer I expected, but don't know what it means. "And the man sitting across from you? What does he do?"

"He makes history."

"He's a history teacher?" I try to clarify?

Brandon shakes his head, but won't elaborate.

"I think I'll finish my soup and go." Something isn't right and he won't tell me what.

## CHAPTER FIFTY-THREE: JAVIER SANTIAGO

Jurgen and I are in his office waiting for the videoconference with Hua Kwan and Xi to begin. It's early for us, but late for Xi. We have another minute or two before the call is to begin so I ask Jurgen, "You've read the brief?

"I thought you weren't activating the sleeper cell until the others completed their work."

"Sabr was advised to act now and she did," I explain. "That has created some problems for us to continue to work in the background. The traditional means of instilling confusion aren't working. Their government is so chaotic the people don't pay any attention to our attempts to influence events. They just assume they are watching their government continue to make matters worse."

Hua Kwan comes into view on the screen. Xi is not with her. "Good Morning," I greet her without the formalities of three-party negotiations. This is a discussion between two federations who have a long history of sharing without the other federation knowing about the special relationship we share. We have to work very hard to continue that. To ensure those discussions do not look like a prior agreement has been reached. Even though in general an agreement has been already put into practice. Only Sabr doesn't know.

"I hope you are enjoying a most fruitful day in your part of the world." Hua Kwan responds.

"We are, thank you," Jurgen responds for us and falls silent to let us know he does not wish to discuss matters until his peer is present.

Fortunately Xi arrives shortly. He nods to us as he takes his seat. Another indication there is no need for protocol amongst us. "Have you implemented the framework from Bergamo between our two federations?"

Xi knows the answer to this question, but he is permitting us to confirm it for him.

"We have," I confirm. That is why I am on this call. To answer that question, not Jurgen.

Now it's Jürgen's turn, "Have you?"

Hua Kwan responds for UaTopia. "We have."

Xi nods in satisfaction. "Then we have a consistency between us on the framework issues, but only the framework issues."

"Correct." I respond as the senior party to the implementation architecture. "You have complete flexibility to insert new criteria into the Ten Commandments framework and the algorithms will present those decisions in a consistent manner."

"In which case they will not seem inconsistent with the Ten Commandments," Xi confirms.

"Yes," Hua Kwan nods to me so I will agree, which I do.

"That is correct."

"Well done," Xi appears to be pleased, but there is always an edge to his pleasure. "We have now brought our two federations closer in our opposition to the hegemons who have sought to restrain our ascendancy to global leadership."

"The hard work has just begun, Xi." Jurgen points out to redirect the discussion. "We must determine what new decision criteria we wish to insert into the common framework. As I remember from earlier conversations the first is, 'what is consistent with party policy and guidelines?' We weren't able to accept that previously since the policies of each federation are very different having grown from very different traditions and circumstances. Accepting them would have driven a wedge between us that would have negated the benefit of aligning the basic Ten Commandments."

Xi is impatient. Apparently we are keeping him from something. Probably another courtesan who has come to his chambers to restore his bliss. "I have read the report. The transition team has done what was asked of them. What else is it you wish to discuss?"

"You are aware that Sabr has activated her automated system," Jurgen responds with annoyance barely masked.

"Of course," Xi responds. "We fed her the false information about the capability of her machine to complete its own installation."

"We are grateful you were able to provide our summary to her secretary of defense," I respond as Jurgen doesn't have all the details, and in fact, neither do I, but can't let Xi know that. "However, she will soon discover it is based on an assumption we have validated previously will not hold up in the long run. Her system will appear to be operating as specified for a period of time. But all the while the actions will vary further and further from the standards, which will in and of themselves vary further and further from the Ten Commandments and the validation decisions from the system's reference group."

Xi glances at Hua Kwan. My Mandarin is a bit sketchy, but I'm able to determine she is telling him I'm taking credit for what his team did. Thanks for undercutting us when the lie she is telling will never be revealed to the great man. As the one person who determines what people learn about the world around them she can control the information flow to him as well. That's a power I'd like to have, but Jurgen is too involved in my area to permit it to happen.

"When her government falls into chaos our candidate will step into the void and impose order from the chaos," Xi recites. "And the result will be a division of the federation on geographic terms. Those closest to UaTopia will come this way. Those closest to EuTopia will join you."

"We have never agreed to the division of the Middle East," Jurgen reminds him. "The geographic distances would indicate the Persian Gulf as the dividing line in our estimation."

"We still believe the Red Sea to be the dividing line. We have never given up the claims that you arbitrarily established western boundaries when the Ottoman Empire was overrun by you at the end of the Great War. But the Ottoman Empire was formed from our nations a thousand years before. We have history on our side in how we make our claim. Your opportunistic exploitation of an ancient civilization is essentially the same as how you treated our nation when our Empire was replaced by the people. And that is the difference. In our case our indigenous people rose to rule our nations. In the Middle East, you brought beggars to thrones because they would support your claims and economic interests in that part of the world."

"Revisionist history will not be the basis for the division of UsTopia. The Middle East is geographically closer to Berlin than Beijing. That is the basis and that is how it will be determined," Jurgen isn't giving an inch.

Xi nods once to Jurgen. "Time will determine the outcome of this difference of negotiating positions. There is little expectation that UsTopia will replace its leadership in the next few months. So we may continue our disagreement while we work towards a resolution that will accommodate historic and geographic realities."

"Another way of saying that you will continue to give away infrastructure projects as a means of bringing the local governments closer and increasingly dependent upon you and your banks," Jurgen pushes back on Xi, since Xi clearly thinks he has the superior position at the moment.

"A moment ago you were the one accusing me of revisionist

history," Xi smiles. He loves to use Jürgen's words against him. It seems he's playing a game of 3D chess, always maneuvering his opponent into a space that constrains him in multiple dimensions.

"Since you have already agreed to disagree for the moment on how we treat the infinite sandbox, tell me, what is it that you most prize in the dismemberment of UsTopia?"

Xi smiles for the first time in this discussion, "There are many things a negotiator never reveals. Just as you would not answer that same question for me, I cannot oblige you with a response. But you pose an interesting paradox we both must confront. A bi-polar world will require us to paint the other as our enemy in order to motivate cooperation amongst the diversity of ethnicity residing within our borders. That is why we will never arrive at a one world solution to the question of what is the ultimate endgame of politics. If there was no external threat to focus neighbors, they would fight amongst themselves and bring the unipolar polity to an abrupt and uncontrolled end. That we cannot permit to occur. So that is the reason we can cooperate now, build commonality so that at our level we can diffuse the conflict that would destroy each other from outside our federations. But each also serves as the glue to keep our federations from destroying themselves from within."

"Chairman Xi, you are a wise leader and a visionary philosopher. You understand the hearts of all men, even though the diversity of our planet creates a wall between us that is hard to penetrate. But since you have raised the issue that will predominate our terms in office once we have brought an end to the current state of affairs, let me paint a slightly different outcome of the coming transition. We may claim the remnants of UsTopia. We may exert military force to ensure compliance. And then our systems of Truth will in time bring those new citizens into our webs of conformity. But that transition period will not be brief. We cannot expect it to take a week or year or decade. We will be consumed by the effort of integration for the rest of our lives. We have spoken in the past of the American democratic tradition that is deep seated in these people. A strange perversion of history that was a doomed experiment from the first. It only survived because oceans and a vast native land mass isolated the colonies and their attempts at self-determination. The Scots fought a series of wars at nearly the same time and were unsuccessful in breaking the hold of the imperialist British. Only an ocean made it impossible for those same forces to impose their will on the Americans. So it was a world of distance that prevailed. Not a superior idea. We can crush that spirit, but it will take twice as long to extinguish the idea as it survived."

Xi glances at Hua Kwan, says something to the effect that Jurgen knows western history but not Asian. "Jurgen. We have a long memory. We are also much more patient than history would paint your people. You have always used armies to cause regime change overnight. You then kept the armies in place to impose order. We build economies. Very different approaches."

The scary thing is Xi is right.

## CHAPTER FIFTY-FOUR: BRANDON McINERNY

After Sheila leaves I drink five cups of Magritte's tea. I know I may get a little loopy as that seems to be a side effect. If I don't, the nightmares will ride through my attempt to sleep. And I'm exhausted from not sleeping even with the tea. The only night I didn't eventually have nightmares was the one where I drank as many cups as I could just before going to sleep. That one night is what I've been trying to recapture since. One dreamless night in as long as I can remember. And now that's all I want. One more night with no visions, no images of little blonde girls, no words shouted in my ears, insulting my intelligence and making me want to puke.

I'm about to start a sixth cup when I hear a faint knock on my door. Has Sheila changed her mind? I hope I can comfort her and not share a night of nightmares when she has her own to deal with. I set down the cup with the fresh tea bags and let the water continue to boil. In a moment I reach the door and open it to find a woman standing with her back to me. It's not Sheila. "Magritte?" is the only name that comes to me.

She spins around and pushes me back into the apartment. Closes the door behind her and bolts it. She then leans against the door listening for footsteps, I presume. "What…"

Magritte reaches around and puts her hand on my arm, but continues to listen. We stand like this for at least five minutes, a very long time to stand there listening to the kettle boil. I only want to pour the cup of tea, but am afraid to move while she listens. Finally she notices the sound of the boiling water, "Do you need to get that?"

She lets me go and I pour the water into the tea cup before placing the kettle on a cold burner. I listen hoping to understand what she's doing as I return to the living area. She has moved away from the door

290

and taken up residence on the ratty couch with the flower cover over it. She seems on edge, her focus flitting around the room, but mostly concentrating on the door, as if she expects someone to knock at any moment.

I ask, "Would you like a cup of tea?" Then I think that when someone comes to visit I should offer something to eat as well, but I only have instant Chicken Noodle soup. "Or cup of soup?"

Magritte looks at me like I must be from another planet. "How can you be thinking of food at a time like this?"

I guess the answer is no, so I sit down next to her balancing cup number seven while it cools. I need probably one or two more to hopefully get that dreamless sleep. "What's the problem? Why are you here?"

She looks at me like she's thinking I'm putting her on. I have to know what's happened, and yet I'm acting like it's no big deal. But then the whole room is starting to be enveloped in a fog. Not a dense one yet, but by cup eight it should be, and hopefully that's all I'll remember in the morning.

"Ichabod."

"He coming over? I thought it wasn't a good idea for us to be seen together, which reminds me…"

Magritte shakes her head, "They picked him up. Ichabod. They picked him up and he's in jail."

The room is beginning a slow spin through the haze of the rising fog obscuring my understanding of the world I inhabit. "They… Ichabod… jail."

Magritte takes the cup of tea from me and sniffs it. "How many of these have you had tonight?"

"I don't know. More than one. Can't sleep... have to have... enough."

Magritte sets the cup on the end table on the other side of her, slaps my face and watches for my eyes to focus.

"What was...?"

She slaps me again, only harder this time.

"Whoa. What did I ..."

Magritte stands up and unbuckles her pants, lets them fall to the floor. She's not wearing any underwear. This is one hell of a way to bring me out of the fog from her herbal tea. But it seems to be working. She removes her top. Same thing. No underwear. She lifts me up under my arms, pulling my shirt over my head. I'm standing in front of her nakedness feeling myself coming slowly out of the fog that had begun to envelop me. She unfastens my belt, opens the fly to my pants and pulls them down. I step out of them without thinking, although a different part of me has begun to think, and begins to rise to the occasion.

I feel her hand around that part of me that has always had a mind of its own. She squeezes it until it stiffens, and then she pulls it and me behind her to the bedroom. Even in the fog I'm struggling to erase I'm complying with her wishes, but conscious that my bed is probably a mess, and I can't remember when I last changed the sheets. Why am I worried about that? She certainly doesn't seem to be.

She pulls me down on top of her. The next thing I know I find my other self inside of her.

It's morning. I see light around the corners of the window shade.

Sheila's here. She's lying across my chest just as she did after the first time. But something's different. She doesn't smell the same. I don't smell the shampoo in her hair I lathered in from when we shared the shower. When was that? How many hours ago? I don't know. Now I notice her hair color's different. This isn't Sheila. Suddenly I remember. Magritte. The memories of a wild night of almost insatiable pleasure exchanged. No matter how many times we climbed to the peak experience she seemed ready to start over. I have no idea how many times we reached that climax, or at least I did. Did she? I don't know. I could ask her, but that would be impolite. I'd probably not like the answer, if she even told me the truth.

She must feel me moving, although I think I'm being still. Maybe she can hear my heart beating faster for I'm sure I'm reacting to the memories. Getting ready in case she wants to pick up where we last left off. Could I even do it? No idea.

Magritte moves her head, brushing her cheek across my chest. She turns and kisses my nipple, licks it and then sucks on it. She rises just enough to come up on me and engage my mouth pushing her tongue in and slowly moving her tongue in and out, then sucking the air out of my mouth before ending in a kiss. She lifts herself up just enough to look into my eyes. She evaluates something about me. I'm not seeing love, like I see in Sheila's eyes. I'm seeing someone evaluating whether she's had the effect on me she wants. Does she have me completely in her power now? Will I do anything she wants? Or does she have to entice me further?

What do I say to her? I don't want to spoil what she's given me. Don't want to end it if there's more to come. But I also need to go to work this morning. While I might be able to come in late, I'm going to have a problem if I don't show up until noon, if at all. Could always call in sick. But don't want to break the spell of the moment. "Was that for me or for Ichabod?" I finally decide to ask.

Magritte runs her right hand through her hair, pulling it back out of her face. She repeats the nipple kiss and moves on to my mouth, ending in the same vacuum kiss. She then reaches down for me, squeezes repeatedly until I stiffen. She pulls me inside and rides me, slowly at first but with increasingly rapid movements, longer and longer movements against me bringing a rising tension I wasn't sure could be found anywhere in my body after so many releases during the night. When it comes, it literally explodes, but is over in only a moment. She has certainly taken everything I had and left me depleted. She won't be able to repeat this I'm sure. However, she surprises me taking me in her mouth and stimulating me with her tongue until I respond and this time the build is even more intense than the one just before. She knows every means of enticing an orgasm out of a guy, and I think she's tried them all on me. I must either be one hell of a turn on for her, or she wants something very badly. Needs to make sure I'm a lost cause. Totally needing her affections.

She returns to lie beside me. Her head on my chest. "That answer your question?"

She runs her hand over my chest, down over my abdomen and then lightly touches that part of me she has come to know so well. Only this time her magic touch does not get a response. I hear her chuckle in recognition that she has finally exhausted my ability to respond to her. "What did you like most?"

"Every second," is my honest response. At least every second I can remember as the early orgasms are just a foggy memory.

"I need to stay here."

"Why?"

"They have Ichabod. They may be looking for me."

I have to reach back to the conversation of last night. Ichabod. Right. "Why do they have Ichabod?"

"FBI came to his apartment. Took him in to custody. They must be looking for me if they have him."

"Why did the FBI take him?" She's not telling me what I need to know.

"It's time," is all she will say in response.

"For what?"

Magritte reaches up and touches my lips, gingerly, tenderly. Almost as if she's not expecting to kiss them again, or am I imagining something? She rises up and sits across me so I can see her, all of her, but most importantly her face. Her eyes. She looks down at me as if she's committing my face to memory, like someone saying good-bye for the last time.

"What is it?" I have to ask.

"I need you to do something..."

"Here comes the ask, the favor I can't refuse..."

## CHAPTER FIFTY-FIVE: SHEILA

I was confused by Brandon's call. I thought we'd reached the end when I realized he was never again going to be the same person I'd fallen in love with. That a decade as an analyst hadn't brought us closer together, but had built a wall of fears that we would only reinforce the nightmares and the warped sense of perspective we'd both developed over the past decade. But then he wanted to do dinner in a real restaurant. Not the hole in a wall we'd been to with Albert. A restaurant with a linen tablecloth and waiters who speak French or Japanese, or some such language. Wherever the food is from.

Brandon picks me up from my place wearing a shirt I've only seen him wear once. In fact, I'd thought it was something he'd borrowed since I'd never seen it since. I don't remember the occasion. Some recognition he'd received from the Department when he was still getting started. Maybe it was when he was recognized for writing the Ten Commandments handbook that became our on-line reference for interpreting the standards we used as analysts. Never thought much about how influential he'd become because of that one thing he'd done on his own time. A tool he'd created for himself that every analyst referred to at one time or another. In fact, as I remember, Albert had discovered it by accident. He was talking with another analyst about what how to interpret the Commandments. The analyst said he'd not had any real issues since Brandon lent him a copy of his 'cheat sheet'. At least that was what everyone referred to it as until management got hold of it. Couldn't use that title as it implied the work was a daily test, even though for many of us it clearly was early on. "Special occasion?"

Brandon semi shrugs as if he wants to down play his own behavior, which includes how he's dressed for the occasion. "I thought it would do us both good to do something different," is his response, although it reveals he's been thinking about us. Hopefully he's come to a realization about the barriers he's erected between us. How we're going to resolve them. But I'll have to wait and see.

The restaurant is white table cloth, but there's still not many tables. Not a hole in the wall, but clearly a small ethnic place. As we take our seats, I glance at the menu to figure out what kind of cuisine. Somali. Never have eaten it so I'm not sure what to expect. "Why did you choose this place?"

"Albert comes here."

I suddenly realize that if all the analysts are gone that maybe Albert lost his job too. "You talk to Albert since..."

"Did I talk to Albert today?" Brandon knows where I'm going. "I told him I wanted to take you out and he suggested this place. Said it was better than the usual place."

"That's not what..."

"He wanted to join us. Commiserate since all three of us are now ex members of the analyst team. But I told him I needed some time with you. Alone."

Alone? Maybe... "What's he going to do now?" I need to ask right out since he's not telling me what I want to know on his own. Why is he being so reluctant to tell me anything?

"Same as us. Get on with life."

"Did you ask?" like I'm pulling teeth.

Brandon shakes his head, "If he wanted me to know he would have said something."

"So you're assuming he's just sitting home and starting the long search for life after a career has come to a screeching halt."

"Is that how you're thinking about it?" Brandon looks at me

curiously. "Life after?"

"My parents advised me not to take this job," I suddenly remember. Hadn't thought about that until he asked. "Said it wouldn't be a good thing for me in the long run, working for the government. Said it would limit me. Not let me express myself."

"Is that what you wanted to do when you were growing up?"

I'm the one who sort of shrugs now. "I didn't really know. Tried a bunch of things in summer jobs and school activities. I originally thought I'd be a journalist. I liked doing the news on television. Bringing truth to the people. Organizing what they needed to know about world and local events. I enjoyed that."

"Was that in school or a summer job?"

"I had a summer job at a local television station in Sydney. They gave me a job as a news writer. I'd go out on an assignment, learn about some event, and then go back and write the summary for the anchor or correspondent to read."

"So you weren't on camera," Brandon is trying to understand what I did versus what I described.

"I was. Got to read my event summary on camera for the weekend news when one of the correspondents went on vacation. She had an accident and didn't get back for a month, so they kept me on until she returned."

"So an unexpected chance," Brandon seems to be wanting to keep this discussion going for some reason, like he has something to say he isn't ready to get to. "If you liked it so much, why didn't you go back when you graduated? They apparently thought you were doing a good job if they kept you on."

"I considered it, but a friend came here." I remember aloud. "Said it was the Promised Land. Life in a big city, guys and important work.

What more could a girl from Australia want?"

"Why do you describe it like that? I don't understand."

"Maybe you've not noticed but Australia's a long way from anything. So to come to the center of the universe is like a dream. To be where all the stories we see or read about in the media? Well, that's like a validation for someone like me. An opportunity to see if I'm really as good as I think. Can I compete with the best of the best? I can I do what they do? I kind of hoped that after a few years in the Department I'd be able to cross over. Go back to the media once I understood how it's regulated here. But what I'd not expected was how you disappear when you go into a job like this. You spend all your time doing the job. There's no time to do things outside work where you could build a credential."

"Didn't you keep a tape of your on-air work back home? Trot that out to get an interview?"

"I have a copy of it, but when you see me on the tape... well, what I see when I look at myself is someone with potential, but clearly raw and not relaxed or polished."

"You're too hard on yourself. You ought to go look at them again. You might see more than potential."

The waiter comes by to take our order. Brandon looks at me, "Albert told me what to order. You good with his recommendation?"

I nod, Brandon orders and the waiter leaves us to our conversation.

"How's your assignment going?" Time to find out why he really wanted to do dinner.

Brandon frowns which tells me all I need to know. "Don't know as I'm any closer to finding the persons of interest than when I started. Know where not to look, but haven't found the digital footprints or signatures that would identify them."

"Anyone else working this with you?"

Brandon shakes his head, "That's part of what I don't understand. If this is such an important deal, why only me?"

"Have you asked?"

Brandon doesn't answer my question, but decides he has to say something else, "You know I've been unable to sleep without nightmares for as long as I can remember. Leaves me exhausted most of the time."

"Albert told me it gets better…"

"He doesn't have a photographic memory," Brandon responds angrily, but I'm not sure who he's angry with. "I can't forget. I can't shut it off. Even during the day now images just keep interrupting whatever I'm doing. And there's this one image my mind keeps playing with until last night. I finally discovered what my mind has been trying to tell me."

I'm almost afraid to ask, but do, "What?"

"There's this image of a little blonde girl. She's sitting on her heels in front of someone on a bed."

Unfortunately my mind jumps to a conclusion about that picture, but I don't know what significance it has for him.

"Both are nude." He completes the picture as I expected. "I saw that picture a hundred times and every time I saw a tiny bit I'd not seen before. The trail my mind was following. Last night I finally saw enough of his face to know who he is."

"What about her?" I ask.

"The man is me. The girl is you. Only I'm real old and you're maybe seven. Don't you see? My mind is telling me my life is nearly over and you're just getting started. You have your whole life before you and I don't..."

"We're the same age," I protest. "So your dream doesn't make any sense."

"It has nothing to do with age. What my mind is telling me is I'll never regain balance in my life because I just can't let go of everything I've been seeing, reading and thinking about for the last decade. You will."

"Is that why you've been pushing me away?" I demand to know.

"You don't want to be with me. Most nights I wake in a panic, sweat soaked, over and over again. I've tried everything to have a dreamless night's sleep. Not going to happen."

"What are you saying?"

"You need to go home. To Australia. There's no future here, for either of us. But you can start over. Do the evening news. You know more about broadcast journalism than anyone I know."

Impulsively I respond, "Only if you'll come with me..."

## CHAPTER FIFTY-SIX: ELIZABETH WARDEN

The cabinet meeting is late getting started because Sabr hasn't arrived yet. The rest of the Cabinet members are all sending notes to one person or another on their cell phones. Everyone's head is down except mine. I'm looking around at the others, trying to understand what is so engrossing. But I need a moment to contemplate what Sabr is expecting of me now.

Sabr enters the room with her entourage following. She takes her seat in the middle of the table and the others take seats along the wall as usual. Everything about this is familiar now, although I sense, what probably no one else in the room does.

"Ladies and gentlemen," Sabr greets us. "Good morning. We have a busy agenda. I suspect we will not get to everything so I would appreciate it if you could be concise. This is intended to only identify the key events of the day, not solve them all here. I know you all like quality time on your issue, but if we did that we would be in this one meeting all week. So there is only one where we may take a little deeper dive than usual and I want to start there. If we get behind schedule early on, then the rest of you will either be short or we simply won't get to everyone. Your choice, but I still need to be aware of anything that could require a decision from me today. Elizabeth?"

I look around the room and take a deep breath. "Morning. Today is a day we will probably look back on at some point and ask what in the world were we thinking? What I mean by that is Arbiter is live. We have stepped through the looking glass and now all of the decisions about what gets posted, what broadcast gets aired, what issues discussed are all decided by algorithms, Artificial Intelligence, the machines are deciding our fate without anyone reviewing and potentially reversing a course of action. So now we will see. Does

Arbiter live up to its promise or does it unleash pent up fury in venues we aren't prepared for? We have to be very aware how people react, how they express themselves differently…"

## JAVIER SANTIAGO:

Jürgen's cabinet meeting has come around to me. I'm the last speaker as I often have immediate actions other members of the cabinet must address as soon as we leave the meeting. Today is no different. "I have added new criteria to the decision matrix for postings. No longer will we accept anything that questions a decision by our government. No dissent of any kind."

Walter Stoessel, Minister of Defense motions to me that he has a question, "Minister, how do we deal with the intelligence service? Are my analysts seeing raw feeds or are they only able to view intermediated situational information?"

"There are no exceptions," I respond. "If your analysts see unmediated information then there is an opportunity for individuals to communicate a different version of a situation. We simply can't have that."

"But Minister," Stoessel continues. "If my analysts can't be sure they are seeing all that is occurring, how are they to know what resources must be dispatched to deal with it? What you are suggesting is totally unacceptable. My analysts must see the situation for what it is. Otherwise the outcome will be much worse."

"What does that matter?" I push back. "No one will know because our system will simply not permit anything but the truth as we wish it, to be communicated. And if the situation does not end as we wish, the world will never know."

"You're creating dissonance," Stoessel points out. "People will come to understand that there is a difference between reality and their reality. What do we do about that? My soldiers respond to events. They are there. They see what happens and how it ends. How do they deal with conversations subsequently where people inform them something else happened? They can show the soldier the blog or describe what they saw on television news. How do my soldiers deal with the difference?"

"You tell them the truth, as our system reports it, is the truth."

**HUA KWAN:**

Xi listens expressionlessly as the Minister of the Economy explains why the recent currency devaluation has not had the expected improvement in export sales. "We are monitoring the situation closely, but at the moment I am recommending patience. The markets will respond as soon as other technical factors work through the system."

I see the nod from Chairman Xi. "Today is a momentous day for our federation. Today is the beginning of a new world order to come. Today our systems to establish the truth have become fully autonomous. Artificially Intelligent is the term everyone uses to describe our systems. But that is not the case. The Party determines what the machines decide. The Party determines what the people know. The Party establishes what is truth and what is not. We are entering an age where our people will only know one truth. When they visit EuTopia, they will see our truth even there. The island federation will truly become more and more isolated as their truth migrates further and further from the truth known around the world. They will experience growing dissonance, greater conflict and greater suspicion of their governing institutions. For when their people visit any other nation of the world, the truth will be different. And how can one federation be telling their people the truth when every other nation knows differently?"

Chairman Xi decides it's time for him to put the whole project into perspective. "We have executed flawlessly on our plan to disrupt those who disrupted our Middle Kingdom in the nineteenth century. Bringing western weapons, western technology and western ideas into our peaceful kingdom. They sought to plunder us, steal our wealth and enslave our population with their opium, their religions, and their naval ships. It has taken over a hundred years for our people to find their voices. A hundred years to learn the ways of the western nations and beat them with their own technologies. A hundred years to harness our potential to lead the world much as we led our world for a thousand years. So now is our time. We watch as the old imperialists implode on their own technologies, their chaotic governance and divisions in their very beliefs."

**ALBERT CARTER:**

Elizabeth found the money to have me write a transition plan. How to keep Arbiter operational without the contractor who designed, built and was under contract to maintain it until Sabr changed her mind and pulled the plug. It's costing a lot of money in termination payments, but Elizabeth was given no choice in the matter. At least that's her side of the story. I don't doubt it. Elizabeth has always been forthright with me. Probably too much so. Giving me insights that were not commonly known, but probably helped me do my job better. Motivate the team when things were up in the air, better manage the final transition. At least I was able to tell the team she was working with the Office of Personnel Services to provide opportunities in other departments as they occur over the next year. Insufficient. But at least it was something. A shred of hope. An indication that at least Elizabeth cared about what would happen to them.

I knew this was going to be the outcome of all the work we put in to bring this system on line. No system ever gets fully implemented because the requirements change during the period the system is being built. So the end point keeps moving. How you get there often has a huge impact on the design limitations and compromises made along the way. This isn't my first rodeo. I saw where things were going, although I followed the Pied Piper's siren song. Believed Elizabeth's ability to manage the contractor. Last time I'll believe a Harvard Law Professor has what it takes to deliver a multi-billion-dollar complex system that breaks new ground. I probably shouldn't blame her. The system was begun under her predecessor, who developed the initial specifications and signed the contract. So she inherited something that fundamentally is a contradiction. A system capable of evolving with us and shaping what we become by determining what information is shared across the spectrum of media. Only face-to-face communication is exempt from Arbiter. And that's only because they couldn't figure out how to regulate that too.

Danny Martin walks by, sees me in my office and stops. "Glad to see you're still among the living," and I can tell he is genuinely happy to see me.

I nod as I am too. "What are you hearing?" I ask.

"More changes coming," sounds like he's not happy about them, which would mean he has some specifics.

"Willing to share?" I ask.

"Sure what little I do know." As Elizabeth's confidant he always knows more than is officially known. He steps into my office and closes the door. Apparently he's going to confide in me. I've had a few beers with Danny and apparently he trusts me since he never heard anything he told me repeated. "Seems the Vice President has been a naughty boy," Danny frowns about how to put this. "Coercive harassment of his Chief-of-Staff. Only came to light when she took an overdose and tried to kill herself."

"Meghan?" I'm incredulous. I know her. Or I should say I've met her. I can see where the Vice President would be tempted. Apparently he was more than tempted. Apparently she felt coerced into going along.

"He's resigning and Sabr is expected to nominate Elizabeth for his position, subject to Senate confirmation."

"Is that why Sabr terminated the Arbiter contract?" I immediately wonder.

"I have no insight on that, and frankly neither does Elizabeth. Something's going on that Sabr got wind of. The next thing anyone knew she threw the switch and tossed the contractor."

"She having someone come in to check the system integrity?" I ask, suspicious of Sabr's behavior. It doesn't make sense, unless…

"Elizabeth is, but don't know if it was at Sabr's request. That's probably why she kept you on. What are you doing, anyway?"

"Transition plan. But it's generic. She didn't give me any instructions about integrity checks." Then another thought occurs to me. "Who's in line to replace Elizabeth here?"

"Rumor is one of the junior Senator's from a safe state, but they're going to vet her first. Don't want a public discussion until Sabr knows she's safe. The VP is a huge embarrassment."

## CHAPTER FIFTY-SEVEN: BRANDON McINERNY

I ease out of bed, sweat covered from the nightmares that have paralyzed me since I fell asleep. Magritte is still asleep. I don't want to wake her. I'm actually surprised she's not awake since today is the day she's been waiting for. She and Ichabod. Although she doesn't seem to know what happened to him since the FBI picked him up. And there's really no way of finding out without drawing attention to herself. Another societal benefit of Arbiter. Since there is no news about terrorist activity, the terrorists have to work at a handicap. One of their team disappears, they have little chance of finding out what happened. Before Arbiter, they would often know before the police, unless the police were watching the blogs and television news. Allowed them to escape detection and leave the area.

The shower is hot, and I let it run longer than usual. More soap than usual. It's like I'm trying to wash away my feelings about what I know. What I'm about to do. Something just totally unimaginable even a few days ago. And thinking about unimaginable, I keep seeing Sheila's face when I told her to go back to Australia. It was like I'd destroyed the last shred of hope she had. She just sat there after I told her going back with her was not possible. That I was past the point of ever being able to lead a normal life. I could never ask her to share the existence I've already been reduced to. She didn't get it. Couldn't see what I was saying. Maybe it was because I was wearing that shirt. I knew I shouldn't have worn it. I was dressed up like when we were making a difference, but saying I was down and out. The two just seemed incompatible. I don't know why I did that. But when l left her on the street outside her apartment for the last time, she looked at my shirt for a long time before turning her back on me and going in.

The hot water runs over my head. I watch it go down the drain, like my life. How did I ever get to this point? Beyond redemption.

Beyond salvation. I have become that which I've spent the last decade deleting. In a few hours I will delete myself. For the greater good, at least that's what Magritte would have me believe. I know she does… believe it. But then she's just sending me off and not doing it herself. But I get it. She couldn't. Not because she's not capable, but she's just not going to be in the right place to do it.

It's getting late. I don't want to draw attention to myself by coming in later than usual. Although there's no one on my floor to see me coming and going anyway. At least there wasn't yesterday. Who knows who all may be working there today? A new contractor maybe? So I towel myself dry, paddle into the bedroom and quietly get dressed. Usual work clothes, with one addition. Today I'm wearing a gray sport coat. I think I've only worn it once. That was my college commencement exercises, where it was required attire. That means it's been hanging in my closet for over a decade without a single use. Have to brush off the dust. There. Presentable even if not fashionable.

I touch my left pocket. Magritte's present is there. Another look at myself in the mirror. I nod to my reflection and close my eyes before walking out the door. I don't want to think about what I'm about to do. If I start thinking about it, I don't know if I can actually go through with it. But between the nightmares, and exhaustion, and being discarded by the department like that. By Albert, who I thought was my best friend, other than Sheila… what's the use?

The bus comes by, picks me up. I try not to think about anything on the way in. I look out the window at the office buildings and shops that constituted my morning and evening commute for a decade. The shops I've visited, the offices I've not. I don't even have any idea who works in them all day. But Washington is the center of government for the federation. It seems to grow almost exponentially in size, the number of people attempting to live here, and the influential place it holds in world affairs. I was drawn here like a bear to honey. Only after a decade, all I have to show for it is the bee stings.

My stop. Time to get off and go through security. Just another day.

"Morning," I mumble as I go through the badge reader and metal detectors. "Happy Friday."

The guard I've known for years responds, "Happy Friday," and a moment later I'm inside walking towards my cube.

Danny Martin comes around the corner as I do. "Hey, Brandon. Albert's still here. Working a plan or something. You ought to go see him. Think he's feeling real stressed out not knowing when his last day for real is going to be."

"Hey, Danny. How you doing?"

"Holding things together, but barely," he glances at my suitcoat. "Special occasion?"

"Trying to change my image," I respond.

"You stop by and see Albert. I think it would really help him," and Danny disappears through the double glass doors into the Secretary's office suite.

The building seems quiet for some reason. More quiet than usual. Even more so than yesterday. Does that mean even more have left for good? What's going on? Are they doing a wholesale house cleaning of staff? No, if something like that was going on Danny would have said something. In a minute I've found my desk. I'm taking my seat, and checking the last background checks. I've now completed the analysis and have a brief report to give to Elizabeth. I have to decide what the next phase should be. I've done all the standard kinds of searches. Even a few like the backgrounds analysis that require special tools and training. I need to come up with a new approach or Elizabeth won't even want my report. She will dismiss the project just like the Arbiter contract. Then where will I be?

How do you find someone who doesn't want to be found? I'm trying to decide what to do next when Albert appears. "Glad to see you finally woke up. Came by at your usual time and no Brandon. What's

310

going on with you?"

He slides into the chair next to my desk that no one ever sits at. I usually throw my coat over it in the winter and sometimes leave a sandwich if I bring one in which, I often do when I'm running a ten-hour shift. But not today. The chair is open and inviting to Albert. "And what's with this suitcoat? Someone die and you got to go to a funeral or something?"

"Hey," I ignore his questions. "I was going to come see you once I get my report done. You got any ideas how I might find persons of interest who don't want to be found?"

"You haven't found 'em yet?"

I shake my head and wait.

Albert seems lost in thought, "I'm sure you've done all the usual stuff, public source, signals and pattern recognition, biometric..."

"I have."

Albert nods and then looks back at me. "I'd do a honey pot."

"I don't know that one. It a new tool?"

Albert shakes his head, "You place ads... In those ads you reference something the persons of interest would want to know more about. You wait for someone to come asking questions. That's either your person of interest or someone who can take you to him or her."

"Honey pot," I repeat.

"Like a pot of honey that attracts bears and other critters."

I nod again in understanding, "How you doing? Danny said the Secretary's got you writing a plan or something. That just a short-term gig?"

"Maybe to the end of the month…"

"What then?"

"Maybe I'll come over and help you, if you're still here," Albert winks as he's probably pretty sure I won't be. If only he knew.

I give him my semi shrug, "Maybe we can do lunch… tomorrow. I've got to give this report to the Secretary today and I'll suggest your honey pot. Thanks."

"You kicking me out?" Albert acts surprised. "Yeah, lunch tomorrow would probably be good. I'll probably be all planned out by then and be looking for some comic relief."

"In that case you've come to the wrong place. Comic relief is down the hall on the left, right next to the bathroom."

Albert puts his hand on my shoulder, "Hang in there Brandon, better days are coming." I listen to his retreating footsteps. Think about honey pots and not making lunch tomorrow.

Five minutes later I have the report finished, complete with recommendations for the next steps in the investigation. Even I think that section is weak. At least Albert gave me something of substance I have been able to use. I check the Secretary's schedule. I knew about when the report would be finished and scheduled time today even before Magritte came to me with her demand. I wonder what the Secretary's response will be to my report. She must believe this problem is very hard to solve, that even the more powerful FBI tool will only take me so far. Does she really think this approach will identify the persons of interest she's looking for?

I stop in the bathroom to wash my hands one more time, get stock of myself, check my appearance before I go in to see her. Only for some reason, after relieving myself, I can't seem to stop washing my hands. I scrub them and scrub them more. I rinse and lather them up anew, scrubbing and scrubbing… I finally get hold of myself and rinse then turn away from the sink with my wet hands dripping. I sit against the sink for a moment, take a deep breath and let it out slowly. I can do this. Must do this. It's the only way…

The paper towel is the final stop before I complete my journey to the Secretary's office. "Morning Ebony. She ready for me?" I ask Elizabeth's administrative assistant, who is smiling at me as I come in. I don't read anything into Ebony's smile as she seems to smile at everyone, even those who have come to complain about one thing or another.

"Sure, you can go on in."

I open the door and see Elizabeth standing at her window, looking out on the White House. Didn't realize until just now that is her view. Coming to work every day and looking out at the place you thought you should be must be just killing her. To report to the one person who had bested her in the election she had prepared for like no other. And yet she still fell short. A constant reminder of her failure to achieve the goal she set. It's not like what I feel. But somehow I understand the dilemma. Continue to serve the country that rejected her, or go back to Harvard and prepare the next generation of litigators and leaders, hopefully. Maybe one of them would achieve what she was unable to.

"Brandon, I hope you have good news for me," Elizabeth turns to look at me.

"I don't have a list of names for you, but I did find patterns of interest, even though I don't have the persons of interest… at least not yet."

Elizabeth nods absently, as if her mind is engaged elsewhere. She is either considering what I've said or something else altogether. I can't tell which. She muses in silence for a long moment then looks up at me. "We believe we have one of them in custody."

Ichabod…

"FBI has photos of a woman he was seen with. We're looking for her as well. It's probably only a matter of time before we find any others."

"Then my work is nearly done," I realize aloud.

"Nearly?" Elizabeth looks at me curious at my choice of words.

"I'd like to point out a couple of the patterns I discovered, which I think you will need to be aware of. I sent you an email earlier this morning with my report. It will only take a moment."

Elizabeth considers my request, "You sent it this morning?"

"Let me show you," I come around behind her desk and stand next to her, looking over her shoulder at the screen. "That's it."

Elizabeth clicks on the email and my report appears.

"If you scroll down I've embedded example images," I point over her shoulder while feeling for Magritte's present. "There. You see the first of a series of images. As you look down you will notice the pattern. Can you see it?"

I remove the hypodermic needle from my pocket, flip off the cap with my thumb as I'd practiced in my apartment, and plunge it into Elizabeth's neck. The venom injects into her veins as I press down with my thumb. Elizabeth is so startled she doesn't seem to know what to say or do. But in only a moment she slumps over her desk. I remove the needle, pick up the cap and return Magritte's present to my pocket. I'm just going through the motions now. The whole thing happened like I'd rehearsed with Magritte. Muscle memory allowed me to do it. No thinking about what I'm doing or the implications of it. Just get into her office and do it. That was what Magritte told me. Just do it.

I try not to think about what I've done as I reach over Elizabeth, use her mouse to close the file I'd sent her, move down to the next email and click it open. I don't bother to read it. Not interested. This is only to make it appear she opened another email after our conversation. After I've left, which is what I want desperately to do now, but I don't. I wonder if Ebony knows I'm probably supposed to be escorted out of the building since Elizabeth and the FBI have solved the mystery of who the terrorists are. Only Ebony didn't see the terrorists have infiltrated her office, placed an agent within arm's length of the Secretary. And that would be the Secretary's downfall. Magritte said I would need to stay here for a few minutes to give the venom time to ensure she is dead. Don't be in a hurry. The longer I linger the more likely I am to be successful. If this can be considered success. To take a life. I know she's responsible for Arbiter taking over our lives. I know I helped in that process. But she also discarded us when we were through. She's responsible for ruining the lives of so many of us. Proud patriots, all of us. We put service to nation above our own interests. Above all else. Sacrificing with long days and nights to make us all safer, more harmonious, to enable a peace that will last. The reward for our dedication is a pink slip and nightmares that haunt our every sleeping moment. And increasingly for me, my day time thoughts. There is no hope for me. At least in this act maybe I can bring an end to the disruption Elizabeth has caused in the lives of so many.

I walk to her door and close it behind me. "She said she has to get something ready for Sabr, so please hold her calls?"

Ebony smiles at me as she always does, "Sure. Have a nice day, Brandon."

I walk out of the Secretary's office suite. I'm not in a hurry as I have Magritte's other present in my other suitcoat pocket.

315

## CHAPTER FIFTY-EIGHT: SHEILA

I'm at the airport. I can't stay another day in my apartment. Can't bear another day in this city. All my hopes and dreams have left me. So there's only one thing to do. Go back and start again. Find my roots. Nourish them. See what can grow from what I once thought I could be. Learn the lessons. Forget the past. Develop new skills, new insights, and new capabilities.

But it's so damn hard.

Brandon reminded me I was someone else once. A promising broadcast journalist. Only I was too immature to recognize the opportunity before, me rather than the promise of one so far from everything I knew. The one thing I'm going to have to confront is that I'm no longer that person either. I have scar tissue rather than promise. I have wisdom and experience rather than raw potential. In life you can never go back. You can never decide to be what you were.

My world has been voyeuristic for so long I have no idea what other people really do for a living. I've watched people pontificate on life, as they would like it, for so long I no longer have any idea of how I'd like life to be. No. That's not true. I know. And he told me to go home. Back to Australia. That's why I'm here. Waiting for the 9:18 flight to Sydney. I'm doing as he asked. Not because that's what I want. Because he said there is no hope for us as a couple. No hope that as two people who love each other, as two people who have so much to give to each other, we can make a life together.

What happened to him? In just the last week or two? I've been searching my brain for anything that would tell me what to do. Any sign that there is a path forward for us. That there is life after being an analyst for the Department of Truth for a decade. But it seems the castle we built in the sky was really resting on a foundation of sand. And with the first strong wind, the foundation gave way, bringing us tumbling down. Disorienting us. Leaving us to dig our way out of the shattered hopes and dreams that helped us build the castle in the first place. But I'm still here. I'm still wanting to persevere. To make that better life where we can be loved and safe and comfortable in the presence of the other. Be in a place where we build a shared life together.

Albert! I didn't say good-bye to Albert. I feel guilty. He's not only been my boss for a decade, but he's tried harder than anyone to convince Brandon that we should be together. He convinced me a long time ago. Why wasn't I willing to tell Brandon how I felt? What I wanted? How I would do anything to help him deal with what we were both dealing with? But I didn't. I wanted him to be the strong one. I wanted him to say to me, I'll take care of you for the rest of our lives. But that simple assurance never came. And last night he assured me it never would.

People are congregating at the monitor. Must be a gate change or a delayed flight. The airline will send me a text if it's mine. I really don't have any interest in the news, knowing that what gets posted isn't the news, but some subset that Arbiter blesses as fit for human consumption. Is that what I really think? It almost sounds like I'm upset that Arbiter put me out of a job. Put both of us out of a job. I shouldn't be. After all, we've known for years now the objective was autonomy. That at some point analysts would be redundant. The smart ones bailed a long time ago. Found a new life, a new career, a new purpose in life. It's only those of us who mistakenly thought we needed to be loyal to the department that are now finding ourselves at sea with no one even pointing towards shore. Is that what happened to Brandon? He was thrown in the water and discovered he didn't know how to swim?

Albert fed into that, now that I think about it. He told us we were the best he had. Made us feel like we should stay because we were the best. It's like any sports team. If you're the best you know that others are counting on you to perform day in and day out. Is that the problem? We both bought into Albert feeding us the line that we were the best.

That he was counting on us to ensure what was posted really did reflect the norms of our society? But all the time, he was just trying to make sure someone was on the desk? Someone making a decision when the rest of his team was calling in sick or quitting because they simply couldn't take it anymore?

All this time I've been blaming myself for staying too long. But maybe Albert was saying the same thing to every one of the analysts on his team. Not because it was true, but to ensure he had a shift covered. To ensure that Elizabeth, and all her predecessors during his nearly two decades with the department, would praise him for getting the job done. Ensure they would put a little something extra in the pay envelope at the end of the year. This whole life I've been living may have just been a colossal mind game. A manipulation to get what Albert needed from me to meet his goals. I don't want to believe it. I hope it isn't true. But I have to admit, it's possible.

Now I'm not so sure I want to call Albert to say good-bye. If he used me all these years… I don't think I could ever forgive him if that were the case. Brandon seemed to think it was the Secretary who used us. He said that. I'm not so sure it was her. While I agree she used us to meet her objective and then just cast us aside, we all knew what was coming. Was it on her to tell us to go find another job, knowing that by doing so she would slow down the completion of Arbiter, which will, without a doubt, be her legacy?

The crowd around the monitor hasn't moved on. They would have if it were just a delay or gate change. So what's so interesting? I look at my cell, I still have two hours… and then a newsfeed pops up. "Secretary Warden found dead in her office. Police looking for suspect."

What? That can't be true. Elizabeth dead? What happened? A suspect? That mean they think there was foul play? How did Arbiter ever let this one get through? But then I realize Sabr would want this information out. Would want to find the person responsible, if that's an accurate indication that someone took her life, rather than she died from natural causes. Elizabeth was in her 70s. And while that's not old, for some people it is a lifetime.

I walk over to the monitor. All those years reviewing video makes me want to see rather than read. Listen rather than try to decipher. The channel is Fox News. Of course. That means they have pushed the truth into a box they want conveyed. We've done a lot to keep them from simply broadcasting extremist diatribes. But still, I don't trust as the truth anything broadcast on that channel. Too much history. Too much personal experience.

"Secretary Elizabeth Warden was discovered dead in her palatial offices at the Department of Truth, overlooking the splendor of the White House..."

As I said, the Fox News view of the world.

"...while evidence is still being investigated, it appears that a department employee may have been responsible. What Fox News has learned, exclusively, is that DC police and the FBI have all points bulletins out for one Brandon McInerny..."

What? Brandon? This doesn't make any sense. Brandon couldn't be responsible... I tune back in to the broadcast, knowing what I'm seeing has been approved by Sabr herself. Arbiter would never have released any of this story.

"... No motive has been established, although the department has recently experienced a significant downsizing. And in fact, while the suspect was working on a short-term assignment, he had been released recently after more than..."

I'm unable to process what the anchor is saying in this broadcast. Brandon couldn't be involved in whatever happened. Those things happen to other people. Not someone you know. Not someone you love...

Is this what he was trying to tell me last night? Was he telling me to leave because if I stay I'll get caught up in the aftermath of whatever

it is he did today? Elizabeth dead? That doesn't make any sense to me.
Why? She didn't do anything that would warrant such a response.
Brandon? There's no way he could have been involved in a plot to
murder someone. That was always extremists. Brandon is no extremist.
But then I remember the Oklahoma City bombing. When was that? The
bomber was a Timothy McVey. Irish. Just like Brandon. But he was
upset with the government. Thought someone was coming to take away
his guns. Take away his liberty. Take away his freedom of expression
and thought. And as I think about it for only a moment, I realize McVey
was right. The government, although it has waffled back and forth on
the subject, has now come around to disarming him and those like him.
They've restricted the right to express beliefs, if not the accepted beliefs
of the administration. And the government has taken away freedoms.
He is only able to exercise those that agree with the belief structure of
the government.

I can't believe I'm sitting here agreeing with the fucking white
nationalists. And I know I'm not. They violate everything I believe in.
But they have a point in how the government has treated them. Treated
all of us. And is that why Brandon did whatever it is that he did?
Brandon spent a lot more time on the blogs and postings of those
people. I only had to deal with them when they debated their positions.
And generally they wouldn't go on those shows, because they knew the
media was going to paint them as a bunch of extremists. This is one hell
of a time to see what's been staring me in the face for so long. Shit.

I return to the televised broadcast, "DC police have advised
anyone who sees or has seen Brandon McInerny to contact them at the
number on the bottom of your screen. At this time, he is wanted for
questioning in the death of Secretary Warden. The reports we have
received indicate he was the last person to have seen her alive. We don't
know what that means, but the DC police have advised to take extreme
caution if you see the suspect, and immediately notify them at the
number on the bottom of your screen."

So they're not saying he did it, just that he was the last person to see her alive. Big difference. But clearly they think he's responsible. Just can't cross the line until they have him in custody. I need to find him. Understand what happened. Why did he do whatever it was he did? And if I don't get to him first, we'll probably never have that conversation.

I watch the broadcast for another minute. Look for the telltale indications that the Arbiter disposition was overridden by someone from the Department. The imprint flashes at the end of the approved segment. The imprint that tells me an analyst reviewed that segment, and it had been released for posting or airing. The fact that all the human analysts had been laid off tells me Elizabeth still has an elite team in place who can step in during unforeseen circumstances like now. And if that's the case why wasn't I ever given a chance to join them? Makes me more convinced Albert was playing both sides against the middle. I wasn't his best or I'd have been on this elite team. This just gets more and more depressing. Do I really want to find Brandon and help him? There's no question. So I stop at the counter, inform the agent that I'll be delaying my flight. No I don't know when, so I just need it put into suspense until I can work things out here.

The first stop is Brandon's apartment. I don't expect to find him there, but hope I'll find something that will tell me where he might have gone. Something that will tell me what he might have been attempting to do. But when I reach his apartment building I can't even enter. The whole building has been cordoned off by the FBI. They're probably tearing his apartment apart to find any clues as to what he might have intended, who he was, and why he was the last to see the Secretary alive. I should have expected this response by the authorities.

I walk up to one of the people on the other side of the cordon. No idea who she is, but I call, "Miss…"

The woman looks up, puzzles for a moment and then comes over. "This is an active crime scene. I'm afraid you will have to come back tomorrow."

"I don't need to go up," I'm looking at his building as I talk. "I worked with Brandon. At the Department of Truth. We were very close," I hesitate, not sure what else to say, but I go on anyway. "I'm still taking this all in, but I might be able to help you find him. If not, at least help you understand what may have happened."

The woman, starts inputting information into her cell. "You said you worked with him?"

I nod. "He was in print media and I had broadcast and signals."

She clearly has no idea what I just said, but she inputs it to her device. "What's your name?"

"Sheila." I only give her my first name because I've not used my last name in a decade. No reason to. My existence has been limited to a small group of friends who would know instantly who Sheila is.

"Sheila what?" she asks.

"Look. I worked at the Department of Truth. I know how this all works." I'm tired of fitting into square holes because every time I try, I lose something. She doesn't appreciate that. But shit. They need me more than I need them at this moment.

"Then you know I need your name to validate who you are."

I shake my head and walk away. The officer calls after me. "Wait Sheila. You can't just walk away…"

But I do. I walk away and don't look back. But now I have to decide what to do. I tried to help, but who was I helping? Elizabeth is dead. At least that's what was broadcast. I have to believe it to be true or Arbiter never would have let it pass. Do I go to the Department? They'll know who I am. They'll listen, because they know I know Brandon. Although I'm sure they've been interrogating Albert, if he's still there. But that's part of the problem. Since Elizabeth terminated nearly everyone Brandon knew, not many who would be left would have any idea what this was all about, or where to find him.

I could go to the FBI. But I assume the woman I just talked to is typical of how the FBI would treat me. Just another person to screen. Another person to process. I don't want that. Don't want to be just another person they force to tell them anything I might know. To tell them what they want to hear because it fits whatever theory they have at the moment. Doesn't necessarily have anything to do with the truth.

Let's hang Brandon. He killed the Secretary of Truth. He's a bad guy. Can't have people like him walking around. Got to be mentally unstable. But instead of seeing who he is, what the department has done to him, they will only punish him for what he's become. Maybe I need to go get on that plane. Go home and forget what I know. Forget I ever tried to make society a better place because society doesn't care. No one involved at this point has any interest in understanding and doing anything about what caused the events to happen. It's crime and punishment. End of story.

I can't go back to my apartment, because I moved out. Gave up the lease, expecting I was never going to return. So where do I go now? The only thing I can think of is the Starbucks where Brandon and I used to meet with Albert. I'm sure neither will be there. At least it's some place familiar. Some place I'll be able to gather my thoughts and decide what I need to do next.

That's about six blocks, so I walk slowly. No hurry to get there. I look in the shop windows and my vision glazes. Not looking to buy anything, because I have no place to take it. It's a strange experience to window shop when you're homeless and in transition. All the shops are irrelevant. They have nothing to offer me now. Even a restaurant has no interest, because I'm just not hungry. And that's unusual. I always want to try something new. Something I've not tried before. But I never want much. Just a taste. A sample. So I know if I'll want to come back and have a larger portion sometime in the future. I seldom do. But that's all right. When someone talks about a dish, if I've tried it, I can at least tell them if I like it or not.

The Starbucks is on the corner. But something's not right. I see a car across the street. That shouldn't be there. I don't know why I know that, but I do. I'm not aware enough to know if this is a set-up, or someone is watching for Brandon, or what, but I'm not comfortable. So rather than going in, I walk by, looking into the window to see who's there.

Albert is in the back, sitting there by himself. He looks bored. He's not here because he decided to stop for a coffee on the way home. He's here because someone is using him to hopefully catch Brandon. I keep on walking. Where do I go now? But before I even get to the corner a woman and a man step out of the shadows and block my path. I glance around and another woman and man are standing behind me. "Are you Sheila Murdock?"

"You are?" I ask even though I know, but want them to prove it.

The woman to my right opens a badge and identification. I read her name and the agency is the US Department of Treasury, Secret Service.

"I can assure you I'm not a counterfeiter," I respond to indicate I know a bit about her agency which, as part of the Treasury Department, was supposed to apprehend counterfeiters and only inherited the protection of the executive branch much later.

"Do you know the whereabouts of Brandon McInerny?" comes straightforward as I would expect. "We know you worked with him. Were close to him."

I glance over my shoulder at Starbucks knowing where they got that information. "I do not."

The same woman continues, apparently conscious of potential charges of sexual mistreatment should a man question me. "Are you expecting to meet him here?"

"I am not." Better not to say too much. I've been briefed on what to do and say if kidnapped. I have to react to this as if that's the case now. Trying to explain is the worst thing I can do, because anything I volunteer will only result in more questions, more attempts to catch me in a lie, and then put me in jail whether guilty or innocent. They don't care. They have a dead Secretary. Someone has to pay.

"I must place you under arrest and ask you to accompany us for further questioning." Same woman. Same unpolished shoes, in contrast to the big guy next to her. I would guess he is really in charge. He looks the part. Big guy, so he intimidates everyone. Spit polished shoes so probably ex-military. Someone who is dying to hit me. Force me. Scare the shit out of me so I'll tell him whatever he wants to know, even if it's not true, just to get him to stop. He has no idea who he is dealing with here.

"I don't think so," I respond calmly. All that training the Department provided because I sometimes traveled to restricted countries for work. They wanted to make sure I never compromised how the Arbiter system works.

I see Mr. Spit-shine have a conniption.

"We have the authority…" she starts.

"And I have the right… to determine the venue of your questioning." I look directly at Mr. Spit Shine, just in case he thinks I don't understand. "I also have the right to object to any coercion you may wish to impose. I understand you may impose such methods where national security is involved. But you also are subject to judicial review of your application of such force and may be dismissed from the service, stripped of your pensions, and possibly be imprisoned for up to ten years for each infraction of civil liberties as determined by a court of your peers."

Mr. Spit Shine takes a step back. "Your profile says nothing about you being a lawyer."

I remember the training and simply don't answer his question, looking at him with disdain. Essentially daring him to step over the line.

Mr. Spit Shine glances at the other agents, makes a judgment call. "When was the last time you saw Brandon McInerny?"

"We had dinner last night."

"Where?"

"A Somali place a couple blocks from my apartment. I don't know the name or address. But you should be able to find it."

"What did you talk about?"

"I was terminated along with the rest of the analysts this week. We talked about what I would do now that I'm unemployed."

"Did you talk about anything else?"

"His nightmares," I'm not sure why I should tell them this, but it's what we talked about.

"Why was he having nightmares?" Mr. Spit Shine seems to be just letting me talk.

"Have any of you spent one day on a Department of Truth Analyst desk?"

Silence.

"If you had, you'd not ask that question," I respond with conviction.

"Did he give you any indication of what he planned to do today?"

I shake my head.

"Did he voice any grievance against the Secretary, personally?"

I look down for a moment and shake my head before responding.

"Nearly every analyst who worked to protect you and your families from the negativity, the race baiting, the misogyny, the nativism, the cruelty, the mutilation, sexual exploitation, pornographic impulses and desires to share those impulses with you all and punish you if you didn't embrace their world view would say they felt used and tossed aside when Arbiter was all of a sudden live. Whether it was ready or not."

Mr. Spit Shine is not ready for that restrained answer. I know it could have been a lot more forceful if I'd been in the mood. "Are you suggesting you never heard him express a discomfort with the Secretary personally that you'd not heard from any other department employee?"

"I take it you were Marine Corps intelligence."

Mr. Spit Shine glances at the woman who had been questioning me. She shrugs. "What is the relevance of your question?" he finally asks.

"Sun Tzu said you must know your enemy."

"I'm not your enemy," he responds, "I'm..."

"Neither am I yours. If you want to find Brandon, if you want to understand what happened today, we can have that conversation. But this will not get you there."

"I'm ready." Mr. Spit Shine responds. "Let's go have that conversation."

"At the White House..." I respond, "With the President."

"That's not going to happen," Mr. Spit Shine reacts instantly.

I just look at him.


After a half hour of silence while Mr. Spit Shine talks to his superiors just out of range for me to hear the conversation, Albert comes out of the Starbucks and approaches me. He is followed by a short muscular man I'd not noticed when I glanced in through the window. Albert seems aware of the man, as if he's uncomfortable about him. As if the man has some kind of control of the situation. Albert appears to be trying to decide how to handle something he's not encountered before. Even in the most extreme situations I've worked with him, I've not seen him with this particular look. I'm not sure how I should respond to him, but they're clearly trotting him out to get me to tell them where Brandon might be.

"Sheila," he acknowledges me but glances around at the man and apparently decides not to say more.

I look at the man following Albert. Seems I've seen pictures of him, or something. Maybe he's been in one or more broadcasts I've reviewed. But his name isn't coming. "Do I know you?"

He steps forward to shake my hand, something none of the Secret Service agents did. Apparently he's decided to take a different tact with me. Not hostile, innocent until proven guilty. "Will Johnson."

I shake his hand while my mind furiously works that name, and then, "Special Counsel to the Senate Judiciary Committee. But you left that job..."

A flicker of appreciation in his eyes, "I did. Returned to private practice until the Secretary asked me to help her find someone."

Is that someone Brandon? Is that why Albert's here? To help Will Johnson find him? I glance back at the Secret Service agents, particularly Mr. Spit Shine then suggest, "I think we should all go visit with the President."

Mr. Spit Shine shakes his head in alarm, but Will Johnson seems surprised, "The President?"

"The President. And I'll need access to Arbiter." I look at Albert to see how he's reacting. But he's subdued as if this is the last place he wants to be. I understand. "An analyst's access." I see Albert puzzle at that request, but he doesn't comment.

"Call it in." Will Johnson instructs Mr. Spit Shine.

Apparently Sabr's schedule doesn't permit my meeting, and I at least have a nice comfortable accommodation for the night. Being homeless that's desirable, although the accommodation in a secure detention holding cell is not. Albert's down the hall somewhere. I heard them lock him in after me.

I lay down and close my eyes. Immediately the images of some of the most extreme 'documentary' films I reviewed in my role begin rolling through my mind. Images I've been trying to forget from the moment I deleted them from the broadcast queue. But they come back. They sneak into my consciousness. They punch me in the face of my moral outrage. I just want them to stop. To leave me in peace for I'm no longer able to delete them, from the broadcast queue or my mind. It's not my job to save us from those of us who want us to face who we are when we peel away the veneer of civilized.

I don't think I got any sleep, having toured my all-time hit parade of hate speech, misogyny, and sexual exploitation. It's a wonder I was ever able to enjoy my night with Brandon since this is the only view of sex I've experienced in the last decade, with that one exception. But that night was special. And I so want to recapture it…

Will Johnson appears outside my luxury accommodations, looks in before saying anything. "You ready?"

"For?" I don't trust he actually set up the meeting I requested.

"Sabr has thirty minutes before her cabinet meeting. She's giving you her normal prep time. So this better not be a waste of her time."

"You don't know me at all. But I assure you this isn't what you think. You will all have answers in a few minutes. But it will be up to her to change what's about to happen to us all."

Mr. Spit Shine is gathering Albert, who looks rumpled and sleepy. Reminds me that I probably look much the same. No stop off for a shower and doing my hair. Don't think a gang shower in a detention facility would exactly be an experience I would want.

We're driven across town to the White House. Not a word is said in the car. Now I have handcuffs, which tells me exactly what they think of the situation. This won't be a pleasant exchange. I need to make sure I'm in the proper frame of mind. Keep myself from being intimidated by who else will be in the room. Make my point, and explain the likely result of the decisions she has already made. Appeal to her to take action and let the rest of the day end where it will.

Mr. Spit Shine leads Albert into a small conference room. Will permits me to enter before him. He's playing the good guy and Mr. Spit Shine is not. Okay. I know what they're doing. Will Sabr really show up? Or will this be an attempt to get me to talk? They could just use drugs on me. But maybe my refusal to just go along and recitation of my rights made them back off. I don't know. But without Will Johnson involved, this probably would have gone down very differently.

Maria Xhe is at the console. That tells me they're taking me seriously. For the first time I'm beginning to think something could come of my demands. "Maria," I acknowledge her. "Could you bring up the raw input files from any day?"

Maria nods. In a moment she has a day selected. "Please just start scrolling through. Five second advance rate." Maria does as I request. When the first image comes up of a Muslim beheading a western journalist I turn away and won't look back at the screen. The others in the room can't take their eyes away from it, with the exception of Albert, who just looks down, unwilling to engage me with his eyes. What did he tell Will Johnson? Is part of the reason they seem to be taking me seriously because Albert vouched for me? Told them I wouldn't deliberately hide anything? That whatever I had to say would be important? I don't know. But I'm still reacting to the possibility I was sacrificed by him as well as the whole department leadership.

Sabr Malik Goldstein isn't as tall as I thought. She enters the room followed by a woman of about my age, dark complexion, probably Middle Eastern, and Danny Martin, who is Elizabeth's assistant for special projects. She doesn't say anything as she comes in. She looks up and is instantly repelled by whatever image the submissions file is displaying. "What's this all about?" Sabr demands, having trouble tearing her eyes from the screen. She finally does to look first at me and then at Albert.

"Madam President, you want to know what happened to the Secretary, who did it and why. I hope you also want to know what you need to do as a result of the decisions you've made."

"Who are you and why do you think you can talk to me like this?" Sabr responds.

"I'm just a former analyst from the Department of Truth, who had to make decisions about whether what you're seeing up there should be posted, or failed to meet the test of the Ten Commandments. I did that for ten hours a day for over a decade. Made those decisions along with thousands of others who are all walking the streets today, used up and tossed aside, because you made a decision."

Sabr frowns, "My decision has spared all of you from having to spend one more day making those decisions."

"But you haven't spared us from the nightmares we sweat through every night as those images…" I nod to the screen behind me, which causes Sabr to glance up again. She gasps, but can't take her eyes off the screen. "…torture us. Disgust us, Fill us with moral outrage. Not because we are asked to delete them, prevent them from airing, but because they represent the worst that exists in each and every one of us. Only most of us successfully suppress them. Find a way of getting through the day without those thoughts or images interrupting what we do. But not for the thousands of us who spent our lives trapped in a cube with the inner beasts of mankind."

Sabr finally breaks from the screen to look at me. "Sheila Waldock is it?"

"Murdock."

"You're Australian."

"Dual citizenship, Ma'am."

"You're suggesting your friend Brandon McInerny took her life because she destroyed the life of her employees by leaving them locked up with this all day? Forcing them to make decisions about those images and words. That was her crime? That was enough to empower him to take her life?"

"No, ma'am," I'm not getting through to her. "We weren't forced to do anything. We were there because we believe in what we do. Make society better. The betrayal was yours. You substituted our judgment, our interpretations, our ability to grasp nuance and see what's only suggested, for a rigid and inflexible system that permits you or your designee to determine the truth. To make our reality the reality you wish it to be, regardless of what it is. You, and the Secretary, and all of your recent predecessors used us to enable your seizure of our consciousness. To shape us into what you find acceptable, by simply making an adjustment to the Ten Commandments. The original ten came from God. Now you want to replace God in the lives of all people. That's not acceptable. You suddenly have the power to change everything. Whatever it takes to keep you in power as long as you wish to be. You now are changing lives daily. And not necessarily for the better. Often times in complete ignorance of the consequences, because you are determining reality and who we are becoming."

"Is that what Brandon McInerny saw? Is that why he took the action he did? Are you saying I caused the Secretary's death by the decision I made to make Arbiter live?"

"I'm saying you're just seeing the tip of the iceberg. There are thousands like Brandon and me out there… carrying nightmares we will never escape from, even in the daytime. We have sacrificed ourselves for a better society. But we are now walking time bombs because of what you've made us. How you treated us when we no longer were needed. Because you now have a machine you can control that will control us. And the bigger bomb is yet to come. The longer a machine decides our reality the greater the explosion that will ultimately occur, changing our society even more in an unpredictable direction."

"Speculation," Sabr looks at Will Johnson, shakes her head. She appears about to leave when Albert speaks up.

"Madam President."

Sabr stops and looks at him, "You are…"

"Albert Carter. I work directly for the Secretary responsible for the analysts and validation of Arbiter."

"You're just going to agree with her, I suppose."

"No ma'am. I'm here because Mr. Johnson found me."

"Will?" Sabr checks with the one expert in the room.

"You need to listen to his story," Will Johnson responds pensively.

"Have you ever heard of Xi and Jurgen?" Albert begins.

"I talk with them regularly," Sabr seems dismissive.

"Are they your friends?"

"World leaders have no friends," Sabr is preparing to leave.

"I can assure you they have decided you are the weak link."

That stops Sabr. "What evidence do you have of that?"

"The people who recruited Brandon McInerny to kill the Secretary of Truth recruited me to kill Arbiter. And they were placed here by Jurgen and Xi."

"You can't kill a machine," Sabr dismisses his claim.

Will Johnson holds up his hand. "Madam President I can verify that an agent known as Ichabod is sitting in a cell two blocks from here. He has confirmed what Mr. Carter claims. His accomplice, a woman only known as Magritte, is still at liberty. We believe she handled Brandon McInerny and provided the murder weapon. They recruited analysts because they saw them as damaged and disaffected. Saw them as feeling abandoned by the government they had faithfully served to their own detriment. They chose them because of what Miss Murdock has described. That's why you have to listen and consider what she and Mr. Carter have to say."

Sabr looks at Albert and then at me. She then remembers. "If Xi and Jurgen are trying to destroy me and our government. The murder of Elizabeth won't accomplish that."

"No Madam President, but I have up loaded code into Arbiter supplied to me by Ichabod," Albert informs us.

Maria's head almost swivels, "What?"

Albert holds up his handcuffed hands so she will listen. "The code, as it was explained to me, will reprogram Arbiter a little at a time. You won't even notice the changes at first. They have taken the boil the frog approach. Turn up the temperature a little at a time. Reintroduce a little hate speech here. Permit an anti-Muslim expression to work its way into a broadcast. Report a killing. Then over time we will begin to see things we haven't seen in a decade or more because analysts like me and Sheila and Brandon have kept them out of the media. Since Arbiter is self-healing, the new code works through those minor adjustments, but moves the decisions further and further from the Ten Commandments."

"That's impossible. I would know if you changed something like that," Maria responds.

"When did I load it?" Albert asks Maria.

"You didn't. Arbiter would log it in and send me an alert."

"I loaded it ten days ago at 7:29 pm."

"Shift change," Maria notes. She considers Albert's claim. "Not a problem. We can delete the program files and restore from the backup."

"Also infected," Albert notes.

Maria has to consider this set of circumstances. "We may need to go back to an earlier instance, but we can recover. May take a while, but we can fix this."

"You're no longer under contract. All your resources have gone on to other programs," Albert reminds her.

"You said Xi and Jurgen see me as the weak link. How did you get there?" Sabr is thinking this all through now.

Will gestures to her, "We should take that off line, but Xi and Jurgen have implemented the Bergamo Accords without us."

"What?" Sabr can't believe what she has just heard.

It's now my turn, "Madam President." Sabr looks up at me as if she's just remembered I am here. "You believe that Brandon McInerny is a cold-blooded killer sent by the leaders of the other federations to cause chaos and distraction while they work together to undermine you."

"That seems to be what you would have me believe," Sabr concludes.

"I think there is another truth. I think Brandon McInerny is a patriot, who dedicated a decade to make his country a better place for all of us. I think he sacrificed himself, not because the leaders of the other federations paid him, or a handler coerced him. I think he sacrificed himself because he knew only something drastic like what he did would bring your attention to the two types of time bombs you set by your decisions. Jurgen and Xi aren't the reason those bombs are out there about to explode. But they're taking advantage of the fact you set them without a plan. How are you going to help your former analysts cope and adapt, help them continue to serve our federation. And I think he also saw that a fully autonomous Arbiter with no checks and balances, that no longer learns from us and adjusts the truth to what we are becoming will only suppress and constrain us as a people. That's your second bomb. Maybe not one that will explode during your administration, but one that will cause the people to explode, to throw off the shackles you would place on us."

Sabr shakes her head, "Another version of the truth."

THE END

# About the Author

dhtreichler is a futurist, technologist and strategist who toured the global garden spots as a defense contractor executive for fifteen years. His assignments covered intelligence, training and battlefield systems integrating state of the art technology to keep Americans safe. His novels grew out of a need to deeply understand how our world is changing, developing scenarios and then populating them with people who must confront how increasingly sophisticated technology is transforming our lives and how men and women establish relationships in a mediated world.

Keep up with all of dhtreichler's latest work and essays at www.dhtreichler.com and www.GlobalVinoSnob.com.

# Also by dhtreichler

*TRUTH*

*A Cat's Redemption*

*CHOICES*

*HOPE*

*Emergence*

*Barely Human*

*The Ghost in the Machine: a novel*

*World Without Work*

*The Great American Cat Novel*

*My Life as a Frog*

*Life After*

*The Tragic Flaw*

*Succession*

*The End Game*

*I Believe in You*

*Rik's*

*The Illustrated Bearmas Reader – Ralph's Ordeals*

*The First Bearmas*